ZOMBIES
"CHRONICLES OF THE DEAD"

A ZOMBIE NOVEL

By Will Lemen

TABLE OF CONTENTS

THE OUTBREAK

As jokes go, we all thought it was a good one, it was somewhat funny and afforded us some laughs while offering everyone a momentary diversion from the job that we were being paid to perform.

We initiated this *joke* over nine hundred days before the possible, or impossible, zombie event was supposed to take place. Just about the same time that television shows were starting to crop up proclaiming all of the possible end of the world scenarios, and speculating on what might happen to us, and what we could or could not do to prevent our world's ultimate end.

Most of their theories revolved around the day when the Mayan calendar countdown was finally to be completed on December 21, 2012.

We chose zombies as the favored way for us to meet our ultimate demise during the undoing of society and civilization as a whole, which was sure to occur at the predicted and appointed time. Provided of course that the ancient Mayans knew what they were doing.

Because, well let's face it, fighting off a horde of flesh eating zombies would be far more fun than say, running scared from a giant asteroid that was destined to smash into our planet, setting off an extinction event that would by far eclipse the one that brought forth the ruin of the dinosaurs so many eons ago. At least that was the consensus at the time.

Besides, where would you run, and where could you hide from a gigantic asteroid? In other words, you *would* be able to run, but you *wouldn't* be able to hide, and you'd just die tired.

However, I can't help but to think that if a vote were taken today among those same people, including myself, who thought that real life flesh eating zombies would be the best alternative, given the number of other apocalyptic choices available to them, that the outcome might be different and some quicker and less painful form of death such as an asteroid impact on our world would be far more preferable to most of them.

It's no wonder nobody took it seriously at the time, and why should've they? Just imagine, hordes of insane cannibalistic dead people roaming the earth in search of their favorite foods (flesh, intestines, and brains), bent on the unwitting destruction of the human race?

Please!

That was the kind of thing that science fiction and horror novels were made of, not something that happened in real life.

We talked about it and laughed, we kidded each other that we were all doomed to become a footnote in the vast history of the universe by the coming zombie hordes.

We even had a Mayan calendar countdown at the hellhole where I worked. It not only kept everyone apprised of the impending climactic results that were predicted to happen, but also gave us something to do and talk about at work, besides work.

I called it a hellhole because the company's owners in all of their infinite wisdom, had hired an impudent little ass clown of a man with inept skills in upper management to run their business.

He possessed a minor degree from some small inadequate vocational school and doubled as a pathological liar and borderline sociopath while he wasn't busy honing his expertise as a libertine and being a skid mark on society's collective underwear at the same time.

His given name was Robert, although he went by the moniker Bob in his nefarious attempt to be accepted as just one of the guys.

However, in private and behind closed doors, *Bob* was commonly referred to by all of the employees at this dysfunctional establishment as *"Batshit Bobby"*. Of course, this was after we got to know him and discovered that he was without a doubt, crazier than a clump of dried *bat shit on a proverbial stick.*

I'm sure Batshit Bobby wasn't the first, and probably not the last (but he might have been considering the circumstances) psycho-nut-case to be put in charge of a money making venture as such. Nevertheless, it sure seemed to all of the employees as though the people running the show were determined to turn what would have been, could have been, and should have been, a paradise to work in, (now that they had *frog marched* the former executive manager out of the building for undisclosed reasons) into a torture chamber from the lower subterranean depths of hell for all of us to suffer in.

At first, this new boss seemed like a regular kind of guy (the persona he strived to propel outward at every opportunity), which was a far cry from the egomaniacal slave driver that he had replaced. Perhaps the stark contrast between the two men's personalities and their management styles was the reason that at first we were all lulled into a false sense of fairness and honesty projected by that functional psychotic schizoid.

At the time, we all thought nothing could possibly be worse than the maniacal tyrant that we had been forced to put up with and cow down to for the past several years of our employment at that joint.

We were wrong!

It wasn't long before the new boss's nice guy facade began to crumble and the true mental derangement of this lunatic began to become very apparent to everyone, that is everyone except the individuals that had hired him.

To this very day, it still baffles me as to why the company owners turned a blind eye to that guy's shenanigans. Perhaps it was because they themselves were no more qualified to own a business than he was qualified to run that business for them.

However, once people really started to listen to him closely, they observed how he would constantly tell people one thing, then turn right around and do just the opposite, thinking his employees were too stupid to notice his lies. The workers started to realize that every conversation tended to end up revolving around him; they began to be enlightened to the true nature of the beast within the man.

By the way, you had better not have noticed any of his lies, that is if you knew what was good for you and your employment.

Besides being a lying sociopathic braggart with ever-increasing delusions of godhood, Batshit Bobby was also very vindictive. If he even thought that someone had crossed him for *any* reason, or in his demented mind thought that they had made him look bad in the eyes of his employers, that someone's employment was doomed to become extinct at some point down the road. Batshit Bobby would stop at nothing to exact his misguided revenge on his imaginary enemies.

Bobby became known to his employees as somewhat of a story teller, among other things. Moreover, all of Batshit's adventurous stories, and he had plenty of them, began to have a kind of superhero flare to them, him being the superhero of course.

We've all seen his type. If he had found out that you had climbed Mt. McKinley at some point in your life, you would quickly be informed by him that he had climbed Mt. Everest years earlier, in record time nonetheless, even with having had to carry a Sherpa on his back.

Because of course, the weakling guide who had lived in the region his whole life, and was well acclimated to the lack of oxygen at that altitude, and had hiked up and down the treacherous alpine terrain since he was a young child, just didn't have the mountaineering skills or physical prowess to keep up with Bobby.

Well as one might guess, it didn't take too awful long before nobody in the company believed a single word that spewed from Batshit Bobby's continually flapping lying braggart lips, again with the only exception to that being the people that had hired him.

Unfortunately, for the workers under his supervision, everyone had to act as though his bush-league fairy tales interested them; after all, he was their boss.

Sometime later, much to everyone's exasperation, he hired a female screw-up with multiple personality disorder and several *manly* features that included large arthritic looking bony finger joints that made many of the male employees rather uncomfortable, which gave rise to speculation about the proper attire which might embellish this androgynous person.

She (provided it was a female) couldn't understand normal thinking, and was just as big of a liar as he was, if not bigger (which is hard to fathom), and that's when the company really started heading in a south-bound direction.

One undeserved promotion after another was given to this woman (?). So many in fact, that many of the people who worked at that *buffoonery* began to think that there might have been some kind of hypnosis involved wherein the promotions were being granted in exchange for certain bodily fluids which were being transferred between the two of them on a regular basis, and possibly, but knowing him not probably, against his free will.

Then with incompetence levels seemingly having no ceiling, and favoritism running rampant along with nonexistent accountability for some, and a keep your nose to the grindstone attitude toward others, the morale within the company began to plummet into a graveyard spin.

Most of the employees began to trudge down the hallways like the notorious zombies that were destine to invade their lives in the near future, wishing that they worked somewhere else, any place else.

However, little did anyone suspect at the time, that in a few short months, the zombie-like stares of the disgruntled employees (with the extra added attraction of *murderous rage* in their eyes of course) and their mindless shuffling would become commonplace around the world.

Yet there would be one very distinct difference between the past and the future: Although the dawdling walk of the discontented employees being wronged by their boss (Batshit Bobby) and his sexually dimorphic concubine mimicked the gait of the zombie hordes to come, and although their glassy eyed stares did resembled the blood thirsty thousand yard criminally insane gaze of the flesh eating monsters that would soon encompass their future lives, these *dysfunctional buffoonery* employees weren't trying to *bite your face off*. At least they weren't at that time.

What I would now give to be back at that buffoonish hellhole, the hellhole that now seems like it was a heaven on earth compared to the living hell that we all are now forced to endure every single minute of every single day.

However, enough about unhinged ex-authority figures and their paramours, and let me not digress a moment longer.

Even with all of the doomsday television shows, t-shirts, coffee mugs, bumper stickers, and countless other items for sale heralding the coming apocalypse. Who would have really believed that there would be a zombie invasion, polar shift, massive earthquakes, super volcanic eruption, gigantic solar flare causing a worldwide power grid shut down, or a myriad of other end of the world scenarios arriving on December 21, 2012 as foreseen by the doomsday prophets?

Therefore, when the *then* current cycle of the Mayan long count calendar ended… well it didn't take a rocket scientist or a brain surgeon to figure out that nothing had happened. No massive electromagnetic pulse (*to speak of anyway*), no alien invasion from the far reaches of the universe (*that we knew of*), no pandemic plague was ravaging the earth (*at least not yet*), no cataclysmic event of biblical proportion of any kind, no nothing.

For one reason or another, some people were very disappointed that no doomsday scenario befell us on that appointed day. One guy I knew even boasted that he was glad that the Mayans were all dead, because they had lied about the end of the world. Nevertheless, nobody was really surprised by the lack of disasters, natural, supernatural, man-made, or otherwise.

The Mayan's Mesoamerican long count calendar ended its 5,126-year-long cycle when it counted down to the end of its 13th Baktun, we all woke up on December 22, 2012, and not one thing out of the ordinary had taken place.

Not one of the predictions, ancient or not, had come true. The world as we knew it hadn't changed in the least, it hadn't disappeared from sight, or otherwise transformed into something abnormal. That abnormality would come later, and when it arrived, it would be so bizarre, so monstrously weird and outlandishly strange, and it would be something that we were not remotely prepared for in any way. Even though in our ridicules arrogance that we had derived from watching television and movies about the dead coming to life, we thought we would be.

Instead, what had disappeared were all of the television shows that were gearing us up for the end of the world. Predictions of the end of days that had been so prevalent just vanished as if they had never existed. Life as we knew it had not changed, and we all continued with our normal everyday mundane existence.

As time passed, the Mayan calendar and the end of the world became a vague and distant memory. The only thing that still remained to remind us of the zombie apocalypse that never was, were the zombie-like stares in the eyes of the *buffoonery* employees as they made their way down the company hallways *wishing* they belonged to a legion of the wandering flesh eating dead, instead of being held prisoner in that place by the financial noose they had tied around their own necks.

Then one afternoon, without any warning, without any predictions, and without any forecast from anybody of the coming event, it happened.

Our world went straight to hell.

I remember it like it was yesterday. I guess that is where our real story begins.

My name is Jack; I live with my wife Gin, and my two sons, Billy 18, and Jacob 16, if you can call what we're doing living, surviving is a more accurate analogy.

The day that it all started, I was on my way home from work, trying to dodge some of the usual stop and go traffic while my radio blasted out some serious 70's rock and roll music from a British band that was invading my vehicle.

Endlessly switching lanes on the freeway, vying for a position that might get me a car length or two ahead of the other drivers, just like everyone else was doing.

Then at one point the traffic slowed and soon after came to an abrupt halt, which is common in stop and go traffic. Thus, the word *stop*, in the phrase, "*stop and go traffic*."

However, this time the cars in front of me did not move forward again. That usually means an accident has occurred somewhere ahead of you, or the police have someone pulled over for a minor infraction of some kind and everyone passing the scene is slowing down to a crawl and rubbernecking, as if they have never seen a cop giving out a ticket.

"Idiots!" I mumbled to myself, as I changed the radio station that had now gone to a commercial for a local car dealership.

I was in the right lane, with an exit lane to my right. I had never taken that particular exit before, and I was unfamiliar with the area that it led to, and taking an unfamiliar exit is not what someone usually does at the height of rush hour, especially when they live nearly fifteen miles away as I did.

From my vantage point, at first I could only see that some cars at the head of the pack had stopped and that people were out of their cars and moving around. My first thought was that there had been a miner fender bender, but there seemed to be too many people milling around the wreck for it to be just a simple fender bender.

Then I thought, well maybe someone had been hit while trying to cross the freeway.

Some years ago I had been in traffic that came to a complete stop on a eight-lane highway, because a woman with the best of intentions was running back and forth across several lanes of traffic, trying to catch a stray dog (or get herself killed) and get it off the road.

As it turned out, someone had been hit; or rather, *something* had been hit.

While I sat in my vehicle glancing back and forth between the group of people that had gathered in front of the stymied automobiles and the empty exit lane beside me, I continued to change radio stations in search of some good traveling music to listen to on the remainder of the drive home, while debating whether or not to bailout onto that exit lane that seemed to be beckoning to me.

I sat there in the stalled rush hour traffic for a few more minutes, and then decided that this wreck, or pedestrian mishap, or whatever it was, could hold up the flow of traffic for hours.

People had already started to exit the freeway, and I thought that I'd better join them before that too became clogged.

I maneuvered into the exit lane and made my way forward rather quickly, and as I did, my view of what was causing the delay became very clear. That's when I first saw the beginning of what would turn out to be the demise of civilization as we had come to know it the world over.

It looked like a severe case of road rage at first glance, all the way up until I saw a short bald man get bum-rushed by four others that from a distance had looked like they had just been milling around. That was not the case.

They were walking awkwardly, ungainly, stumbling around as if they were drunk. The four of them had the short man surrounded but they weren't beating on him, they were biting him, biting big chunks of flesh out of his face, arms, and neck and one was gnawing at the top of his skull.

As I got closer to the scene, a few cars in front of me were stopping, forcing me to stop too. One car had pulled over and the driver was running toward the imperiled man in what seemed to be an attempt to help him. An attempt that would prove to be the last good deed this man would ever do.

The waylaid man was now on the ground in a puddle of his own blood, with the four attackers now on their knees hovering over him.

The man's high-pitched screams alerted drivers many rows back to the danger that was waiting for them just a few car lengths ahead, as the four *zombies* ripped the flesh and muscle from his body, exposing the off white color of his stripped bones and the marbled grey of his blood covered intestines, as they feasted on his mutilated body.

From out of nowhere a fifth attacker lunged upon the Good Samaritan from behind, and in a blink of an eye, had the man on the ground and was tearing his scalp off with his teeth.

Many of the other drivers were setting in their cars frozen with fear, staring in disbelief at the grisly spectacle that was being played out before them.

As the Samaritan's scalp dangled from his attacker's mouth like a blood soaked toupee, he let out a blood-chilling scream which seemed to pull the mesmerized onlookers out of their shock induced trances, and set off a chorus of shrill screams from all directions as many people jumped from their gridlocked vehicles and tried to run to safety.

Others quickly locked their doors hoping that would bring them safety, but in the end, they would find that they had trapped themselves, and through the glass windows of their four-wheeled metal coffins watched the end of world as they knew it unfold before their eyes.

These people, that had chosen to trap themselves inside their vehicles, found themselves surrounded and waiting for help that never came. They never left their cars again, and died of thirst or met their doom through starvation, or in some cases, self-termination was the chosen method to end their torment. Their cause of death no matter how it occurred would later prove to be irrelevant. As shortly after their demise (provided that no brain trauma had occurred) they would reanimate, ultimately joining the innumerable forces of our undead arch-enemies, and become one of our greatest nemesis, as we the *still* living would later attempt to commandeer transportation amid the abandon vehicles that were strung out along our country's highway system.

Others tried to plow through the impassable mass of stopped automobiles in front of them that was blocking their escape; the result of their panicked effort turned the road into a no rules *rush* hour demolition derby.

As people were being crushed between the violently colliding automobiles, some of which were then being run over and left wallowing in pools of their own blood and screaming in agony, while others were pinned under or between some of the crashed vehicles with no hope of evasion or survival. Others might have been the lucky ones, as they were killed instantly and didn't have to suffer the torment of watching themselves being eaten alive by the former road warriors that they had recently shared the thruway with. As the scenario unfolded, the sound of crunching metal and smashing glass added a phantasmagorical element to the surreal scene as it filtered through the high-pitched human screams of terror and resonated throughout the countryside.

In their panic to save themselves, some people were backing up and spinning their tires on the pedestrians they had just trapped under their cars, jetting blood onto cars and people equally, like a crimson waterspout.

This caused even more panic as blood splattered men and women alike scurried among the moving cars, pounding on their windows in a panicked attempt to find a safe haven in the midst of the ensuing carnage.

A young girl, who looked as if she was just barely old enough to drive, was naive enough to believe that she could help one of the panicked pedestrians that was clawing at her door.

The girl began to roll her window down and at the halfway point, the man's demeanor quickly turned from a helpless panicked victim begging for help, to an enraged brute determined to commandeer the young lady's vehicle, and she was immediately dragged out of her car through the window by the brawny man she had chosen to aid.

As the young woman was pulled screaming and kicking across the top of the half-open window, the pressure of her thrashing body movements battering on the fragile glass broke the window and the remaining shards of glass disemboweled her in the process.

Her screams of terror and pain were short lived as her intestines spilled out of her lower abdomen and were left draped on the outside of the driver's door as the spark of life quickly departed from her earthly husk.

Her attacker was also in the process of becoming short lived. Before the ruffian could shove his victim's limp and what I thought was her lifeless corpse away from the door so he could take control of her vehicle, the young girl regained consciousness and began furiously gnawing at the man's left ankle.

Pulling himself into the car using the steering wheel for leverage, the man began to scream like a six-year-old spoiled brat throwing a temper tantrum as he sat behind the wheel of his hijacked prize and pulled his bleeding leg into the vehicle. All the while not realizing that he was all ready dead.

As we would come to find out later, it only took one bite from the ravenous monsters to seal your doom. Once bitten by a member of the walking dead, unless your limb (if you were lucky enough to be bitten on one of your extremities) was immediately hewed off above the bite, your chances of survival was zero. You would feel fine at first, then after about forty-eight hours, you would begin to feel ill. After several more hours, you would become drowsy and lethargic, then comatose. Soon after that, you would wake up *dead*, and very hungry!

As he sat behind the wheel, he watched his enamored and attached young female victim bite her way up his leg onto his body, and back into the car with him.

At that point, I knew his quest for safety had ended and mine had just begun, as I saw the girl put an end to the man's torment by ripping a bite sized chunk of flesh out of the side of his neck and swallow it whole.

I could feel my heart thumping rapidly in my chest as my foot slid slowly off the brake pedal. As my vehicle began to slowly inch forward, I could see several bloody bodies on and around other stopped cars, and I instinctively knew that if I didn't do something fast, that I would soon be joining them, but it seemed that my mind and body were both frozen in time and I could not move; I could only stare blankly into the apocalypse that now surrounded me as if I were hypnotized.

Now as the chaos began to reach a fever pitch, one of newly sighted victims who had been knocked down and flattened by one of the panicked drivers, and who looked as though she should not have been moving, was dragging her mutilated body out from under the vehicle that had rolled over her.

Her jaw had been crushed and broken off from her skull; it was hanging down passed her collarbone like a grotesque necklace, held on only by her scratched and torn facial skin. Flesh and muscle looked as if it had been peeled from her right forearm and hand by a jagged piece of metal, leaving several inches of shredded skin dangling from the exposed bone, held on only by the bloody oozing veins and arteries that were stretched to their very limits.

Some of her skin was left hanging from the underside of the car that had ravaged her body, and was dripping blood onto the road.

As I watched the crimson droplets fall into the puddle of blood beneath them, the noise from the chaos around me disappeared, and it seemed I could hear each drop as it splashed into the gory liquid as if I were listening to a leaky faucet in the dead of night sending shock waves of sound ripping through the serene silence as it dripped.

The woman somehow had managed to stand up and move; and she was moving toward me.

Her wobbling motion snapped me back from what I can only describe as a daydream in the middle of this nightmare I was experiencing.

She too, was unwieldy and clumsy. Walking as if she was intoxicated, yet her head seemed stabilized and steady like a marionette's head, floating above her body and not affected by the erratic movements of the rest of her swaying body as if the two weren't attached.

The look in her overly blood shot eyes was not one of pain, but one of anger and rage, it was the look of a crazed maniac bent on destroying something, and that something was me.

After seeing what had just happened to some of my fellow freeway travelers, and the growing number of what seemed to be reanimated dead people on the scene, the feeling that my life was now in serious jeopardy overwhelmed me. I felt that my escape was now paramount to my survival, and like many of the other people, I also panicked. My panicked state released my body and mind from its former stupor and I was able to think and move once more.

I hit the accelerator pedal hard and my spinning tires squealed loudly as the concrete road stripped the rubber from them.

I swerved around the car in front of me, narrowly missing another vehicle and a panicked woman who was screaming and flailing her arms about like a scarecrow on a windy day as she cried for someone to help her.

As I passed the hysterical woman, I had a momentary thought.

"I should stop and pick her up!"

That thought quickly passed as another thought pushed it out of my mind.

"Hell with her, the bitch wouldn't stop for me!"

No more thoughts of helping anybody (but myself) seeped into my brain after that, as I sped between a truck and the car that the Good Samaritan had abandoned and raced up the exit ramp, now only able to see the gruesome fracas in my rearview mirror.

With the mayhem far behind me now, my heart was still pounding hard in my chest, and my breathing was labored as if I had just ran a mile in under four minutes.

I had sped onto the surface streets where the traffic was sparse, and in my endeavor to traverse the area I meandered through the unacquainted streets with my mind still reeling from what I'd just witnessed, trying to digest the horrific scene and rationalize some semblance of sense to it.

My momentary panic subsided, and I told myself that what I had just experienced was just an isolated incident, probably people using PCP, or Bath Salts, or some other synthetic drug that caused them to act in such a heinous way.

I continued on my journey homeward, and while driving through an oak-shaded residential area I caught a glimpse of what I thought was an aircraft flying overhead, but I never got a good look at it because of the lush foliage above me.

"News helicopters most likely," I thought, figuring that I would turn on the local news when I got home and they would have the whole story of what really had happened back there on the freeway.

Moments later and long before I would arrive to what I thought would be the safety and security of my home, an emergency broadcast blasted across the radio waves. The broadcast was alerting everyone listening, that there seemed to be some kind of outbreak, and many random and extremely violent acts were taking place all across the region, and more incidents were being chronicled even as the report aired.

That's when I began to fear for my families wellbeing.

I began to run stop signs and stop lights if I could see that no other vehicles were in the immediate area.

Rolling stops became the norm for me and every other driver on the road that was aware of the so-called outbreak, and I just narrowly avoided several accidents along the way.

Trying to call family members was of no use, the cell phone carriers were deluged with an avalanche of calls, and the result was that nobody was getting through.

As the miles fell behind me and I made my way closer to my home, I couldn't help wondering if my family was there, and if so, were they safe?

By now, things had gotten so bad that most of the radio stations had stopped airing their regular formats and were giving constant updates on the upheaval that was gripping the area, and as I would come to find out later, the whole nation and the world.

Along the way I began to see more and more of the violent acts like the ones that I had witnessed during the life and death struggles on the highway, and that the radio was now reporting on. Not all of which were confined to the streets and roads.

While passing an old Victorian house, I watched a woman run out onto her front porch screaming, only to be dragged back inside by two teenage girls with what were becoming the all too prevalent crimson stains on the front of their clothes, and the same color liquid dripping from their mouths and hair.

As they paused their attack momentarily to stare at me as I passed, before refocusing their attention back onto their captured prey. I could see that they both had a chilling glare in their eyes that made the hair on the back of my neck stand up. The woman who had climbed out from under the car and lumbered toward me on the freeway had the same murderous gaze in her eyes.

It was witnessing scenes like that which made me more resolute than ever to make it back to my home and my family at any cost.

When I did finally make it to the subdivision where I lived, I approached my house, and with my goal in sight, a sense of relief fell over me.

I could see my wife Gin and my two sons Billy and Jacob huddled together in the driveway. When my wife saw me coming down the street, she started to wave her hands over her head to get my attention, a gesture that was unnecessary considering the dire circumstances.

When I pulled into my driveway, the three of them hurriedly approached my van.

"I thought you'd never get here!" Gin said, as the panicked look on her face was replaced with one of concerned joy.

"Have you heard? It's all over the television."

"You mean about the attacks? Yes, it's all over the radio. I saw it close up too; there were multiple homicides on the freeway right in front of me. People were screaming and running everywhere, cars were wrecking into each other and running over people, and I just barely got away myself."

I could see the look of fear growing in her eyes again.

"What are we going to do?" She asked, now shaking with fear as tears welled up in her eyes.

"The first thing you're going to do is get into the house while I turn the van around and back it into the driveway; just in case we need to make a quick getaway later." All the while thinking that it was more of a gesture than anything else, and it wasn't *really* necessary.

"Now! Let's go boys, Gin, everyone in the house," I ordered sternly, as I put my vehicle into reverse and began to back it out of the driveway.

With our vehicle now backed in and ready for a fast retreat, I joined my family in what we thought was the safety of our home.

WELCOMING THE NEIGHBORS

Locking the door behind me, I asked my family.
"Have any of you seen anyone being attacked?"
"No, but a lot of cars have been speeding in and out of the subdivision," Gin answered, still shaking.
"Probable people like me trying to get home or leaving to find their family members. You're lucky you haven't seen an attack, it's not a pretty sight," I said, issuing them a warning.
Suddenly we heard the sound of glass breaking in the kitchen.
"What's that?" Gin asked, as she grabbed my arm.
Without hesitation, Billy ran toward the kitchen, and seconds later we heard him shout.
"Dad, Dad!"
At that moment I knew what had happened. Someone was trying to get into the house, and from the sound of it, they probably had succeeded in their endeavor.
I jerked my arm from Gin's grasp.

"Stay here honey, I'll be right back!" I said, as I quickly followed Billy into the kitchen.

Upon joining Billy in the kitchen, we stood there, momentarily stunned by what we saw.

A person had made it halfway through the patio's glass door; his clothes were saturated with blood, and his intestines were draped over each side of his twitching body as he sat there eerily straddled on the remaining pillar of broken glass that was still attached to the bottom of the doorframe.

During his attempt to enter our home, he had hit the door at the top, breaking out the glass down to several inches past the door handle.

The shattering glass falling on his body had cut him in numerous places causing massive hemorrhaging, which in turn resulted in puddles of blood outside the patio door, and on our kitchen floor.

When he attempted to step through the opening, he had slipped in his own blood and fell on the remaining glass that was still in the door.

That glass was broken at about a forty-five degree angle, and as he fell, the glass had acted like a serrated knife-edge cutting him in half vertically from his crotch to his sternum as he slid along its razor sharp periphery, spilling his perforated and severed guts onto our kitchen floor as well.

"That's Jon from down the street, Julie's husband! That's him all right," Billy announced.

Just then, Jacob bolted into the kitchen from an adjoining room, leaving his mother alone in the hallway still waiting by the front door.

"He's split in two!" Jacob yelled.

"But he's not dead!" Billy said, excitedly glancing back and forth as he began to show signs of a person who was about to go into full panic mode.

"But he's split in two!" Jacob repeated, again yelling.

"He's almost in two separate pieces, he should be dead," Billy said, shaking his head in disbelief.

"What's the problem in there, is everyone all right?" Gin yelled, as her curiosity was starting to get the better of her.

"Don't come in here honey; you don't want to see this," I yelled to her, fighting back a sickening feeling in my stomach.

I had seen combat in two different theaters of operation while in the Marine Corps, I had watched as men kicked and screamed as they were handed their own limbs to hold as they were transported to a waiting helicopter to be medivaced out of the LZ (Landing Zone, for you non-military types). I had seen young boys with both of their legs blown completely off, and their intestines hanging out of their shirts. I had seen many horrendous things, but I had never seen anything that even came close to this.

There in front of us was a man that I had seen many times at a distance; however, I had never talked to him. This man was hanging on my patio door almost cut into two pieces; he should have been dead. Instead, he was snarling and growling, spitting up blood, mucus, and some pinkish-whitish foam. The look in his eyes was the same as I'd seen before, first on the women's face who was going to attack me on the freeway, then on the two girl's faces as I made my way home that day, it was the look of fury.

"Don't come in here, honey!" I called out again to my wife.

Of course, telling someone not to look at something is always an open invitation for him or her to want to look even more. So of course, into the kitchen Gin came.

It would have been bad enough for her to enter the kitchen and see our neighbor's body cut in half and suspended on what was left of our patio door. It would have been bad enough, just to see his intestines bulging out of his torso and cloaked over his legs, with the balk of them in a pile under one of our kitchen chairs.

But neighbor Jon was still alive, or so we thought at the time, and he was snarling and growling, and inadvertently spitting at us, and as his head lurched as he snapped at us, his upper torso bobbed up and down on the large shard of glass in the door, sawing ever so slightly on the front of his rib cage.

Pain did not seem to be a factor in Jon's world; only anger and ferocity were displayed as we watched his teeth slowly turn to a deep dark-yellow color, which then quickly began to exhibit a putrid brown hue with a tinge of baby-shit green as his gums transformed from a normal pink hue, to a sickening bluish-green tint with a hint of gray.

Pinkish-red tears began to flow down Jon's cheeks, as we watched his eyes become more and more bloodshot while his head twisted and jerked on his compressed and bent rotating neck.

As soon as Gin got a glimpse of the horrible sight, she stopped for a moment staring in disbelief, and then let out a blood-curdling scream so loud that the boys and I had to put our hands over our ears to block the pain from the overload of decibels it caused.

Before I had a chance to think, I blurted out.

"Calm down honey, it's Jon from down the street."

She screamed again, this time not as loud as before, more like a high-pitched moan. It was almost like she was confused, and now trying to decide if this were real or not, and if Jon was all right or not.

My tone now became somber.

"Don't worry, we'll help him," I said, knowing that there was nothing we could do, and my experience in the Marine Corps told me that Jon would be dead very soon. After all, he was in far worse shape than many men that I had seen die before they could get help.

Moreover, I knew that help wasn't coming, at least not in the normal time frame that we were accustomed to.

"*Jon is dead meat,*" I thought to myself. Little did I know at the time, just how right I was?

By now, Gin was crying and shaking uncontrollably, I put my arms around her as she turned to me and buried her face into my shoulder sobbing.

The sight of our neighbor split in half and dangling on the broken glass door was just too much for her to take, hell, it was too much for all of us to take.

"It's going to be all right honey," I said, trying not to show her how frantic I felt too.

We could hear the television that was on in the living room, and like the radio, all regular broadcasting had been preempted and the emergency broadcasting system was now issuing all of the warnings, and live video feeds from numerous violent occurrences around the area were being shown.

"What did the television just say," Jacob inquired.

"They said, don't do something?" Billy said, glaring at him. "Go find out!"

"Right," Jacob said agreeably, finding this to be a good excuse to leave the horror that was being played out in our kitchen.

We turned our attention back to our neighbor Jon, who was still jiggling his head around and snarling at us.

Many of Jon's muscles, tendons, and nerves had been severed, so he was unable to move anything below his neck, but his shoulders swayed a little from the momentum of his head movement as he tried in vain to bite us.

To add to the gruesome chain of events, Jon had begun to gurgle and spit up small chunks of his intestines and pieces of his lungs as he continued to growl and snap at us like a mad dog.

Gin then asked sadly.

"What are we going to do?"

"We could try to get him off the door, and maybe lay him down," I said reluctantly.

"Don't do that Dad, stay away from him," Jacob muttered in a low tone as he returned from the living room.

"The television says if you get bit or he scratches you, or maybe even gets his blood or any of his bodily fluids on you, or in your eyes or mouth, you could get infected with whatever it is he has, and turn into what Jon is now."

29

I quickly yelled. "Stay away from him, everybody get back!"

We all stepped back a few feet and watched as our neighbor spewed blood and thrashed his head around violently, all the time staring at us with that murderous look in his eyes that was becoming all too familiar to me.

Then, as quickly as it had started, it was over.

The constant vibration of Jon's head lurching back and forth in his futile effort to get to us had inadvertently loosened a large shard of glass that was still clinging to the top of the doorframe.

When it fell, it buried itself deep into the top of Jon's skull like a dagger, and suddenly all of his movement ceased, and his head slumped to the side at a ninety-degree angle.

"We need to do something," Gin whimpered, still in tears and shaking.

I could see it in my wife's eyes that she was scared. Hell, we were all scared. But Gin in particular was having very hard time watching the chain of events that were taking place in our home.

"Well there's nothing we can do for him," I said. "We need to lookout for ourselves now."

In the chaos caused by our neighbor's untimely visit and subsequent unwelcome stay, we had failed to hear the crackle of the surrounding gunfire outside.

Now with our domestic excitement and noise abated, we could hear the pandemonium that was ravaging our neighborhood, and it sent chills down our spines.

Jacob was the only one of us that had actually heard any of the warnings that were being broadcasted on the television, so I asked him.

"Jacob, did the news say what's causing this?"

Jacob tilted his head slightly to one side and said.

"I don't think so. But I came to tell you how they said it might be spreading, so I didn't hear everything they said."

Leaving our neighbor Jon in somewhat of a pile, still perched on the broken glass of the patio door, we rushed into the living room to see if we could obtain any new information from the news bulletins.

What we eventually gleaned from the constant flow of news flashes was that the police, military, and political structure was breaking down extremely fast, and that hospitals and urgent care facilities were immediately overwhelmed.

They weren't of any help anyway, there wasn't a cure. Once you were infected, you didn't go to an emergency room; you attacked people and tried to eat them.

Therefore, the only people that were going to the hospitals were people that had not yet become infected, and were just hoping to get some kind of vaccination, or a pill, or something that would keep them from getting the parasitic virus if they were to come in contact with someone or something that was carrying it.

Live newscasts from some of the medical centers, showed some of the doctors and nurses, had already contracted the disease, and were attacking these people as they entered the facilities.

Several months earlier, the Center for Disease Control in Atlanta had isolated a zoonotic virus which was found in the feral dog population, and now they thought that *it* might be the possible offender, and with the dogs numbers having had exploded in the United States in recent years, the disease was spreading ridiculously fast. But even the CDC wasn't completely sure.

They put out several possible scenarios. One of which was the Typhoid Mary scenario. This stated that the feral dogs were immune from the disease that they were carrying, and had spread the virus months beforehand. It lay dormant for an undetermined incubation period, and then when something of an unknown nature triggered it, it became active in some people.

That is why initially, such a great number of cases were so prevalent, with some estimates ranging as high as eighty-five percent of the population. It was almost as if someone turned on a light switch, only in this case a *zombie* switch.

Apparently, death was the trigger that activated the dormant virus in people that seemingly, had not yet been affected, and their ultimate demise awakened the quiescent sickness. Whether it was chemical activity in the brain, or lack thereof, death by any means other than forced trauma to the head, meant that you would return to the living, undead, with a voracious appetite for consuming human flesh. Therefore, within the short span of several hours, there was total anarchy across the globe.

A "*Zombie Apocalypse*" had begun!

As we somberly walked back into the kitchen again, to focus on how we were going to cope with the predicament that was facing us.

Billy looked puzzled.

"What's that buzzing sound?" he asked.

"It's coming from the kitchen." Jacob said, with the same puzzled look on his face.

The gruesome sight of our former neighbor Jon who we all were expecting, yet dreading to see, had grown even more macabre.

During the time we had watched the news unfold in our living room, the smell of the contents of Jon's carved up entrails had attracted a multitude of flies who's constant buzzing had impaired our hearing to the point that we were unable to hear the real danger that awaited us in the next room.

Later as we learned more about the menacing creatures that were roaming our world, we would find that the smell of the rotting flesh of the zombies would usually be the reason that flies were attracted to them, but in this case, Jon had not been a member of the undead long enough for his body to start to putrefy. Therefore, the feces leaking from his ripped and torn intestines was the culprit in this instance.

When we reentered the kitchen, we found that the immense rabble of flies was not the only thing that was hovering over our former neighbor Jon, Julie his wife had made her way to our patio doorway and was making a meal of what was left of Jon's now cadaverous corpse.

Now seeing her, and hearing her over the hideous buzzing of the massive amount of flies, we watched in horror as our new visitor snarled and spit, all the while biting and tearing away the flesh from her now dead husband's bones, partially chewing it, then gulping it down, reminiscent of a wild dog wolfing down its prey.

It was clear Julie too was infected; extremely dangerous, and bound to attack us as soon as she realized we were in her presents.

Without uttering a word, I turned and ran as fast as I could to my bedroom closet where my gun safe was located.

I thought to myself.

"Hurry Jack, faster!"

I fiddled with the safes combination for only a few seconds before I was able to swing the door open, but that few seconds seemed like hours.

My first choice was my Glock 19 which was fully loaded and hanging from a gun hook right in front of me.

Even though many of the experts will tell you to unload your gun and store the ammunition in another area, I was taught a long time ago, that if your gun isn't loaded when you need it, you might as well not have it.

Trying to locate your ammunition and load your weapon (probably in the dark) while the bad guys are bearing down on you, is not only illogical, but also unadvisable. That is if you wish to stay alive.

That advice served me well during those first hours of the apocalypse, and still does to this very day. An unloaded gun is just another blunt force object like a club; you might as well be carrying a stick or a rock.

But enough for now on gun safety and tactics.

In a split second, I had a fully loaded gun in my hand and I was rushing back to the kitchen hoping that

Julie was still preoccupied with her husband, and hadn't noticed my family standing mere feet away.

Returning to the kitchen, I found Jacob and Billy standing in front of Gin, Billy with a kitchen chair held over his head, ready to club Julie senseless, and Jacob with an iron skillet poised to do the same if the diseased man-eater were to bolt in his direction.

Julie had yet to notice any of us standing there, but I knew it was just a matter of time until she did. We all knew that one of us was going to have to put Julie out of her misery before she threatened us, and being the one with the gun, I knew that I was the most likely candidate for the distasteful (no pun intended) yet necessary job.

I stood there for a moment hesitating, watching the repugnant pantomime, waiting for Julie to make a move toward us so I could justify in my mind, the heinous act that I was about to commit.

"What are you waiting for?" Gin asked anxiously, and in my opinion a bit too loud.

"We can't just kill her! Jon's already dead, so we won't be saving him, and she hasn't done anything to us yet," I said naively, as I reluctantly raised my pistol, not yet fully realizing the scope of the cataclysm before us.

Jacob now repeated the warning the emergency broadcast had reported.

"Don't let them bite you, or scratch you, or get any of their blood in your eyes, nose, or mouth."

"Right! Shoot her, shoot her now!" Gin pleaded.

Again, in my humble and meager opinion, she said it a bit too loud.

Because at that moment Julie looked up, and noticed the four of us tasty morsels standing nearby watching her scarf down her husband's diseased body.

Gin, seeming less afraid now, yelled.

"She's seen us!"

Julie quickly lost all interest in the *post-marriage* meal before her, and concentrated her full attention on the seemingly fresher live meat in her midst.

She leaned forward putting her left hand on the remains of Jon's right leg, digging her fingers deep into the gashes she herself had caused during her feast, and reaching up over Jon's head with her right hand in an attempt to pull herself to her feet; she grabbed the razor sharp edge of the broken glass that had sawed her husband in half.

Julie put most of her weight on the glass with her hand, which was covered with Jon's blood, and between her slippery blood-soaked fingers and the angle of the glass, there was little friction to aid her grip.

Unable to maintain her grasp, her hand quickly broke free and slid down the glass, instantly her fingers were cleanly severed off between her knuckles and the first finger joints, causing her to fall face first into Jon's hollowed out torso where the glass neatly sliced her head from her neck.

Her head fell to the floor leaving a trail of blood behind it as it awkwardly rolled under our kitchen table; her body went limp except for a slight twitching of her fingers (the ones that were still attached) and dropped on top of Jon's half eaten corpse.

Her *severed* fingers quivered on the floor beside Jon's dead body for a few moments, and then slowly began to exhibit signs of stiffening before they too became lifeless nubs on our kitchen floor.

That is when we knew the true horror of this disease. Although Julie's head was now detached from her body, her head was still alive.

The eyes in Julie's decapitated skull rolled back and forth and up and down as they had when her head was still connected to her body.

Although she still moved her jaw in an attempt to bite us, and I'm sure she would have if an opportunity would have presented itself, she was not able to spit or spew blood or saliva now that her lungs were several feet away, still enclosed in her detached body.

Earlier we had wondered why Jon was still alive after his body had been cut in two. Even when the shard of glass fell and finally put him out of his misery, we didn't make the connection that the diseased brain would have to be destroyed before the infected ones would ultimately find peace.

The official broadcasts had not mentioned anything about how to kill the people that had been infected, the warnings were more generic, like stay inside, lock your doors, don't get bit, that kind of thing.

Gin turned away from Julie's grossly animated head. "I think I'm going to puke."

"Me too!" Jacob said, his face turning a little green. Boom! Boom!

I watched a fist size chunk of the back of Julie's skull careen off one of the kitchen table legs as my Glock 19 sang out, sending its 9mm hollow point bullet through Julie's left eyeball and smashing into the interior of her cranium shortly before pushing through the bone

37

and taking pieces of her brain with it, and finally putting an end to our neighbor's torment, and her furious menacing stare.

The only sounds now were the ringing in our ears from the gunshots, and the sickening buzz of the hundreds of flies in the room, along with the constant crackle of gunfire in the distance.

Our neighbors had now ceased all movement except for a slight random twitch occasionally, and for the moment, I felt safe as I slid the pistol into the back of my waistband.

We stood there for a while, pondering what to do next. Gin still had her back to the atrocious scene.

"I'm going to call the police!" she said.

"I tried calling you several times on my way home, but couldn't get through, everybody is calling 911. But go ahead and try, maybe you'll get through." I said, doubtful that she would get any results.

Gin dialed the emergency number again and again to no avail.

"You're right the phone is still useless, I can't get through to the police," Gin said, as she tossed her cell phone onto the kitchen counter just barely missing the sink.

"We can't stay here, it's not safe," I said.

Billy waved his hands around in front of his face, as he shooed away the flies.

"Well I'm not going to stay here with all these flies," he exclaimed!

"The cops aren't coming, the ambulance isn't coming, nobody is coming, I think we're on our own," Jacob scowled.

"He's probably right, after what I saw on my way home, what the television said, and now this, there might not even be a police force now, or army, or anything," I said, as I shooed away some flies that were now tormenting me as well.

Gin leaned toward me, her face now beginning to turn the same shade of green that Jacob's face had turned earlier and muttered.

"This is disgusting, how are we going to clean up this mess?"

I tried not to think of just how disgusting what we had to do was really going to be, and I said.

"I've got an idea. You boys go get the snow shovels, and that old paint drop cloth that's out in the garage. Hurry up! Bring some duct tape too!"

"And some insect spray if you can find any," Gin added loudly.

When the boys returned with the paraphernalia I'd sent them to retrieve, we began to shovel our repugnant former neighbor's piles of guts and dismembered body parts, along with Julie's severed head outside onto the patio.

We didn't get very far before hearing the heaving sound of Gin vomiting from the sight of the disjointed corpses and the smell of fecal matter from Jon's shredded bowls.

The odor had already permeated the room, and was spreading quickly throughout the rest of the house. Now with the vomit added to the mix, the reeking stench in the room was almost too much for any of us to bear.

Jacob's tint was greener still, as he covered his mouth.

"I think I'm going to throw up too," he complained.

"Try to hold it down," I said. "Leave the room if you have too."

Jacob turned his head away from the pile of intestines he was pushing out the door and dropped his shovel to the floor.

"I'm going to the garage, it doesn't smell out there," he said before covering his mouth with his hand once more.

"Go with him honey, you don't look so good either," I said to Gin, hoping Billy could tolerate the smell long enough to help me finish the distasteful (again, no pun intended) job at hand.

"How are you doing Billy? Are you going to make it?" I asked.

Looking up at me with a scowl on his face, he answered.

"I'm okay, but let's hurry, this really stinks."

Trying not to slop blood on each other, or ourselves, we worked as swiftly as we could, shoving the almost unrecognizable human remains out the doorway, which had the effect of drawing most of the flies outside with them.

We sealed off the broken glass door with the paint tarp and the duct tape to keep the flies out, sprayed the kitchen with insect spray killing most of the flies and masking the reeking stench of Jon's feces and Gin's added mix of puke a little bit, then swatted the few remaining flies with a couple of folded newspapers.

As we finished the morbid cleaning chore, Billy looked out a back window and spotted another disease-infested neighbor none of us recognized wandering around our backyard.

"There's another one Dad, looks like he's headed next door to Don's house."

"Don will just have to take care of himself, we have our own problems," I answered. "Hell, for all I know Don's already one of them."

"You go see if there's anything new on the television, I'll go get your mother and Jacob," I said, as I turned and walked toward the garage.

Opening the door to the garage, I was glad to see that the normal color had returned to my spouse and son's faces.

I looked at Gin and repeated my previous statement.

"We need to leave; it's not safe here anymore."

"Where can we go?"

"I don't know!" I answered shaking my head. "But I know that we can't stay here much longer."

I motioned for her and Jacob to come back into the house.

"Come back in here, the smell isn't as bad now, smells more like bug spray," I said, hoping they wouldn't get sick again.

"Let's grab a few things, and then we've got to go!"

"Hey, everybody, come in here, there's a disease update on the television," Billy yelled from the living room.

While we entered the living room and converged on the television, we all hoped the new information that Billy had summoned us to hear was good news, but it wasn't.

"They say that the diseased people are dead!"

Grabbing the remote from the coffee table, I pointed it toward the television, and pressing the plus on the volume button I shouted.

"Quiet, I can't hear what they're saying."

The faceless voice behind the emergency warning screen repeated the announcement over and over, as we stood there dazed, listening in disbelief.

We now learned that the disease first kills you, and within seconds, you reanimate with an insatiable appetite for human flesh and organs, not to mention brains. If you die first, say you're hit by a car and killed, then the disease takes you over immediately and you get up and attack the first person that you see, as I had witnessed in the beginning on the freeway.

It was clear now why Jon and Julie didn't die immediately after their horrendous mutilating fates; they were already dead.

Now the broadcasts were no longer focusing on how to save the living, they seemed more intent on spreading information on how to kill the living dead.

Five or six minutes passed while we stood in front of the television, all of us in an almost trance like state. Then without warning, the television went dark, snapping us back to the cruel reality that confronted us.

"Great, now the electricity is out," Gin said angrily.

Then trying to comfort herself by convincing herself that everything would be all right, she mumbled. "Maybe it's a rolling blackout, and it'll come back on in awhile."

"I hope you're right," I said, also trying to comfort her. "But we can't wait here to find out. If we're still here when it gets dark, and the lights are still off, things could get really ugly."

"Uglier than what happened in the kitchen?" Jacob asked sarcastically.

Smiling sarcastically back at him, I replied.

"Well I for one don't want to go to sleep with this lingering smell in the house, and dead stark raving flesh eating homicidal maniacs walking around outside the house with only a canvas tarp and duct tape between us. So like I said before, let's grab a few things and get the hell out of here."

A sheepish grin creped over Jacob's face and he responded.

"Indeed!"

It wasn't long before the electricity in our house did come back on. In the beginning, there *were* rolling blackouts, but each time the electric went off, it stayed off longer and more areas were affected, until ultimately total blackouts came, and the power grid never did come back up. Ever again!

GET THE HELL OUT OF DODGE

We walked back to the garage carrying a few meager items we had collected in the house, mostly food, some water, and heavier clothing that we thought we might need later.

Fortunately, I had made some preparations in case of a regular emergency, if there is any such thing, by collecting a hodgepodge of equipment. To which I now added to the list, guns, ammunition, and some camouflage army surplus clothing I had acquired along the way. But I was not remotely prepared for anything like this cataclysm.

My home was in a subdivision and it had too many windows and too many doors, I didn't have a fireplace for heat, a generator for power, or a well for water. It wasn't a place that I felt we could hold out for very long, from the living or from the living-dead. That belief was confirmed by how easily Jon and Julie had entered the house. I knew I had to find someplace, someplace safe, someplace my family and I could survive this horrific new world that we had been thrust into, but where.

Then, on the short walk to our garage to survey my inadequate pile of emergency equipment, I had an idea.

Once in the garage, Billy asked. "How are we going to get our stuff in the van without being eaten? There are *eaters* in our back yard, and all over the neighbor's yards. They're probably out in front by the van too!"

Before now, we had been referring to the "Zombies" as diseased one's, or the infected one's, but after Billy called them "Eaters", well it kind of stuck, and after that, most of the time we called them eaters.

"We're not going to put our stuff in the van. You saw what I had to do to our neighbor Julie and you hear all that gunfire out there."

Billy and Jacob both nodded their heads, affirming that they understood.

"People all over are doing the same thing to their neighbors. We wouldn't get fifty miles from here in the van. Someone would block the road or shoot out the tires, or the way people were acting when I drove home, we would probably be in a wreck before we got to the county line. In any case we'd end up dead and eaten before nightfall."

Billy tilted his head slightly to the side as Jacob had done before, and added a turned up upper lip on the left side of his mouth showing his confusion.

"We're not going to walk are we? We definitely wouldn't get fifty miles if we try to walk. Would we?"

I was able to muster a smile for the first time since this whole zombie thing started. Partially because of the look on Billy's face when he asked if we were going to try to walk to some place safe, and partially because I was about the reveal my idea to my family.

"No, not the way it is out there now, we *will* need the van, but not to carry our things, we'll need it to pull our boat."

"The boat?" Gin asked sarcastically, shaking her head back and forth as if she thought I was going to say that I was just kidding.

Nodding my head in an effort to convince her that I was deadly serious, I quickly answered her question without a hint of sarcasm in my voice.

"Yes, the boat, we can't stay here, and we can't drive the van, and we can't walk, the boat is our only logical choice. Hell, logical or not, it's our only choice!

Look at it this way, in the van or any car for that matter, the roads will surely be clogged with wrecked and abandoned vehicles, not to mention filled with

45

panicked motorists that are driving like stark raving maniacs as they run for their lives. Plus, we'll need gas and a lot of it if we want to get very far.

With the boat, we'll just float down stream most of the time, and only use the motor when we absolutely need to. We still might need to obtain some gas at some point, so we'll take that little squeeze pump I have along with us."

Trying to convince myself as much as I was trying to convince my family, I said. "We don't know everything this disease does to people, but one thing I know for sure, it's not going to make them break the laws of physics, which means, they can't walk on water."

"But can they swim?" Jacob asked.

I thought about it for a moment, and then answered.

"I don't know if they can swim or not, but if they can't swim any better than they can walk, we'll be safer in a boat until we can find some place safe to hold up (of course that was said when we all thought that there were still some places that were actually safe) while we try and get our shit together."

Before civilization as we knew it ended, some zombie connoisseur's blogging on the internet about an *imaginary* zombie invasion, said to go north where it is cold, zombies are made of flesh and blood and are subject to freezing, and once they're frozen, your problem of being eaten by the dead is over.

The way I see it, the problem with that theory is, you would have to go far enough north that zombies (or as we called them, "Eaters") would never thaw, even during the summer months.

If you miscalculated and didn't trek far enough north, all that it would take is for one warm front to come through overnight and thaw out the zombie hordes, and you'd wake up to an unexpected horde of nimble and very hungry zombies intent on having you for breakfast.

The only advantage I could see by going north into a constant frozen climate was the snow and ice could be melted, giving you an abundance of water. That is, until you ran out of fuel for the heat source that you were using to melt the frozen water. Then you would probably freeze to death before you would die of thirst.

Not to mention the fact that I was never too fond of cold weather, and the thought of subzero temperatures all day, every day, day and night, all year round for the rest of my life, did not appeal to me at all, not one bit. Therefore, I quickly rejected the idea of a miserable existence in a perpetual winter.

Besides, going north in our boat would mean that we couldn't just float down stream; we would be going up stream against the current all the way, using more gas than we could possibly carry.

Not to mention we would never be able to pass through the locks on the Mississippi River just north of St. Louis. Our only option was to go down south to a warmer climate; somewhere that had a lot of wild game seemed to me to be a much better idea.

Now that the apocalypse was no longer a matter of conjecture, and the zombie virus didn't seem to affect animals, even the feral dogs were just carriers, at least for the moment anyway. So with that said, hunting and eating animals seemed like a viable answer for a food source if scavenging for food in abandon houses was not possible or practical for some reason.

I hoped my hypothesis on this issue was correct, and that eating the meat of wild animals didn't cause us to catch or spread the disease, because at this time nobody knew how long the incubation period was for the dormant infection, and eating anything that you weren't absolutely sure of was risky to say the least.

Fortunately, we had enough food in the beginning that we could contemplate this matter at a later time. Although if we were to hunt animals for food, we weren't about to eat a feral dog first to test the theory.

We lived close to the Mississippi River, and very close to one of its tributaries. Because of this location, I had purchased a small boat to cruise the waterways with my two sons, do some fishing, and generally enjoy the warm summer days.

The boat was only a fifteen-foot bow rider with a forty-eight Evinrude outboard motor, but it served the purpose for which I bought it.

I had named the boat Morphodite, because at the time I thought it was funny, and I still do, even in the middle of a zombie apocalypse. However, I never thought I'd be taking a boat as small as the Morphodite on such a monumental journey, but it was all we had, so it would have to do.

When Armageddon came, there was little time to formulate a plan, most people headed for their local stores and started grabbing things off the shelves, and it didn't matter what. Panic was wide spread and most of the gunshots we were hearing were coming from the direction of a strip mall in our neighborhood, and I didn't want any part of it.

We would stick to our rough-and-ready plan, and stay away from the stores and shopping malls, at least until things died down a little (no pun intended).

Our boat's two gas tanks were five gallons each and portable, I would usually take them out, drive to the gas station to fill them, and then bring them back to the boat and put them in it again.

They fit under the back seats of the boat on either side of the battery, which sat in the middle. A gas line ran from the fuel tank to the motor, and when one tank is empty, you simply disconnect the fuel line from the empty tank, and attach it to the full tank, and off you go again.

"Grab the siphon pump and bring it over here."

Jacob looked around the garage.

"I don't see it, where is it?"

"I think it's over there behind that toolbox," I said, pointing to an old gray partially rusted toolbox in the corner.

Sliding the toolbox over and spotting the small plastic pump, Jacob announced.

"I got it!"

Gin picked up the almost empty gas can we used to fill our lawnmower and asked. "Do you want this one too?"

"Yes, we're going to need all the gas we can take with us!" I answered.

"Well this one doesn't have very much gas in it!" she said,

"That's the next problem we'll have to solve!" I said.

"How are we going to do that?" she asked.

"We're going to have to go outside and siphon some of the gasoline out of the van," I answered solemnly, thinking that taking a chance filling a gas can while standing around outside in the midst of a zombie outbreak might be more of a risk than we really wanted to take.

But, at the time I felt that we would probably need the fuel at some point down the *road* so to speak, or to be a little more specific, down the *river*, and not having any other gasoline source, the van was the plan.

"Do we have anymore containers we can use?" Billy asked, as he looked intently around the garage.

"I don't think so, we have the two boat tanks and the mower can, and that's it," I answered.

"So we can take fifteen gallons of gas with us, right?" Billy asked sounding a slight bit frustrated.

"Right, unless we can find something else we can put gasoline into, real quick, and I don't see that happening.

But the good news is, since I had intended to take the boat out on the river this weekend, the two boat tanks are full, so all we have to do is fill up the one gas can and we're set."

Gin turned to me with a very worried look on her face.

"How long will that take? To siphon the gas I mean."

"Not long I hope; it depends on how much trouble the eaters give us," I replied confidently, unaware of how bad things were deteriorating outside of our house.

Then pulling my pistol from my waistband, I tapped the butt of the gun saying. "But first things first, we'll need more guns than just this Glock."

"I'll help you get them," Billy said quietly, sounding somewhat excited.

"Me too!" Jacob added, with the same excited tone.

"Let's all go back in the house and take another look around, maybe we can grab a couple of things that we missed the first time," I said, as I led the way into the house.

I gathered together all of my firearms, ammo, and the relevant equipment that I had.

We pulled the pillowcases off the bed and put the rifles, pistols, magazines, and ammo in them, and the remaining equipment such as holsters and slings were bundled into one of the bed sheets.

Each of us took as much as we could lift, and carried it to the garage.

You never really know how many guns you have, or how much they weigh, until you try to carry all of them at once, including their ammo, holsters, and assorted accessories. But that's most likely true with the equipment from any sporting or recreational endeavor one might choose to partake in. Fortunately, I had chosen firearms related endeavors for some of my recreational pursuits. Guns work a little bit better in a zombie apocalypse than do golf clubs, tennis rackets, and bowling balls. Although in a pinch, anything you have on hand that can be used to bludgeon, stab, beat

51

down, cut, squash, sever, or in essence generally destroy the brains of the living dead is far better than being eaten alive. Of course, that's just my opinion on the subject and other's opinions may vary.

Passing Gin in the hallway she looked perplexed and asked. "Do we really need all of that?"

Without any hesitation, I answered her question.

"Honey, when you absolutely need a gun, there is no substitute! Remember, when *seconds* count, the police are only *minutes* away. And I think in this case, I would venture to guess that the police are never coming."

Seemingly not totally convinced by my mini-lecture, Gin gave me what might be called a knowing look and said in a monotone voice.

"O...kay."

The weight of our equipment made the trek back to the garage seem longer than it really was. Even after each of us stopped once or twice along the way to give our hands a quick rest, by the time we got to the garage our hands and arms ached, and we were unable to maintain our hold on the makeshift transporters any longer, and they began to slip from our grasp as we entered the garage.

"That was harder than I thought it would be," Jacob said, as he rubbed his hands together to get the blood circulating again.

"You think everything is harder than you thought it would be," Billy said, as he too rubbed his hands together.

We dumped the contents of the pillowcases and sheet onto the floor in a pile, and we wasted no time preparing to go outside and pump enough gas from our vehicle to fill the remaining gasoline container.

Peeking out the side and only window in the garage, Billy said. "I only see two on this side; they're just stumbling around out there."

"We don't know how many more might be on the other side of the garage door. There could be one, or none, or a whole lot more of them! So here's how we're going to do this," I said, with the sound of authority in my voice.

"We might run into more than just eaters out there, so we're going to dress the part, besides, we don't want to go out into a world full of eaters in street clothes, so grab those camouflage uniforms over there. Mine is the multi-cam, there's some army digital that should fit Jacob. Billy you get older stuff, I think it'll fit you."

"I always get the old stuff," Billy said jokingly, as he reached for the older garments.

It was good to hear Billy joking; I hoped it meant that he was getting past the grisly episode in our kitchen with the neighbors.

Smiling at him, I said. "Just start changing and I'll tell you the plan."

As we changed our clothes, I shared the details off my plan with the boys. I call it my *plan*, but really, I was just making it up as I went.

"Billy, when I say go you open the garage door, do it as fast as you can, if there are any of them out there we want to catch them by surprise, not the other way around. From what we've seen so far, they haven't demonstrated any semblance of speed. So, I think they're probably not capable of moving very fast, but I don't

53

know that for sure. If they're close, they could be on us quick. Billy you carry the gas can, and I'll carry the siphon. While I'm sticking one end of the hose in the van's gas tank, you put the other end in the gas can, and I'll start pumping the fuel. Jacob you cover us with one of the rifles, I don't care which one, I would use either the AK-47 or the 9mm carbine if I were you. On second thought, use the carbine, it's better for close quarter's battle, and that way we can save the AK ammunition for longer range targets."

Nodding his head, Jacob agreed and grabbed the pistol caliber carbine.

"Billy, you and I will use pistols, pistols will give us plenty of fire power and we can quickly holster them to free up our hands to do the siphoning," I said, as I pointed to the pile of guns and assorted equipment.

Billy rummaged through the mixed heap of firearms and equipment we had dumped on the garage floor.

"I'll take this one; do we have a holster for it?" he asked.

"That's the 92 right, here it is," Jacob answered, as he handed him the holster.

Reaching behind me, I pulled the Glock 19 that I had used on Julie earlier from my belt.

"I'll need a holster for this too, it's in that pile somewhere, Jacob see if you can find it."

Reaching into our equipment mound, Jacob pulled out two holsters, one in each hand, and held them up in front of me.

"I think it's one of these."

"It's this one!" I said, taking the one in his right hand.

After finding what we needed, we geared up and took our positions by the garage door.

"Billy, look out the window again and see if anything has changed," I ordered.

Billy moved quickly to the garage window and peeked out.

"Still only two of them over here," he said as he made his way back to his assigned position at the garage door.

"Okay, everybody knows what to do, everybody ready?" I asked.

Both boys replied.

"Ready!"

"Okay, on three, one, two, three, open the door!" I shouted.

Billy tugged hard on the garage door handle, and the spring-loaded door clattered and squeaked as the somewhat rusty wheels road up along the metal tracks.

As the door opened, and revealed the driveway, our worst possible nightmare had come true, and we immediately found ourselves exposed.

At least fifteen zombies were in the driveway and surrounding area, two of which were within arm's reach of Jacob. The shrill squeak from the wheels had attracted the zombie's attention, and in the split second that it took to open the garage door, the closest zombies were already on the attack.

It all happened so fast that Jacob didn't have enough time to raise his rifle to his shoulder.

Holding his gun at his waist, he raised the barrel of the carbine slightly and began to fire the semi automatic gun as fast as he could.

As Jacob fired the nine-millimeter carbine repeatedly, the muzzle rise lifted the gun up, and before his target's hands could grab him, Jacob's bullets were smashing into the zombie's face.

"Close the door!" I screamed.

Billy had lifted the door with so much force, that when it had reached its pinnacle, it bounced back and was already on its way back down.

Jacob had already pointed his gun at the second zombie, which had now turned and taken one staggering step in his direction. He again began to rapidly fire his weapon.

Two more shots rang out, the first one hitting the zombie in the neck and the second one boring its way through the garage door that was quickly on its way down.

Lowering his rifle, Jacob said. "I think I got both of them, but that second shot, I don't know."

With my heart pounding, I said. "Billy, make sure that door is locked, we don't know what those things are capable of."

"Got it," Billy said, as he jiggled the latch. "They're all over the place," he said, as he once more tested the door lock.

Little did we know it at the time, just how much of an understatement that was.

While Jacob had been dispatching the two zombies, his gunfire had drawn the attention of other zombies in the neighborhood, and they too were now descending upon our home.

"Holy shit," I shouted. "That wasn't good; Jacob you almost got bit, we all almost got bit! That was stupid!" I said, disgusted with myself.

"I've always told you boys, laziness *will* cause you pain. We were so intent on grabbing our guns, and planning how to get the gas out of the van, that we overlooked the obvious," I said sternly, scolding myself more than anyone else, and thinking *"so much for making it up as I go."*

"We should have taken the time to gather more intelligence; we should have looked out the front window. From now on we've got to be much more careful; we've got to think things through a little more."

Only this time I was thinking.

"We, meaning me!"

With that said, we began to formulate a new plan.

"We're going to forget about filling that third gas can, we'll take it with us, but from the looks of things, we're going to have enough problems just getting the boat out," I said, my heart still racing from the shock of the near fatal encounter we had just experienced.

"Jacob, go see what your mother is doing, we need everybody out here."

"Okay Dad, I'll tell her," Jacob said, as he hurried back into the house.

"Billy, crank up the trailer hitch about a foot, once the garage door is opened again, we don't want to be out in the open any longer than we have to be," I said. "And check the tire pressure on the trailer; we can't afford to have a flat tire on the way to the river. I'm going to oil those squeaky wheels on the door, no point in announcing we're coming out."

Billy was eighteen when this all started, a typical teenage boy, cars, girls, and texting was his main concern, but fishing was still high on his list of things to do. Therefore, I tasked him with gathering up all of the fishing equipment that we might need on our journey.

"And put your fishing stuff in the boat, we don't want to forget that," I said, knowing that he would make sure that we had all of the fishing gear we would need to help us survive in this new apocalyptic world.

"I'm going in and see what's taking your mother so long; she's probably packing way too much stuff," I said, as I glanced into the boat, and quickly realized how little room for supplies there was.

"What's going on in here Gin?" I asked, trying to sound confident that everything was going to be fine.

"We're packing things, like you said to," she answered, speaking with a hint of sarcasm.

"I said grab a few things we might have missed, not pack the whole house!"

Looking at me sheepishly, she said, "I know, but everywhere I look, I see something we missed."

"All right," I said. "But some of that stuff we don't need and don't have room for, like all those pillows."

"We're going to need pillows! How are we supposed to sleep without pillows?"

"Okay, we'll take as much as we can, but remember, the boat is only fifteen feet long. I guess we can always throw something overboard if we need more room," I murmured as I turned away.

Now the sarcasm in her voice was more pronounced.

"Okay honey," she said.

"This is going to be more fun than I thought," I muttered as I walked into the kitchen to gather some more food for our journey.

I made a point of not telling Gin about our close encounter with the zombies on the driveway. The sound of Jacob shooting them blended in with the gun fire we were hearing all over the neighborhood, so that didn't get her attention. She seemed to have put the encounter with our neighbors Jon and Julie behind her for now, so I saw no reason to upset her all over again. After all, she would find out soon enough how difficult and dangerous this excursion was going to be.

Jacob was already in the kitchen grabbing food off the pantry shelves, and as I joined him I suggested.

"Get the canned food Jake. It's heavier, but the canned vegetables have water in them, and we're going to need all the water we can get," I told him.

I hurried to grab the last few cans of green beans off the shelf and added.

"Get those jars of peanut butter too; they don't need to be refrigerated."

"Come on Gin, bring what you've got, and let's go!" I yelled with a sense of urgency.

Rounding the corner and dragging two full suitcases Gin announced.

"Here I come, and by the way, where's my camouflage suit?" She asked.

"Probably in one of those suit cases," I replied.

"Very funny," she said, not at all amused.

"We'll get you some later, at some sporting goods store or someplace," I said, thinking that it shouldn't be too hard to find camouflage clothing somewhere, hell now days even department stores sell it. At least they did before the outbreak, now of course they'll be giving it away.

We made our way back into the garage, toting the last of our possessions that we would be taking with us.

That's when the reality of the situation hit all of us. There was a calm silence, because we all knew that once we left, we would never be coming back to this place.

THE MORPHODITE

Normally I would have installed the gas tanks back into the boat when I returned from filling them at the gas station. However, as fate would have it (probably knowing of the impending apocalypse), I got distracted with another of life's little emergencies at the time, and left the full fuel tanks on the floor of the garage to be loaded at a later date. That later date of course, just happened to be in the middle of an apocalyptic outbreak of the undead, with life and death balanced precariously on our timely departure from this zombie-infested locality.

"Billy let's get these tanks in the boat, hook'em up, but don't open the vent cap," I said, again trying to implant a sense of urgency that was desperately needed. "We've got to get moving, we want to be on the river before dark. Jump in the boat and I'll hand them to you."

With only two hours left until sundown, we weren't remotely ready to leave for the river.

"We don't have much room so let's pack these supplies as tight as we can," I stated, again with authority. "Guns and ammo go in last; we have to be able to get to them fast when we need too! We've only got two sleeping bags, put them in front, and tie them to the bow cleats."

"I'll put the rest of the food up in the front compartments," Jacob said, as he stashed several cans into the front hold of the boat.

It took us another half an hour to fill the boat to capacity with our supplies and weapons, and still leave enough room for ourselves.

As I stepped up on the side of the trailer and handed Jacob the last box of ammo, I asked. "Are all of the magazines loaded?"

"Yes, all of them are fully loaded," Billy answered, nodding his head.

"Well, that's it then," I said. "We need to hurry, we don't have a whole lot of time before it gets dark, and if we have to fight our way to the river, we don't want to have to do it in the dark."

"Well, are we ready to go?" Gin asked.

"Not quite yet," I answered, motioning to Jacob. "Go in the house and look out the front window and see if you can see how many eaters if any are in the driveway, and be careful, take a gun with you, remember we only have a drop cloth for a back door now."

"Okay," Jacob said, picking up the same carbine he had used earlier as he headed into the house.

"Do you think there might be some of those things in the driveway?" Gin asked, unaware of our earlier experience trying to fill the gas can.

I knew there were zombies on the other side of the garage door, but I didn't want to alarm her anymore than she already was, so I said. "Well it can't hurt to check."

"Right, it can't hurt to check," she agreed.

We had been working rather somberly, but that mood was broken quickly a few minute later when we heard three gunshots coming from inside the house.

Before we had a chance to react, Jacob came bursting back into the garage.

"I just shot three of them on the patio, I heard them growling on my way back from checking the driveway."

"Are you all right?" Gin asked.

Smiling Jacob replied. "Yes, I'm okay Mom, but we have three more dead neighbors. I mean *really* dead neighbors."

"Jon and Julie's smell must have attracted them. What did the driveway look like, any eaters?" I asked.

Looking confused, not knowing that I was trying to spare his mother any more grief by not telling her about our previous failed attempt to get to the van, Jacob answered cautiously.

"Yes, there're lots of them, twenty-five, maybe thirty, they're all over the place, in the driveway, in the yard, the street, the neighbor's yards, everywhere."

With nightfall closing in on us, I now felt an overwhelming sense of desperation. We had to come up with a workable plan, and fast.

"So, if we were to break out the front window, could we get a clean shot at most of them?" I asked.

Nodding his head Jacob answered.

"I think so?"

"So if one of us was to shoot from the front window, and one of us shot from the garage, between the two, they could cover the one's hooking up the trailer to the van?"

"I'll shoot from the garage," Billy said quickly.

"I guess that leaves me at the front window," Jacob said.

"Then your mother and I will hook up the trailer," I added.

Shrugging her shoulders and stating categorically.

"I don't know how to do that!" Gin said, scowling as she informed us.

"All you have to do is just back up the van a few feet, and I'll do the rest," I said, hoping to convince her. "You *can* back up the van can't you?"

"Yes, I know how to back up the van; you just put it in reverse and stomp on the gas pedal, right?" she said, in her all too familiar sarcastic tone.

After our disastrous attempt to fill the gas can earlier, which I felt was my fault, I wanted to do my best to make sure that everyone knew what to do, and how to do it this time.

"All right!" I said ignoring my wife's feeble attempt at sarcastic humor. "Here's the plan. Jacob, you'll go to the front window, break it out, and leave as many shards in the frame as you can, since you won't be going out that way it might afford you a little more protection, remember Julie's hand? Then shoot as many eaters as you can see, and hopefully the sound of your shots will draw the ones on the driveway toward you. We'll wait a couple of minutes for them to migrate to the front window, then Billy you'll open the garage door, and we'll shoot any stragglers. Gin, when it's clear, you make a run for the van and back it up to the trailer. Once the trailer is hitched, we'll yell for Jacob and hold off any eaters that might have turned back toward us while he makes his way back here. Then we all jump in the van and get the hell out of Dodge. Any questions?"

Jacob piped up, "Nope!"

"Are you sure you want me to back up the van?" Gin asked.

I looked at her nodding my head, which gave her a visual affirmative answer to her question, and said.

"We don't have a choice, I might need Billy to help with the trailer, and he can't do that and drive at the same time. Don't worry, you'll do fine."

Not sounding very confident Gin replied, "All right, I'll do it, give me the keys."

"Okay then, here's the keys, let's do this thing," I said, as I handed Gin the keys to the van.

Jacob turned and began to walk into the house.

"Lucky you turned the van around Dad!"

"Yes, if you want to call this luck," I answered. "I guess if I hadn't of backed it in, we would really be up shit creek without a paddle."

"We'd be up shit creek without a paddle and without a boat," Gin added.

"Indeed we would," I proclaimed.

"Jacob, we'll wait two minutes after we here your first shot," I said. "Keep shooting and give us a minute or two, and then listen for your name, when you hear it,

64

get back here as fast as you can. And watch your back. Get me?" I barked.

"I get you Dad," Jacob barked back as he headed into the house.

We barely heard the glass breaking as Jacob thrust the butt stock of his rifle through the front window. But we heard very clearly the repeated blasts of that same rifle as he began to eliminate the threats in front of our house.

"One minute," I said as I looked up from my watch.

Now Gin's adrenalin was starting to course through her veins as she screamed, "I counted seventeen shots!"

Worried that the zombies would hear her yelling, and might not follow the sound of Jacob's gunfire, I whispered back.

"Not so loud, he's trying to draw them off."

"Seventeen shots, how many bullets does that gun hold?" Gin asked, whispering this time.

"It uses Glock magazines, and the one in his gun is for the Glock eighteen, and it holds thirty-three rounds fully loaded."

Looking very concerned Gin asked. "Was his fully loaded?"

"Billy told me earlier that all the magazines were fully loaded, right Billy?"

"Right Dad, all of them are, or at least they were before he started shooting."

"Anyway, knowing Jacob and his attention to detail, my answer would have to be yes, even if Billy didn't concur," I told her.

I really hoped that I was right, and that Jacob had loaded his magazines to their full capacity.

65

I looked down at my watch and checked the time again.

"A few more seconds and we go!"

Billy put his hand on the garage door handle, and quietly spoke.

"He's still shooting; he's not out of ammo yet."

With a solemn look on my face, I started a slow countdown leaving three or four seconds between each number.

"Three..., two..., one..., open it!"

Billy again quickly raised the garage door.

Outside we saw dozen's of zombies, many of them were on the ground in pools of their own blood with chunks of their brain's oozing out of their skulls.

Our plan was working. Some of the undead had bullet holes in their neck or their chest from some of Jacob's near misses, but were still walking, they were staggering a little more than normal, or should I say abnormal, but all of the zombies that were still able to move, were moving in the direction of the front window of our house.

Others were converging on our front yard from across the street; again, all in the direction of the window from which Jacob was sniping.

"It's working," Billy said, lowering his pistol and moving toward the trailer.

Gin didn't have to be told, she sprinted to the driver's door of the van and jumped inside, and before we knew it, the engine was started and she was backing the van toward the trailer.

"A little more, more, stop," I shouted, as the hitch ball was now lined up with the trailer.

The trailer was slightly high, so I began to turn the crank to lower the tongue coupler onto the hitch ball. The weight of the trailer pushed down on the back of the van as I lowered it into position.

"There, it's hooked," I said, slapping down the locking latch and quickly cranking the trailer's gear jack wheel up and out of the way.

Rising up, I said to Billy.

"Call Jacob back here now!"

Then we all realized that we weren't hearing anymore gunfire coming from the front window.

As fast as I could, I holstered my Glock pistol and I grabbed one of the AK-47's out of the boat with one hand and a seventy-five round drum magazine with the other, and as I ran back into the house, I yelled.

"Something's wrong, get in the van, I'll be right back."

Entering the house I saw that the tarp that we had put up to cover the back entrance of the house had been pulled down and was lying several feet from the kitchen, and in the middle of the living room floor.

It looked as if it had been dragged from the kitchen in the direction of the front window, leaving a trail of Jon and Julie's blood on the floor.

I quickly made my way into the living room and saw Jacob by the front window he'd been shooting from, he was struggling with a zombie, as several other zombies tried to climb through that same window without much success.

Jacob had done what I had told him and left some large shards of glass along the window frame, and the zombies were slicing the flesh from their hands and arms all the way down to the bone, leaving big pieces of slightly greenish tinted skin drooping over the windowsill.

On the floor in front of me, was Jacob's spare magazine that he had unknowingly dropped. He had emptied his first magazine, and when he reached for the spare one that he had brought with him, it wasn't there, and that undead killer had attacked him before he could pick it up off the floor.

I rushed across the room and struck the zombie in the side of the head with the metal reinforced wooden butt stock of my rifle. It tumbled off to the side of the couch and landed face first on the floor next to the wall.

Although the stock on the rifle had a metal butt plate on it, the zombie was only temporarily stunned, and almost immediately began to stand up.

Sticking the barrel of my rifle to the back of the assaulting zombie's head, I pulled the trigger and blew a gaping hole in the back of its skull, and at the same time the exit wound my bullet made was even bigger, which caused most of the zombie's face to be splattered all over the living room wall.

"Are you all right?" I asked, quickly scanning Jacob up and down looking for any wounds he might have suffered.

"I'm fine Dad," he said, not really looking the part.

Just then, I heard a noise behind me and saw Jacob lift his rifle as he screamed.

"Look out!"

He pulled the trigger, and we both cringed as his carbine spit out a deafening *click*.

During his struggle with the zombie, he'd forgotten that he'd run his gun empty.

I swung around and saw a rather large blood stained male zombie staggering toward me and closing the gap between him and me rather quickly.

Having no time to acquire a proper sight picture, or even enough time to raise the muzzle of my rifle slightly, I fired from the hip, just as Jacob had done in the garage during our failed attempt to fill the extra gas can.

Putting the first bullet just below the mutant's belt buckle, this slowed the zombie's momentum a little, as the 7.62mm full metal jacketed round drilled through its innards and crashed into the back of its pelvic bone.

I pulled the trigger several more times in rapid secession, and watched my bullets slam into the zombie's body.

As the muzzle climbed a small amount with each shot, my bullets impacted the living corpse from its crotch to its eyeballs before it collapsed onto the floor just inches from me.

The power of the AK-47 shot at point blank range, not only slowed the oncoming undead cannibal somewhat, but it also ravaged its body to the point that pieces of its spine and intestines were hanging out the back of its torn and blood soaked shirt.

I looked down at the gory mess that was in a pile at my feet, and I thought to myself, "*I stitched up this subhuman, Chinese Gangland style!*"

I stepped over the crumpled body in front of me, and told Jacob to pick up the spare magazine that he had dropped and then said. "Let's get out of here."

Ejecting the empty magazine from his rifle, he quickly inserted the fresh one into his gun and racked a round into the chamber.

"I'm right behind you," he said, as he crammed the empty magazine into his pocket.

We dashed out of the living room thinking that we would again go through the kitchen as we attempted to make our way back to the garage.

That plan was suddenly thwarted when we ran head long into three more of the undead maniacs that had come in through the patio door and were now blocking our path through the kitchen as they investigated the sound of gunfire they had heard coming from the living room.

We instantaneously and simultaneously changed direction, reminiscent of a flock of birds changing direction in flight, and scrambled for the only remaining exit left unobstructed by zombies, which was the front door of our house. Zombies were also rapidly overrunning it, from outside *and* from behind us. There was no time to lose.

Moving as fast as we could, we ran down the hallway making for the front door. Fortunately, no zombies had infiltrated that far into the house yet, so we were able to reach the front door without having to dispatch anymore-poor souls on our way.

A split second later, we were at the front door with the three feral zombies following close behind.

I grabbed the door handle and jerked the door open; I threw my shoulder against the storm door, bending it somewhat as I opened it past its maximum and slammed it hard into the side of the porch.

"Come on Jake," I yelled as I raised my rifle and fired a shot into the head of a female zombie that was standing in the middle of the walkway blocking my path.

As the snarling cannibal dropped in front of me, what was left of its head hit the concrete and made a nauseating thud.

I heard the storm door slam behind Jacob as he lunged quickly through the doorway and onto the porch.

Without breaking stride, Jacob hoisted his carbine to his shoulder and popped off two rounds into the head of an undead that I hadn't seen as it stumbled toward me from the side of the house.

By now, Gin had moved over to the passenger seat of the van, and Billy had jumped into the back of the van and opened the side door that faced the house.

We ran for the van through a plethora of those homicidal maniacs, firing as we went, dropping most, but missing some, nonetheless, we were creating a vista of horrible carnage in our wake, that under any normal circumstances would have sickened us to the point of vomiting.

We were only a few feet from the safety of the vehicle, when shots rang out from our neighbor's front yard.

Jacob's friend Norton and his father Joe had been forced out of their house by another group of degenerate zombies, and were engaging them in a life and death struggle on their front lawn.

"It's Norton and his dad," Jacob yelled, as he abruptly stopped.

"Get in," I shouted. "There's not enough room in the boat for any more people."

"Hurry up, get in," Billy screamed, as he saw zombies approaching from the other side of the van.

Jacob screamed back.

"Can't we help them?"

"No we can't," I answered. "There's nothing we can do for them, they're on their own son, just like us. Now get in the van!"

Jacob looked very sad as he climbed into our vehicle and closed the door behind him, still watching his friend Norton and his father fending off a growing number of the undead.

Fortunately for us, and unfortunately for Joe and Norton, they had unwittingly aided us in our escape, as the sound of their gun shots drew into their front yard some of the zombies that had previously been focused on us.

Jumping into the driver's seat, I crammed the van into drive and stomped down on the accelerator pedal, the vehicle lurched forward causing my door to slam, and as we launched ourselves out of the driveway and into the street, I saw Jacob in the rearview mirror staring out the back window at his friend Norton still battling zombies at his father's side.

"We could have helped them," he said, almost in tears.

"We just barely made it out of there ourselves. We were lucky none of us were bitten, or scratched, or something. If we would have gone to help them, there was a very good chance that we all would have been killed." I said, trying to justify our leaving them to fend for themselves.

"It's too late now," I said sadly. "We've got to concentrate on getting the boat in the water, we're not far from the river, but we don't know what we'll run into on the way, or what will be there to greet us when we get there."

"Besides, Joe is an ex-marine just like your dad, and they were still alive when we last saw them, we got away, and maybe they'll get away too." Gin added, trying to comfort Jacob.

TO THE RIVER

It wasn't long before we would find out what awaited us along the way.

We had only traveled a couple of blocks, during which we found ourselves dodging the first of many wrecked and abandoned vehicles that we would encounter during our travels through the zombie upheaval, when we encountered a large dead dog lying in the middle of the road; it was being feasted upon by two female zombies. Between the three of them, they had unintentionally blocked our way, along with the help of a cable TV truck that had wrecked, and in the process had dropped ladders all over the road.

With little or no shoulder on the road, we had only two choices. We could speed up and try to ram our way through, and hope that any damage to our vehicle or trailer would be minimal, which wasn't likely.

Or I could stop the van, one or two of us could get out and lure the zombies to the side of the road and dispatch them there. Then by moving a couple of the ladders, we could continue on to the river.

It was imperative that we get the boat to the river. The boat was our plan, and without it, we had no plan.

Zombies seemed to be everywhere we looked, and we certainly didn't want to be stuck out in the open without a means of transportation. Therefore, I felt that we couldn't risk damage to the van or to the boat trailer.

If we were to get out of our vehicle for a short time, we could eliminate the immediate threat quickly, get back into the van, and be on our way before the sound of our gunfire brought more of these monsters down on us. That is if nobody mistook us for the undead, or just wanted what we had and started shooting at us. That was a chance we would have to take, after all we couldn't return to our house, and we couldn't stay there.

I slowly applied the brakes and brought our vehicle to a crawl as we approached the roadblock ahead.

"I'm going to stop the van about ten yards from them. Billy, Jake, you two get out on opposite sides and get their attention, lead them into the ditch and blast them.

Then toss those two ladders off the road and get back in here as fast as you can."

As we came to a stop, the side doors of the van opened, and Jacob and Billy slid out of their seats onto the asphalt, raised their weapons and began to yell.

"Hey! Hey, you eaters! Look, here we are!"

Both of the female zombies tilted their heads up quickly as if they had been startled, their teeth still clinching the same leg bone of the deceased mutt, one at the foot and the other at the hip.

They paused for a moment, glaring at the boys with the usual murderous look in their eyes that all self respecting card-carrying zombies seem to have, snarling, and dripping a dark red colored blood marbled with foaming white and pink saliva from their mouths.

Suddenly, without warning and in unison, as if they had choreographed their moves, they rose to their feet lifting the body of the dog with them until the weight of the canine's cadaver caused it to tear away from the semi-devoured leg and drop to the ground in front of them.

They moved toward Billy and Jacob, each choosing a different boy to attack. The two zombies now conjoined by the dog's leg that they refused to release, tugged at each other, and swaying back and forth they struggled to move forward toward their chosen victims.

Under different circumstances, this spectacle would have been rather humorous, but these weren't different circumstances, this was a life and death situation, and those were *my* boys, *my* children that were in grave danger.

I quickly rolled my window down and yelled.

"Lead them into the ditch and kill them, and be careful."

"We are Dad," Billy answered.

"Come over by me Jacob, they won't let go of the dog's leg," Billy shouted.

Without hesitation, Jacob ran to his brother's side.

"Now they're coming, just a little bit closer," Billy mumbled, as he pulled the trigger on his AK-47.

Boom! Boom! Boom! Boom!

The two undead females first dropped to their knees like marionettes whose strings had been cut, and then they fell face first into the ditch, again in unison. Their jaws still clutching the leg bone of the dead mongrel even though the tops of their heads were now missing due to the effect of the 7.62 projectiles fired at close range.

The gunfire had drawn more zombies to us faster than we had expected, considering we could hear gunshots in the distance coming from all directions.

I'm sure it was just because of our life threatening dilemma that it seemed to us, that *we* were the only ones being targeted by all of these crazed killers.

"Move those ladders and get back here, hurry!" I yelled as loud as I could.

"We gotta go, more of them are coming!" Gin screeched, as she hastily scanned the area for more zombies.

"Hurry, get in!" I screamed, as three of the newly arrived zombies were now within five yards of our vehicle and stood between the boys and the safety of the van.

With their rifles slung over their shoulders, and with panicked looks on their faces, the boys picked up the last ladder that was blocking the road.

With one at each end, they ran side by side back toward the van, and using the ladder as a weapon, they took down two of the zombies by hitting them neck high and pushing them into the ditch along with the ladder.

As the boys tossed the ladder and the two zombies into the ditch, they left the third diseased monster staggering toward my window and lined up down the sights of my Glock 19. I quickly took advantage of the close range shot by dusting off the skull of the zombie with two well-placed shots in rapid succession, sending one bullet crashing through the front teeth of the monster on its way to the Medulla Oblongata, and the other one directly into the middle of its forehead.

The zombie dropped dead onto the asphalt just inches away from my window as the boys ran to the van and jumped in.

The side doors were still open as I pushed down on the gas pedal hard. The tires squealed as we swerved around the cable truck and the dead mutt's remains and continued on our trek to the river; allowing the remaining assaulting zombies still in the ditch with the ladder, and the ones that were arriving late onto the scene, to concentrate their attention on the bodies of the two dispatched female mutants, the zombie I had neutralized, and the damn dog.

"I guess they like *dead* animal flesh too," Gin said, watching the zombies feast on what was left of the deceased K-9 as we drove away.

Glancing into my rearview mirror and seeing the brains of the original two female zombies being munched on and fought over by even more newly arriving rogue zombies, I added.

"Evidently, flesh is flesh, and any body part will do! But it looks to me like they consider brains a delicacy!"

The boat launch was only about 3 miles from our house and the dog in the road, was about half way between the two.

Therefore, after a few more minutes on the road, we could see the boat ramp, and what we thought were several abandon vehicles in the parking lot, some with empty trailers, and some without trailers at all.

This could have indicated that some had been left by fishermen already on the river when this thing broke, or that other people had the same idea as us, and got to the river before we did.

However, because the ramp was clear of abandoned vehicles and trailers, the most likely scenario was that anglers were already on the river at the start of the zombie apocalypse.

Either way, it meant that at some point we were likely to encounter other people on the river.

Pulling up to the boat ramp, I reminded everybody.

"Just because we don't see any danger at the moment, that doesn't mean that we can't be in great peril at any time. Those eaters back there came out of nowhere. If it can happen back there, then it can happen here. We have to hurry! We can take it a little easier once we're on the river."

I turned the steering wheel hard to the left, and maneuvered the trailer into position so that I could back it into the water.

"Boys, unhook the straps holding the boat to the trailer and everyone get into the boat," I ordered.

"I'll hold onto the boat while you park the van Dad," Jacob said.

"No need to son, we won't be coming back, get in the boat."

"Oh yeah," Jacob said sheepishly, as he and Billy continued to release the stern of the boat from its trailer.

"Look out Dad!" Billy yelled, just as the cracking sound of Jacobs's carbine ripped through the calming sound of the small waves breaking on the riverside.

Boom! Boom! Boom!

"Got'em Dad," Jacob proclaimed, smiling.

"Where did those two come from, I didn't see them until Billy yelled and they were almost on me," I said, feeling my heart pounding wildly in my chest. "They scared the shit out of me, figuratively speaking of course."

"They were behind that tree, they must have just been standing there until they heard us," Billy said.

"We are going to have to be more aware of our surroundings if we want to stay alive, *we* of course meaning me," I said aloud this time.

"Let's get out of here," I said, as released the boat from its front restraint and gave it a shove, just before hoisting myself up and onto the bow.

"Start it up Billy. Jake, you open the air valves on the gas tank," I commanded.

Billy started the motor as I made my way through our hurriedly packed supplies and took my place at the boat's controls.

As the sky became dark and the warmth of the sun abandoned us, I slowly maneuvered our little craft toward the middle of the river where the current was the strongest.

I took one last look back at the dock, and at my mini-van that I had abandoned there.

That solitary vehicle left there on the boat ramp. That familiar mini-van that I had driven for so many miles sitting there alone by the water's edge, sadly reminded me once again that we would never be returning to this place.

The river was high, but not even close to flood stage as we putted out to the middle, and as we did so, a cool breeze began to blow in from the north. We were on our way to parts unknown, and we even had a tail wind to help us on our journey.

There was no turning back now.

THE RIVER

"We didn't have much time to organize our *stuff* back there, so let's get some of these things moved around a little and everyone find a spot to bed down for the night. Billy, go up front and watch for anything that we need to be concerned about, and take an extra drum magazine up there too," I said, pointing at the riverfront with one hand and handing him an AK drum magazine with the other.

"Do you want me to shoot at the eaters on the bank?" Billy asked, looking a little puzzled.

"Not unless they pose a threat to us, and out this far that is highly unlikely," I answered. "But that doesn't mean we'll never shoot one of them on the shore. There are going to be times that we will be in very close to the shore, and I don't know how far these diseased dead bodies can jump, or even if they can jump, and I don't want to find out."

Turning to Jacob, I said. "You make sure you help your brother keep watch, especially keep an eye on the bridges we'll be going under, who knows what will be on them."

"Sure thing Dad," Jacob replied.

"Okay, the currents pretty strong here, time to turn off the motor and drift," I said, as I turned off the Morphodite's outboard motor and our boat began to sluggishly float down stream.

"We only have so much gas, and we don't know when or where we can get more. So we're going to stick to the plan and drift most of the way. The only time we're going to start the motor is when we get too close to the shore and we can't paddle back out into the current, or we need to high tail it out of Dodge in a hurry." I said, trying to get my point across before they were told that one of us was going to have to stay awake and on watch at all times.

Then Gin inquired. "Are you saying we're going to just drift along at this slow pace, it's going to take forever to get anywhere?"

"That's right, it will, but if we run out of gas we're going to end up drifting anyway, and we won't have any way to get out of trouble quickly if we need to," I replied. "And I have a feeling we're going to need to at some point!"

"I guess you're right," Gin mumbled. "I mean what's the hurry anyway; we don't know where we're going or what we're going to do when we get there anyway, right?"

81

"Right, at this point that's about it in a nutshell," I agreed, nodding my head.

"Let's put one of the oars in the front of the boat and one in the back, that way we can push things away from the boat or push the boat away from the shore at any angle," Jacob suggested, as he reached for one of the oars.

"Yeah," Billy said. "And we can use them as a club if we need too, instead of firing a gun and drawing the attention of other eaters in the area."

"That sounds like a good idea," Gin said, handing the second oar to Billy.

As the night wore on, we each burrowed out a small area to sleep in among our stacks of supplies, then I announced that I would take the first watch and assigned Billy the second, and Gin the third, and Jacob the last one; each of us taking a two and a half hour shift.

To my surprise, there was no resistance from anyone regarding the imposed sentry duties. I guess they all realized that it was a necessary evil and an unavoidable chore that had to be done to ensure the safety and security of our family.

Although the temperature dropped to an uncomfortable level that night, we didn't suffer too much, as our coats, blankets, and sleeping bags were thick enough to keep us warm, and the gentle rocking of the boat on the river along with the pillows that Gin insisted on bringing, allowed us to get some sleep.

The night passed uneventfully, and the sunrise signaled the start of the first full day of our journey south. It was to be the first of many days that we would never forget on our way to our new life under the dark cloud of the horrific disease that was plaguing the world over.

When I woke up, I saw Jacob at the bow of the boat aiming the .243 Steyr hunting rifle off the port side of the boat, pausing for a moment, and then slowly rotating to the starboard side, pausing again, and rotating back to the port side and back again.

"What are you doing son?" I inquired.

"I'm checking out this scope Dad. You know I could take out any one of them, or *all* of them easily with this rifle."

"Any or all of what son?" I asked, a bit confused.

"All of those eaters. Look at all of them!"

I sat up, looked over the side of the boat at the riverbank, and I could hardly believe my eyes.

Hundreds of zombies were standing on the bank snarling and snapping at us. Of course, we were too far away too distinctly hear their hungry growls or the clatter made by their teeth pounding against each other as they mimicked chomping down on our delicious flesh and bones, but we could clearly see their ominous presents and menacing body postures.

Some were just swaying back and forth leering at us as we slowly floated downstream past them. Others were stumbling around in a somewhat controlled frenzy as if they were going to charge into the river in pursuit of us, yet stopping short of entering the water and then quickly backing up, acting as if they were afraid of the flowing liquid. Some had walked to the edge of the river but no further, and stood there drooling as they ogled us with their minatory stares.

With the voracious appetite for flesh and brain that these undead cannibalistic abominations had exhibited in the past, along with their undaunted resolve to satisfy that hunger, it was hard to believe that something as simple as water would be enough to halt the onslaught of these horrendous monsters. However, it was all too clear that they had a deathly fear (another opportunity for a pun) of the water.

However, one thing was for sure. Almost every one of them had taken notice of us and would have attacked us if it weren't for the fact that we were at a wide part of the river and there was about fifty yards of water between them and us.

"This is very interesting," I said, as I rested my elbow on my knee and my chin on my hand. "The CDC did say that they thought the sickness had come from feral dogs. Maybe it mutated from rabies, you know *hydrophobia*, the fear of water."

"Okay Jake, you want to check out that scope, let's see if it is sighted in."

"Okay Dad, what do you want me to do?"

"Pick out one of them that's close to the water and see if you can take out its knee. Try to get it to fall into the water," I instructed.

Jake pulled the bolt back and then slammed it forward, inserting a bullet into the chamber of the hunting rifle.

"How about the one in the yellow shirt?" Jacob asked, as he raised the rifle up and rested his cheek on the stock of the gun.

"Sure," I said. "Go for the left knee though, it's closer to the water and you might have a better chance of

84

knocking the eater off balance and dropping it into the drink."

"Roger that," Jacob remarked, as he gently pressed the trigger back toward the rear of the gun.

The violent report of the rifle broke the morning silence and echoed off the surrounding landscape, and the left knee of the zombie in the yellow shirt exploded.

The zombie didn't have a chance to catch its balance. It belly flopped into the river, and it went crazy.

While flopping and flailing around, it wasn't swimming, I don't think it could swim, it just churned up the water floundering around and splashing violently.

After awhile it was able to find its way back onto the riverbank, accidentally I think.

Even after making it out of the water, the hydrophobic dead man continued to shake and flail his arms around for a while, sometimes shaking like a wet dog and flipping water droplets onto other zombies, which caused them to quickly move away from him and form a kind of empty aura around him.

Jacob started laughing hysterically at the comical way the zombie looked flopping around in the water, and at the antisocial way the other zombies reacted to their wet comrade.

The shot woke up everyone in the boat. Moreover, the shock of seeing the large horde of zombies on the bank soon rendered everyone wide-awake.

"What's going on?" Gin yelled, as she rose up quickly, startled by the gunshot.

"We're experimenting," Jacob answered, barely able to contain his laughter long enough to get out the words.

"Well that thing is loud, next time give me some warning before you scare the hell out of me," Gin replied angrily.

"Okay Mom," Jacob said, laughing.

"What's so funny Jake?" Billy demanded, just before he stretched his arms and yawned, a little pissed at being woken up so suddenly.

"Well, we know for sure those things don't like water!" Jacob chuckled. "You should have seen that! Look at it trying to stand up with only one good leg. Let's see if I can do that again."

He raised the rife to take another shot and I quickly stopped him.

"Don't shoot another one, it's a waste of ammo, and besides, I think we're drawing too much attention to ourselves. We don't know who or what might be within earshot of us. And we don't need any unwanted company."

"Looks like we already have some unwanted company!" Billy exclaimed.

"Yes we do," I said, noticing that the now one-legged dead cannibal that had just crawled out of the water seemed to be trying to convince itself to go back into the water and come after us. Yet it just couldn't seem to gather enough testicular fortitude to take another dip in the river.

It was obvious that this zombie didn't like the water and was very afraid of it, but the drive that it had to get to us was almost as strong as its dread of the hydraulic fluid it had just crawled out of, and that scared us.

I had to ask myself how long it would be before the humongous hunger for human flesh in these things might overcome the only fear that we had seen in them since this whole zombie apocalypse thing had started, and be able to attack us in the water.

We slowly drifted down the river past the creatures that had gathered on the riverbank, some of which tried to follow us, but the riverbank was too uneven and filled with bushes and trees, making it impossible for any of those ungainly sub-human aberrations to keep up with us for long.

Moments before we were out of sight of the horde, we heard gunshots and saw several zombies fall to the ground as their heads exploded, leaving a red cloud of mist in the space that their heads had once occupied.

"Someone is clearing out that group," Gin said, as she settled back in her seat.

"With extreme prejudice I might add!" I said. "Oh well, better them than us!"

"Indeed! Way better *them* than us," Gin then added.

"It takes a serious high powered rifle to vaporize somebody's skull like that, and a bigger caliber than our .243 I think," Jacob remarked.

"You're probably right, we need to be extremely vigilant," I said. "And stay as low as we can in the boat, no reason to give someone a bigger target than need be. Whoever is thinning that horde must have seen us too; we're luck that they didn't take any pot shots at *us*."

"They most likely figured that it wouldn't do them much good to shoot at us, considering that our boat is out in the middle of the river, and even if they could kill all of us, they still wouldn't be able to get their hands on the boat and our supplies," Gin speculated.

"Not to mention the massive horde of hungry dead bodies marching around on the riverbank probably posed a greater threat to them than they were willing to take for a boatload of undetermined articles belonging to someone else," I said, adding to Gin's speculation.

"Or maybe they just wanted to kill some eaters," Jacob added.

"That too," Gin agreed.

The next several hours passed without incident. Therefore, during that time, I decided that this would be a good time to come up with some rules for our survival.

"We need to think of some rules," I said, breaking the serene silence that we were just beginning to become accustom too.

"What kind of rules?" Gin asked.

"Rules to live by, and survive by," I answered.

"That's not much of an answer; give us an example of one of these rules of yours," Gin asked, acting a little annoyed.

"Well," I said. "They're not just my rules, we need to brainstorm and come up with as many ideas as we can to help us survive this insane holocaust."

Putting a thoughtful look on my face, I stated.

"For example, nobody goes anywhere alone, never ever, not to look for food, not to look for supplies, not for anything or for any reason, not even to go into the woods to take a crap. Never go anywhere alone. Ever! Get it?"

"I get it," Jake excitedly answered. "You mean like always carry two guns on you all of the time!"

Smiling, I replied. "That's right, somebody write these down so we can go through them and sort them out when we're done."

"I will, anyone have a pen or pencil?" Jake asked, as he started looking through one of the backpacks we had on board the boat.

When we were franticly rushing around trying to pack things that we thought we would need on our journey, pen and paper were not high on the list. However, Jacob did manage to find a crumpled spiral notebook and a pencil at the bottom of a backpack that he used to take to school.

"Okay, I'm ready!" Jacob stated proudly.

"Did you put the first two rules down yet?" Billy asked sarcastically, shaking his head back and forth, indicating that he didn't think Jacob had.

"Oh, hold on," Jacob insisted, and moments later, he announced. "Okay I got'em," he said, as he held up the paper for everyone to see.

"Nobody goes anywhere alone and always carry at least two guns."

"How about always keep a gun within reach, I mean if you put your guns down when you lie down to go to sleep, you keep them close to you," Billy added.

"That's a good idea," Gin said enthusiastically, for a change.

"What else?" Jacob spouted, excited about this new boredom breaking exercise.

"What about always keep a backup weapon with you? You know, a knife, or a club, or something," Billy recommended.

"I think a club might be a little awkward for a backup weapon, but you could certainly use one as a primary weapon. I mean when a gun isn't suitable, like when you have to be quiet and not attract a lot of attention," I countered.

"You mean like all of the time?" Jacob wisecracked.

"Indeed, I have taught you well my son!" I wisecracked back.

As we continued down the river we managed to compile quite a few rules, some we made up ourselves, and some we remembered from zombie movies or television shows.

We weeded out or modify the rules that probably weren't workable in a real zombie world, and one thing was for sure, we were definitely in a real zombie world, it didn't get any more real zombie than this.

With our list completed, we began to memorize the following rules to avoid being...

EATEN, DISMEMBERED, DISEASED, SHOT, BITTEN, MUTILATED, or otherwise KILLED, CAPTURED, or MURDERED by zombies, normal humans, insane maniacs, or other diverse mentally deranged entities etc.!

1. Watch for eaters (zombies) and rogue humans! Always assume one is near.

2. Never have less than two (2) guns on your person! Fully loaded!

3. Always, have a gun within reach, always!

4. Never, go anywhere alone, anywhere! Ever!

5. Always, carry a backup weapon, i.e., knife, hatchet, sword, bat, etc., always!

6. Always, keep a lookout on duty, day and night, all of the time, 24-7!

7. Never camp out in an open area, unless it is unavoidable, if unavoidable, refer to the first six rules!

8. Gather as much ammo as possible, check everywhere you go.

9. Look for and take, as many guns and high capacity magazines as possible, always check!

10. Take anything you think might be useful in the future, if possible, but don't over burden yourself, you still might have to move fast.

11. Look for food and water all the time!

12. Learn as much about the enemy (eaters or non-eaters) as possible, and share the information!

13. Watch your back! Watch everybody's back!

Of course, there is always an exception to every rule.

Take rule number 2 for instance, it sounds *really* nice to always have two fully loaded guns on you at all times.

However, what if you just got finished dusting off several zombies and you haven't had time to reload, when another one or two undead homicidal cannibalistic maniacs come along with visions of having you for their breakfast, you're certainly not going to take the time to reload before you deal with the new threats unless you have no other choice.

If your gun is completely empty. Then you might reload by quickly replacing your empty magazine with a full one (provided your weapon of choice is magazine fed, not a revolver or some such other nonsense), depending on how urgent the need to dispatch the zombies might be.

Alternatively, maybe you would do what they call a *"New York reload"* and pull out your second gun and blast them back to hell where they belong.

On the other hand, you could say to the aggressor. Oh, please Mr. Eater, don't bite me yet, wait for me to reload my lethal weapon so I can blow *your* head clean off! Well you could do that, but I don't recommend it. However, if you do choose to try that option, *please* let me know how that works out for you.

As you can see, there seems to be several options that could be used with this scenario. Therefore, we would do our best to adhere to our rules, but we all knew that they were more like strict guidelines rather than set in stone unbreakable rules.

It took longer than I had expected to float down the tributary to the Mississippi river. I had been there before, but had always got there under power.

When we did finally enter the mighty Mississippi River, of course, the current was much faster, and the river was much wider than the tributary from which we had started.

Faster was better because we would reach a warmer climate quicker, and wider was also much more desirable because we were farther away from the bank, farther away from zombies, and farther away from people that might want to take our boat, or might just want to kill us and take our supplies, or all of the above.

One thing about the Mississippi River we hadn't counted on, or even considered, even though we had encountered several completely dead bodies floating in the water on our way to the Mississippi.

Whether we floated or powered our boat down the river, we encountered an enormous number of bodies floating in it, more in some places, less in others. But no matter how you want to look at it, none of us had ever seen such a vast amount of death in one place prior to our journey down the Mississippi River.

Some of the many bodies floating around us were that of unfortunate ones that had come down with the disease and had been put down by people like us that so far were untouched by the devastating plague. They were killed before they had had a chance to do anyone any harm, and then their bodies were dumped into the river.

Other diseased persons that had turned into full-fledged killer zombies and had attacked people in an attempt to devour them, had had their brains destroyed and their bodies thrown into the river as well, again by someone that was so far unaffected physically by the disease.

Many had more than likely just been murdered, and their property taken by panicked people during the first hours of the outbreak, and their bodies were dropped into the river as well.

In any case, every corpse in that river had a hole in its head that had led to the destruction of at least part of its brain, which had rendered them dead, all the way dead.

Most of the bodies had begun to rot and were hideously bloated, and many had been partially eaten, either by zombies before they entered the water, or by the fish and turtles in the river, or sometimes by both, which made them all the more repulsive.

The riverbanks were littered with bodies that had washed onto them; some were hung up on derelict boats or barges, others on outcroppings of trees that were sticking halfway out of the water, and some had just floated out of the current and been beached by the river itself.

There were hundreds of rotting corpses floating in the river around us; we would see one or more, and usually more, spit out by the river at least every forty or fifty yards, and many times, they were ejected out of the river in grotesque clumps onto its banks.

Unfortunately, for us, the smell at times was overwhelmingly repugnant.

Crosswinds seemed to help a little most of the time, but when the river meandered, and the breeze blew parallel with the river, the stench of hundreds of rotting human bodies floating around us, and on the riverbank, was almost too much to bear.

It was like the smell of road kill, only much stronger and always present. Added to that we had the unforgettable memory that was seared into our minds of the mutilated rotting bloated fish bait corpses floating all around us; so we were afforded the perfect mix of constant smells, visual effects, and psychological brain twisting, which was enough to drive any normal person totally insane.

Fortunately, I didn't consider myself to be a normal human being, with my combat experience I had seen death many times before, but never on such a vast scale as this. However, I was concerned about the affect this hideous terrain would have on my family's psyche.

It's a funny thing though, about the way the human nose processes smells, if the odor is constant, after a while you get used to the stink and don't notice it nearly as much. I believe it's called *sensory adaptation*, and if not for this human anomaly, we would have had to abandon our plan of using the river to travel, as the stench was relentless.

As for all of our fishing equipment that we had with us, it was useless to us. With the river filled with rotting and diseased dead bodies, there was no way we were going to eat any of the fish we could pull out of that water. They had been feeding on the zombie carcasses and were no doubt carrying the disease in one form or another.

"Billy, we might as well throw the fishing poles overboard, along with the rest of the fishing stuff. We're not going to eat anything that comes out of this river," I declared.

"Okay Dad," Billy replied. "There's no need to keep it, all the rivers, lakes, and ponds are probably contaminated by now too."

"Well, even if they aren't, we can't take the chance. I mean how would we know whether or not there were bodies up river, or on the other side of a lake, or bodies that had sank to the bottom and were releasing the virus into fish that had nibbled on them?

I mean hell, if we're going to eat the fish we would catch, we might as well cut to the chase and grab one of those zombie corpses floating in the river, and drag it into the boat and feast on it!"

"Thank you for that visualization honey!" Gin said. "Is it dinner time yet?"

"Sorry dear, just trying to get a point across."

"So, should we throw all of it away?" Jacob asked.

"We might as well, it's just taking up space," I said. "We'll find food and water somewhere else. Meanwhile, we brought enough to last us a week or so if we ration it, and who knows, we might stumble across something sooner."

We drifted along for a couple of hours without seeing anything of consequence, except for the dozens of bloated bodies in the water, and we tried not to dwell on them too much (especially after my comment about pulling one aboard and eating it).

Then all of a sudden, Billy shouted as he pointed behind us.

"Look over there!"

I turned around, and in the distance, I could see a small boat coming toward us. This boat was not just floating down river as we were. This boat was at full throttle and gaining on us fast.

"Boys get your guns ready! Gin, you too!" I shouted, as I quickly reached down and grabbed my AK-47.

"I've got my pistol right here, rule number two," Gin replied.

"Everybody stay low and keep your guns pointed at these people! If these guys start shooting, don't hesitate, shoot back, and shoot to kill, don't worry about head shots, we can do that later."

"Okay Dad," both boys answered, as they too picked up their rifles.

96

As the small boat approached us, we could see three people moving about in it, and as it came even closer, it looked as if the three were struggling with each other.

"Take your guns off safety guys," I said softly, as the boat was now almost to us.

It was now clear that there were not actually three people in the small boat, there was one person, a woman, and two zombies in that boat, and it was not going well for the woman. She was losing the battle with the zombies. She was still alive and fighting, but she was being badly bitten and bleeding profusely.

Somehow she had managed to get to the controls of the boat and shut off the motor just as it came alone side of us. She started screaming for help, but it was clear to all of us that even if we killed the zombies it would still be too late for her. She was already diseased.

"Help me please!" She pleaded with a sad panicked and desperate look on her face, as she pushed one of the zombies away.

I raised my rifle to my shoulder and fired at the zombie that was closest to her.

The bullet left the barrel of my gun and slammed into the zombie's spine, severing it just above its torso at the base of its neck, causing the head to drop forward as if it were bowing its head to pray.

Blood gushed out of the neck and poured down the front of the creature, and over the woman's arms and chest. She desperately tried to push it away from her as I had not hit its brain and it was still trying to grab and bite her even though its head was hanging down almost to its stomach, held on only by the skin at the front of its

97

neck, which was now elongated by the weight of its head.

By now the other monster had maneuvered behind the women and was about to lunge on her when I heard the crack of Billy's AK slice through the sound of the women's screams.

His shot was true and hit the zombie in the head just below the right eyebrow, blowing out the back of its skull and dropping the zombie like *third period French* over the boat's windshield.

All of the sudden in an attempt to kill the first zombie that was grappling with the woman, everyone on our boat, even Gin, open fire on the remaining zombie, not with just one shot, but with many.

When the guns finally went silent, what I had secretly hoped would happen, had happened, both zombies were dead and the woman was dead too.

Between our rapid firing, the zombie moving around as it attacked the woman, and the waves on the river rocking both boats, our aiming had been compromised somewhat.

Secretly we all had hoped this would happen, because in the back of everyone's mind, we all knew there was no hope for the imperiled woman, she had been bitten, therefore she was diseased, and therefore she was doomed to become one of the undead eventually.

In addition, we all knew it would be very dangerous to keep her with us for any length of time, when she died; she would turn quickly and attack us, so it was better this way.

We also knew that if she had lived through the ordeal on her boat, one of us would have had to shoot her in the head while she was still alive, not wanting to take the chance of waiting for her to die and turn into a flesh eating killer.

So maybe her death wasn't an accident, maybe somewhere deep in our psyche, our subconscious had taken careful aim.

We sat there for a short time, stunned by what had happened, and maybe even feeling a little guilty.

Although I had a fair amount of combat experience under my belt, my family members were all still novices at their new occupation of serial killer.

We knew that the zombies were very dangerous, and would kill and eat any living humans every chance they got. However, they still looked like people in most ways, for this early in the apocalypse the *living* undead had only just started to slowly rot, so it was a very traumatic experience for us to shoot them, especially for Billy, Jacob, and Gin, even though at times it was hard to tell.

The next chore needed my immediate attention. Although we had killed the woman, her death had not been caused by massive head trauma.

Unlike the two zombies, her fatal wounds were to her heart, and lungs, which meant that she would be reanimating in a matter of moments.

So I leveled my rifle and took aim at her head. I squeezed off one round that permanently ended her ordeal.

Not long after that our boats started to drift apart, but I decided to start our motor and substantially extend the gap between us.

We didn't bother to search the woman's boat for supplies, as it was now speckled with tainted zombie blood, and any scavenged items we found would probably be carrying the disease.

However, before we left, I fired a few rounds into the side of the boat just below the water line, so that in time it would sink, or at least run aground at some point. Either way, that boat would be far from us and wouldn't be a constant reminder to my family of what had happened.

We cruised down river with our Evinrude forty-eight at top speed, and after about ten minutes of dodging floating corpses in the water, I picked a spot in the river that seemed to have a gap in the body count and turned off the motor, and we began to drift once more.

"How long do you think it will take us to get where we're going? And by the way, where are we planning to go?" Gin asked.

"We are heading for a warmer climate," I said, trying to sound confident and reassuring.

I didn't really know where we were going to end up. In all the excitement of the world-ending apocalypse, I hadn't given much thought past getting to a warmer climate.

"Well that's a pretty generic answer," Gin charged, in her usual sarcastic manner. "I guess that means you don't know?"

"Sure I do," I muttered, thinking that she didn't remember our previous conversation, when I had told her I had no idea where we were going or what we were going to do when we got there.

"We're going to Texas," I proclaimed, quickly conjuring up a makeshift plan.

"Why Texas?" Billy asked.

"Because we're on the Mississippi River, when we get far enough south we're going to have to go either east or west before we get to the Gulf of Mexico.

We're in a fifteen foot utility boat; I don't think an ocean voyage will be conducive to our safety. Plus where would we go, even fully loaded with fuel, we'd get maybe far enough out to sea to die of thirst in a few days.

So, when we get down to Vicksburg, we're going to jump ship and follow interstate twenty into Texas. There are a lot of animals in Texas, feral hogs, steers, and some exotic game brought in for exclusive hunting," I answered. "Although hogs might not be any better of a choice than the fish, considering that they'll eat about anything, dead zombies included. So we probably should just hunt for vegetarian animals like cows."

I had been in Vicksburg once several years ago, and knew that interstate twenty led to Shreveport, and then to Dallas.

Jake piped up asking. "Are we going to walk to Texas from Vicksburg?"

"We are going to do exactly what we have to do to survive. If we have to walk all the way to Texas, then that's what we're going to do," I answered.

Billy cringed, and said. "That sounds like fun."

"Well hopefully we won't have to walk the whole way," I continued. "A truck might be the best option to have; we could carry other modes of transportation with us such as bicycles if we can find any. We need to keep an eye out for anything and everything that we might be able to use in some way."

"Rule 10," Gin said smartly.

"Have you ever been to Vicksburg?" Jacob asked.

"Yes a long time ago, but not on the river, that's why I made sure I packed the GPS. The satellites are still working, and as long as the batteries last in the GPS we'll know where we are."

"The reason we're in this boat instead of our van, is because you said we wouldn't get fifty miles on the highway, and now you're saying we're going to take interstate twenty hundreds of miles into Texas?" Billy barked, seeming quite annoyed.

"Look, I said we wouldn't get fifty miles the way things were when we left home, it's going to be a few more days before we get to Vicksburg, and maybe by then things will have calmed down a little. And it's not like we really have a choice."

I leaned back against the side of the boat and said. "Listen everyone, I don't have all the answers, and I really wish I did, but I don't. Life is going to be tough from now on; living is going to be tough from now on. We're just going to have to do the best that we can. We're going to have to lookout for each other and protect each other, and just take things as they come. And let's face it; we can't stay in this boat forever."

"Okay then," Gin said. "Do you have any idea how long we're going to be on this stinking river?"

"Well, it's about five hundred miles to Vicksburg from where we started, and it looks like we're traveling a little over one mile an hour, let's say one point two miles per hour. If we divide five hundred by one point two."

"Never mind," Gin interrupted, rolling her eyes. "I guess we'll get there when we get there."

"I'm hungry, can we eat something?" Jacob asked.

"Me too," Billy said. "Hand me one of those cans of tuna, and a bottle of water."

"The bottled water is in that box beside you," Gin said, pointing to the box.

"Did we bring a can opener?" Billy asked.

"I didn't," Gin said.

"Neither did I," Jacob added.

"Great, we have all of this canned food and no way to open it," Billy stated nastily.

"Everybody calm down, I have a P-38 on my key chain. Lucky I put my keys in my pocket back at the dock, force of habit I guess." I replied as I reached into my pocket.

"You have a WWII German gun on your key chain," Billy said smiling, trying to add a little levity to the situation.

"No," Jacob said, also smiling. "He's got a WWII fighter plane on his key chain."

"You two are so silly, it's a can opener, even I know that," Gin said.

"Yeah, some people call it a John Wayne," I said, as I pulled a lump of keys out of my pocket and held it up for them to see.

"See, it flips open like this, and you hook it onto the side of the can. Toss me your tuna can Billy and I'll show you guys how it works."

I gave them a quick demonstration on how to use the John Wayne can opener, then cans of tuna and bottled water were handed out to everyone, and as we slowly drifted along surrounded by the floating bodies of the dead and inhaling the foul stench of their bloated and decomposing flesh, we choked down our meager meals.

The next several days were pretty much the same as the days that had preceded them, groups of zombies were occasionally sighted on the riverbanks, stumbling around, snarling and growling at us, but still afraid to venture into the water.

However, except for the woman in the boat, we had yet to see living people that hadn't been stricken by the outbreak.

Abandoned boats were becoming a common sight along the way, but an uncanny absence of the people who had left them made us wonder; had they given up on the river because of its grisly demeanor, or had they reached their destination and no longer needed their boats.

Yet, with some, their reasons were blatantly clear, they had not only abandoned their boats, they had abandoned the will to live too, and suicide was their way of relieving themselves of the horrors of the new world.

Many times, we came upon vessels that had washed ashore, with its occupant still clutching the weapon used to achieve their ultimate demise.

Sometimes whole families had meant their end at the hand of one of their family members who had turned the weapon of choice on themselves after their spine-chilling deed.

We could have stopped at many of these "suicide boats" and rummaged through what gear they might have had. However, those scenes were ghastly, and very sad, and I didn't want to subject my family to any more emotional trauma than they were already having to endure, even if we were in violation of some of our survival rules.

Night was beginning to fall on day eleven, when Jacob suddenly shouted.

"Seventeen!"

Billy was just drifting off to sleep, and now was wide-awake; awakened by Jacob's yell.

"Seventeen what?" He demanded, not happy about being disturbed.

Jacob proudly answered. "Seventeen days from home to Vicksburg, it should take us seventeen days."

"You woke me up for that? You... idiot," Billy scolded.

"I've been thinking about it on and off since Mom asked a few days ago, I thought you guys wanted to know," Jacob said in his defense.

"Thank you sweetie, I did want to know, so we've been out here for ten days."

"Eleven, this is the eleventh day, tomorrow will be the twelfth day," Jacob again gloated proudly.

"That means we have six more days on this horrible river," Gin said scowling.

"I think we have just enough food and water to get us there, I guess in about five days I'll take out the GPS and see how close we are. We don't want to run the batteries down, so we need to use it sparingly," I stressed.

It was dark now, the low light of a crescent moon made the bodies in the water almost indiscernible, and as usual I took the first watch while everyone else settled down for the night.

The river was unusually calm, and our boat made an excellent platform for stargazing. The lack of light coming from cities and towns due to most of the electricity generating plants in the country shutting down; increased the amount of stars that were visible at night. So I had adopted the hobby to pass the time on watch during periods when the boat was in the middle of the river and well away from its banks.

As the current was beginning to speed up as the river narrowed slightly, I watched a shooting star flash across the night sky.

Bam! Splash! Splash!

Suddenly something hit the bow of the boat hard. Things were falling in the water all around us.

"What's going on?" Gin asked, only half awake.

Now there was more splashing in the water around us.

"I don't know," I said, just as another object slammed into our boat, this time on the side just behind the windshield, and a severed foot landed on one of the ammo boxes next the our water supply.

"Eaters!" I screamed.

Looking up, I could no longer see stars directly above us.

"The bridge, they're jumping off the bridge."

At this point, at least eight more had fallen into the water beside our boat and were thrashing around trying to get to us. The two that had hit the boat were not a threat, so many of their bones were broken in so many places that even though they were right beside the boat, they couldn't even lift their arms to grab the railing on the boat, and quickly sank out of sight.

The zombies that had jumped off the bridge and missed our boat were quite a different story. With all of their seemingly panicked flailing, some of them were actually making their way closer to the Morphodite.

As we floated under the middle of the bridge, the zombies that were still jumping into the water had no chance of getting to us. Our main concern now were the zombies that were already beside the boat, and the ones still on the bridge that may leap into our boat, or maybe even onto us when we pass under the other side.

"Shoot that one!" I yelled, pointing to a zombie that was close enough to us that we could hear its fingernails scraping the side of the boat.

Those words had hardly left my mouth when Jacob, being the closest one to the zombie, spun around quickly and with one smooth fluid motion, pulled his 9mm pistol from his side holster, leveled the gun at his hip, and fired two shots into the zombie's face, effectively extinguishing the seemingly artificial life from the hungry brute.

"Nice shooting son," I said, as I turned the ignition key and started the boat's motor.

Slamming the throttle forward, the bow of the boat lifted as the boat lurched forward, almost knocking Jacob and Billy off their feet. They both sat down quickly as we began to pick up speed.

Zombies were now dropping off the far side of the bridge in large numbers, apparently unable to see through the night's veil of darkness that we were no longer below them, and unaware that their fall would ultimately land them in the middle of millions of gallons of the liquid that they feared and despised. Or, maybe their diseased brains were making them act like lemmings, and they were just following the zombie in

107

front of them off the side of the bridge, ignorant of their final destination.

Whatever the reason for their leaps of faith, they were dropping like proverbial flies off that bridge with no chance of landing on their prey.

I turned the boat to the left and headed toward the riverbank several yards away at a rate of speed that was somewhat unsettling to my wife.

"What are you doing?" Gin screamed.

"I'm going to turn around," I yelled back at her.

"Turn around, are you crazy?" Billy snapped, looking back at all of the zombies thrashing in the water and still jumping off the bridge.

Once more, I turned the boat to the left and we began to go back up stream toward the relentless pack of hungry zombies treading water and the ones doing belly flops from a height that would put an Olympic diver to shame.

"Everybody hold on, we might hit some eaters," I shouted, as I again turned the boat to the left.

"One more turn, and we'll get out from under this bridge," I said, as the boat now roared close to its top speed.

Making one last left turn, a zombie's head bounced off the deep V-keel of the Morphodite, cutting a large gash into its skull and killing it instantly.

"I hope that eater's head didn't damage the boat," Gin shouted over the roar of our boat motor.

"That's doubtful, we split its skull like a ripe watermelon hitting a brick wall," I shouted back.

Looking back and seeing chunks of that zombie's blood gushing brain floating in the choppy river water.

"Kind of *looks* like pieces of a watermelon too," Jacob said, seemingly unaffected by our ongoing harrowing experience.

Now at top speed, our small craft hydroplaned atop the choppy waters induced by the floundering and flailing of the undead in the river, along with the splashes of their high diving cohorts.

Closing fast on the intermittent curtain of zombies now dropping from the backside of the bridge, I yelled. "Everyone get down as low as you can."

As our small boat breached the curtain of the undead, one of the falling zombies hit the point of the bow about half way down its chest and was ripped apart, spraying a fine mist of blood onto the windshield of the boat, along with one lung and an internal body part that was unrecognizable after impact.

A second zombie hit face first on the top and back of the boat's outboard power plant, embedding its top row of brownish-yellow teeth into the hard plastic cover of the motor.

A third jumper landed feet first midway down the right side of our boat, snapping both legs at the knees, compression fracturing most of the vertebra in its back, and impaling the lower portion of its skull on a cleat. With most of the bones in its body broken or cracked in one way or another, it was left hanging there only half dead off the outside of the boat, peaking into the bowels of the Morphodite, and reminding me of the old "*Kilroy was here*" cartoon.

Cutting the power and letting the boat drift again, I inquired.

"Is everyone all right?"

"Everyone's okay, but there're a couple of messes we'll have to clean up," Gin replied, shaking her head in disgust.

"Yes, I can hardly see through the windshield," I said, looking around for something to wipe off the copious amount of blood and gore.

"I'll take care of this one," Billy said.

I watched as he held on to one of the cleats on the right side of the boat to steady himself, and with a karate type yell, he kicked the "Kilroy" zombie in the face, tearing its head off the cleat that attached it to the side of the boat.

The zombie splashed into the water and slowly drifted away, and as we watched, it sank to the bottom of the river.

"We should leave those teeth in the motor," Jacob said. "It'll remind us of the bridges we have to pass under."

"All right, but throw some water over them and wash off some of the blood, it already stinks enough around here," I said, while I dipped an old t-shirt into the tainted river water.

"This is great, all of this gore on the boat is going to attract even more flies," Gin said. "I don't think I can take much more of this bullshit."

We spent the rest of the night cleaning the blood and body parts from the boat; the best we could in the dark. None of us could sleep anyway with all of the excitement from the encounter at the bridge and the mess it left us with, not to mention the realization that there might be many more bridges further down the river.

The next few days we drifted down the Mississippi without any substantial episodes, except for the increase in the fly population on and around the boat.

We decided to change our tactics and began starting the motor and speeding under the bridges at a high rate of speed, then drifting again until we approached another bridge where we would then repeat the process over again. We continued to use this maneuver at all of the bridges we passed under until we concluded our river voyage at Vicksburg.

We quickly learned that the zombie's sense of timing was far from optimum. With their wavering gate and their clumsy staggering, it proved rather easy to avoid their attempts to drop on us, as long as we were aware of an upcoming bridge.

When the zombies would see us drifting up on them, they had a tendency to gather in a group, trying to position themselves in a spot in line with our passing. If we powered up and changed course slightly, by the time they stumbled over each other trying to reposition themselves, we had already gone by and would watch some of them fall into the water well after we had passed.

As long as we didn't drift under them giving them enough time to make their way to a vantage point directly above us, it was not much of a challenge to avoid them.

One disturbing note; we noticed that the zombies that had jumped into the water, tended not to run out of energy or become tired.

They would splash and flail around in the water until they finally made it to the riverbank, no matter how long it took.

At one point, we were able to anchor our boat in the shallow water above a sandbar in the middle of the river and watch a zombie tread water, after an hour we decided to continue on, and the zombie was still showing no signs of fatigue.

Fortunately, for us, not every bridge that we passed under had a horde of zombies laying in wait to fling themselves down onto us.

That fact caused me to wonder why any group of zombies that were scared senseless of the water, would gather in the middle of a bridge that spanned the largest river in the country in the first place, but some did, even though during the daytime they could clearly see the river from their vantage point.

DAY 13

Day 13 was the day that everything changed for us, and changed everything for everyone we would meet going forward.

The previous days had been similar to each other and our routine was about the same. We would wake up at sunrise, force down a little food amidst the gruesome landscape, revolting smell of the gradually disintegrating bodies all around us, and the morning congregation of flies that always over stayed their welcome. Then spend our time trying to fight the boredom of slowly drifting along, all the while waiting for the next round of terror that could be just around the next bend in the river.

Day 13 was different; right out of the box things took a downhill plunge.

Gin and I had just finished a paltry breakfast consisting of a shared can of peas and the last three slices of a loaf of bread that weren't spotted with mold.

Meanwhile, Jacob and Billy were arguing over the only chocolate granola bar that was left on the boat.

Gin suddenly turned to me, and looking rather forlorn, said. "Here we go again, look."

She pointed over my right shoulder at a boat approaching in the distance.

"Boys, get ready, there's another boat coming," I warned them.

Billy quickly snapped the granola bar in half, crammed one piece in his mouth, and tossed the other piece to Jacob.

"Everyone get down, like before," I said, reaching for my rifle.

As the possible new threat came nearer, we could see only one person in the substantially larger boat. It was a man and he didn't seem to be in any distress.

"There could be more than just the one we can see, others might be hiding, same rules apply as before, if we have to shoot, shoot to kill and worry about head shots later," I said, reminding my crew of our first encounter with the woman and the two zombies.

With the stranger's boat upon us, he cut the inboard engine of his large cabin cruiser and shouted.

"Ahoy, ahoy there!"

I returned his greeting by shouting back.

"Ahoy to you stranger!"

The man looked to be about six feet tall, rather husky, with short white hair and a well-groomed white beard. I estimated him to be somewhere in his late fifty's or early sixties.

He cast a rope into our boat as his vessel slowly drifted along our starboard side.

"Tie it off boy," he said, as Jacob grabbed the rope. "We'll all compare notes, if that's okay with you folks?"

"Are you alone?" I inquired, as I stood up, my rifle at my side and pointing in his direction.

"Just me, myself, and I," he replied, putting his hands on the side of his boat and leaning in our direction.

"Where you folks from?" The bearded man asked cheerfully.

"Saint Louis," I answered with a smile, as my finger slowly slid closer to my rifle's trigger.

This man wasn't acting like you would expect someone to act in the middle of a "Zombie Apocalypse", especially an apocalypse that had started less than two weeks earlier.

"All the way from Saint Louie, you must have seen some things along the way," he said, not really seeming too concerned as his eyes scanned back and forth checking out our boat.

"That's right, we've seen some things, what's your name, and where did *you* come from?" I asked him still smiling.

114

"That's a really nice trophy you got there," the man said, pointing to the teeth sticking in our boat motor. "I'd like to have that trophy."

Noticing his behavior getting even odder, I replied.

"You wouldn't want to get it the way we got it."

"Well I recon not, if you say so," he muttered softly.

"Where did you say you're from," I asked again, becoming even more suspicious.

"From a little place north of here, called Friars Point Mississippi, you don't want to go there; it's crawling with those dead people."

"We call them eaters," Jacob said smiling.

"Eaters you say! Well speaking of food, you folks hungry; don't see how you can have much food in that little boat of yours. I've got plenty of food, MRE's."

"MRE's?" Jacob asked, as he turned toward Billy for an answer.

Billy shrugged his shoulders and answered. "I don't know!"

Wondering why this stranger that we had only just met, would want to share his food with us so readily, I answered Jacobs's question.

"Meals-Ready-to-Eat is what it stands for, they're mainly made for the military."

"That's right, meals ready to eat, I got plenty of meals ready to eat, got some cooking below as we speak," the man said, pointing to the hold of his boat.

"Say those are some mighty fine looking weapons you got there, *I'd* like to have those weapons," he announced giddily.

I glanced over at my two boys and my wife, and I saw that Jacob had already slung his carbine over his shoulder, and Billy had sat the butt stock of his rifle on one of the sleeping bags we had tied to the front of the boat and was holding onto his gun by the barrel.

Although her pistol was still pointing in the general direction of our newfound *friend*, Gin had lowered it, and she didn't look ready to handle any surprises.

They all had been lulled into what could be a false sense of security by this man's cheerful and generous demeanor.

"Sorry, we don't have any to spare, no spare ammunition either. Don't you have a gun?" I asked suspiciously.

"No gun, just a fishing knife. I was fishing when all this started; don't normally bring a gun with me when I'm fishing."

"I'm Jack, this is my wife Gin, and my two boys, Billy and Jacob. I didn't catch your name."

The smile sank from the man's face, his voice lowered, and he said slowly.

"How old is your woman, I'd like to have that woman."

With that statement, he turned away from me for just a moment.

Keep in mind, after several days of drifting down the river and having to endure the sight of bloated dead bodies constantly floating around me, along with the accompanying stench of their rotting flesh that was always present. After just barely surviving the attacking zombies that were jumping off the bridge into our boat in the middle of the night. Seeing a suicide boat filled with the dead bodies of whole families at least once every day (and usually more). Not to mention the memories of

116

seeing our neighbors butchered on our patio door, and having to put one of them down as if she was a mad dog, and having to leave Jacob's best friend Norton and his father Joe battling a large rabble of assailing zombies in their front yard and not being able to help them.

I was in no mood to play this guy's game.

I had already shouldered my AK-47 as the man was turning back to face me. He clumsily tried to shield the pistol he had in his left hand.

"If you have to know my name," he shouted. "It's your worst nightmare!"

I'll never forget the surprised look on his face, when he completed his turn and saw me standing there staring at him through the iron sights of my Romanian manufactured assault rifle.

Before the man could react, I pressed the trigger toward the rear of the gun, and fired a shot that hit him in his left lung.

Then rapidly, I fired another, and then another, and another, and another, and the man fell back onto the deck of his boat, dead and riddled with bullet holes.

Jacob had tied our boats together with the rope that the crazed man had tossed to him. So it was rather easy for me to jump onto his vessel and send one more round crashing into his forehead at point blank range, which exited through the back of his skull and splintered the wooden deck below, destroying his brain and making sure he wouldn't reanimate.

Having to shoot, hit, or run over humans or sub-humans was becoming the norm. Therefore, I figured with the crazy way this man was acting, plus the fact that he was in the process of pulling a gun on us, a gun that earlier he had claimed not to have, one more self-defense killing wouldn't matter much in the long run.

After shooting the stranger in the head, I quickly surveyed the deck of his boat to make sure no other threats were present.

When I turned toward Billy and Jacob, they were standing there staring at me with very confused looks on their faces.

From their position in our boat, they could not see the gun the man had picked up. Gin caught a glimpse of the gun, but everything happened so fast, that by the time she reacted to what was happening, it was over.

Jacob then asked. "Why did you do that Dad?"

Gin quickly spoke up.

"Because it had to be done, he wasn't normal."

"He seemed normal to me; didn't he seem normal to you Billy?"

"He seemed a little weird," Billy retorted.

"He also lied to us," I said. "He said he didn't have a gun, that's a 1911 Colt .45 he's still clutching in his hand, and here's another one right here by the cabin door." I said, as I picked up the second pistol and shoved it into one of the large cargo pockets of my multi-cam pants.

"He may have lied about being alone too, so stay alert. I'm going to check down in the cabin."

I slowly eased down the three wooden steps that led down to the cabin below deck. The cabin door was ajar; allowing the aroma of what the bearded man that I had just killed had called his MRE's that were still cooking on a small propane stove to seep out into the claustrophobic hallway where I stood. Before I entered the cabin, I caught a whiff of the simmering meal inside and thought, *"we're going to have a delicious warm meal for breakfast for a change."*

However, when I peeked inside the cabin through the half-inch gap provided by the partially opened door, a nightmare that I had not even dared to imagine confronted me. I had suspected that the man from Friars Point Mississippi wasn't alone, but nothing could have prepared me for what I found in the cabin of this lunatic's boat.

Before me was a hideous sight, the maggot infested torso's of a woman and three children. A girl about sixteen years old, a boy around twelve, and another girl maybe four years old, all dead with their body parts teeming with maggots, separated and stacked neatly in piles around the cabin which was overrun with flies.

It was apparent that they were the man's, meals ready to eat. He had been carving on them for some time it seemed, using a set of butcher knives and a carpenter's handsaw that were placed on a small butcher's block near the woman's torso.

Pieces of them that he had cut up like round steaks were still sizzling in a large frying pan on the stove, emitting the scent that just moments before had titillated my taste buds, but after finding that the slaughtered humans were the source of the once pleasant smell, my now queasy stomach churned with every inhaled breath.

What was left of their bodies was starting to decompose, and the introduction of scores of fly larva most likely made the meal unpalatable for even the most ardent of the criminally insane. This is probably the reason that this maniac interrupted his breakfast. He saw us and decided he needed fresher meat.

Until that moment, I had never smelled the odor of human meat being cooked. If not for the reeking of all of the rotting and bloated bodies that had been floating around us for almost two weeks, not to mention the carnage that we had seen and the atrocities that we had been forced to commit leading up to this horrific scene, I probably would have puked my guts out right then and there on the floor of that boat's cabin.

I could hear footsteps on deck, so I quickly glanced around the cabin.

"There's nothing we need in here," I said aloud to myself as I climbed back up the steps to the deck.

"Is everything all right," Gin yelled.

As I emerged from the cabin, Jacob and Billy were looking at the dead man lying on the deck.

"Don't go down there," I said.

"Why not," Jacob asked.

"Because it's worse than our kitchen, that's why, so don't go down there, get it?" I answered gruffly.

"Is everything all right?" Gin asked again.

"Yes, it is now," I answered. "We must have disturbed his breakfast."

"MRE's?" she replied.

"If that's what you want to call them," I answered. And by the way, we were almost his next MRE's!"

"What's that supposed to mean?" Billy asked.

"I'll tell you what that means. I was talking to that maniac for every bit of three minutes, and I looked over at you and Jacob and both of you had put your weapons in a position that you couldn't have possibly used them if your lives depended on it, and by the way, from what I saw down below, your lives did depend on it. Both of you were acting as if this guy was your best friend, like you'd known him for years.

Gin, are you listening to this, you're our ace in the hole, your job is to sit there all pretty like, with a gun in your hand, and if need be, shoot somebody. You're most likely the last one anyone will shoot at because they think you're the least threatening of all of us."

"He seemed like a nice guy," Jacob said, with a slight sound of guilt in his voice as he raised his eyebrows and lowered his head.

"That nice guy was going to *eat us!*" I shouted, hoping to make an impression on all of them. "The MRE's he spoke of; happen to be the people below deck he butchered and has cooking on the stove as we speak; most likely members of his family."

Shocked, Gin asked. "Are you kidding me?"

"I wish I was. One of you boys grab that Colt pistol from his hand, and let's get the hell out of here," I snapped.

As I employed my greenhorn sea legs to make my way to the port side of the larger boat where the Morphodite was tied, silently and posthumously I extended my condolences to the unknown deceased people below decks.

But most of all I wanted to express my deepest gratitude, and thank the Friar's Point "*filleter*" for making it possible for me, until the end of my days on this miserable planet, to never be able to smell the aroma of any type of meat cooking on a grill, without having flood back into my mind the memory of the horrendous culinary act that he had performed that day in the galley of his boat.

So with Billy and Jacob already on board the Morphodite, I stopped momentarily just before jumping aboard my small craft and pulled the man's confiscated stainless steel Colt .45 out of my pocket, held the big bore pistol close to his head and emptied the magazine into his face. He was already dead so my gesture was just one of meaningless and selfish gratification, but he had pissed me off, so unloading his own gun into his face made me feel a little better.

Then after jumping aboard my boat, I cut the thin rope that bound our two vessels together, and pushing the crazy man's boat away from ours, I once more aimed just below the water line and fired several shots, only this time, I used the crazy man's other .45 caliber pistol to accomplish that task.

"Start the motor Billy, and take us out of here, let's put some distance between us and this nut-job," I asserted.

We cruised at full speed for about fifteen minutes, then shut down the motor and again resorted to a slow leisurely pace floating down the river.

"I think we need to add another rule to our list," I said. "It might sound harsh, but maybe something like, when in doubt, shoot first and ask questions later. I think we came very close to the end of our journey back there. If that guy would have been a little less insane, he might have fooled all of us."

I could tell by the way that Gin was acting, that she was a little angry with herself for letting her guard down so quickly.

That's when she said. "We almost got killed back there, for real, didn't we?"

"I think we came very close, if I hadn't seen the gun in his hand, he would have shot us all," I replied. "The way it looked in that cabin, he certainly didn't have a problem killing people."

"I think you're right, from now on we should shoot first if anyone we meet does anything weird," Gin insisted as she reached for one of the newly acquired Colt .45s.

"I think I'll just put this one right here by me," she said, while dropping the Colt's magazine to check the ammo in the gun.

Slamming the magazine back into the 1911, she said. "It's got a few bullets left in it. Now I'm beginning to understand why you brought all those guns with us."

Pointing to our stockpile of ammunition, I mentioned.

"What's in that Colt is all of the .45 ammo we have; the rest of the pistol ammunition is 9mm."

"Well I'm going to start with this 9mm," Gin said, tapping the Beretta 92 that was resting on her lap. "I'll use the Colt for back up."

"You boys hear that, we shoot first and ask questions later, we never put our guard down, if we're going to make it in this world we need to stay suspicious of everyone we meet. Get it?"

"We get it Dad!" Billy replied.

"What about you Jake, do you get it?" I asked sternly.

"I get it Dad, shoot first," Jacob answered with his usual teenage sarcastic tone.

Day 13 seemed to be longer than any of the previous days, nevertheless, night finally dropped its dark curtain on the day, and like all of the nights before I took the first watch.

Perhaps it was because of the stress our voyage was putting on me, or the lack of quality sleep I was getting, or our new diet, or possibly all of the above plus some.

Nonetheless, that evening I felt extremely tired. I was fighting to keep my eyes open, and slowly losing that battle.

In this new hellish existence, with so many threats coming from so many sources, to fall asleep on watch could easily mean the death of us all.

My heavy eye lids began to close one last time, when I was brought back from an inevitable sleep by a blinding flash of light, at least I thought it would have been blinding if I had had my eyes open.

The flash of light quickly brought me back to consciousness, but by the time my eyes could focus, all I could see was a distant streak in the sky that resembled a shooting star, and it was gone just as quick.

I thought this light must have been caused by some kind of jet aircraft. However, I hadn't heard any noise that accompanied the light, but that could have been either because I had already drifted off to sleep, or maybe because it was some type of new top secret stealthy jet out of Scott Air force Base in Illinois, or maybe Whiteman Air Force Base in Missouri.

If that were the case, it would mean that there are still some military forces out there fighting this plague. It would also mean there still is a United States government somewhere out there.

Then another thought crossed my mind, maybe it was just some pilot fleeing for his life like the rest of us, but instead of floating down the Mississippi River in a fifteen-foot bow rider named Morphodite, he had commandeered the latest stealth fighter to make his escape.

In either case, we were still on our own, in the middle of the country, and in the middle of the apocalypse, and there was no immediate help coming.

However, the flash of light and my conjecture of what it was, or might have been, and where it might have came from, had stifled my desire to sleep, and I was able to finish my watch wide-awake.

PIRATES

The next morning, Jacob awakened me with an urgent tone in voice.

"Dad, wake up, Dad wake up!"

"What's wrong?" I asked, rubbing my eyes.

"Look over there," he said, pointing to a boat in the middle of the river ahead of us.

"It's not moving and we're coming closer to it, it must be anchored."

"It could be a suicide boat?" I said.

For the first time since we started seeing suicide boats, I actually hoped this would be one of them. It was early in the morning and I had just been awakened, I really didn't want to deal with something like we had dealt with the day before.

"We're still a few hundred yards away, hand me the hunting rifle, I'll take a look at it through the scope."

Jake handed me the scoped rifle as I leaned forward onto the bow of the boat. I extended the legs of the rifle's bipod and placed them on the part of the bow that was wide enough to support them and that didn't have any residual goo from the high diving bridge zombie that had smashed into it.

Lying as flat as I could, I turned the zoom knob to infinity and adjusted the focus knob in kind.

"What do you see Dad?" Jacob asked, the urgency still in his voice.

"Well, it's for sure not a suicide boat, I see at least three men, and two of them are moving around. Looks like the third one is watching us through a pair binoculars, so they know we're coming."

"Everybody, wake up!" I said in a loud voice.

Gin slowly sat up.

"What going on now?" She asked, yawning as she spoke.

"We're going to have company, we need to get ready, Billy get up," I shouted.

"Okay, I'm up," Billy replied, stretching his arms and yawning too.

"What's the big deal?" he then asked sarcastically.

Annoyed with his lack of seriousness and sense of urgency, I answered harshly.

"The big deal is, we're floating toward a boat that's anchored in the middle of the river, and it has at least three men on it. Do you remember what happened yesterday?"

Billy looked at the boat in the distance.

"Shoot first, right?" he replied.

"If we have to," I confirmed calmly, seeing that he now understood the possible grave nature of the situation that was about to confront us.

We floated along for several more minutes as we prepared to meet this new potential threat, and when we felt that we were as ready as we were ever going to be, I started the motor and we cruised at half speed toward the anchored boat.

The Morphodite was not a fast boat, relatively speaking. Its 48 Evinrude could push it along at a top speed of only about 32 miles an hour. So a great many boats were easily capable of out running it.

With that in mind, I decided that we should meet this possible danger head on instead of trying to out-run a probable faster vessel, and thus having to shoot from a less stable platform, that is if we indeed did have to shoot.

Just out of earshot of the boat we were approaching, I said calmly to everyone. "Stay alert, watch these guys, and keep your gun pointed at them and your finger on the trigger."

"Halt," shouted the man that was pointing his rifle at me. "This is a toll point. Your group will have to pay the toll!"

He was as dirty as the two men on either side of him who stood like sentries with their AR-15's held at a

127

forty-five degree angle across their torsos, trying to look as though they were doing this deed in some official capacity.

We weren't much cleaner, with the blood splatters from past zombie encounters, and having not been able to wash for over a week.

With the river tainted with rotting bodies, no one in their right mind would wash themselves with that water. So hygienically speaking we weren't much different from them, but then again, we were not stopping people and demanding that they pay us a toll.

The man pointing the gun at me and mandating the toll, who I presumed was their leader, wore a red bandana wrapped over his head. He had adorned himself with two crossed bandoliers filled with shotgun shells, even though he was carrying a rifle identical to the firearms his minions were holding. His boots were knee high and resembled cavalry boots; his white shirt had over sized puffy sleeves and was opened half way down the front to show off the two gold chains he wore around his neck.

His partners were comparably dressed, and they all were sporting a 1911 .45 cal. automatic pistol as their main sidearm, guns similar to the pair that we had confiscated a day earlier. They also had one or two extra pistols of different varieties stuck down the front of their pants.

My first impression was that they were doing their best to imitate 18th century pirates. The only thing that was missing from their buccaneer costumes was a cutlass.

"How much is the toll?" I inquired of the man.

"Pretty much everything you have, except your lives. We'll take them too if you insist, so lower your weapons pay the toll and be on your way," the pirate said, answering my question.

On both sides of me and from behind, simultaneous shots rang out. A bullet whizzed past my ear so close I could feel the disturbed air in its wake just before it planted itself deep in the chest of the "want to be pirate" that a fraction of a second earlier was demanding our every possession.

More and more shots were forthcoming as I watched all three of the men do a spastic pirate jig prior to collapsing on the deck of their boat as they were peppered with projectiles spewing from the guns of "my group" as the leader of the would be pirates called them.

When the gunfire stopped, Billy quickly spoke up.

"You said to shoot first!"

"Yes I did. You all did well, they were going to take everything we have, and then probably kill us too! Even if they had let us go it would have been the same as a death sentence to be left out here without food, water, or weapons," I proposed.

"Now we can take their stuff," Jake added.

"Exactly," Gin agreed.

"Let's go on board and take a look around. Gin you stay here and cover us, there could be more of them on that boat." I said, to Gin's displeasure.

"I always have to stay in the boat," Gin remarked, sadly.

"Trust me; it's *always* safer in the boat," I replied in a wittily incisive manner.

"Boys kill anything that moves, and don't forget to give these fine gentlemen their well deserved head shots," I said without remorse.

We climbed aboard the pirate vessel, and after making sure that the pirates wouldn't bother us again by returning from the dead, we began to inventory their stockpile of ill gotten gains.

"I think these guys had been at this from the beginning, look at all this stuff, clothes, guns, jewelry, gas cans, food, and several marine flare guns, not to mention everything else," I elaborated.

Along with the many items we acquired from the pirate's ship, we salvaged all of their weapons, and even more importantly we obtained a plethora of ammunition that they most likely confiscated (took at gunpoint) from others on the river which were not quite as quick on the trigger as Billy, Jake, and Gin.

We loaded as much of the pirate's booty as we had space for, including a couple of extra containers of fuel.

"That's it Dad, we don't have any more room, at all," Billy said, while he bounced up and down on a pile of blankets, trying to shove them down below the edge of the boat without much success.

"One more thing," I shouted, from the far side of the soon to be ghost ship.

Picking up a nearby gasoline container, I proceeded to remove the cap and splash gas on and around the remaining piles of goods we were leaving behind. I then opened several of the plastic gas containers that were stored on deck, and tossed them onto various parts of the pirate ship. Then I grabbed one of the flare guns and a couple packs of flares, and I rejoined Gin and the boys on our boat.

Upon returning to our boat, I maneuvered the Morphodite around the pirate's craft, turned our motor off, and again we began to drift.

However, this time I didn't shoot below the waterline to sink the boat, this time I loaded the newly procured flare gun and fired a bright red emergency flare onto the gasoline soaked deck of the freebooter's vessel.

When the gasoline ignited, we heard a loud swishing roar as a large black and orange mushroom cloud of smoke and fire bellowed into the sky. We were approximately forty yards away from the flame, yet we had to shield ourselves from the uncomfortable heat we could feel reflecting off our skin.

Soon the whole ship was totally engulfed in a glowing yellow-orange fire, which produced a black sooty smoke that rose high into the air.

The flaming boat was anchored in the middle of the Mississippi River and it would be out of our sight in less than an hour.

However, we could see for many miles the pillar of black smoke that had risen into the clouds. The fiberglass and plastic construction of the larger boat while burning produced a column of stark contrast between the puffy white clouds and the azure sky.

Finally, the trees along the riverbank obscured our vision of the distant dark monolith that served as a memorial in the sky that announced the death of the pirates that had tried to waylay the wrong people.

You might wonder why I would choose to stay in the smaller Morphodite boat to complete our journey south; instead of commandeering one of the larger crafts that we had acquired access to along the way.

The answer is that most of the boats that we encountered were either disease infested, (not that the Morphodite necessarily wasn't after some of our encounters) which most of them were, or suicide boats which psychologically we wanted no part of, or they were just too big and less maneuverable even though they were faster than our small boat. But considering that most of the time, speed was not a great concern to us, and we were already very familiar with our own boat, I felt it made more sense to stay on the Morphodite. You know, *"if it ain't broke, don't fix it!"*

We fought the boredom of the rest of the day's journey by sorting through and separating the pirate's booty we had appropriated earlier that day. Then we settled into our usual ritual of preparing for sleep as the grayness of dusk fell upon us once more.

TARGET PRACTICE

The next morning soon arrived, and we awoke feeling restricted in the midst of the massive stockpile of supplies we had scavenged from the river pirate's boat, and along with other things such as the chill in the air and the never-ending foul smell of the river, had helped produce a rather uncomfortable night's sleep for all of us.

We ate our breakfast cramped among our newly obtained hoard of resources, with each of us secretly wondering how we were going to be able to finish this boat ride in such constricted living quarters.

Jacob was the first to speak up.

"I think we might have over done it," he said, pointing to the large pile of pirate weapons.

"More than just the guns," Gin added.

"We don't have any room to move around, we didn't have much room to begin with, and now we don't have any," Billy stressed, throwing the empty can of roast beef he'd eaten for breakfast into the river.

"You're right, we did over do it, so let's fix it," I said, as I picked up a bundle of blankets and tossed them into the water."

"We've only got a few more days on the river, and we can't carry all of this stuff once we leave the boat. So let's pitch a lot of it overboard and only keep the food and anything that's absolutely essential," I instructed, as I hurled more junk over the side.

"The guns too?" Billy asked.

"No, not yet, keep the guns and ammo, I have an idea," I answered.

We spent the next hour going through our supplies, separating it and flinging whatever we deemed unnecessary into the Mississippi.

"That's better, I feel like I can breathe again, I mean if it weren't for the foul smell of this God forsaken river," Gin said, sprawling out over one of the passenger seats.

133

"Much better," Jacob agreed, as he too stretched out his legs.

Billy leaned back against the boat's windshield and pointing to the stack of firearms and ammunition, he then asked.

"What about your idea Dad? We still have all of this ammo and all of these guns, and they're heavier and harder to carry than most of the things we just threw out of the boat. What are we going to do with them?"

Having thought of this idea the night before while mostly unsuccessfully trying to sleep on a mound of miscellaneous items, I answered his question.

"I think we should pick the guns that we're going to take with us, most of which we brought from home, keep as much ammo for those guns as we can possibly carry, and use the rest of the guns and ammo for target practice."

"You mean you're going to let me shoot at the eaters on the riverbank?" Jacob giddily piped up.

"That's right, we're going to use up the spare ammunition shooting at eaters and anything else that looks like it needs to be shot," I happily answered.

"Cool," Billy said. "But I thought you wanted to save our ammo for when we really needed it, and didn't want to attract any undue attention to ourselves?"

"That was before the pirate ship," I replied. "We have tons of ammo now, way more than we can possibly carry without a vehicle. And we don't know how long it will be, or how far we'll have to go before we can commandeer one.

As for attracting attention, we'll probably attract so many eaters to the riverbanks and surrounding areas by firing the guns, that anyone that's out to get us is going to have their hands full with all of the crazed eaters running around.

Besides you can never practice too much, you know what they say, practice makes perfect.

Plus, it will give us something to do instead of being bored to death for the next couple of days."

We spent some time going through the heaped hodgepodge of weapons we had collected from the pirate's boat.

First, we separated the rifles from the pistols, and then we paired them with the proper ammunition for each gun. We chose the weapons we wanted to shoot, and waited for a cluster of the undead to appear on the riverbank.

It wasn't long before we found ourselves floating by a fairly large horde of the hungry dead beasts that watched us pass while uncontrollably salivating at the mere thought of devouring our succulent cerebrums.

Anxious to begin our tedium breaking exercise, we quickly began taking turns picking out targets for each other from the glut of homicidal maniacs that peppered the countryside.

"Remember, it counts as a miss if you don't hit them in the head," Jacob said, taunting Billy.

"I never miss! Haven't you been watching?" Billy replied jokingly.

"Keep an eye on the one with the red hunting cap," Billy said, as he leaned the barrel of the M1 carbine he had chosen to shoot onto the side of the boat.

"Boom!"

The muzzle blast of the gun sounded seconds before the report of the powerful military rifle echoed back to us off the cliff face near the far riverbank.

The targeted zombie dropped onto the water saturated ground by the edge of the river as its red hunting hat was ripped from its head and fell onto the muddy terra firma as well, along with chunks of its brain, hair, scalp, and skull (possibly a couple of teeth too).

"That's five for me. Who's next?" Billy gloated.

"Anyone can do that using the boat as a rest. Stand up and shoot like a man, off-hand, like this," Jacob pointed out, as he stood up, shouldered a world war two bolt action rifle, and blew the top half of a zombies head clean off.

"Did you see that, the bullet lifted the top of its skull off like a trap door, and ejected part of its brain out and onto that other eater?" Jacob announced as he laughed.

"Yeah, yeah, I saw it, that was nothing watch this," Billy insisted as he took aim at another zombie.

The boys bantered back and forth shooting the undead that wandered the riverbanks and turning our first practice session into somewhat of a competition resembling the game of H.O.R.S.E.!

"Okay, my turn," Gin said, standing, and raising the Winchester 30-30 lever action rifle she had picked.

"Pick out a target for me honey, don't make it too hard!"

"Too hard?" I answered. "You did pretty well shooting at those pirates; you shot them before I even knew what happened."

"Yes, but they were a lot closer than these eaters are, and they didn't have all of those flies swarming around them," Gin replied with a smile. "I think that makes them harder to hit."

"Okay hit the fat girl; she should be easy to drop!" I said laughing.

"Very funny, her head is still pretty small from this distance," Gin retorted, making a pre-shot excuse just in case she missed.

"All of their heads are small from this distance Mom, that's what makes it fun!" Jacob remarked as he pressed the trigger back on his rifle and harvested another zombie.

"No, fun is when I hit them, that's when it's fun for me," Gin pointed out.

"Boom!"

The lever action rifle reeled Gin back.

"This thing kicks more than I thought it would," Gin claimed, lowering the rifle and rubbing her shoulder. "I think I like shooting the pistols better."

"Maybe, but you need to learn how to shoot as many guns as you can, you never know when we might have to employ a *battlefield pick-up*," I stated, hoping she would understand that philosophy.

"You need the practice Mom, you missed the fat chick," Jacob said, pointing out the obvious.

"You were holding the gun wrong, you weren't holding it on your shoulder right," Billy instructed as he proceeded to demonstrate.

"See like this, with the butt of the gun seated snuggly in the small of your shoulder."

"I guess all those trips to the range paid off," I boasted, watching Billy instruct his mother in the art of properly holding a rifle.

"Yeah, thanks Dad," Billy declared sarcastically, as only a teenager would. "You were my inspiration."

The sound of our practice session drew many zombies to both sides of the river from the surrounding areas. At times there were as many as seventy-five to one hundred undead targets staggering around at the edge of the water, staring, drooling, and snarling at us.

Again, like earlier in our journey, many tried to follow us along the banks of the river, but were soon blocked by steep banks or thickets of bushes and trees, the one's that we didn't shoot I mean.

Even if they could keep up with us, at some point they would have to wade into one of the tributaries that spilled into the mighty Mississippi, and they weren't about to do that, at least not yet. For at this time, still none of the zombies we'd seen had knowingly dared to venture into the water willingly. It seemed at least for now their hydrophobic tendencies were proving stronger than their seemingly insatiable appetite for human flesh and *brain food*.

The bridge jumpers that had dove, belly flopped, cannon balled, or otherwise landed in the water during their attempt to board our vessel, had actually thought that they would plop down *in* our boat, thus avoiding a midnight dip before they indulged in their dinning pleasure. Of course not realizing that even if they were successful in their leap of faith, that the sudden stop onto the deck or any other part of the Morphodite from the height of a bridge that spanned the Mississippi River, would most likely suppress their appetite permanently.

"Can we move in closer to the bank and use the pistols now?" Gin asked, as she was frustrated with all her missed shots.

"Okay honey," I said. "But we'll have to keep the motor running, there are an awful lot of eaters, we don't want to get too close and get overwhelmed."

"I'm going to shoot the Berretta pistol," she stated.

"Nobody is going to shoot any of the 9mm ammunition; we can carry twice as much of the 9mm as we can the .45 cal. stuff. So we're going to shoot those Colt 1911s. The Colts have more knock down power, but the Berretta holds more ammo, just like my Glock.

It doesn't do any good to knock down an eater, they just get back up with a couple of broken bones and maybe some of their intestines hanging outside of their skin. A head shot with a 9mm is just as good as a head shot with a .45, except the .45 takes out bigger pieces of the eater's brains.

We'll practice with the Colts. Thanks to the pirates we have plenty of ammo for them, and we won't be taking them with us when we abandon the Morphodite anyway," I countered.

"All right, that sounds like a good idea, give me the one with the snake engraved on the grip," Gin said, seeming to be *okay* with my decision.

With the motor running, we eased toward the riverfront.

The closer we came to the zombies that awaited us on the riverbank, the more frenzied they became. Vicious growls, drooling snarls, and snapping jaws,

139

greeted us as we slowly made our way to within ten yards of a tightly grouped horde of the living dead.

Putting the boat in neutral, I watched my wife release a half full magazine from the 1911 and insert a full magazine back into the pistol, then perform a press check by pulling the slide back slightly to view the large .45 cal. round that was seated in the chamber. Satisfied that her gun was now fully loaded, she then let the stainless steel slide slam forward allowing the gun to go into battery. She was now ready to reap the hungry zombies drooling before us.

She lifted the handgun to eye level, and without a moment's hesitation, she let loose a withering barrage of full metal-jacketed projectiles that slammed into several of the undead.

We all watched as the back of the head of one of her intended targets splattered across the face of the zombie standing directly behind it, knocking both of the reanimated corpses to the ground.

"Way to go honey," I said enthusiastically. "Seven shots, one eater minus the back of his skull, one blinded by bone fragments, two with massive spinal cord injuries, and two more with debilitating skeletal trauma. I guess you really do need to practice, you missed one," I jested.

Gin laughed, and exclaimed. "Yes, I do need to practice, give me another magazine!"

Billy quickly tossed her another fully loaded magazine.

"Here Mom, see if you can do it again."

Dropping the empty magazine from the magazine-well of the gun, she again loaded the pistol, pushed down on the slide release, and began to fire upon the stumbling mass of former humanity.

As she fired her pistol into the crowd of wavering zombies, more grayish-yellow brain matter with a tinge of pink was mercifully released from the calcium-fortified enclosures that sat atop the necks of her victims and splattered onto the bodies of the surrounding horde.

Not wanting to be left out of the pistol portion of our practice session, the rest of us joined in the impromptu one-sided firefight and accompanying zombie massacre.

As we fired our pistols, we watched pieces of *our* targeted zombies explode onto other nearby and still standing living dead corpses just as Gin's had done.

However, as the gruesomely sloppy skirmish continued, we were all so caught up in the macabre action, that we failed to notice one of the many wounded zombies that had fallen into the water, had in its panicked flailing to exit the river, inadvertently made its way to the back of our boat and had managed somehow to climb in.

While doing a magazine change, Billy was the first to see the gory intruder in our boat. It had made its way forward, and was now only a couple of steps from Jacob who was oblivious to the immediate danger.

"Look out!" Billy shouted as loud as he could; trying to be heard over the sound of three Colt 1911's engaged in a rapid fire drill.

It was no use; none of us could hear him screaming the alarm. The noise from the guns and the loud ringing in our ears from the many previous shots had deafened us to his warning.

With his gun empty, Billy was left with no other choice if he wanted to save his brother, another method of termination would have to be employed.

Gripping his 1911 as tight as he could, he lunged toward the intruding undead cannibal, and swinging the pistol like a hatchet; he buried the magazine-well of the gun deep into the top of the attacking zombie's cranium, releasing the living-dead life force of the animated monster back into the wild.

With the attacker neutralize, Billy stood over the carcass that was now oozing bodily fluids onto what was left of our food supply.

We had just killed a multitude of zombies on the riverbank that day, and as we each in turn ran out of loaded magazines for our Colts, we could now hear Billy shouting over the ringing in our ears.

"Hey look, stop shooting and look!"

Looking behind us, we saw Billy pointing to the dead zombie that he had dispatched, which was discharging its putrescent secretions into our boat.

"How'd that thing get in here?" Gin quickly asked.

"It's ruining our food supply, we have to get it out of here," I yelled.

Dropping my gun, I scurried over to the festering body and began to pull on its arm, attempting to drag it to the side of the boat.

"Don't just stand there, help me Billy," I scolded. "Jacob, steer us back out to the middle of the river before something else happens."

With a plethora of new zombies descending onto the nearby riverbank with a hungry desire (pun intended) to replace the soulless corpses that we had just eliminated.

142

Jacob jumped into the pilot's seat of the Morphodite and shoved the shift lever forward out of neutral, thereby engaging the prop to the motor. As he did so, he turned the steering wheel to the left and we sped back out to a safe distance from the infested riverbank.

Billy and I dragged the blood-oozing zombie's remains to the side of the boat and dumped it into the river, while Gin threw much of our now tainted food over the side as well.

"That little exercise almost cost us dearly," I said.

"We don't want to do that again, that was stupid," Gin admitted.

Billy then added.

"We just went in too close, we need to stay further out."

Jacob had been quiet up to this point, but he now agreed.

"A lot further out!" he said with an amount of authority that he had yet to acquire.

"Well I think we've had enough target practice for today," I told my family. "We'll do it again tomorrow, only at a greater distance, and I think we might need to start using some hearing protection too, my ears are still ringing.

I have some of those foam earplugs somewhere in this pile of stuff. We're all going to go deaf with all the shooting we're doing, we can at least use them during practice.

Let's eat and get some rest, as usual we don't have any idea what's in store for us tomorrow," I said, while picking through the small amount of food that we still had on board.

The following morning we were awakened before dawn by a thunderstorm that brought torrential rain to the river.

The thunder woke us up before the rain arrived, so we were able to throw some tarps over most of our supplies, and raise the boat's canopy.

We floated down the river until well after sunrise, huddle together under the boats canopy to stay dry.

"I'm bored," Jacob said, almost whining.

"Me too," Billy said frowning.

"Okay, we've gone through a lot of hardships on this trip, and we're probably going to have to endure a lot more in the coming weeks, months, and maybe years," I responded. "So we're not going to let a little rain defeat us, are we? Let's look on the bright side, the rain has dispersed most of the flies, so I say we grab a couple of guns and get even with a few of those epidermis eaten sons-a-bitches. Are you with me?"

"Sure," Jacob said.

"Me too," Billy added as the frown melted from his face.

"I'm with you too, honey," I heard as my wife chimed in. "This will be like shooting fish in a barrel, the way they're all clustered together."

"Good, I'll find the hearing protection, and you guys get some guns and ammo," I said, as I began to grope through one of the backpacks we had transported from our former home.

After finding the earplugs and handing them out to everyone, I asked the eager shooters.

"Everyone got their earplugs in?"

"What?" Billy said jokingly.

"Yes, we're all ready, let's start getting even with those evil bastards!" Jacob yelled.

Two of us used the Colt pistols, and two of us used the AR-15 carbines we had liberated from the river pirates. The carbines we took from the pirates were a shorter version of the normal AR-15 rifles and allowed us more maneuverability in the tighter spaces underneath the boat's canopy.

The distance to our chosen targets was at the limit of the .45 cal. pistol's effective range, but in our confined space, trying to maneuver four rifles, even short-barreled ones, would be too much of a chore and potentially dangerous to *our* health.

It rained most of that day, so we spent a good deal of the time shooting at the unfortunate undead from a seated position within the restrains of our boat's rainproof canopy.

By the end of the second day of so-called practice, we had put a serious dent in the excess amount of ammunition we had seized from the pirates, and a serious dent in the zombie population that lined the riverbanks on our journey south. All of which were huddled together under trees and any other shelter they could find to avoid the relentless rainfall.

Few of them even noticing us floating by them, as their fear of the water falling from the sky overwhelmed their hunger for flesh and their most favored of rare delicacies, human brains.

Gin was right when she said that using these huddled masses of fearful cannibalistic killers for target practice would be like shooting fish in a barrel. If it wasn't for our penchant for making head shots, it wouldn't have been any sport at all.

With the ammunition for many of the guns used up after our target practice, I made the hard decision to reduce the amount of firearms that we had been stumbling over as we moved around the boat, by throwing them overboard.

I weathered the pre-explanation vexation of Billy and Jacob as we began tossing several guns into the river to free up a little more room in the boat, because they were just taking up space now. Not to mention, we still had more usable guns and ammo than we could possibly carry once we abandoned the Morphodite and left the river.

"This is ridiculous, throwing all of these nice guns into the river," Jacob attested, as he slowly picked up one of the guns in question. "It's ludicrous!"

"Dad, are you sure this is a good idea?" Billy asked, as he tossed a Winchester rifle into the water.

"Yeah Dad, we might be able to use these weapons to barter with later," Jacob contended. "You know, trade for something we need."

My idea to throw the ammo-less weapons overboard wasn't a spur of the moment thought that I chose to act on summarily without reflection as my two boys seemed to think.

I had given it some thought and had concluded that it was the most logical thing to do under the present circumstances.

As long as we were in the Morphodite, the firearms weren't a major burden, although they might have been a little inconvenient to maneuver around while adjusting

146

our positions on the small craft, their weight was really not an issue.

However, our plan was not to spend the rest of our miserable lives floating around the zombie apocalypse in a fifteen-foot bow rider.

As I mentioned before, we already had more weapons than we could carry. And knowing that when we got to the point on the river where we're going to abandon our boat and continued our journey on foot. Well, the overflow of the for all intent and purposes, useless, heavy, and cumbersome firearms, that we might have to carry for who knows how many miles before we could relinquish them for some piddly amount of needed supplies, to someone that may choose to use them against us, would be a great and maybe impossible burden to bear.

Therefore, in defense of my inferred ridiculous order, I gave this response.

"Well boys and girls," I said, not wanting to leave my wife out of the mix just in case, even though she had yet to comment on my perceived ill-conceived notion. "You're right, we could use these heavy steel weapons for the purpose of barter, after all, we don't have any idea how far we might have to carry them into the abyss of this diseased and dangerous land.

We've spent all of the ammunition that can be used in them, but I suppose we could always use them as unwieldy clubs against the masses of attacking undead that I'm sure we'll encounter at some point along the way, at least until we run across some suitable ammo for them. I'm sure nothing could possibly go wrong in that scenario.

I mean we could always leave the guns we brought from home. You know, the guns that we *do* have ammo for, the guns that we *are* familiar with and know how to use very efficiently and effectively.

We could leave them, their ammo, and all of the other heavy and useless items that we don't need, like food and water.

I mean who wants to carry several pounds of food and water with us, when we can carry several pounds of guns to barter with later for food and water?

That way we can traipse through the wilderness, carrying untold pounds of unmanageable dead weight (no pun intended), in search of some dumbass turds that were too stupid to head out into an eater infested wasteland with their *own guns*, so we could save their dumb asses and beg for their food and water at the same time.

That's a brilliant plan, now why didn't I think of that?

Better yet, while you're stumbling around like a drunken eater, weighed down with your *really cool* bartering goods strapped all over you. When an attacking eater decides to make a meal of you, all you'll have to do, is say.

Excuse me hungry zombie, could you be so kind as to wait for me to unfurl myself from all this heavy awkward shit I have wrapped all around my body before you take a bite out of my brain.

That should workout well, after all, we've ran across so many congenial zombies that seem to be more than willing to work with us during our pursuit of their ultimate demise. Don't you think?"

"Very funny Dad!" Jacob said sarcastically, his eyebrows forming a straight line across his brow.

"We get your point Dad," Billy agreed, as he threw another gun into the river.

Never being one to know when to stop, especially when I wanted to instill something deep into my children's heads, I continued.

"No, no, if you guys want to carry two or three hundred extra pounds on your back while we look for more friendly people like we've already met, so you can supply weapon to them, be my guest.

I'm sure you'll have no trouble at all keeping up with your mother and me either, you know, while you search for your new friends to hand over your firearms to," I chortled, as I dangled a long gun over the water waiting for a reply.

"Go ahead and drop it in the water," Billy conceded. "I told you, you made your point."

I did as Billy directed and dropped the expendable weapon into the rippling current, then with my wife and boys in agreement, we seeded the bottom of the river with the rest of the nonessential firearms, making a little more room in the boat for ourselves.

When the rain did finally stop, the clouds gave way to blue skies and we removed the protective tarps covering our supplies.

Raising the canopy was quite a lot of work, not because it was hard to put up, because it wasn't, it just rotated up and snapped onto the windshield, the hard part was moving everything we had laid on top of it during our rush to get our supplies packed in the boat.

We decided to leave the canopy up. If we took it down it would not fold all the way to the deck as before, it would lay on top of the supplies that once covered it and would really be in the way. It would be easier to duck under it while moving around the boat, than it would be to constantly step over it or to move everything again to get it all of the way down.

Moreover, if it rained again it would already be in place, and when it wasn't raining, we could use it as a sun shade.

Not to mention, it would impair the ability of any rogue zombies to move around our craft freely if another one gained unauthorized access to our boat.

After almost two full days of shooting different guns, and sending thousands of rounds of ammunition down range into the brains of our undead enemies, thereby destroying a mere fraction of the zombie populace. Not to mention some constructive criticism, friendly competition, and friendly critiquing, we were becoming quite good at making head shots on zombies at a variety of distances, and with a variety of firearms. We decided that we would continue our daily practice sessions until our surplus ammunition ran dry, or we came near to our departure point on the river. Whichever came first?

FOOD SHORTAGE

We initially thought the damage was minimal from the zombie that had boarded the Morphodite uninvited, and through its ultimate demise had rendered part of our food supply uneatable.

However, as we foraged through the remainder of our stores, we found that the diseased fluid secreted on them from the marauding zombie had contaminated even the cans.

We couldn't open them with the John Wayne can opener without pushing the now dried emission into the contents of the can.

We surely didn't want to wash the cans off in the river, and we didn't want to assume that washing the cans with what was left of our drinking water would clean them well enough to insure our safety.

"I can only find two cans of food that for sure have not been affected by that eater," Gin said, as she held up two cans of green beans for inspection.

"Then get rid of everything else, throw it in the river," I said with disgust.

"Jacob, have you still been keeping track of how many days we have left on the river?" I asked.

"Yes Dad, about two and a half to three days left," he answered.

Gin broke in.

"We can't go three days without food! What are we going to do?"

"We're going to have to make an unscheduled stop. As soon as we see the next house, we'll stop and see what we can find," I replied in answer to her question.

After making the decision to essentially loot the next house we saw along the way, the river carried us along for nearly an hour before Billy stood up, pointed at a house, and shouted.

"Hey, there's a house, way over there."

It was a large white farmhouse setting back from the river about five hundred yards on the Illinois side of the river and partially obscured by a few trees, and we were about a mile from the point that we would want to land our boat.

"Quick!" I said. "Grab a gun and start shooting."

Looking around at both riverbanks and seeing no zombies (which was rare indeed), Jacob asked. "Shoot at what, I don't see any eaters?"

"Just shoot, the sound will draw all of the eaters in the area in this direction," I pointed out, just before I shot several rounds into the air. "Then we'll quietly float past them and dock the Morphodite perpendicular to the farmhouse," I stated as I fired a few more rounds.

Billy and Jacob joined me in my noise making effort, followed by Gin, and for the next couple of minutes the four of us fired volley after volley into the air creating deafening cannon like reports. Each volley thundered along the rivers channel, summoning any roving zombies that were within earshot to our location.

"Enough!" I yelled, "Hopefully that will do the trick."

"Now we'll just quietly float down the river past all the eaters that are investigating where that sound came from," I said.

"I hope you're right," Gin said apprehensively.

"It should work, every time we've shot at them, no matter how many we put down, more keep showing up," I concluded confidently.

"It won't be too long before we find out," Billy added.

As Billy had predicted, it wasn't long before we were cautiously approaching the riverbank and looking for a suitable place that the Morphodite could be moored.

"This looks like a good spot, not too steep and the current is slow here, and no eaters in sight. Hand me the anchor and I'll tie it off short," I said, jumping out of the boat onto the stone speckled sandy bank.

"Looks like the noise making ploy worked Dad," Billy said quietly. "I don't see any eaters around here."

"Keep an eye out for them anyway," I warned. "You know as well as I do that just because we don't see any of them, that doesn't mean that there isn't one or two of them or even more lurking in the area."

"Let's gun up people, and stay quiet while we're doing it," I ordered, using my best ex-marine whisper.

"Everyone strap on your pistols, Billy, you and I will bring the AKs and one drum magazine each. Jake, you bring that 9mm Sub-2000 you're so handy with and at least two spare high cap magazines. Honey, just bring your pistol and a couple of magazines, and you can carry the backpacks," I ordered again.

Outfitted, and on the march, our small band trudged through the thick knee-high brush toward the farmhouse in the distance.

"I'm just carrying these empty packs, and this walk is wearing me out," Gin said, in her best complaining tone.

"This is nothing; wait until we abandon the boat in a couple of days, then we'll be on foot until we can find some other means of traveling. With a lot more to carry than we have now," I explained, thinking after the fact that I probably shouldn't have mentioned the coming hardship to my wife, she was already starting to complain about walking with two *empty* backpacks.

"Thank God, we're almost there, I think your noise ploy definitely worked, we haven't seen one eater so far," Gin said softly.

"That's what I said back at the boat Mom," Billy announced. As if there were a trophy for the first one to state the obvious.

"We don't want to draw attention to ourselves if we don't have to, so don't shoot any of them if you can help it. Use the butt of your rifles to smash in their skulls if we run into any and there aren't too many to deal with by hand," I whispered. "Maybe we can find a hand tool or something at the farmhouse to use as a weapon, something a little less noisy than our guns."

When we arrived at the front door of the house, it was standing wide open. I entered first, but not before giving Jacob strict instructions to stand watch outside, and not to enter the house unless he heard a lot of gunfire coming from inside or he saw zombies approaching, then Billy followed me in, and Gin hesitantly followed him.

The inside of the house looked like the people that had lived there had left in a hurry. That wasn't too surprising, I figured a lot of people left their homes in a

154

hurry when all of this started. Nonetheless, we still needed to be very careful, we couldn't afford to assume that no one was living there, dead or alive.

"We need to stay together, and keep alert, we've got to watch our backs," I reminded them.

"It looks like that's the kitchen just ahead of us through the next room. Most of these old farmhouses have a pantry, that's where we'll most likely find the food if there is any," Gin explained quietly.

She was right; the kitchen was straight ahead through the dining room which we were about to enter. A few more steps and we'd be in the kitchen.

"That's probably it, that door on the left with the broom beside it," Gin whispered softly, as she pointed to the door.

"Billy, you jerk the door open, and if there's an eater in there I'll clobber it with this," I said, as I snatched an iron skillet off the stove.

Lifting the heavy frying pan over my head, I signaled Billy to open the pantry door. He leaned forward and slowly turned the door handle, then quickly pulled it toward himself. The door opened slightly and then slammed closed again as if it were spring loaded. My wife's eyes told me that she was frightened, as she proclaimed in a deep solemn tone not even trying to whisper.

"Something's in there!" She said.

"Who's there? Who's in there?" I asked in a stern yet low voice.

"Was that a growl?" Billy asked, thinking that he'd heard something.

Gin answered quickly.

155

"That's what it sounded like to me, sounds like an eaters in there!"

"Billy," I said. "Pull as hard as you can, Gin you help him, ready, on three, one, two, three."

Billy and Gin tugged on the door handle with all of their might.

The door flew open, and upon seeing a dark red mucilaginous liquid smeared all around the mouth and running down the front of the large entity hiding in the shadowy darkness of the old farmhouse pantry. I swung the iron pan vertically down onto the top of its head; the pouring spout acted like a spearhead and effectively crushed a gaping cleft in the top of the skull of the oversized occupant loitering on the floor of the food closet.

"That's not blood all over his shirt," Billy revealed. "It looks like strawberry jam!"

"It is strawberry jam, there's the jar between his legs," Gin said, pointing to a large jar nestled in the man's crotch.

"Doesn't look like that's the first jar of jam this guys eaten, he must weigh five hundred pounds. He's probably been hiding in here off and on since the outbreak began," I said, showing little or no remorse after butchering an innocent and defenseless citizen. "He couldn't hold the door closed because his hands were covered with jam."

"And he sounded like an eater because his mouth was full of it," Gin added as she scanned the shelves of the pantry for *our* much needed food.

"Well, better him than us, Billy can you step over this behemoth and reach what's left of the food in here?" I asked.

"I think so," he replied, stretching to step over the corpulent corpse.

"Take it all, I don't want to have to do this anymore," Gin complained.

"You better get used to it, once we ditch the Morphodite, this will be standard operating procedure like it or not," I interjected. "This is going to be our way of life from now on."

Just as Billy cleared the last shelf in the pantry, Jacob appeared at the kitchen door.

"They're coming," he whispered.

"How many are there?" I asked.

"A herd of at least ten, coming from the same direction we came from."

"You mean horde?" Billy scoffed.

"Herd, horde, whatever, they're coming," Jacob answered sharply still whispering.

"Did they see you?" I urgently asked.

"No, I don't think so," he answered, shaking his head.

"Quick, let's go out the back door," I blurted out, probably a little too loud considering that there were as Jacob had put it, a *herd* of hungry zombies close by, a *herd* that may or may not have been stalking us.

We dashed out of the kitchen and through the screened-in porch at the rear of the house, and through the door that led outside to the backyard.

A barn was only about fifty yards from the back door of the house, so we sprinted across the yard and through the three-foot wide opening between the two large sliding doors on the barn.

"Hurry, close the door!" Gin puffed, trying to catch her breath.

A loud rusty squeak accompanied the diminishing gap between the two barn doors as Billy and Jacob quickly pushed the mammoth wooden door closed.

"They must have heard that, it couldn't have been much louder," I concluded.

"Nothing we can do about it now," Billy asserted, shrugging his shoulders.

"Right," I agreed. "Let's check out this barn and make sure there are no eaters in here!"

As he pointed to several rusty hand sickles with sun bleached and worn wooden handles hanging at eye level on the wall of the barn, Jacob apprised us of their presents.

"Look at these!" he said.

"That's just what we're looking for, everybody grab one," I insisted, tossing my frying pan onto a nearby bale of hay.

With sickles in hand, we searched the barn for any rogue zombies that might be skulking there.

"No eaters Dad, but look at this," Billy directed, as he motioned for me to look into one of the animal stalls.

The barn was devoid of life, or death, except for one starving horse, and of course us.

The horse had been locked in the stall without any food or water, and left there by its owner, most likely from the first day the apocalypse started.

"What are we going to do with it?" Jacob asked.

"I don't know, I've never owned a horse," I replied. "Look around, there must be some food in here that it will eat, what's in those sacks over there?" I said, pointing to a pile of neatly stacked gunnysacks.

Billy pulled his knife from its sheath, and stabbed it into one of the sacks.

"It's oats, horses eat oats don't they?" He asked, already knowing the answer.

"Yes!" Gin responded. "Horses eat oats!"

Billy put his knife back into its sheath, and proceeded to lift the opened sack and throw it into the horse's stall. The starving horse slowly ambled over to the open gunnysack and began to feast on the first meal it had seen in almost two weeks.

"Billy, open the stall so it can leave when it's ready, it needs water and we don't have any in here. When it leaves the barn it'll find some outside."

"Speaking of leaving the barn," Jacob announced. "I don't think that's going to be so easy. Those eaters did hear the door squeak, and now they're right outside."

I rushed over and peeked through a crack in the wooden slats of the barns siding.

"Looks like all of them followed the sound, but I don't think they know we're in here yet," I whispered. "That means we have the element of surprise on our side."

Looking around the barn, almost in a panicked state, Gin asked. "Are those big doors the only way out?"

"There should be a smaller, regular door somewhere, so the farmer can enter the barn without having to wrestle with those big doors every time he goes in or out."

"It's over there, over in the corner, I saw it when we first came in, and it opens to the side of the barn, close to the front," Jacob informed us, pointing to that corner of the barn.

"Still, we're going to have to fight our way through those eaters, the tall brush surrounds the farmhouse and barn, and where it is cleared, there are fences. We don't want to be caught trying to climb a fence, and we know how hard it is walking, not to mention running through the undergrowth. I think our best bet is to meet them head on, and use these sickles, not our guns, to chop our way through them," I suggested. "Unless someone has a better idea?"

No one offered an alternative to my plan, so we prepared to make our escape from the barn, and hopefully trek back to the Morphodite in one piece.

"Sling your rifles over your shoulders like this," I said as I demonstrated. "We're only going to use our guns if we absolutely have too. We know gunfire attracts eaters quickly, and we already have enough of them to deal with as it is." I maintained, as I loosened my sling and slid my head and arm into the gap between the rifle and the sling, and mounted my AK-47 on my back.

I walked with resolve toward the door we had slated to be our exit point.

"Let's go," I ordered. "We'll line up in front of the door, I'll go out first, Jacob, second, honey, you go third, and Billy you bring up the rear, and keep an eye on your mother," I demanded.

We took our positions by the side door of the barn, lining up as I had instructed, and on the count of three, I shoved hard on the rickety wooden door, accidently

160

folding it back far enough to break the top hinge off of the dilapidated frame. This led to a loud crash as the old wooden door slammed into the side of the barn, resulting in the bottom hinge also tearing loose from the ramshackled doorjamb.

Needless to say, the inadvertent noise of the door being ripped off its hinge's and subsequently smashing into the side of the barn, instantly attracted the attention of every one of the zombies that up to now had been silently and aimlessly wandering around the outside of the barn.

The usual snarling, snapping, and drooling ensued as the attack commenced, and our second land battle was on. Only this time, our van was not sitting thirty feet away in the driveway, this time five hundred yards of dense vegetation separated us from the safety of our boat that was moored on the river that we had grown to hate, but hate it or not, we were still going to disparately try to return to it.

The first of the undead that tried to attack me came at me from my right side. It was a young woman, while living she had matured to somewhere between eighteen and twenty-five years. She had blonde hair and green eyes; however, they were severely bloodshot now. She was of average height for a girl, about five feet three inches tall. She was just the right height, so that when I swung my sickle horizontally at her, I didn't have to bend, or stretch, or reach up or down. I just swung the sickle in a very natural swing, like a pimp might backhand one of his whores in his stable, and hewed her head off, slicing right through the very middle of her

161

neck and dropping both her head and her body to the ground.

Her head rolled in front of me and settled on her right cheek, she looked up at me from the ground still working her jaws, not yet willing to give up on her attempt to feast upon me, just like Julie our former neighbor had done several days earlier on our kitchen floor.

"Not a bad cut, for a rusty sickle," I thought, as I kicked her severed head out of my way, knocking her front teeth down what was left of her throat at the same time.

Billy had taken another approach to using his sickle. After my first kill, I turned to check on my family and saw that he had driven the point of his farming implement into the crown of a zombie's skull. The result of which was twofold.

First, the point of the sickle had penetrated clear through zombie's head and seemed to be lodged somewhere in the attacker's throat. I could see Billy was having a hard time lifting the sickle vertically out of the now falling undead killer, as his weapon was stuck in the zombies head.

Second, before I could render him any assistance, he grabbed the sickle with both hands and tugged hard on the handle back toward his stomach, pulling the rusty concave blade through the face of his advisory, splitting it down the middle and exposing its now semi-divided brain along with a multitude of dark red liquid that splattered onto the front of his pants, covering him with zombie juices.

The hewing, slicing, and stabbing was over in a remarkably short period of one or two minutes, and when we left the farm, the body count was at eleven. The sickles had done their job well.

On our way back to the river, we encountered four more of the diseased homicidal maniacs and dispatched them summarily.

Arriving back at our boat, we found it exactly the way we had left it.

"Jump in and let's get going before more of them show up," Gin said with a sigh of relief. "I never thought I'd be glad to see this stinking river again!" She said, shaking her head.

"It wasn't that bad Mom, we went through those eaters pretty quick," Jacob jeered happily.

"Don't get cocky son, remember, the eaters only have to get lucky once, like the one that managed to crawl into the boat, we have to get lucky every time!" I countered with as much passion in my voice as I could muster.

Before climbing into the Morphodite, I reached down and picked up a smooth round rock from the bank.

"Here, Jacob catch!"

"What's this for?" He asked.

"It's to sharpen our sickles," I replied.

I picked up the anchor and placed it on the bow of the boat. I pushed the boat away from the sandy bank, and using the head of one of the numerous corpses that had washed to the shore all along the river as a step; I pushed off and jumped into the boat.

My weight shoved the cadaver's face into the mud as the toe of my boot peeled off a chunk of hair and scalp that stuck in the tread of my boot sole.

"Start it up Billy, and let's get out of here," I prompted, with a quick shake of my foot, flipping the rotting toupee from my boot before stepping onto the deck of the Morphodite.

Billy started the motor and backed the boat away from the riverbank. About twenty yards out, he turned the boat to the starboard side and crammed the shift lever into its forward position and we slowly made our way to the middle of the river once more.

GROUP THERAPY

"Hey Dad, what do you think happened to that horse?" Jacob asked, looking rather dejected.

"I guess it'll be all right. I managed to rip the barn door off its hinges and all, so it had a way to get out of the barn. We killed all the eaters in the immediate area, so it probably left the barn in search of water; it's most likely fine," I said, trying to cheer Jake up.

"I hope so. How could anyone do that to an animal?" Jacob inquired, still looking forlorn.

"I doubt if they did it on purpose. Remember how fast this whole thing started, nobody had much time to

164

do anything except run for their lives," I maintained. "That's what we did."

"The horse is fine," Billy interrupted. "It's just fine."

Then Gin added.

"We'll never really know for sure, but animals are very resourceful and resilient. I bet right now that horse is drinking water and getting its fill of grass. One thing is for sure, he's not on this horrible river like us."

"The river didn't seem like such a bad idea when we were in that barn honey now did it?" I said sarcastically, reminding her of our latest close encounter with the Grim Reaper.

"No it didn't, but I still don't have to like this damn river, and I don't care what you say, I'm never going to get used to this smell. This river stinks!" She snapped while holding her nose, giving her voice an adenoidal tone.

"Well you won't have to put up with the smell of the river for too much longer. Tomorrow I'm going to break out the GPS and see exactly where we are, and how much farther it is to Vicksburg," I said, growing tired of her complaining. After all, it wasn't helping any, and certainly wasn't doing anything to diminish to odor the river was emitting. But I didn't want to start an argument, things were bad enough without us fighting among ourselves. So I chose to change the subject and hoped that she would follow my lead, which she did.

The next morning after everyone was awake; I dug through our stuff and found the GPS device that I had made sure to bring along with us. I turned the mechanism on and was glad to see that it had held a charge and was operating with seventy-six percent of its battery life left. After making a few calculations and formulating an interim plan, I made an announcement.

"We should be able to pick up some kind of a vehicle in Vicksburg, if not; Tallulah is just west of there fifteen miles or so down interstate twenty. Vicksburg is right on the river, and it should be a short walk into town. I can't see not being able to find something to drive in one of those towns. By my estimate we should reach Vicksburg some time tomorrow afternoon barring any kind of delay."

"You mean like pirates," Jacob asked.

"Yes!" I said. "Like pirates."

"Or like getting killed," Billy interjected.

"Thanks for the positive input Billy," Gin said sarcastically.

Ignoring his mother's comment, he asked.

"Hey Dad, I noticed something about the eaters. They always seem to be traveling in groups. The only one we've seen not with another eater was our neighbor Jon, and it wasn't long after he arrived at our house that Julie showed up at our patio door. Why do you think that is?"

"I don't know, but you're right," I answered. "We've seen a couple of massive groups on the riverbanks. At the farmhouse there was a bunch of them. Then on the way back to the boat there was that group of four of them."

"Two on the road on the way to launch the boat," Gin quickly divulged.

"Don't forget the two at the boat launch standing behind the tree. I saved Dad remember," Jacob proudly added.

"Maybe it all goes back to what the CDC was saying about the virus possibly being from feral dogs. We know the eaters are afraid of water, like hydrophobia," I reminded.

"Yeah, they're funny when they try to swim," Jacob said laughing.

"They're not so funny when they end up in our boat, are they?" Billy fumed, recalling Jacob nearly being bitten.

"If it is the feral dog syndrome, maybe it's like wolves, and there's some kind of pack mentality that has evolved. Whether it's pack mentality or a mutated strain of the disease, or maybe they just like each other's company. We might be able to use the group therapy thing to our advantage at some point," I mentioned.

"How are we going to do that?" Gin asked, tilting her head to the side and raising her eyebrows.

"I'm not sure right now honey," I answered. "But let's keep it in mind anyway; the more we know about our enemy the better we'll be able to fight them."

Gin nodded her head in agreement.

"We know they're afraid of water, and they like to travel in packs," she said.

"They have pretty good hearing," Billy interjected once more.

"They like to eat people, it's lucky for us that they're kind of slow and off balance most of the time," Jacob quipped.

"Especially lucky for you," Billy said sarcastically, again reminding his brother of his near encounter with a gruesome death.

"Anything we can think of that might help us fight off these monsters we need to consider, so keep thinking, and in the mean time let's sharpen our sickles, it's only a matter of hours before we get to Vicksburg and I'm sure we're not going to have time to do it there," I maintained. "We're going to need these sickles to be sharp until we can find something better if we're going to make it to Texas."

We settled down and shared the rock that I had picked up to sharpen our sickles. The sickles had worked pretty well at the farmhouse, and we really didn't need them much sharper than they already were. Even though they were old and rusty, the farmer had maintained them well enough to be able to split a zombie's skull rather efficiently. But, I wanted to give everyone something to do for awhile to keep their minds occupied with something other than the smell of the river, and the memories of the horrors that we had encountered along the way.

The rest of the day dragged sluggishly by, as did most of the days that had preceded it. All of us had a sense of joy and relief when the days ended and we could lie down and close our eyes for a few hours, and hopefully dream of more pleasant times in the past, and maybe even in the future.

VICKSBURG MS

We had spent the early portion of the following day packing what we were going to carry with us into the small town of Vicksburg.

Humans have a tendency to develop an emotional attachment to inanimate objects, and it doesn't matter what those objects are, how large or small they might be, or even how long we've owned them. The attachment can be very strong, and the detachment can be quite traumatic. Therefore, we found ourselves in a mild state of melancholia as we prepared to deal with releasing the emotional hold we had on many things we would be leaving behind.

In my case, it was my small 15-foot utility boat I had named Morphodite. We had already left behind most of our possessions when we were forced out of our home days earlier, which made leaving my boat on the bank of the Mississippi river that much harder. Nonetheless, it would soon have to be done and there was nothing that I could do to prevent it, so I would just have to grin and bear it, and put it out of my mind as soon as possible, for there were far more pressing matters at hand.

Shortly after 2 o'clock in the afternoon, the GPS showed Vicksburg MS less than a mile away.

"Vicksburg is a mile ahead!" I announced. "We'll be paddling to the bank; we don't want to take the chance that the noise from the motor will bring any eaters our way."

As we rounded a large bend in the river, two long steel-truss bridges that spanned across the water connecting Mississippi and Louisiana came into view.

"That's Vicksburg there on the left by those bridges," I stated. "Let's start paddling!"

The river meandered to the east about five miles before Vicksburg. Then it abruptly turned to the southwest at Vicksburg. The effect of which was that the current was somewhat stronger on the outside of the curve, resulting in an accumulation of corpses that had been ejected from the river and washed onto the bank as the river made a 45° southerly turn and began to flow southwest.

"Great, even more dead bodies, I suppose we have to walk over them now?" Gin said with disgust.

I didn't feel there was a need to try and rebut Gin's comment. After all, spending weeks on a river that had the smell of death constantly in the air, along with hundreds if not thousands of rotting human and sub-human bloated bodies floating all around us. Not to mention the numerous hordes of slobbering zombies lining the banks of this river from hell, intent on having us as the main course of their next meal. We all felt the same way, so all I said in response was.

"Let's try to get to the bank before we get to the majority of them."

Then I paddled even harder, hoping my family would follow suit.

The stronger river current spit us out toward the bank as it had done with the decaying carcasses already littering Vicksburg's waterfront.

We made our way to the shore, and as the Morphodite scraped upon the sand and rocks, I jumped from the bow and pulled as hard as I could on one of the forward cleats, dragging the boat farther up onto the bank.

"There're only a couple of bodies right here, try not to step on them when you get out of the boat!" I explained, pointing in the direction of the beached remains

"They squish pretty easy after being marinated in the river for who knows how long."

"I'll say, you scalped that one back by the farmhouse, and its hair stuck to your boot!" Jake said giggling.

"I hope you find it as humorous when it happens to you," I said sarcastically as I smirked at my youngest son.

"Let's grab our stuff, we've got to get moving, we're burning daylight. We need to find some kind of vehicle as soon as possible, so let's get going," I quietly barked.

We unloaded the equipment we had separated from what was to be left behind. Each of us gathered up what we had assigned ourselves to carry, toted it up the riverbank, and marched into Vicksburg.

We had landed about a thousand feet north of a place called Riverfront Park, and found ourselves walking through a fairly large field. We walked south toward some buildings, and soon we were standing in the parking lot of a small business.

"This stuff is heavier than I thought it would be! What exactly are we looking for?" Billy asked,

171

concentrating more on his heavy load than on searching for a new mode of transportation.

"A vehicle to start with, that's our main concern," I answered. "And be glad that you didn't talk me into bringing all of those guns we threw into the river."

"Yes, any vehicle, I'm beat already and we've only walked a few hundred yards!" Gin interrupted, puffing as she tried to catch her breath.

"Keep your eyes open for a sporting goods store or a gun shop or army surplus store, something like that. A pharmacy or a grocery store would be nice, if we could find one that hasn't been looted to the point that it's completely empty. A National Guard armory would be great to find if we can, any place that might have something of value to us, equipment, medicine, weapons, food, anything like that!" I continued, ignoring the interruption by my wife. "But first we need to find a ride."

"Look over there!" Jacob yelled, pointing to the next parking lot. "Maybe that's the National Guard armory over there."

"Keep your voice down, eaters will hear you!" I scolded in a low voice.

"Sorry," Jacob said grimacing as he whispered. "But look over there!"

Jacob had pointed to a small gap between the buildings through which we could just barely see several military vehicles in the parking lot ahead. We cautiously hurried across a street that divided two parking lots, I believe it was Lee Street, most likely named after General Robert E. Lee; after all, we were in Vicksburg.

Across one parking lot and through the narrow spaces between the buildings we went. We crossed another road that led to a destroyed dock on the river. Something, maybe a runaway barge or a large boat, who knows what, had torn the dock from its mooring. Whatever had run into the dock had continued down the river and left it no longer operational.

When we arrived at the location of the military vehicles, we found them abandoned; no living persons were around, just more dead bodies, a lot more dead bodies. Some of which were in uniform, some in civilian clothes.

"This isn't an armory, but it looks like they made a stand here," I said, surveying the carnage.

"If any of them lived through it, they're gone now," Billy responded, also surveying the death and destruction.

"Maybe, but they left us some cool stuff, look at this!" Jacob remarked, as he climbed into a turret that was built into the roof of a discarded National Guard Hummer that was equipped with a Dillon Aero M134 mini-gun.

"There's still plenty of ammunition left!" He announced, grabbing the handles of the gun and pressing the trigger.

"It's got to be turned on first," I said.

"It is on!" Jacob answered. "See this switch is in the *on* position, it should work?" He said scratching his head.

"Whoever shot it last either got killed or ran away and left it on, it's electric, and it runs off a battery which is probably dead," I informed him. "So you might as well turn it off."

"Yeah, dead like everything else in this world. Are we ever going to get away from this stench?" Gin asked, frowning and wrinkling up her nose.

"Maybe it won't be so bad once we're away from populated areas, or once populated areas I should say, and remember, we're still really close to the river," I replied in answer to her question.

Turning my attention back to the task at hand, I instructed my son.

"Billy, see what kind of battery that mini-gun uses, maybe we can find one that's charged. Check those gas cans too, see if they're full. I'll see if they left the key in this vehicle," I said, opening the Hummer's door.

"They're both full Dad!" Billy said, informing me of his findings.

"The keys are in it too!" I remarked happily.

I turned the ignition key to the right and the powerful Hummer started up.

"Looks like we found our means of travel, throw your things in."

"Billy, you and Jake check a couple of the other trucks and see if we can use one of their batteries for the mini-gun," I ordered.

"And watch out for eaters!" I added.

The boys chucked their equipment into the Hummer, all except their guns and sickles, and then set out to search the other trucks.

The boys lifted the hoods on several of the abandon trucks, checking their batteries to see if they were still charged, and might work the mini-gun, while Gin and I packed the families supplies orderly into our newly acquired means of transportation.

About the fifth vehicle, another Hummer, Billy waved and pointed at the battery. I shifted our Hummer into first gear and slowly moved to the soon to be cannibalize truck.

"This looks identical to the battery the Dillon uses," Billy said. "Now all we have to do is find some tools to get it out."

"I'll look back here; these mini-guns run their batteries down pretty fast so there might be some tools close to our new gun!" I said, searching the back of our Hummer.

"Here's the wrench they use, catch," I said, as I tossed the wrench to Billy.

"This looks like it will work," he replied.

Moments later Billy was lifting the battery from the donor truck.

"Here Jake, put this with the mini-gun," he said, handing Jacob the salvaged battery.

"Bring that wrench over here Billy and let's see if we can get this gun working," I said.

Billy tossed the wrench to me.

"Here catch Dad!" He called out.

"Thanks!" I replied, catching the tool.

"Just one more second and we'll try to shoot this thing." I said jovially, anticipating shooting a mini-gun for the first time in my life.

I had shot many guns up to now, in the Marine Corps I had had the opportunity to shoot grenade launchers and set off explosives, throw hand grenades, and fire various other military weapons.

Before the "Fit hit the Shan" so to speak, I belonged to a gun club and participated in some organized shooting disciplines such as I.D.P.A. and I.P.S.C., and occasionally a three gun match at the shooting complex near Sparta, Illinois. Not to mention, once or twice a year, me and a buddy of mine liked to make the two hour drive to Sikeston Missouri, to enjoy a day shooting different makes and models of machine guns, by *invitation only* of course.

There we shot anything from a Browning 1919 belt fed machine gun to a full auto Uzi, and about everything in between. However, I never got the chance to shoot a mini-gun. So even in the midst of this brave new world, I was still excited to have the opportunity to fire this weapon at last. Not to mention, I could not think of a better gun to use to defend ourselves against a hard charging horde of hungry zombies.

"That's it, now it should work," I said, laying the wrench down by the battery.

"Boys, get in the truck!" Gin said, sounding alarmed.

"What's wrong honey, eaters?" I remarked looking around, yet seeing nothing.

"No, I don't see any eaters, that's what's wrong. We haven't seen one eater since we left the boat. I mean there are plenty of dead ones, but none of them are walking around. All throughout this trip, we've seen eaters. The riverbanks were crawling with them most of the time, the barnyard was infested with them, but here, nothing. Something is not right!" She asserted.

"Maybe it's just luck?" Jacob said, optimistically smiling.

176

"Now days there's no such thing as luck. We have to make our own luck. So get in the truck and let's see if this gun works," I answered.

This time it was *me* that climbed into the turret. I pointed the weapon at the building adjacent to us and flipped the mini-gun's switch to the on position, and the machine began to hum. I pulled the trigger to the rear and the six barrels of the modern Gatling gun began to spin and spit fire, tearing through the side of the sheet metal walls of the targeted structure.

Not wanting to expend all of our ammunition on testing the gun, I quickly halted the test.

"Seems to work," I boasted.

"Well if there are any eaters around here, they should be on their way now," Gin softly hinted.

"Right, so let's get out of here!" I agreed, as I climbed down from the turret and jumped off the Hummer.

"Billy, you get on the mini-gun, same rule applies, shoot first and ask questions later," I reminded him as I climbed into the driver's seat.

As we pulled out of the parking lot and made our way onto old U.S. 80, I handed Gin the GPS and said. "Turn it on and let's see how far it is to the Texas boarder."

As our navigational device booted up, a sign signaling our approach to interstate twenty appeared.

Just at that moment, a large brown dog leaped onto the hood of our vehicle snarling and barking at us on the other side of the windshield. Then another dog joined the first one on the hood of our Hummer, viciously snarling and barking and dripping saliva as well.

Glancing in the rearview mirror I could see more dogs running behind our truck, twenty, maybe thirty of them.

"They're over here too!" Gin screamed, as a large mange covered German Sheppard bounced off the door on her side in an attempt to get at her.

That's when I heard the mini-gun's zipper like sound, as the three thousand rounds per minute weapon laid waste to the pack of dogs that trailed behind us.

The dogs to the side of us, and the dogs on the hood, were too close to the vehicle for the gun to be of any use.

Vertical stops on the mini-gun's mount, put there to prevent the gun from chopping through parts of the Hummer, also prevented the gun from tilting down far enough vertically to get a sight picture on the attacking cur's positions.

The engineers that had designed the turret could not have imagined that the operators would be fighting off a pack of vicious dogs at point blank range in the middle of a zombie apocalypse.

"Grab something and hold on!" I yelled to everyone.

Then I hit the brake sharply, sending the two dogs that were standing on the hood, flying off onto the road in front of us. Then quickly removing my foot from the brake and stomping down on the accelerator pedal, the massive Hummer plowed into the feral dogs, knocking both of them ten or so feet in front of the mammoth truck's bumper.

Then as the heavy vehicle rolled over the ferocious canines, everyone aboard heard the bones of the animals being crushed and broken as they tumbled beneath our truck.

The dog's broken and splintered bones penetrated their skin, some of which was ripped from their bodies as the exposed metal on the underside of the truck tore away pieces of bare muscle and flesh. Then the mutilated dogs were spewed out the back, coming to rest in the middle of the road in an unrecognizable blood soaked and hair infused heap of bones, guts, and skin.

I veered back and forth across the road, bumping into the feral dogs that continued to menace us from the sides of our vehicle, slightly injuring a few of them and causing them to fall behind.

This enabled Billy, using short bursts of fire from the mini-gun, and Jacob, who had begun shooting at them through the back windows with his carbine, to picked them off one at a time along with other stragglers of the pack that were struggling to keep up, yet still had not given up their pursuit of us.

As the Hummer gained speed, tired and out of breath, the remnants of the decimated but yet still dangerous feral dog pack trailed further and further behind us.

"Holy shit!" Gin gasped. "That was close, are you boys all right?"

"We're fine, but I used at least half of the mini-gun's ammo," Billy answered.

"Well, get ready to use the rest of it if you have to!" I said. "In all the excitement we missed our turn, we've got to turn around and go back."

Gin shaking her head, said. "I don't think that's such a great idea."

"We don't have a choice, interstate twenty is back there, if we turn around now we might be able to catch them by surprise while they're still worn-out and haven't had time to regroup," I insisted. "We've got to go back at some point, and our best chance of surviving another attack is to go back right now!"

I pulled the Hummer to the left side of the road and came to a stop with the left front tire just slightly on the shoulder; I put it in reverse and slowly backed up while turning the steering wheel to the right, making sure not to allow the front tire to go down too far into the ditch. When we were perpendicular to the road with the back tires about to go onto the opposite shoulder, I stopped, changed gears, turned the wheel to the left, and we proceeded to return to interstate twenty and to the bridge that would take us into Louisiana.

"They've seen us and here they come again. Honey speed up!" Gin urged, nearing a panicked state.

"Hold on everyone, I'm going to ramming speed! Don't worry about shooting them unless they jump on the truck," I ordered; as I crammed my foot down onto the little peddle on the right.

The Hummer engaged the two lead dogs head on at about fifty miles per hour, tearing their bodies to pieces and killing them instantly. The impact splattered portions of their blood and intestines across a wide path that encompassed several other canines, causing them to hesitate for a moment and rethink their attack.

That slight moment of hesitation, gave us the time we needed to break through their ranks and make it to the bridge.

Once safely on the bridge, and with the malicious mongrels behind us, we saw the feral dogs reorganize what was left of their pack, and amble back in the direction of Vicksburg.

"I *knew* there was something wrong back there!" Gin declared. "I'm starting to think the CDC might have been right about the feral dog connection and this disease."

"But why no eaters back there? It doesn't make any sense," I asserted.

"Maybe the eaters know the dogs have the same disease as they do so they're not interested in eating them, and they move on in search of something else to eat?" Jacob speculated.

"That didn't stop Julie from chowing down on Jon in our kitchen!" Billy argued.

"That's right," I said. "Jon was just as infected as Julie, and she didn't hesitate to make a meal of him. And how about those two female eaters you guys dusted off on the way to the river? They were eating a dog carcass on the road, of course we don't know if that dog was infected or not, but chances are it was."

"All dogs are probably infected," Gin then added. "Whatever the reason, CDC feral dog connection or not, the next time we don't see any eaters, I think we need to leave the area as soon as possible."

"I think you're right, the dogs are much faster than any eaters we've encountered so far, which makes them a lot more dangerous," I agreed. "So the shoot first rule applies double for dogs. You see a dog you kill it. Do you hear that boys?"

"We hear you Dad, double for dogs," Jacob responded.

ON TO TEXAS

We traveled west on interstate twenty for only a few miles when we came to the town of Tallulah. There we decided to try to replenish our food supply before driving further west.

Not wanting to run the battery down on our GPS, we didn't use it for mile by mile directions, and not being familiar with the area, we took the first Tallulah exit off the interstate. That exit turned out to be the long way into the town.

However, that mistake did have an upside. The route took us all the way over to state highway eighty, and then past a cemetery that was infested with zombies. Not that zombie infestation is necessarily an upside by any stretch, but it did reveal to us that there was a good chance that no nomadic packs of feral dogs were in the vicinity. At least that was our theory.

"No feral dogs here," Gin stated.

"Not in the cemetery anyway," I replied, hoping that she was right and the whole town was free of roving packs of dogs.

"They're in groups!" Billy said, seeing several large throngs of zombies meandering through the cemetery. "Look at them, some are stopping and scratching and clawing at the graves."

"Just like all of the others, they're always in a group," Jacob acknowledged in agreement. "Even the ones that are trying to dig up the graves are in a cluster!"

"They probably can hear their brethren wallowing around inside the buried coffins scraping and tearing at the casket lids trying to get out, and are trying to help set them free," I said, turning my attention back to the road ahead.

"Well good luck with that," Gin said, rolling her eyes and shaking her head in disgust.

"As long as they're preoccupied with trying to dig up their friends they won't be preoccupied with trying to eat us," I stated. "So they can dig until their rotting fingers fall off for all I care."

Gin agreed, and we again focused on our main endeavor, which was to find food and supplies.

Shortly after passing the graveyard, we found ourselves crossing a small bridge that led into a residential area.

"This looks like the perfect place to scavenge for food," I said. "But we'll go a little bit further from the cemetery and that bunch of eaters before we stop."

We continued for only a couple of blocks, and to our surprise, we had left the residential development and were in the middle of an industrial zone.

"This is a hell of a place to put an industrial area, right in the middle of a neighborhood of residential homes!" Gin said shaking her head.

"They probably didn't put it here, it was most likely here first and they built all of these houses around it," I told her.

Without even glancing in my direction, Gin pointed to another group of houses, and in her typical quasi-sarcastic fashion, she stated.

"Well whatever the case, stay on this street, there are more houses up ahead."

We traveled along Kimbrough Drive until it dead-ended into a thoroughfare named Johnson Street where I stopped the Hummer and asked Gin.

"Which way now honey, left or right?"

"It looks like left will take us back the way we came, and I can see more houses down there," Gin answered, pointing to the right.

I turned the Hummer onto Johnson Street toward the houses Gin had pointed out.

"Good choice honey, look a hospital sign, maybe we can pilfer some medicine there, we might need some antibiotics or something later. My guess is, in a small town like this the odds are pretty good that there will be some medicine left at the hospital. At the very least there should be some aspirin at the nurse's station," I speculated. "But first things first. We need to find some food, and those houses over there are where we're going to look."

We turned down one of the streets that led into the residential area across from the hospital.

"I see eaters," Billy said calmly. "Only two so far and they are together," he said, pointing in the direction of the two zombies.

"We'll go a few houses down, keep looking for eaters," I said. "We don't need any surprises."

"What about that big brick house?" Gin asked.

184

"No brick houses, unless we are going to hold up in them for a while. If we get trapped in a brick house, we wouldn't be able to chop through the walls and escape if we had to. A house with wood or vinyl siding is strong enough to keep the eaters out, but would at least give us a chance to break through the drywall and siding and get away, and we could probably do it with only our sickles if we had no other choice. With that said, we're going to stay away from the older houses too, at least until we find a place that we're going to stay for a while. The older homes were built a lot stronger than the modern one's are. When we need some real security, then we'll choose an older, or brick house or something better."

"That's what we're looking for, a one story home; we don't want to be caught upstairs, so we'll stick to ranch style houses. Let's not go down into any basements either, you hear that boys, no basements, it's too easy to get trapped in a basement," I stressed, as we pulled into the driveway of the ranch style house that I had indicated.

"Everyone keep alert, keep quiet, and keep your eyes open for eaters," I warned. "Use your sickles first, and your guns only if you have to. We want to get in, get what we can, and get out, everyone understand?"

After an affirmative nod from my family, we tentatively approached the side door of the house.

"It's open," Gin whispered, clutching her Berretta 92 with both hands.

"Put that back in your holster, sickles first remember?" I said, reminding her of the one sided conversation we had had not two minutes earlier.

"Honey," she said. "You go first, and if you can't handle whatever we run into in there with your sickle, I'll blow their brains out with my gun, all right?"

"Hey, you can't expect me to think of everything," I said in agreement, not finding it to be an appropriate time to have a debate.

I went first as agreed, and the rest of the family followed me. As we sneaked through the side door and into the house, I noticed that for the first time in many days, I didn't smell the stench of rotting flesh.

"Smell that?" I asked.

"Smell what?" Gin asked.

"Exactly," I said. "There is no smell," I maintained, inhaling a deep breath.

"That's great Dad, but we're here to look for food, not to smell the roses along the way," Jacob interjected snidely with a smile.

"Very funny son," I replied, tilting my head back and forth and adding a sarcastic smile.

"Cut it out you two, let's find the food and get out of here," Gin said, shaking her head and gritting her teeth as she spoke, signaling her disgust. "This place is creeping me out."

"Let's separate, Mom and Dad you go that way, and Billy and I will go this way, we can search the house faster that way," Jacob claimed.

I quickly countered.

"Never split up, haven't you ever seen any scary movies? They always split up, and then one by one they manage to get themselves killed. We are not separating, we may need to leave at a moment's notice and we don't want to have to go looking for the other group. In the scary movies, they always have to go looking for somebody that wandered off too, and then someone that would have gotten away gets their ass killed.

As far as we're going to separate, is as far as we can see each other, no farther. In other words, we're not separating, not in this house, or any other, you get me?"

"We get you sir," the boys whispered in unison.

"Okay, enough of the movie references, let's find some food."

Upon locating the kitchen, which wasn't too hard in this relatively small ranch style home, we began our search for food.

"Billy you watch the door we came in through, and Jacob, you keep an eye on the door that leads into the other parts of the house. That's your separation boys, you're separated across this room," I said, trying again to get my point across to them.

Gin and I began to rummage through the cabinets looking for any eatable food.

"Peanut butter is still a good choice, no refrigeration is needed and it has plenty of protein and calories," I needlessly reminded her.

"Forget about things like cereal and bread, cereal will probably be stale, and any bread we find is going to be so moldy it will be unrecognizable, so let's look for mostly canned foods," Gin then added, needlessly reminding me.

One of the lower cabinets was heavily stocked with many different kinds of canned vegetables and fruits and even a large box containing granola bars.

We had no sooner filled our satchels with the food from the cabinet, when we heard a voice coming from another room inside the house.

"Are you getting Pa his food, Pa is hungry again," the elderly sounding female voice announced.

The tone of the yet unseen woman suddenly changed from inquisitive to angry.

"Who are you? I'll get you," the voice challenged, as the shadowy figure of a frail old woman emerged from the dark hallway and through the door that Jacob had been tasked to guard.

The woman looked to be in her late eighties or early nineties, and she was clutching a baseball bat with both hands and wielding it over her head like a *Bushido Warrior* would hold a samurai sword, almost losing her balance as she was now unexpectedly top heavy.

Using a baseball bat in the middle of an outbreak of flesh eating homicidal maniacs is not at all a bad choice for a silent yet deadly efficient weapon to use for cracking skulls. Taking into consideration that zombies are generally slower and less coordinated than your average living human beings are; at least the ones that we've been unfortunate enough to have had to deal with have been.

Except for the ones that ended up in the water, then they move a lot faster than they normally would had they stayed dry.

With that said, it always amazed me, how so many people, mostly women I think, kept a baseball bat by their bed or by the front door of their home to fend off intruders.

I guess they thought that when the time came to use the clumsy weapon on someone that's more than likely, bigger, younger, and stronger than they are, that they'd rise to the occasion and wallop the snot out of the larger aggressor. Even though they had never played a single game of baseball in their life, aren't familiar with the weight or balance of the sporting implement, and the only time that they really touched their bat was when they placed it in the corner umbrella stand in anticipation of the next formidable intruder.

The reality of such a situation is; people tend not to rise to the occasion, instead they tend to default to their training. Of course, their training consists of noticing the bat in the corner once or twice a week, or month, or year, maybe.

Therefore, the bat sits in the corner for months, sometimes years, collecting dust without being touched by the would-be home run hitter; giving them a serious false sense of security.

If the time ever would arrive and they needed to use their weapon of choice, the bad guy, usually, and without much effort, would take it away from the owner and bludgeon them half to death with their own weapon; and that is exactly what I did.

The hunched over old woman who was ravaged with a case of acute osteoporosis, charged toward Jacob as fast as she could, of course at her age, if she'd been moving any slower she would have been going backwards. Jacob backed away from her and with a quick side step; he easily avoided her feeble attempt at hitting that ever elusive home run.

I dropped my bag of pilfered goods and bum-rushed the old hag. She swung the bat downward, aiming at my head with as much force as she could gather with her aging atrophied muscles; which wasn't very much.

Using my left forearm, I blocked the bat forcing it to deflect to my left, and in one fluid motion, I grabbed the baseball bat close to the knob with my right hand, and grasped it tightly with my left hand just above the old woman's hands.

I stepped forward with my right foot, and swung my right elbow hard into the elderly woman's lips. As the old woman faltered backwards, her false teeth now crammed deep into her bleeding mouth, she released the bat quickly as I twisted it from her weak arthritic grip.

I now clasped the bat with the standard baseball players grip and twirled around. With the bat in hand, and with a powerful two hundred and seventy degree swing, I buried the barrel of the baseball bat into her temple, collapsing her left eye socket and cheekbone, forcing her left eyeball to bulge out onto her crushed cheek, somewhat resembling a blood-shot boiled egg dangling from her face.

The powerful blow from the baseball bat reduced the old woman to a twitching sack of bleeding skin and broken bones, as she softly whimpered while wallowing on the floor in a mixed puddle of her own urine, feces, and blood.

"Quick, let's check on Pa," I said, as I dropped the baseball bat beside the convulsive elder, and pulled my sickle from my belt.

Clutching my trusty sickle in my hand, I cautiously led our somewhat shocked little band into the hallway that the old woman had appeared from earlier.

"Pa might be armed," I whispered.

That's when the refreshing smell of the fresh air left us, and the stink of rotting zombies that we were so accustom to, along with the subtle hum of hundreds of flies buzzing replaced it.

"There's the smell, I knew we couldn't get away from it for long," Gin stated, wrinkling up her nose.

"I think Pa might be an eater, look at that," Jacob said, pointing to a door that had towels stuffed against the crack at the bottom. "And listen, remember that sound."

The closer to the door we came, the stronger the smell of rotting flesh was present, and the louder the muffled sound of the flies buzzing behind the door became.

"I can hear growling too, it's coming from inside that room for sure," Gin concluded confidently. "The one with the towels stuffed along the bottom of the door."

"No reason to open the door. We got what we came for, and I don't feel like fighting my way through a swarm of nasty flies that are tending to their larva that's busy feeding on Pa's decaying carcass. Not just to croak an eater that's not a threat to us anyway. Let's get back to the Hummer and get the hell out of here," I ordered, motioning for everyone to turn around and head back into the kitchen.

We hurried out of the house, pausing only briefly to pick up the canned food we had scavenged, and long enough for Jacob to make a somewhat sick joke.

Pointing to the baseball bat that I had used to beat down the old woman, he said. "An old bat, for the old bat!"

Then with a swift vertical downward swing, he dug the point of his sickle into the deep gash on the left side of her face that I had provided with the baseball bat, and with a rapid twist, ended her convulsions along with her future will to eat flesh.

Gin didn't find Jacob's humor at all funny, however, Billy and I had to hide our smirks from her as we walked single file out of the house.

Even though I found Jacob's callous demeanor slightly disturbing at the time, the old bat (no pun intended) had to be terminated with head trauma, or she was going to be *zombiefied* at some point. Jacob had just preformed that duty flawlessly without blinking an eye, just seconds after making a joke about the weapon used to bludgeon her. Well after all, what did I expect? Only moments earlier he had watched me break several bones in the arthritis stricken elderly woman, and leave her bleeding and squirming in pain on her own kitchen floor.

Therefore, I couldn't help but smile at his timely attempt at humor, thinking that it was probably his way of dealing with the stress of the situation.

Back onboard the Hummer, Gin wondered.

"Are we going to the hospital now?"

"I think we've had enough adventure for today, don't you?" I answered, while fastening my seatbelt.

Gin leaned over and locked her door, looking out her window for any signs of zombies.

"Yes I do," she said. "There'll be other hospitals along the way; we can look for medicine somewhere else."

We spotted several groups of zombies walking through the neighborhood as we pulled away from the old woman's house, and one by one, as they too spotted us, would begin a fruitless attempt to close the gap that separated our groups.

Out of the town and back onto interstate twenty, we drove west, systematically dodging abandoned and wrecked cars and trucks along the way. We found that the highway wasn't as clogged as we thought it might be, but tractor trailer rigs posed definite problems at times.

Our speed was moderate, but constant for the most part. Zombies were present most of the time. The ones that were a threat to us were the ones that were huddled around some of the derelict vehicles we passed; many times the cars and trucks blocked the road, forcing us to slow down as we maneuvered by them, giving the zombies a chance to stumble our way. However, the Hummer sat high enough off the ground, and our speed was still fast enough that the undead corpses that did manage to get close were handled with a quick close range head shot from our small arms, or we just swerved around them altogether.

Of course, there was always the exception to the rule, which was the occasional felony hit and run that was dealt out to over aggressive zombies that staggered into our path and we couldn't shoot or avoid hitting.

However, most of the zombies we saw could be seen loitering around distant houses and buildings and were not an immediate threat to us.

We drove on for hours, and when we weren't avoiding or shooting zombies, we talked about many things, many things except the spontaneous pounding that I had given to the old woman back in Tallulah. I wasn't sure whether that was a good thing or not.

The woman had attacked Jacob, and she was keeping and apparently feeding a zombie she called Pa, probably her husband, which she had locked up in one of the rooms. We could smell Pa as we approached that room, so Pa was getting overly ripe and had been attracting flies for quite a while, and at some point in time would have probably over powered the feeble female, and made a meal out of her, or at the very least turned her into one of his cannibalistic ilk.

So we most likely did her a favor, me by giving her a righteous beat down, and Jake by finishing her off with the point of his rusty sickle. Obviously, she had lost her mind, just like the man on the river that had eaten his family. Although, not as much of a threat as the maniac on the river, in my mind she still needed to be handled in a like manner.

It's just too bad that she attacked us with a baseball bat and not a "*Maceball*" bat!

Maceball bat [mayssball bat]

1. A baseball bat with long spikes driven through the end of the barrel of a bat so that the pointed end of the spikes protrude several inches out of the other side.

194

2. A medieval apparatus used in conjunction with playing deadly war games in ancient times, and usually incorporated by a nine-man uniformed team on the field of battle.

For had I hit her with the sharp metal obtrusions on a maceball bat, it would have terminated her instantly, and saved her the embarrassment of flopping around on her kitchen floor, floundering in her own waste products.

Not to mention it would have spared Jacob the trouble of spearing her brain with his sickle, and putting her out of everybody's misery.

ASSASSINS

Dusk was only an hour away when the outskirts of Shreveport came into view.

"This is the first night in weeks that we won't be sleeping in a boat," Gin said, seeming happy about the prospect.

"Maybe," I answered. "I had hoped we'd get here sooner than this, we need to find a secure place to sleep tonight, and we don't have very much time to find one."

"We can always sleep in the Hummer," Billy yelled down from the machine gun turret.

"Only if we absolutely have to," I yelled back. "We've been in this truck all day, and there's not much room, I would rather find some place better to sleep tonight, even if we have to find another boat to sleep in."

"Either way we better find somewhere fast it's going to be dark soon, and I really don't want to be clearing houses, or buildings, or boats, or anything else in the dark," Jacob maintained adamantly, as he shook his head.

"We won't be clearing houses or anything else in the dark, at least not tonight," I said, as I nodded my head in the direction of a large two-story brick house that was just ahead.

"It has an upstairs; I thought you said we weren't going into a house that has an upstairs, or a basement?" Billy asked.

"That's just for when we look for food and supplies; we need a secure place to sleep tonight. So we're going to clean this house of eaters if there are any, and we're going to do it before it gets dark, and we'll bed down here tonight," I responded, as I pulled the Hummer into the circular driveway that ran in front of the house we intended to sleep in. Then I backed it in as close to the front door as I could.

"Everyone stay put, I'll check the front door; and watch for eaters," I ordered, as I slowly departed the safety of the driver's seat with my sickle in one hand and my AK-47 in the other.

I hooked my sickle around the horizontal handle on the front door and pulled up on it, and then I pushed down on it with the curved weapon.

"Damn, it's locked, I'll try another door," I whispered to Gin.

"Be careful honey," she said, very concerned that I was walking around the yard alone.

"Wait, what about the rule about nobody goes anywhere alone?" Gin reminded sternly."We're not going to separate, remember?"

"Right, thanks for the reminder," I replied, already thinking the same thing.

Then motioning with my head, I said. "Billy, you come with me, and bring your AK. Jacob, you stay up there in the turret and keep your eyes peeled."

"Don't get out of my sight," Gin reminded again.

"One of us will stay in your sight at all times," I promised.

"Make sure you do," Gin threatened with a glaring look.

Billy and I reconnoitered the situation, slowly walking to the corner of the house where the attached garage was located. As I turned the corner hoping to find an unlocked side door leading into the garage, two zombies, one male and one female, immediately confronted me. The female zombie reached out and grabbed me by my arm, and pulled me toward her, or it?

Before I could react, the head of the feminine zombie exploded onto the red brick wall of the garage. In the blink of an eye, the neck, head, and lower back of the male (masculine) zombie also exploded, sending blood, brain matter, intestines, pieces of bone, and an assortment of bodily fluids against the wall, onto the first dead zombie that lay at my feet, and onto me.

"Don't move mister, I don't want to kill you, but I will if you force me to," a gruff voice called out.

"*Now where have I heard that kind of rhetoric before*," I thought, remembering the words the leader of the river pirates had spoken.

"I wouldn't think of moving, moving is the last thing on my mind," I stated, trying my best to act unafraid.

"Are you diseased, or is anyone with you diseased, or bit?" The voice asked, as a man pushed his way through a row of tall bushes where he had been hiding.

"Well I wasn't diseased, but now that you've slopped eater blood and guts all over me I'm not too sure," I said, being a little pissed off and unable to suppress my sarcasm.

"I'm not going to asked you again mister. Are you or any of your party diseased?"

Thinking that this guy might not be in the mood for backtalk, I decided to play it straight with him.

"No, nobody's sick or bit, or undead," I answered, now more angry than afraid.

"Well not yet anyway," the man laughed. "You all are lucky we came along," he said, as five more heavily armed men and two weapon-laden women stepped out from behind the same clump of shrubs and into the open.

"I think I'm lucky you people are such good shots, otherwise you might be talking to a dead man right now," I contended, looking back at Billy and grimacing.

"That your family with you?" the man asked, walking slowly toward us.

198

"Yes it is sir, we don't mean you any harm," I said, unsuccessfully trying to convince the group that we were docile.

"Mister, if we thought you had any intention of doing *us* harm, we wouldn't be having this conversation," the man said, very convincingly I might add.

"We call ourselves the Assassins, although we don't regularly kill people, I mean unless we have to, just the ones that are already dead are the ones that we're after. That's why you still have possession of your firearms. We saw you come into town, and you just happened to pull up right next to the area that we were hunting in," the man claimed.

"What's your name mister," I asked the man, thinking back to what happened on the river, when I asked another man the same question.

Before he could answer, I said. "My name is Jack, this is my son Billy. My wife Gin and my other son Jacob are in the Hummer over there."

"My name is Frank, last names don't mean too much anymore. Let's mosey on over to your truck, but first tell that boy manning that Gatling gun of yours to stand down, we're friendly folk," Frank insisted.

I turned toward the Hummer and called to Jacob.

"Jake, don't shoot, we're coming over!"

Billy and I led the way to our truck, followed by Frank and the seven other *Assassins*.

"It's going to be dark soon, you people need to come with us back to our camp, it's not safe around here," Frank insisted. "Especially at night!"

199

"I'll ride with them," he told the others in his bunch. "The rest of you get back to the fortress, I'll meet you there, now get moving, it'll be dark soon."

As Frank crawled into the back of our Hummer, he said chuckling, as if his comment was a joke.

"You drive, and hey, if you people kill me, none of you will make it out of this town alive! You have my word on that."

I laughed at Frank's aphorism, as I too climbed into the truck, but we all knew that Frank wasn't joking.

An eerie silence inundated the inside of our vehicle from the first moments of the ride to the very last, only interrupted by the directional orders barked by Frank as he guided us out of the neighborhood, and to what I hoped would be a safe haven for at least that night.

We drove for a few blocks in a westerly direction, not daring to even whisper of any plans of how we might handle Frank and his people, for fear Frank would overhear us.

It wasn't long before we came to the outskirts of a commercialized area and Frank directed me to turn into the parking lot of a big-box membership store once owned by a now defunct company.

"Go around to the back, by the dumpster," Frank ordered.

I followed his instructions, and pulled up facing a huge sliding metal track door.

"Honk your horn, two short beeps," Frank prompted. "And I mean *short* beeps; we don't want to bring any unwanted company to our door."

I complied with Frank's request, and within seconds, the large garage type door before us began to open.

"Drive in and park over there," Frank mandated, pointing to an open spot between a minivan and a large military truck.

We had just meant Frank and his friends, and I wasn't to the point in our relationship where I trusted him. We were outnumbered back at the brick house, and even though we could have killed some of his people, we would have been committing suicide had we fired upon his group. His comment, that if he were killed, we wouldn't make it out alive, told me that we were being watched all the way to our present location, probably by snipers. I felt we had no choice, it was dark now and Frank had let us keep our weapons, however uneasy I felt, I drove my family into the building as Frank had directed.

Within the confines of the thick concrete walls of the once thriving retail club store, the casual demeanor of the people we initially saw conveyed an atmosphere of calm to us. The only guards in view were placed high atop pallets of store merchandise on either side of the door we had entered through. However, of the several people in the room, nobody was devoid of some kind of a weapon.

"You can stay here tonight and maybe for a couple of days, but not any longer," Frank explained. "It might look like we have a lot of supplies, but we also have forty-seven people to feed, forever."

"Or until they get killed," I thought.

"We did have forty-nine until three days ago," Frank, informed me. "And sixty-four before that."

"What happened three days ago?" I asked, finally breaking my silence.

"Three days ago, Sally and Kevin got careless, we were out on a search and destroy mission similar to the one we were on today when we found you and your family. Those two, for some unknown reason, decided to break one of our cardinal rules. They broke off from the group and began searching a building alone, just the two of them," Frank said, shaking his head.

"Eaters get'em?" I asked, thinking. *"They probably slithered off by themselves to get naked together, and instead got themselves killed for their trouble."*

"We call them Out-Breakers, but the answer to your question is no," Frank answered. "Another bunch killed them. Live people, we're not the only organized band; there are some other smaller groups in this town.

Probably every town of any size in the whole country, maybe the whole world, has more than just one collection of military, paramilitary, or want-to-be military people, and they, like us, are all probably fighting with each other. One group of people always wants something that the other group has, and always seems willing to try to take it by force."

As my family and I tried nonchalantly to scrutinize this troop of seemingly friendly zombie fighters, the leader of the box store band of *"Assassins"*, continued to tell us about the premature deaths of his former follower.

"Counting Sally and Kevin, we've lost a total of twelve people to the living, and five more to the Out-Breakers. The live ones are the most dangerous, Out-

Breakers, or as you call them Eaters, don't shoot guns and they don't carry weapons, except for their teeth," Frank insisted. "Sally and Kevin were just the last to go, and they died because they were stupid. We have rules for a reason, and they broke the rules, and now they're both dead," Frank explained, noticeably upset.

I never knew Sally or Kevin, and I didn't really give a shit if they were dead or not, but I didn't want to lather up Frank any more than he already was, so I said to him applying my best empathetic face.

"I'm sorry for your group's loss Frank. We have the same stick together rule. We were actually practicing that rule when we ran into you and your people."

"You're safe here for the night, and tomorrow you can decide whether or not you want to rest up here for a couple of days, maybe even go on a search and destroy mission with us before you hit the road again," Frank suggested.

I had no intention of going out on some, as he called it, search and destroy mission with a bunch of strangers that were armed to the teeth. So I responded to Franks offer by saying.

"I'll talk it over with Gin and the boys, but she is pretty set on moving on to Texas. She has family there and she wants to join up with them as soon as possible if we can find them."

None of what I said was true, but I felt I needed to say something that would give us an excuse to get the hell out of there when the time was right.

"Well we've rigged up a gas generator to the electrical box, so we have lights in most of the building, and we have another one hooked to the freezers so the frozen food won't rot. No heat or air-conditioning yet, and we haven't gotten to the gas pumps outside yet either, but we're working on getting both of them up and running at some point. At any rate, let me introduce you to some of our people," Frank insisted, as he led us over to a man and woman standing by a pallet of diet soda.

The man was tall and muscular with short brown hair, a bushy mustache, and a serious five o'clock shadow. He was wearing a blue jump suit with the name Mike embroidered onto a patch sewn above the left front pocket.

We could see the footprint of a large frame automatic pistol that he had stuck in his right side pocket, and his rifle, an old Russian made SKS that had been imported from some Eastern Bloc Nation that no longer needed it, was lying on top of the pallet beside him.

The woman was medium height, thin, well built, with bleach blonde hair with six or seven weeks of dark roots showing. She was sporting a shoulder holster that housed a revolver that looked too big for her to handle, but who am I to judge.

Both of them paid little attention to us as we approached.

"This is Mike and Sondra, they were janitors working over night here when this whole end of the world thing came about," Frank explained.

Mike was still wearing his janitorial uniform, but Sondra was far too well dressed to be on the job as a custodian, so I figured she had appropriated her wardrobe from the sales floor. I can't blame her for that, everybody else is taking whatever they wanted from wherever they can get it, including us. The old rules don't apply in this new paradigm.

"Hi, I'm Jack, and this is my wife Gin, and these two are Billy and Jacob, they are my sons," I said with a smile, introducing my family to Mike and Sondra.

The two were civil with their greetings but quickly turned away from us, engaging each other in conversation and making it clear to all that they had no interest in becoming friends with us anytime soon.

Frank introduced us to every person that was holed up in that building that night. Some seemed happy to meet us, others, not so much.

Some were concerned that we might be thinking of staying, and others concern that we might be thinking of leaving. Frank had already made it clear to us that we would be leaving, however I saw no reason to mention that to any of his people.

The leader of the so-called Assassins guided us over to a display of camping equipment that had been set up in the middle of the store prior to the apocalypse.

"You and your family can sleep here tonight. Get settled in and I'll be back later and then we can talk," Frank stated as he walked away.

Gin looked around, wondering if any of the assassins were watching us.

"What are we going to do honey?" She asked.

"Yeah Dad, what are we going to do?" Jacob added, as he sat down on one of the cots.

"We better do what we've been doing, namely, keep a lookout tonight, take the same shifts as usual, and try not to look too obvious, we don't know these people and some of them weren't too friendly when we were introduced. If we're not careful we could wake up dead," I asserted. "So for now, keep your weapons close to you at all times just like we've been doing. Except for killing them, we need to treat them as if they're eaters, keep your guard up at all times. Don't think for a moment that it was a coincidence that Frank put us out here in the middle of the store. This camping equipment isn't the only thing on display."

We each picked out the spot that we would be spending the night, and it wasn't long before Frank, came back, and he had brought Mike and Sondra with him.

"You've meant Mike and Sondra, they're second in command around here. We brought you people some good food to eat, I figured you and your family most likely haven't had a real cooked meal for quite some time," Frank said, as he and the janitorial crew handed out plates heaping with steaming meat and vegetables.

"There's no shortage of barbequed meat around here, we've got plenty of propane tanks and brand new grills, eat up," Frank urged.

We looked around at each other, everyone silently asking the same question. Is the food poison, or drugged?

Frank shook his head and stabbed a fork into my steak.

"If we wanted to kill you, you'd already be dead," he said, just before taking a big bite of the meat he had pulled from my plate.

"It's good that you're cautious though," he added. "We could use a little more of that around here sometimes.

I thought that remark was rather strange, coming from a man that had let a group of armed strangers into his stronghold.

"We didn't get this far from home by being careless," I stressed, not willing to mention some of the careless and thoughtless mistakes we had made along the way.

Frank plopped my steak back down onto my plate, his fork now standing erect in the middle of the meat, and with a loud gulp, he swallowed.

"You said your people are assassins, and you go out on search and destroy missions. What exactly does that mean?" I asked, handing Franks fork back to him.

"Like I told you before, we don't kill humans unless they attack us first; we try to help them if we can, just like we're helping you now," Frank insisted.

"The Out-Breakers, now that's a different story, we try to eliminate as many of them as we can.

Our reasoning is this; there hasn't been a lot of people traveling through this city like you and your family are. That makes the population a finite number for the most part, living or dead.

It's true if you get infected or just plain die, you turn into one of those things. But we think we can control that to a certain extent by being vigil and aggressive when the need arises. We go on search and destroy missions, and put down as many of the diseased ones as we can find, acting on the theory that once we get rid of all of them, we will be able to manage with relative ease any strays that happen to wander into town. And if we deal with the people that die of natural causes or accidental death immediately, we will be able to sustain some semblance of a normal life. At least that's the theory," Frank explained.

"Why call yourselves assassins, why not exterminators, or eradicators, or maybe eliminators?" I inquired, as my curiosity was getting the best of me.

"When we first started the process, the three of us decided that it would be better to first give ourselves a name. That way we would bond every member to part of a team, which would help maintain a sense of esprit de corps within the group. We didn't want some warm and fuzzy name like the cupcake brigade, we felt that a name like Assassins was more suited to the grisly tasks that had to be preformed, and there would be no second guessing about what the Assassins were all about, thus mentally helping us deal with the psychological trauma involved," Frank elucidated.

"That's pretty cerebral coming from a couple of janitors," I quipped with a smile.

Mike and Sondra had remained quiet up to this point, and then Mike leaned over and put his face within twelve inches of mine, stared at me with a cold glare that would freeze molten rock, while saying snidely.

"You people seen much combat?"

His threatening demeanor brought out the ex-marine in me and I immediately responded by saying.

"If by combat, you mean having your dead neighbors break through your back door and try to eat you alive, while getting the pleasure of letting your two young sons watch as you splatter chunks of their brains all over your wife's kitchen? Or having to shoot your way out of your own home, while half of the people that were once your friendly neighbors, tried to kill you or eat you alive.

Or are you referring to having to hack your way through ten or fifteen eaters with these sickles, hewing off heads and limbs as you go, while trying to escape from a stranger's barn," I replied sarcastically (it's one of my many gifts you know), describing a few of the horrible circumstances we had encountered along the way.

This was the first time that we'd seen Mike actually smile.

"I think I like you," he chuckled, backing away from me.

"Don't be too hasty," I joked. "I haven't even mentioned the river pirates, or the speedboat eaters, or the stench of the river that was enough to puke a maggot off a gut wagon," I said, again proudly employing the same gift as before.

Now both Mike and Sondra laughed.

"I like you too," Sondra agreed.

"It's too bad we can't let you stay here," she claimed.

"It's okay, Frank already told us we can't stay, and we're fine with it, we've got places to go, and people too see," I said, sticking to my earlier lie.

"Tell us about the humans, earlier you mentioned other living people," I asked, subtly trying to collect some intelligence about the other groups that occupied part of the town.

Mike and Sondra stopped smiling as Frank replied.

"Remember back at the house, I told you that if you killed me, you wouldn't make it out of town alive."

"I remember that," Billy spoke up.

"We all remember that," Gin replied, adding her own brand of sarcasm. "That was right neighborly of you."

Raising an eyebrow and glancing at Gin, a slight smile cracked the straight line of Frank's thin lips as he explained further.

"Well it wasn't just because I had people watching you through the crosshairs of their sniper rifles. Sure, they would have killed you, no doubt about it. But even if they hadn't, the odds are you would have either been killed or captured by one of the marauding bands that hold certain parts of the city. If you don't take a specific route back to the highway, you end up traveling through their turf, and I'm confident that they would put an end to you one way or another. You're lucky you ran into us first."

"So what's your theory on them, I mean after you clear the town of eaters?" I asked.

"At some point we'll have to deal with them totally. We run across them from time to time, but so far our numbers have been equal too or greater than theirs have been, so they usually leave us alone," Frank explained.

"Usually? Say usually a couple of more times, and there won't be any of your people left," I thought to myself, thinking of the twelve dead members of the Assassins that had been killed by maunders.

"What about your sniper's, do they stay out all night?" I asked thinking. *"That's a job I certainly wouldn't want."*

210

"No, they follow us in after every mission, as a matter of fact they got back while we were cooking your food," Frank confirmed.

"By the way Mike, you know those lights we've been seeing at night?" Frank asked.

Mike nodded.

"Well, Jim saw one tonight, and Rick's team reported seeing the weird shadows yesterday." Frank told him.

"Weird shadows?" Jacob asked.

"What do you mean weird shadows?" Gin broke in. "That sounds creepy to me."

"Creepier than a zombie apocalypse? Really Mom?" Billy challenged, tilting his head down, raising his eyebrows, and staring at her.

Frank then interjected.

"Since this thing started, some of us have been seeing these strange lights at night and shadows during the day. I've seen them myself, well kind of, you never really see them. You'll see a light or a shadow out of the corner of your eye, and when you turn your head to look at it, it'll be gone. Or if you're outside sleeping, or about to go to sleep, the light seems even brighter, and when you open your eyes to see what it is, it's gone, at least that's what the sentries doing double shifts on the roof say anyway. But they're never inside, at least not yet; they're *always* outside, so far anyway."

"I've seen them, the first time was within minutes of the start of this catastrophe, and I thought it was a news helicopter, but thinking back there wasn't any noise and the gaps in the tree tops couldn't have totally blocked my view.

Then again on the river, I almost fell asleep on my watch and was awakened by a bright light that was gone when I opened my eyes," I recalled.

"You almost fell asleep on your watch?" Jacob prompted.

"Yes once, and only once, and *almost* is the key word here," I answered, defending my indefensible position.

Frank quickly interposed. "It's getting late, get some sleep now, and we'll talk some more in the morning."

The three leaders of the Assassins stood up and walked away, Frank stopped momentarily, turned to me, and with a big grin on his face, he said. "Cerebral? Before this zombie war, I was a psychologist."

Turning away once more, he briskly walked away.

"That was interesting," Gin said, pulling her blanket over her shoulders.

"Yes, informative too, I'll take the first watch as usual," I replied, as I lay on my back with my eyes wide open.

"Try not to *almost* fall asleep Dad, you know how you are," Jacob quipped.

"Very funny son, your grossly mistimed, and flagrant endeavors at humor, are so amusing that I *almost* forgot to laugh," I quipped back, ending the families last conversation of the day.

Billy was on watch when he woke us up in the early hours of the morning.

"Get up, something's going on, everyone's freaking out," he said, sounding the alarm.

The sounds of a seemingly controlled panic echoed through the cavernous building as the Assassins were running in all directions.

Amidst the confusion, Mike ran by shouting.

"Grab your guns and come with me," he ordered, not bothering to look our way.

We quickly armed ourselves and ran to catch up to Mike.

We moved to the front of the store where two large boarded up and blocked doors were located.

"Our guys on the roof say there's a huge gathering of Out-Breakers outside, most are here in the front of the building," Mike explained calmly. "We're going to take this door as our battle station; you people have a problem with that?"

Before any of us could answer Mike's question, the familiar sound of Jacob's 9mm carbine pierced our eardrums.

While the rest of us were busy listening to Mike query us about our willingness to fight alongside the Assassins. Jacob had seen a zombie pushing through the door blockade, exposing its arm, and allowing several of the all too prevalent houseflies to enter the building.

Jacob's full metal-jacketed lead projectile slammed into the humerus bone of the dead assaulter's right arm and chipped off a large portion of the epicondyle, rendering the arm useless, but not deterring the zombie from clawing and shoving at the barricade with its left hand, allowing even more of the common flying pests to intrude into our sanctuary.

"Does that answer your question, Mike?" I asked, again using my best sarcastic tone.

Mike didn't answer, instead he lunged toward the open portion of the barricade, stuck the barrel of his SKS through the opening provided by the now wounded zombie, and pulled the trigger, effectively shattering the top of the eaters head and splattering its cranium juices into the faces of the surrounding undead.

As soon as that attacker fell, another one took its place at the opening and was eliminated in turn the same way. Then another took its place, each more grotesque than the previous one, having been soaked and pummeled with its predecessor's bodily fluids and the remains of their formally intact body parts, namely their brains and the backs of their skulls.

Rushing to the barricaded door, we each found a port that allowed us to attempt to fend off the army of the undead that had congregated on the other side of the wall.

"There must be a hundred of them," Mike yelled as he fired through different gaps in the protective cover.

"At least a hundred, looks like you Assassins have your work cut out for you if you're planning to rid this town of all of these eaters," I insisted, while using my sickle to cleave off the intrusive fingers of an overly aggressive zombie that had managed to stick his hand through a narrow crack.

Sondra had taken her place by the other door, and was joined by four other female Assassins. They were struggling just as much as we were to repulse the onslaught of flesh eating brutes whose numbers were starting to influence the structural integrity of the once solid fortification.

"There're too many of them," Sondra screamed. "Our door is starting to give way."

"Ours isn't doing much better," Gin screamed back as she fired her pistol point-blank into the face of an unrelenting pre-teen zombie.

Little by little, the surge from the mass of post humanity inched our barricade inward. Most of the Assassin's group had gone to the roof by now, and were firing down into the mob from there, leaving our small troop to defend from inside.

The surrounding walls muffled our shots that originated from the inside; however, the shots fired from the rooftop, although very effective in thinning the herd, the noise of the gunfire served to invite even more of the hungry fiends to our location.

"If they break through these doors we're through," Mike announced loudly.

"I've got an idea," I said. "I'll need a couple of your people to come with me."

"Sondra," Mike yelled. "Take Megan and go with Jack."

"Billy, you come with us. Honey, we'll be right back," I assured Gin, as if anyone could give reasonable assurance of anything during an outbreak of the undead.

With my new backup crew in tow, we ran to the back of the building where our Hummer was parked.

"Billy jump in the turret and warm up the mini-gun, we're going outside," I said. "Sondra, you and your friend, what's her name, open the door and shoot any of them that try to get in."

Megan, a short brown haired girl dressed in what looked like store bought urban camouflage sneered at me, and said. "It's Megan, not what's her name."

"Whatever, just shoot anything that's not human, we don't have much time," I shouted angrily, not being in the frame of mind to want to deal with some moody little bitch celebrating her time of the month; that seemed more intent on hearing her name pronounced correctly than doing her job.

Sondra pushed the green button that activated the electric door, and as the gap in the entrance grew, I blurted out to Billy.

"Ready Billy?"

Billy responded with a resounding.

"Ready!"

Sondra and what's her name began shooting at a few zombies that had gathered close to the back door, and that were now walking toward the doorway. When the door opened enough to accommodate our vehicle, I floored the Hummer and out the door we sped, cautiously but with malice, mowing down at least one unfortunate zombie that was either to slow, or too stupid to move out of our way. *"Chalk up another felony hit and run for me."* I thought, as we raced around the building.

Retracing the route we had taken on the way in, we quickly found ourselves at the front of the building facing a considerable amount of zombies.

Acting without an order to shoot, Billy released the fury of the mini-gun on the crowd of undead citizens that were trying to force their way into the Assassin's fortified sanctum.

216

We eased forward along the front of the building, close enough to crush some of the bodies of the zombies that we had killed or wounded earlier from inside the store.

As we inched forward, I hoped that Mike and the other Assassins still inside, would hear the buzzing of our mini-gun, and would hold their fire as we passed.

We cleared a wide swath moving slowly forward, painting the front of the building red with the spattering of blood, and adding texture to the mix with pieces of brains, chips of bone, and strands of shredded intestines and hair.

It was the usual blood and guts scenario we were growing accustom to seeing exiting from the mutilated zombie hordes, as we slaughtered countless numbers of the undead vicious monsters that night.

Once we had made the first pass by the front of the building, killing zombies, enduring the usual putrid stench, and swarming flies (yes, even at night) that seemed to always accompany the undead, I threw the Hummer into reverse. Using the path that we had just created, we backed over many of the zombies we had just put down, breaking most of their bones that had remained intact, and rendering immobile those that were only wounded, as Billy laid waste to the monsters on the outlying area of the parking lot with the mini-gun.

"There's not much ammo left Dad," Billy yelled.

"There's not many of *them* left either," I yelled back. "Hold your fire for a minute."

I turned the vehicle toward the parking lot exit and we drove into the street. We could hear the mop up effort of the Assassins on the rooftop as they picked off the remaining small clusters of zombies that were scattered throughout the parking lot.

"Where are we going?" Billy asked, concerned about Franks warning of marauding bands of humans.

"Just down the street, hold on," I answered as we turned down a dark residential street two blocks from the Assassins hide out.

After passing a few houses down the gloomy street, I turned around in a driveway, pulled back up to the corner, and stopped the Hummer facing the box store.

"I can see the parking lot pretty good from here," Billy whispered, as the turret sat him a good three feet higher in the Hummer than me.

"I can just barely see it from down here," I whispered back, as I pushed the barrel of my AK-47 out the driver's window and fired several shots into the air.

"No need to whisper now," I yelled, firing even more shots into the air.

"Hopefully, these shots will lure them away from the store's parking lot; that is if Frank's people will stop shooting."

After a few minutes, the Assassins on the rooftop had cleared the remaining zombies, and had stopped firing their weapons, leaving only the buzzing sound of a few thousand airborne flies to attract more zombies.

I fired several more shots into the air and now that the parking lot had fallen silent, the noise from our location was starting receive the attention of the zombies whose previous target was the big box store, but hadn't as yet made it to its parking lot.

"Some of them are turning toward us Dad, they're coming this way," Billy yelled.

"Keep an eye out for eaters that might already be here, or that are coming from another direction, we don't want to be ambushed," I told him, this time firing my AK through the picture window of a house across the street.

"What the hell, I might as well bust some stuff up while I'm at it." I thought to myself.

"It looks like all of them are coming now," Billy announced loudly.

With that, I again fired several more shots, this time into some other nearby houses as I backed into another driveway.

"We'll go down the back street, that way we'll bypass the eaters we drew toward us, and we'll get back to your mother and Jacob unscathed," I promised, whispering once again.

For a change the plan worked flawlessly, we drove slowly around the block and down the street that ran parallel with the zombie's route. We entered the parking lot and quickly sped to the back of the building once more, willfully committing two more felony hit and runs along the way. Two short beeps at the back door and within seconds we were back inside the big box store.

"You're pretty good at killing Out-Breakers," Mike said, as he, Sondra, Frank, and what's her name approached, leading Jacob and Gin and a few other people from their team.

Hugging my wife, I smiled and replied. "It's one of my many gifts."

"We've got people upfront repairing and reinforcing the barrier, and on our way back here we took a vote. We

219

decided that if you and your family want to join us, you're more than welcome to," Frank remarked.

"Like I said before, we've got places to go and people to see," I answered. "It'll be light soon, and we'll be on our way, but if we ever get back this way we'll be sure to stop in and say hello."

We all knew that the odds of us ever seeing each other again were pretty much slim to none, but it sounded good and was reminiscent of the way things used to be. So we all pretended that it was a real possibility and carried on that way until we had parted ways with the Assassins.

We spent the early hours of the morning in preparation of our departure; we used the time to organize our equipment and fill our gas tank with the generous gift of gasoline that Frank's people had siphoned out of the underground tanks that were buried beneath the gas station on their parking lot.

The Assassins even donated enough of the right caliber ammo to replenish our mini-gun half way. I didn't ask were they got the ammo, or if they were sure that they could spare it, I just accepted it and kept my mouth shut. We needed the mini-gun ammo desperately, and I wasn't about to jinx the deal by asking too many questions.

I figured it this way, if they were stupid enough to give us their ammunition; we were going to be stupid enough to take it.

Finally, Mike and Sondra put some of what Frank called real food into a cooler, and sat it in the back of our Hummer; we were now ready to depart.

Then an unexpected turn of events took us totally by surprise. As we were about to leave, and saying goodbye to our hosts, what's her name came sauntering up, followed by another woman about her same age.

"Remember me, I'm Megan, and this is Mary," she said, pulling to her side the skinny red headed girl who was in her early twenties that was following her.

"Sure we remember you. What's your name?" I asked jokingly.

Tilting her head and putting her hands on her hips, Megan gave me one of those looks that women give you, and without saying a word, they're saying "really".

I couldn't help but to laugh.

"Megan," I said. "I could never forget you."

She smiled at me, and said. "That's kind of what I wanted to talk to you about, I wanted to ask you. Can we come with you?"

"What? You two want to come with us?" I asked. "Why? Do you know what it's like out there?"

"We heard you and your family are on your way to Texas, both of us have family in Texas," Megan whined, protruding her lower lip.

"We want to be with them."

I looked at Gin, and she had a complacent look on her face as if the decision was up to me.

Then Jacob added.

"We can make room, it'll be tight, but there's room."

Stepping forward, Billy then added his opinion.

"There are times when we could use the backup Dad," he said smiling.

I could see the sparkle in both of my boy's eyes. Billy was right, there were times when we could use the back up, but I suspected that back up was not the main reason that my two teenage boys wanted the company of two young women.

"Mary, are you trying to tell me that you really want to leave all of this, join up with a group of people that you literally just met, and try to make it all the way deep into Texas?" I asked, wondering why these two girls were making this strange request.

Mary's response caught me off guard.

"All of you are going to leave all of this, and try to make it all the way deep into Texas, aren't you?" She asked.

"You've got a point Mary, that's exactly what we're going to do," I answered, smiling and nodding my head.

Megan abruptly broke in.

"So what difference will two more make?"

Again, I looked at Gin. This time she shrugged her shoulders as if she didn't care, signaling to me that it was all right with her.

"Okay fine, you two can go with us," I said. "But you'll have to do as I say, when I say, do you understand?"

Not bothering to answer my question.

"Great!" Megan said. "We'll get our things."

The two girls turned and hurried off to retrieve their belongings while Billy and Jacob hurried to try to make room in the Hummer for both them and their worldly possessions.

A few minutes later Megan and Mary returned, each carrying a backpack and toting their guns. We packed their stuff and said our final goodbyes, waving to Frank and his Assassins as we departed.

We were led by Mike driving one of their fortified vehicles, he would escort us safely back to interstate twenty where we would all part company.

LONE STAR STATE

After leaving Frank's group, we were across the Texas-Louisiana boarder in less than a half an hour, despite the heavy congestion on the freeway that was prevalent before we passed a highway called the Inner Loop Expressway.

We had gone about one hundred miles into Texas and we were making good time; because there were some long stretches of highway in the middle of nowhere that weren't cluttered with wreaked cars and trucks.

When out of the blue, Megan commented.

"Neither one of us have relatives here in Texas."

"What?" I asked. "What do you mean neither one of you have relatives in Texas?"

"We just said that because we didn't want to stay there any longer, we didn't think it was safe anymore. Frank was making some *really* stupid decisions, and everyone was just going along with him.

"Like what?" Gin asked, curious to find out why the girls would want to leave what appeared to her to be a fairly safe environment, except for the occasional zombie horde surge.

"Take you guys for instance, no offence, but Frank picked you up, didn't know anything about you, and brought you back to our compound and let you in. He didn't ask anyone's opinion; he didn't take a vote, nothing, he didn't even take your weapons away from you," Megan answered, visibly stressed. "So we'll ride with you until we get to wherever your people are in Texas, and we'll go on by ourselves from there."

Thinking that Megan and Mary were sharper than I had first thought, I confessed to them as well.

"Well ladies, I hate to bring you down with the facts, but we don't have any relatives in Texas either, I initially told Frank that in case we needed an excuse to leave. I noticed the same thing you did; the fact that he let us keep our guns was a huge red flag to me. Guns would have been the first thing that I would have taken away from strangers, and then any other weapons that they might have, at least until they had proven themselves not to be a threat. Frank and the rest of them have a pre-zombie-holocaust mentality; they think there's some good in everybody. That may have been true before this plague happened. I never believed it myself, but that's just me. Anyway that kind of thinking is going to get them all killed now days."

"It *was* kind of weird that they let us keep our guns," Gin said.

I looked over my shoulder at Megan.

"Frank told me that before doomsday he was a psychologist, I think that might be his problem, Frank is just thinking *too* much," I told her.

"He never told me that, I don't think he ever told anyone that. That's just great, he tells a total stranger all of his deep dark secrets, but doesn't tell his closest brothers and sisters in arms, that's just wonderful," she spouted.

"All it's going to take is for one of those outsider groups to devise a plan to infiltrate their lair, Frank let's them keep their weapons, and they all find themselves waking up dead in the morning," Billy stated.

"That's why we left son, that's why we all left," I said, agreeing whole-heartily with him.

"We're definitely not as congenial as Frank, but we have a set of rules too," I said to the girls.

"Jacob, show Megan and Mary our rules," I insisted.

Jacob dug around in his pocket and pulled out a wrinkled and tattered piece of paper.

"Here, read this," he said, handing the paper to Mary.

"There's one more rule that's not on that paper, it's our shoot first and ask questions later rule. It goes like this. When in doubt, shoot first, and later ask yourself if it was the right thing to do," I told the girls.

"That rule has saved us a couple of times," Gin added, nodding her head in agreement.

Billy leaned over to Megan and looked her in the eye.

"So don't be afraid to use it," he interjected.

The two girls reclined in their seats and leaned against each other as they began to read and memorize our list of rules.

"If you think of anything that you think might be useful, don't hesitate to mention it, one of those rules states share your information," I imparted to them.

Our gas gauge read three quarters full as we continued west. We were traveling at a reduced rate of speed, not nearly as fast as the freeway was designed to handle, so we weren't in need of a fuel stop at the moment.

However, as on any road trip, post apocalyptic or not, the call of nature will dictate certain mandatory delays.

As we passed a road sign that informed us that a rest area was three miles ahead, Gin spoke up.

"We need to stop up ahead, I have to use the restroom, anybody else have to go?" Gin asked, taking a poll.

Most everyone agreed that a restroom break was indeed needed, so instead of dropping trou along the roadside, we decided to make a stop at the rest area.

"Everyone take your rifle with you, and cover each other," I said, coaching the new members of our troop as I turned onto the exit ramp.

When we arrived at the normal parking area, I drove the Hummer over the curb and parked it about ten yards from the stone building where the restrooms where located.

"Billy, I want you to climb into the turret and cover us, you can go in last. Jacob and I will go in first and make sure it's safe inside. All of us will use the women's restroom, that way we only have to clear one room, and the ladies will have, well, whatever ladies have in their restrooms. When we come out, you girls can go in and we'll stand guard. Billy will watch over all of us with the mini-gun."

"Remember Dad, we only have a half full belt in this gun and we need to make it last, so I'm only going to shoot a couple of bursts at a time and that's it," Billy reminded me. "Unless of course a large horde of eater's show up, then I'm going to let loose on them."

"Then keep your AK close, and shoot them with it," I insisted, as we began to move away from the Hummer. "And stay inside the truck, don't get out, shoot if you have to, if the noise brings in a bunch of eaters, we can always leave and drop a deuce in a roadside ditch somewhere if need be."

I entered the restroom first as planned, Jacob followed close behind me, and after checking all of the stalls, and pulling the handle of what was probably the locked door to a supply room, we determined that the restroom was safe.

"It's clear in here, we'll be out in a minute," I called to the women.

"Okay, but hurry up, we have to go too," Mary yelled.

"Keep your voice down," Billy said calmly, as he scanned the area for any roaming freelance zombies.

After everyone in the group was relieved of their urinary and other pressures, we decided to check the information center with the hopes of finding a road map.

Even though we had our GPS device, in our hurry to leave our home, I'd forgotten to pack the unit's charger;

if we couldn't find a car charger to fit it soon, it would become useless to us.

I pulled the Hummer up to the building with Billy again on watch in the turret; the others followed using the vehicle as cover. Again, I parked the Hummer ten or so yards from the door of the building, I stopped the truck and led our group cautiously to the front door.

The glass door was broken along with all of the other windows, so entering the building was not a problem. However, entering the building quietly was impossible.

The broken glass from the windows covered the floor and crunched under our feet with every step as we walked. The maps and tourist brochures were scattered everywhere, making finding the map that we wanted a bit of a chore.

"What do you want?" A man's voice suddenly came from behind the large semi circular counter setting in the middle of the floor. We all froze in our tracks. Only slight crunches were now heard as even the slightest movement crushed more glass under our feet, making it impossible to be completely quiet for more than a couple of seconds at a time.

"Who's there, I know you aren't any of those crazy people, they can't stand still. So who are you and what do you want?" the voice once more asked.

"You're right, we're not the crazy people, we're just a group of people traveling through," I told him while pointing to the counter, informing our group where the man was hiding, just in case anyone had any doubt.

"We just want one or two of your maps and we'll be on our way, if that's all right with you," I said.

I was trying to convince the man that he had some semblance of authority in this matter, all the while motioning to Jacob and Megan to watch each side of the counter, and to Gin and Mary to be ready in case the man decided to attack us from the middle of the counter.

"Come on out and let us take a look at you. We won't hurt you unless you try to hurt us first," I told the man as I leveled the barrel of my AK-47 at his position.

I did not intend to kill this man right off; or at all for that matter; however, if he made any kind of hostile moves toward me or anyone in our group, he would be dead before he hit the floor.

From behind the counter the top of the man's head appeared, rising ever so slowly into view.

"I want to see your hands, put your hands on the counter," I ordered forcefully, in the style of a police officer giving commands to a suspect.

By now, we could see the man's eyes and nose as he continued to stand up.

"Our weapons can easily penetrate that counter you're behind," I told him.

Still not able to see the man's hands, I was becoming impatient.

"Put your hands on the counter," I repeated angrily, as my index finger began to tickle my rifle's trigger.

"Okay, okay," the man said, slowly sliding both hands onto the counter as he stood all the way up.

"Stay there and don't move," I said, as I moved toward the man, pointing the muzzle of my rifle directly at his nose, just out of his reach.

Tilting my head toward Jacob I informed the man.

"This is my son Jacob, he's going to come around the counter and search you. If you move a hair, outside of blinking your eyes, I'm going to put a big hole in your face and blow out the back of your head. Nod your head one time if you understand," I said slowly and concise.

The man nodded one time as ordered, and I motioned to Jacob to go around the counter and search the man, saying.

"Check him for weapons Jake."

The glass crunched loudly under Jacob's feet as he moved swiftly to the back of the counter.

"He's got some stuff here on the floor," Jacob claimed, kicking the man's rifle a few feet away in one direction, and his pistol a few feet away in the opposite direction.

Upon searching the man's person Jacob found no more weapons, so I removed the muzzle of my gun from in front of his face and asked him his name.

"What's your name mister?"

"Clyde, my name is Clyde," the man answered.

"Well Clyde," I said. "Like I said before, all we want is couple of maps and you'll never see us again.

Girls, see if you can find a road map, there should be some around here some place."

"You people aren't going to try to get through Dallas are you?" Clyde inquired, shaking his head.

"We're not sure yet, that's one reason we're looking for a map," I answered. "What do you know about Dallas?"

"I came through Dallas on my way here, I'm an over the road truck driver, well, I mean I used to be a truck driver. I was hauling a load of computers out of San

Diego; and I was a few hundred miles on the other side of Dallas when all this shit hit the fan. Things went kind of smooth until I got to Dallas, trust me, you don't want to go there," Clyde said, as he continued his story.

"Roving gangs of people, and roving gangs of those sick people, and I mean a lot of them, all trying to kill everything they come across, men, women, children, dogs, cats, and each other. It was just dumb luck that I made it out of there alive."

"How are you surviving living here?" Gin asked. "All of the snack machines are empty, where are you getting your food?"

"Oh, you miss understand, I don't live here," he explained. "Like I said, I drive trucks; trucks supplied this nation before all of this shit happened, everything that you used to buy at the stores where you shopped, trucks brought it there.

I've been stopping at rest areas and breaking into abandon trailers for food, and just about anything else I need. All you have to do is find the right trailer.

I was searching the trailers outside when I heard you people coming. It's not like there's a lot of traffic nowadays, you can hear a vehicle coming for quite a long way. I thought you might be doing the same thing, searching trailers I mean, so I ran in here to hide until you left," Clyde elaborated.

"I didn't think of that, we were going to avoid the trucks, I figured there were too many places for people and eaters to be hiding," I told Clyde.

"I didn't say you didn't have to be careful, you have to be ready for anything. Making sure there's nobody hiding in the cab is the hardest part. The cab sits up high and those crazy people can drop down on you in a second, you've got to be ready for that," Clyde warned. "If you and your people decide you want to start going through trailers for supplies you'll need a pair of bolt cutters, big one's I recommend, and make darn sure that you find some way to block the back doors from closing all the way. Otherwise someone might lock you inside, and that will be the end of you," Clyde said, imploring us to take his advice.

"You wouldn't happen to have an extra pair of bolt cutters on you would you Clyde?" Mary asked politely, as I detected her slowly moving the barrel of her gun in Clyde's direction.

Although Mary had asked Clyde nicely for spare bolt cutters, I could almost read her mind, she was ready to kill Clyde and take his cutters.

It was too early in the zombie invasion for me to have lost all of my moral fortitude.

Sure, I had killed during the war, and of course, I have no qualms about putting down any number of zombies in any number of ways. Yes, I had accidently fatally clobbered the obese man in the pantry while he dined on fruit jam, and yes I was ultimately responsible for the untimely demise of that frail elderly woman (but remember, I thought she needed killing). Oh yes, there was the maniacal cabin cruiser cannibal (he needed killing too, if you will remember).

But hey, in my own defense, you might recall that I had nothing to do with the river pirates death, and we're really not sure who actually killed the woman in the speed boat now are we?

However, putting aside any of my past indiscretions that some people might take issue with, I did not feel that Clyde deserved to die over a pair of bolt cutters. He was friendly and cooperating with us, he'd shown no signs of aggression toward any of us, and he didn't seem to be a threat to our group. So I chose to give him the benefit of the doubt, while keeping my weapons close (as usual), and my mindset in combat mode (as always), ready to kill him quickly if by chance I had misjudged his character.

On the other hand, it did give me some insight into Mary's own mindset, so I quickly but casually stepped in between Clyde and Mary's gun.

"No, but you might find one in one of those trucks out there. Sometimes drivers carry a pair with them just in case they lose the key to the lock on their trailer," Clyde answered, trying to be helpful.

"Here's the map we're looking for," Gin said, handing a map to me.

At that moment, the sound of Billy's AK interrupted our conversation.

"We've got company," Megan shouted, as she ran to assist Billy.

"I'm right behind you," Mary called out.

"Me too," Jacob said, following the two girls out the door.

As I said, Clyde had shown no hostility toward us whatsoever, and it seemed like he was trying to be helpful, I mean with his suggestion of searching semi trailers for supplies, and with that old saying in mind, *the enemy of my enemy, is my friend*, I said. "Clyde, pickup your guns, and let's go."

Without hesitation, Clyde grabbed both his rifle and pistol and followed me out the front door, not realizing that Gin had him covered the whole time and would have weighted him down with lead had he made the slightest belligerent move toward me.

Billy had killed two of the zombies that were approaching us; we could see their remains lying about seventy-five yards out, just passed a group of small trees. A good distance behind them we could see three more of the walking dead maniacs stumbling our way.

Tucking his pistol into his waistband, Clyde raised his lever action rifle, took careful aim, and dropped one of the zombies in its tracks.

"That was at least three hundred yards away," Clyde bragged.

"That was a good shot Clyde, no doubt about it," I concurred.

"Who says a 30-30 isn't effective," he boasted. "It doesn't have the fire power that your guns have, but it's pretty good for long range," he boasted once more.

"Well then take out the other two, they travel in groups you know, only head shots count," I said, challenging him to repeat his first shot.

Racking another round into the chamber, Clyde again took careful aim and pulled the trigger, and again a zombie dropped to the ground.

"One more Clyde, and that's the last of them," I said urging him on.

Racking another round into the chamber, and again taking aim, Clyde dropped the hammer on his model 94 Winchester and the last of the undead that we could see bit the dust.

"Hat trick," Clyde announced laughing, as he ejected the empty cartridge case from his rifle and eased another bullet into the gun's chamber.

"Indeed," I said. "I've got to admit, you're pretty good with that thing, all three shots were off hand."

"We better get out of here Dad, that noise is sure to bring more eaters," Billy warned.

"It's been nice knowing you Clyde, but we've got to go, you better go too," I said, as I got behind the wheel of the Hummer.

"Get in everybody, we're leaving," Gin announced, as she too boarded our vehicle.

"Goodbye," Clyde yelled, as we drove off. "Keep your head down and your powder dry, and don't forget, don't let them trap you inside a trailer!"

We could see Clyde still standing by the information center, waving, and shouting something. But as the distance between us grew, his voice faded and we could no longer hear his words.

"He's not going to make it," Mary said, shaking her head.

"Not if he keeps standing there yelling and waving like an idiot," Jacob added, also shaking his head.

"All that shooting is bound to attract eaters, and he's nowhere near his truck, and he won't last long hiding in a building with no doors or windows," Billy shouted down, still perched in the machine gun turret.

"I think we need to take his advice though, let's steer clear of Dallas, maybe we should go further south, down to Corpus Christi or Galveston," Gin added, pointing to the newly acquired map.

"Okay, sounds good to me, if Clyde was telling the truth about Dallas we don't want any part of it. You plot our course honey, and we'll detour, avoid Dallas, and go south. But try to keep us on the interstates as much as possible, their width gives us room to maneuver most of the time, and we've done pretty well so far sticking to I-20."

As we approached Dallas, Gin asked me.

"Do you think we should stay on I-20 to I-45, or should we cut across to I-45 on highway 34?"

After taking a long look at the map, I answer her question.

"If we stay on the road we're on, we'll scratch the outskirts of Dallas, which according to Clyde could be dangerous. On the other hand, if we take the diagonal route, it's shorter, but it's narrower and easier to block, so we could end up getting stopped by a rogue gang, or it could just be blocked by wrecked vehicles from the initial panic. Either way, we'd have to turn around and drive back to the outskirts of Dallas. Or it could be a lot worse you know," I told her, not doing a very good job of instilling a sense of confidence in her. "Let's take our chances and stay on the interstates for now," I decided, hoping I'd made the right decision.

"Boys, it looks like your mother has decided to go to Galveston, so that's where we're going. The map shows several fresh water lakes nearby, not that we're going to drink any of the water out of them, but some of them might be clean enough to take a bath in, and it's right on the Gulf of Mexico too," I said.

"It's close to Houston too, I was in Houston once," Mary said. "I was pretty young, so I don't remember much about it."

Billy had climbed down from the turret, and chimed in on her comment.

"Houston is a big city isn't it?" he asked.

"Bigger than Shreveport, but not as big as Dallas-Fort Worth, according to this map," Gin answered abruptly.

"You think it will be safer there than in Dallas?" Billy asked, questioning the wisdom of his mother's choice.

"There's no place that's safe, we know that, we'll avoid Houston just like Dallas, and see how things are in Galveston," I answered, hoping my answer would suffice.

Our journey was uneventful until just after we had turned onto I-45 heading south. On our left was some state prison facility.

A flash of sunlight reflecting off the shooter's riflescope, announced that it was from there that the bullet was fired from the rooftop of a building that sat adjacent to a basketball court within the fenced jail.

The bullet that came smashing through our back left window, causing Megan to be wounded, and literally scarring the hell out of all of us.

The snipers round had hit its target, which was our vehicle, but had missed hitting any of us; however, shards of glass were hurled throughout the interior of the Hummer as the window exploded. Some of which had landed in Megan left eye, causing her to scream in pain.

"My eye," she cried. "There's glass in my eye."

Gin quickly crawled into the back seat and pulled Megan's hand from her now profusely bleeding eye to assess the damage.

I on the other hand, slammed my foot down on the accelerator pedal, increasing the speed of our massive vehicle.

"Is anyone else hurt," Gin asked, now looking for something to bandage Megan's wound.

"I'm fine," Mary answered.

"Me too," said Jacob.

"I'm not hurt, I just got glass tossed all over me," Billy replied.

It turned out that the sniper's bullet wasn't intended to kill anyone, although it would have been fine with the shooter if it had. Its real purpose was to make the driver do exactly what I did. Which was speed up, and be distracted enough by the chaos inside the vehicle, that when we approached the roadblock that had been put there by the sniper's comrades, no one would notice it until it was too late to stop and turn around. Their plan had worked and nobody did notice it.

The prisoners, or the friends of the prisoners, or whoever had built their blockade, had built it in a fashion that at first glance, looked as if a person could drive through by weaving between the vehicles in the center that were blocking the road. However, once they started through the middle, the trap was set, and the prey would encounter some tractor-trailers that had been tipped on their sides, making the road impassable.

I had been glancing back and forth, from the road ahead, to the back seat where Gin was attending to

Megan's eye, all the while Megan screamed and cried, still bleeding all over herself and Gin.

"Holy crap!" I yelled, looking up from the back seat and seeing the road blocked by several vehicles.

I quickly slammed on the brakes, hitting the brake pedal too hard. The oversized truck skidded sideways and headed for the right side of the blockade.

Fortunately for us, the trap worked best if the prey headed straight through the middle of the barricade. Our Hummer was bigger and heavier than most private passenger vehicles on the road, and the barricade was setup so that the prisoners could drive their vehicle the wrong way down an entrance ramp, and make their way back to the confines of the prison after they had looted, and who knows what else to any unsuspecting passersby.

Our hefty truck plowed into two of the cars the inmates were using to ferry themselves to and from the prison, knocking them forward and out of our way. The impact brought us to a stop forty feet passed where the cars had been parked.

Caught off guard by my display of inept driving prowess, the bushwhackers scrambled over and around the blockade, attempting to salvage what was left of their carjacking efforts.

Before the Hummer had come to a complete stop, Billy and Jacob had already grabbed their guns and had them pointing out the broken back window, waiting for their first targets to appear.

They didn't have long to wait, within seconds the hijackers dressed in prison garb appeared, climbing over parked cars and trucks, running at us, screaming, hollering and firing their guns wildly, like a World War II Japanese *banzai* charge.

I guess they were trying to scare and panic us. They probably assumed that we would be panicked and running scared.

However, after all we'd been through up to that point, all of the grisly scenes we'd had to endure, and all of the killing we'd done, all they accomplished with their banzai charge, was to announce their presents and give us closer and easier targets.

If you've ever tried to shoot a gun, and actually hit what you're aiming at while running, you know that even with some practice it is nearly an impossible task at any distance. Not to sound over confident, but the outcome for the ambushing prisoners was predictable from our standpoint.

In prison, they might have been bad asses, but out here in the middle of an apocalypse of biblical proportion, we six people in the Hummer were the real bad asses.

They came at us hard, thinking that with their numbers we would cowl down and surrender without a fight. Some of them were even laughing as they ran toward us, some of their bullets even hitting our truck.

Billy was the first to open fire on them, and with his AK-47 resting on the door of the Hummer where the window used to be, he had a stable platform on which to make his shots more accurate. He shot three of them, killing the third one before the first two hit the ground.

Jacob and I then joined in, Jacob firing his Sub-2000 over the top of Billy's head as he crouched down taking advantage of the makeshift rifle rest.

"Keep your head down Billy," he yelled over the sound of the gunfire.

I knew it would be difficult to get my AK wrestled passed the steering wheel in a timely manner, so I settled for my pistol.

Steel challenge shooting on the weekends had prepared me for this exact scenario. In steel shooting, most of the targets are twelve-inch diameter, round steel plates (about the size of a human head), anywhere from ten to twenty yards away; the goal was to hit each of the plates with one shot as fast as you could. Five targets, five shots. Moreover, any hit is a good hit.

As fate would have it, several of the attacking road pirates just happened to be ten to twenty yards away, so just like shooting steel plates, my bullets ripped through the heads of five of our advisories killing them instantly, while preventing them from coming back from the dead.

The melee was over almost as fast as it had begun. Gin and Megan were down on the floor, with Megan still reeling from the pain her eye injury was causing her.

Mary had raised her weapon, but was afraid to pull the trigger; fearing that she would hit Billy or Jacob.

With the immediate threat extinguished, we watched two of the prisoners that were still alive, abandon their makeshift fortress, and run from the scene back in the direction of the prison.

"Forget about the ones that were killed without a headshot. Our truck is damaged and Megan is hurt, we don't have time to deal with them, we need to leave before they turn into eaters and attack us again, or the noise brings more eaters this way," I said, as I started the engine, hoping the Hummer was still drivable.

"Some of them are just wounded, still alive," Mary mentioned unemotionally.

"Hell with the wounded ones, their buddies will take care of them when they come back from the dead," I said, also without emotion. "Anyway, let's face it, the bastards got what they begged for, so who are we to deny them their just dessert?"

With the two front tires flat, and the radiator leaking fluid, our crippled Hummer limped down the road away from our latest battlefield.

"We're not going to get very far, we need another ride, and we need it fast," I said, struggling to steer our vehicle.

"I've stopped the bleeding, but she needs some pain medicine and some real bandages, we need to find a drug store or a hospital, and soon," Gin said, as she cuddled Megan in her arms.

I knew from experience's that I had had as a teen, that we wouldn't get far in the wrecked Hummer, once you have a radiator leak, especially one as large as the one in our vehicle, you're only going to go about four miles before the engine overheats and locks up, and that's if you're lucky.

I didn't know exactly how far the next exit was, however, it wasn't long before a road sign informed us that it was only two miles ahead.

By now, the Hummer had shed the rubber from its front wheels and we were riding down the road on just the rims, spewing sparks and making a horrendous noise.

"Only about a half mile to the exit, with all the noise we're making we're going to have to abandon this ride quick, and get some distance between us and it," I shouted over the screeching of metal scrapping the concrete.

A short time later, the freeway exit came into sight.

"Here's our exit," I informed the group. "Start looking for a parking lot, or someplace that we might be able to get another ride," I directed, as we left the interstate.

"Look, there's some kind of truck place over there," Jacob said, pointing to a large lot filled with trailers.

"Dad, look, there's a truck stop on the other side," Billy shouted.

"Truck stop means fuel, and like Clyde said, supplies," I added.

"They'll probably have first aid kits there," Gin added, still holding Megan close.

"When we get to the bottom of this ramp we bail out. Weapons and ammo are our main concern, we'll come back later if we can for anything that we leave behind," I ordered.

We stopped at the bottom of the exit ramp; the Hummer was smoking from the friction of bare metal scrapping the road, and the steam from the almost dry radiator.

"We got here just in time," Jacob said, jumping out of the truck. "This thing is about to catch on fire."

"Grab our stuff and let's get Megan over to that truck stop," Gin urged, helping Megan out of the Hummer.

We had no sooner gathered our belongings and started in the direction of the truck stop that three zombies appeared in our path.

"Most likely attracted by the noise, I'll take care of them," Mary said, pulling a machete from her backpack.

Billy, with his sickle in hand, added. "I'll help."

As the zombies came nearer, Billy and Mary approached them head on, and as the lead zombie made an awkward lunge at Billy, Mary swung her machete upward diagonally as hard as she could, like a tennis player might hit the ball with a backhand stroke.

The razor sharp machete sliced through the nose of the zombie and continued into its skull, stopping half way through and sticking in the rotting corpses head, wedged between the sliced bone.

Nodding his approval of Mary's quick reaction, Billy stepped to his left and planted his sickle deep into the brain of the next stinking animated carcass standing in line, but unlike Mary's kill, when the zombie dropped to its knees, Billy's sickle effortlessly slid out from the crown of its blood gushing head, as Billy had now mastered his technique.

Mary struggled for a moment trying to free her weapon from the skull of her first kill, but with her third and final upward yank, the top the insane monsters cranium snapped off, making a dull popping sound like a muffled firecracker.

Her large brush clearing knife now free, Mary set her sights on the third attacker. She quickly and without hesitation, walked up to the zombie and rammed her machete straight through its right eye socket and into the brain of the last attacker.

She then turned to me and said. "That takes care of that, now let's get to the truck stop!"

The truck stop was close to the freeway; it wasn't more than one hundred yards from our location, so within minutes we had arrived at the gas stop and cleared the building of a few zombies that had taken up residence there. It took some time to extract the now dead, *undead* bodies we had created, but before long, we were searching for supplies as Billy stood watch at the front door.

"Here's some first-aid kits," Mary said, bringing two of the larger ones to the front of the store.

"Here's some pain killers," Jacob called out, raking several different brands off the shelf and into his arms.

"Find her some water, or something to wash down the pills," Gin shouted.

Billy reached down and pulled a can of soda from a display beside the door.

"Here catch," he said, as he tossed the can under handed to his mother.

Gin gave Megan a couple more pills than the recommended dose stated on the medicine's label, then asked Mary and Jacob to find some sleeping pills.

Most of the aids for sleeping at the truck stop were not to help you sleep; they were to aid you from falling asleep. However, together Mary and Jacob managed to find what Gin had asked for, and delivered it to her.

"Lay on this counter Megan, I need you to be asleep, I can't get the glass out of your eye while you're moving all around," Gin said to her softly, as she helped her onto the counter.

Again, Gin gave Megan more than the recommended dose, and as the pain medicine was beginning to take effect, so too were the sleeping pills, and as Megan drifted off to sleep, Gin looked through the first-aid kits in search of some kind of ointment for Megan's eye, and ordered Jacob to find a tool kit of some kind.

"Here Mom, mostly all they have are big tools, except for these needle nose pliers, but you might be able to use this," Jacob said, handing his mother an eyeglass repair kit. "It has some really small tweezers in it."

"These are perfect," Gin declared, pulling out the tweezers.

When the sleeping pills took effect and Megan was sound asleep, Gin carefully operated on her, and was able to find and extract all of the glass that was embedded in her eye.

"That should do it, all of the glass is out, and I smeared some anti-bacterial ointment on the eye, it should heal up in a couple of weeks, but she's going to be blind in that eye. We're going to have to get her an eye patch too, she's going to have to wear one from now on.

We were far enough away from the prison, and there was no way that the prisoners could know that we were just a few of miles down the road from them, and with Megan in the shape she was in, we decided to stay the night at the truck stop and look for a new vehicle the next morning.

We made ourselves as comfortable as possible, and settled in for the night. With no electricity, there were no lights, which made it easier to fall asleep.

I had taken the first watch as I always did, and near the end of my watch, I was getting ready to wake up

Mary, who had volunteered to take the second watch. I heard someone moving around and assumed it was Mary preparing to relieve me.

"Just in time Mary," I whispered, not wanting to disturb the others.

Mary didn't answer.

"Mary," I whispered again.

Still there was no answer. Seeing some movement several feet behind me, I pulled my pistol, transferred it to my left hand, then pulled my sickle from my belt and grasped it firmly in my right hand.

The faint glow from the moon cast long and almost indiscernible shadows across the dark room, but as one particular shadow moved toward me, I realized that a zombie must have somehow entered the building.

As the shadow moved closer to me, a gurgling sound was emanating from the darkness, and that sound quickly turned into a growl, there was no doubt now, a zombie was present.

I backed up and put my back against the front door. The dim moonlight was just bright enough for me to see a figure within striking distance. I lifted my sickle and brought it down as hard as I could. However, in the pale moonlight my aim was not as accurate as it might have been in full daylight. My sickle sliced down along the side of the zombie's head, separating the scalp from the bone all along the side of its skull, and peeling off its left ear as it went. My sickle finally stopped at the bottom of the monster's jaw, and left its ear, and scalp from the whole left side of its head laying across its shoulder.

After missing the killing blow to the head with my sickle, and with the flesh-eating maniac nearly upon me,

I kept my left arm tucked in by my waist, and I tilted my pistol up at a forty-five degree angle and fired two shots at the trespassing zombie's head.

My first shot hit the left collarbone, shattering it and causing the maniac's left shoulder to slump down in front; my second shot hit its mark by way of the nose. My bullet sailed straight up through the monster's left nostril, and popped a piece of bone out of the top of the zombie's skull that was about the same size as a silver dollar (an Eisenhower Dollar, not a Butch Buck), taking a portion of its deranged brain along with it.

The homicidal brute dropped to the floor at my feet, it was no longer a threat. Its bloody but eerily familiar face was illuminated for a split second by a flash of light coming from outside. I turned expecting to see some idiot with a flashlight walking around the parking lot in the middle of the night attracting zombies and feral dogs with its beam, but there was nothing.

It was another case of those strangely elusive lights that Frank had spoke of, and I had experienced on the river.

I turned back to the body in front of me, now only visible by the soft moonlight that fell upon the floor of the truck stop.

"What's going on?" I heard Gin ask.

"What's happening?" The sound of Billy's voice came through the darkness.

"An eater got in," I said.

"Is anybody hurt? Billy, Jacob, are you two all right?" Gin asked them.

"I'm fine," Billy answered.

"Me too," Jacob said.

"Mary how about you, are you all right?" Gin asked.

"I'm fine, did you kill it?" Mary responded.

Nobody had checked on Megan, and I didn't know how Mary was going to handle it, and I didn't know how I was going to handle Mary if things got ugly. But I was going to find out in a matter of moments.

"It's dead," I said, bracing myself for Mary's wrath. Because I knew who the dead zombie once was.

"Where's Megan? Is she still sleeping?" Mary asked.

"She's not on the counter, where is she?" Gin asked, with real concern in her voice.

"Someone look behind the counter, maybe she fell off. Megan where are you?" Mary called softly.

With no answer from Megan, the reality of the situation began to filter into everyone's consciousness. Mary slowly walked over to me, and the body at my feet.

Pulling a small flashlight from her pocket, she illuminated the fresh corpse's face.

"Turn that light off, eaters will see us," I quickly scolded. "It's bad enough that I had to fire my gun."

"Is that Megan?" she gasped. "Did you kill Megan?"

"She turned, she was an eater!" I stressed, still holding my Glock 19 at my side. "It was either her or me; I chose me."

"You killed Megan!" Mary stated, staring down at her friends body.

Let's get one thing straight right now. *Eaters* get killed, we kill them. I killed Megan because she *needed killing* (funny how that term keeps popping up). If I die, or get bit and turn into one of those flesh eating killer cannibals, I expect every one of you to do the same for me!" I told them all emphatically.

"She must have died in the middle of the night," Billy said.

"How did she die?" Jacob asked.

Mary turned to Gin as she answered Jacob's question.

"Your mother killed her, she gave her too many sleeping pills, didn't you?" she said, looking at my wife.

"If I did, I didn't mean to, she was in pain, and I had to get that glass out of her eye. I was just trying to help her; I didn't mean to hurt her," Gin explained, now feeling guilty.

To my surprise, and I think to everyone's surprise, Mary shrugged her shoulders, turned, and walked back to where she had been sleeping, and coldly said. "I'm not going to clean up that mess in the dark; it'll have to wait till morning."

With that, Mary curled up in her blanket, closed her eyes, and in a moment was fast asleep again. She had evidently forgotten that she had volunteered to take the second watch.

We had thought that Megan was Mary's best friend, but she showed very little emotion over Megan's death. I wondered if she was just putting on a show for us. Maybe she felt outnumbered at the moment and wanted to wait for a better opportunity to get even with Gin.

At daybreak, I would try to delve deeper into Mary's psyche in an effort to ascertain if she could be trusted to remain traveling with my family. Only time would tell, but I was going to watch her closely until I was sure she wasn't going to seek retaliation against Gin. So I took the second watch as well, not bothering to remind Mary of her promised obligation.

Everyone was awake at dawn, and Megan's body still laid by the front door. In the daylight, we could see the gruesome results of her termination, and my failed first attempt at that goal.

Parts of her decaying yellowish-gray brain were scatter on the floor next to her body, mixed among pieces of broken cranium and bloody strands of hair, as dark red goo seeped out from the portion of her head that my sickle had skinned, and a two-foot wide puddle of purplish ooze had pooled underneath her broken skull.

"Why do you think she died," Jacob asked, staring down at Megan's corpse, not directing his question to anyone specific.

Gin chose to answer his question as her eyes welled up with tears.

"She had lost a lot of blood; maybe her body couldn't handle the sleeping pills in her weakened conditioned."

Mary then calmly added.

"Don't forget the pain pills you gave her. Well, she's dead now, and I made a mistake last night. There's no reason to clean up the mess if we're not going to stay here."

This seemed like a good time for me to intervene.

"Mary, I thought Megan was your friend?" I asked.

"She was my friend," Mary answered, showing no emotion.

"You don't seem too broken up that she is dead," I remarked.

Mary moved over to where Megan had fallen asleep, pushed herself up and sat on the counter.

"It's like this," she said. "It was my grandfather's birthday, he was ninety-four years old and not in very good health. The family didn't think he would last another year, so they decided to celebrate his birthday with a big party at my uncle David's house. The party just happened to be the same day of the outbreak.

On that day, I watched my ninety-four year old grandfather, who had been confined to a wheelchair for the last five years of his life, stand up and walk over to my six-year-old cousin Lucy, and rip her to pieces," Mary continued emotionless. "I was the only one at the party that left that house alive. Half of my relatives turned into zombies that day, and attacked the other half. It came as such a surprise to everyone, that most were killed or bitten before they could fight back. I had to kill my father, and my baby brother who was only eleven, with the knife we had used to cut my grandfather's birthday cake. Since that day, I've seen countless people die, and had to kill at least fifty of the undead, and that's not even counting the one's I put down that night with you and Frank.

So, to answer your question, I'll be your friend, I'll watch your backs, I'll fight with you, and I'll fight for you, but don't expect me to get emotionally attached to any of you. That's just the way it is, and that's just the way it's going to be, that's just the way it has to be."

It made sense now, Mary's lack of emotion, her cold comments; I probably would do the same, had I seen my whole family killed, not to mention having to kill some of them myself.

However, I thought, now it is my turn to turn off the emotion.

"Well Mary, I'm sorry to hear that you've had it so rough, but everybody's had it rough. We killed our neighbor's in our own kitchen; that was quite a gruesome mess. Then we had to fight our way out of our house, and watch our friends and neighbors battling eaters in their front yard as we left them behind. The list goes on and on, so everyone has had a hard time from the start," I told her.

"I know," she said. "Let's find a ride."

With her last comment, I decided it was a good time to drop the subject and get the hell out of that place.

The good news was, there were no feral dogs around, the bad news was, zombies had wondered into the parking lot and were close to the vehicles we needed.

One might think that in an apocalypse like the one that we were enduring, transportation would not be an issue. Just find a car or truck with the keys still in it, and off you go. It wasn't that simple.

It's true that there was a multitude of abandon vehicles, some wrecked, some not. People had jumped from their cars in a panic and ran, or died inside their cars from starvation or the elements, while waiting for help that never came. The problem was; most of those that ran away left their cars running, and at some point, the car either ran out of gas, or over heated and rendered the engine useless.

The cars that the people died in had plenty of gas, but most of them also still had a rotting dead body in them. An animated rotting dead body that will surly kill and eat you if given half a chance. One that has

253

decomposed enough to make the car stink to high hell and attract a multitude of harassing flies, and who knows what diseases they're carrying after feeding on the zombie hordes, therefore making the vehicle uninhabitable, even if you could release the zombie within back into the apocalyptic wilderness.

We had already had our fill of the smell of death on the river. Maybe in two or three years you could toss out the skeletal remains and the smell might have dissipated, that is unless zombies rot slow enough to still be active after two or three years, but nobody knew the natural life span of the dead at that time.

We did know that the undead were slowly rotting, but we had no idea how long it took before they ceased to be a threat in their menacing quest to eat flesh. It had been less than a month since the beginning of the outbreak, and the abandon cars with their windows rolled up and the sun shining in were like convection ovens, and the living corpses inside were too stupid to open the doors and escape the vehicles on their own, so they were becoming exceedingly ripe, yet still very dangerous.

We didn't have two or three years to wait for a new vehicle, we had to begin the search immediately, so with our weapons in hand, we stealthily left the safety of the truck stop building to dispatch the zombies walking among the abandon trucks.

I led the way into the parking lot but was quickly overtaken by Mary, who promptly hewed the head off a little girl who looked to have been about ten years old when she was alive. The little girl was the first living corpse in the pack that was within our killing radius, and

Mary, without forethought, kicked the still snapping head clear to get to the second zombie in the bunch. It was clear that Mary was attempting to take out some of her frustration on the small assembly of famished zombies before us.

With one eye on Mary, I pursued the rolling head, and as I caught up to it, I stomped down hard on it several times with the heel of my boot, crushing the cranial cavity flat upon the asphalt, and leaving a bloody impression of my boot heel imprinted on the temple of the lifeless girl's head.

Mary took care of the second threat as quick as she had the first, however, more efficiently the second time around, as she didn't decapitate the zombie, she chose the more traditional method of harvesting a drooling corpse, by splitting its skull down the middle as far as the upper lip and instantly killing it. Then jerking her machete sideways, she widened the gap in the zombie's head and smoothly slid her weapon out.

Billy and Jacob dealt with a few eaters that were flanking us, and Gin acted as the rear guard.

"Look in the one's that have the big sleeper units first," I ordered. "Knock on the doors before you open them, if there are any eaters inside that should get them riled up."

"Will do," Mary said, as she jumped onto the running board of a red tractor-trailer and tapped on the driver's door with the handle of her machete.

Gin kept watch as we checked the lot; we were having no luck at first, but in the last row sat a big blue tractor with a huge sleeper.

"Jackpot!" Billy yelled, waiving to the rest of us through the open drivers window, as we all heard the powerful diesel engine start up.

We gather by the truck's cab, and Billy informed us that the gas tanks were full and it looked like there would be plenty of room for everyone.

"The trucker that owned this rig must have been getting ready for a long haul somewhere," I said, thinking the driver must have been killed just before he was about to leave the truck stop.

The only thing left to do now was to check some trailers, stock up on any food and water we could find, and get back on the road again.

"Anyone find any bolt cutters in any of these trucks?" Billy asked, sticking his head out the window. "Every trailer I saw had a lock on it."

Pulling a small pair of bolt cutters from behind his back, Jacob answered with a smile on his face.

"Do you mean like these?"

"Those are kind of small, but they'll probably do. I doubt if we have to open every trailer," I said, patting Jacob on the back.

"Let's try that one over there," I suggested, pointing to a trailer that had the logo plastered all over it of a national food chain that no longer existed.

After Jacob tried numerous times to cut the lock off of the back door of the chosen trailer, and found that he lacked the strength to squeeze the bolt cutters together hard enough. Billy wrenched the cutters from his hands, and moments later, we were in the trailer.

"I could have done it," Jacob complained.

"We didn't have all day," Billy, answered sarcastically.

"I probably weakened it for you," Jacob hinted, implying his brother couldn't have done it without his help.

"Enough bickering," Gin scolded, from outside the trailer. "Is there anything in there we can use?"

"I think there's lots of stuff we can take with us, maybe we should hook up this trailer and take the whole thing with us Dad?" Jacob suggested.

"I don't think we'd get too far hauling this or any trailer for that matter, remember we need to be maneuverable, and trying to get around all of the vehicles that are parked all over the roads would be hard for a seasoned truck driver, and nearly impossible for any of us," I explained.

"There's some bottled water back here," Mary shouted.

"Help Mary with the water boys, get as much as you can carry, we don't know when we'll find more," I maintained, lifting two cases of the precious cargo.

From that one trailer we ended up with enough food and water to last the five of us a week or more. We packed most of the food in the sleeper unit, leaving enough room for us to sleep when need be. We found that there is an amazing amount of compartments inside and outside of the cab of a tractor-trailer rig that small items can be stored. Not to mention, by strapping most of the cases of water in between the cab and the fifth wheel, we had plenty of room for the rest of the supplies.

With everything packed, the boys and Mary in the back, Gin riding shotgun, *literally*, and the rest of our guns at the ready, I pulled our new ride out of the truck stop and back onto interstate 45.

"Next stop Galveston Texas!" I proclaimed, adding an extended *Indian war whoop* as we hit the freeway.

ON THE ROAD AGAIN

The road to Galveston was about the same as the road to Dallas, or the road to Shreveport, or probably the same as the road to anywhere in the country.

It was peppered with abandon cars and trucks and staggering zombies that for the most part we tried to avoid.

We drove for a while, until I saw a billboard sign that read "Military Surplus" next exit.

"I think we'll take this exit, we might be able to find something of interest in that surplus store," I announced. "Remember, I told you we'd find you some camouflage clothing honey, there should be a lot of it there."

Jacob stuck his head out of the sleeper.

"I'm going to look for a machete like Mary's, I want another backup weapon."

"That's not a bad idea, maybe we all should look for an extra backup weapon, I'm thinking of a tomahawk myself," I added, turning onto the exit ramp.

"There it is!" Jacob hollered, pointing to a storefront that was painted olive drab green, with artillery shells on each corner of the building.

"Calm down. As my grandmother used to say, we *ain't deef*," I said, smiling. "I see it, we all see it, how could you miss it?"

We used our usual tactic, and pulled up as close as we could to the front door. We sat up high in our semi-tractor, and that high vantage point allowed us to see not only the surrounding area, but allowed us to see what, if anything, might be lurking behind most of the parked cars that were near.

Several blocks over, we could see zombies milling around, but they were too far away for the noise of our diesel engine to make them aware of us. Even the hissing sound coming from the airbrakes did not attract their attention.

"Eaters, that means no dogs, let's go," I said, as we all exited the vehicle.

"I'm going to lock the doors, I don't want to leave somebody behind to guard the truck by themselves, and I don't want to leave the doors unlocked and take the chance that someone, or some *thing* might crawl inside while we're away."

"What if we have to leave in a hurry?" Gin asked, stepping onto the sidewalk.

"What if we have to leave in a hurry, and there's an eater in the truck?" I answered. "I think we can unlock the doors faster than we can get rid of an eater that's hunkered down in the cab of our vehicle, and a lot faster than we can clear the truck of someone that has a gun trained on us."

259

Mary stepped down from the truck, and in her snarkiest tone added.

"Unless of course, you get killed with the keys in your pocket?"

I then responded back to her in my snarkiest tone.

"Right, so you better make sure I don't get killed, problem solved, see how easy that was?"

The door to the shop was open, the glass was broken out, and the door had been propped open with an empty ammo can.

"We're not the first ones to have this idea," Billy said, as we started to enter the building.

"I'll go first, and then Mary, then Jacob, and then Gin, Billy you come in last and watch our backs," I ordered. "Who or whatever was here is probably gone by now, but we don't know that for sure, so stay alert everybody."

We slowly entered the surplus store; it had been ransacked, the shelves that were still attached to the walls were empty, and what was left of their goods were now on the floor.

Clothing racks had been turned over, the merchandise was scattered among the usual array of dead rotting bodies and severed body parts that we had grown accustom to seeing almost everywhere we went.

"It looks like more than just one or two people were here," Mary whispered, pushing aside one of the racks.

"It looks like this store was crowded during the beginning of the outbreak. There are lots of signs of a brawl, and as you can see some died right here," I said, gently nudging a carcass with my foot, of what was left of an old man with half of his head missing.

"Let's get what we came for and get the heck out of here," Gin said, as she rummaged through some used camouflage uniforms.

"Army digital is fine, that's what Jacob is wearing, there's some used Marine Corps digital, and some brand new multi-cam over here," I explained, picking up a pair of multi-cam pants.

"Billy, you've got that old school camouflage design, now's your chance to upgrade if you want too."

"I'm fine, these are really comfortable, and I like the big pockets," Billy answered, standing by the door, manning what had come to be his usual guard post.

"I like these," Gin announced softly, holding up part of an air force uniform.

"Good choice honey, grab a bunch of different sizes, get some for Mary too, you two can try them on in the truck and find one that fits."

"That's a cool camo pattern Mom, and look what I found!" Jacob announced excitedly.

We looked in Jacob's direction, and he was holding up a display of edged weapons.

"This is just the display, there's a bunch of this stuff all over the floor over here, even a tomahawk for you Dad," he said. "But no machete for me."

Mary tossed him a large duffel bag that she had found.

"Put the stuff in that, we'll sort it out in the truck," she ordered. "We can't stay in here all day."

We gathered a small assortment of equipment that was on hand, which could be easily carried or worn, such as a couple of tactical vests and a compass, and of course, the new edged weapons; and Jacob stuffed it all into the bag.

"Let's get going, we've been in here too long," Mary asserted, moving toward the front door.

"Billy, is it clear?" I asked, passing by Mary, smiling and dangling the key in front of her.

Billy cautiously crept outside. He turned back and motioned for the rest of us to follow. We bolted across the wide concrete sidewalk and up to the truck, I unlocked the passenger door, and as I opened it, I said. "Get in and unlock my door."

They piled into the cab of the truck and dumped the surplus booty into the sleeping area while I ran around to the driver's side to join them. Billy had leaned over passed the steering wheel and reached for the door lock as I came around the front of the truck. I heard his startled warning even though the driver's window was up. At the same time, I noticed what he had seen; there was someone at the rear of the cab.

The entity had its back to me and was a few steps away, and cutting one of the cords that held down our cases of water. It was simply reflex that caused me, without any hesitation what so ever, to pull my pistol and fire two shots into the back of the head of the would-be thief.

As the body fell to the ground, a screaming woman appeared from behind a car that was parked across the street. She ran straight at me waving a butcher knife over her head. Again my reflex's kicked in. I turned my body and swung my pistol in her direction, I double tapped her with two 9mm slugs in the chest from a slightly off balance modified Weaver stance. The woman dropped

262

face first onto the asphalt street. She had no sooner hit the pavement, than three more people appeared, all were men, two came from behind the same parked car that the woman had been hiding behind, and the third from a nearby abandon truck. All of them were running toward me, and all of them were brandishing knives.

By now, Billy had jumped out of our truck and was leveling his AK in the direction of the men in the street. We fired on the attackers, Billy taking the two on the left, leaving me to attend to the one to our right.

Malingering street zombies alerted by the gunshots, now began to appear on the scene, as well as more humans wielding knives.

Fortunately, for us, whoever this group of people was who were trying to steal our water, for some reason or another they hadn't managed to acquire any firearms, at least none that they were using to attack us.

The street in front of the surplus store was starting to become rather crowded with beings that were trying to kill us, some of which were alive, and some of which were *un-alive*.

"Get back in the truck!" I shouted to Billy, who wasted no time complying with my request.

I shoved my pistol back into its holster and jumped upon the running board of the truck, opened the door and slid inside.

"Lock the doors!" Gin yelled the unnecessary advice, as Billy crawled over her into the sleeper.

I inserted the truck keys into the ignition and started the engine, threw the truck into first gear, and we began to move.

Some of the faster knife-wielding attackers were upon us before I hit second gear. Holding onto the side mirrors on each side of the truck, they began to hammer on the windows with the handles of their knives.

"They're going to break the windows," Gin screamed, leaning toward me.

"We'll see about that. Hold on everybody," I shouted, just before I tapped the brake pedal.

Now in the truck's third of many gears, we were approaching twenty-five miles per hour. That's when I suddenly hit the brakes rather hard, and then quickly let off them again; I then crushed the accelerator pedal to the floor once more.

The sudden deceleration and subsequent acceleration, the surprise of the lurching motion forward and backward, and the laws of physics, caused the attacker's grip to be violently torn from the side mirrors and both of the attacking hitchhikers were thrown from our vehicle and tumbled along the pavement beside our truck.

"Can anybody say road rash?" I asked laughing, as I rammed two zombies that were clad in business suits and had wandered into our path, tossing them to the side as well.

"Another felony hit and run Dad. How many is that for you now?" Jacob joked.

"Not enough," I answered as I swerved to hit a hapless older looking jaywalking corpse.

After several more felonies under my belt, we found our way back onto the interstate, and again heading in the direction of Galveston.

"We seem to be having a lot of close calls, almost every time we stop, we end up having to fight our way out of some dilemma," Gin commented while sorting through her new camouflage uniforms.

"Indeed we do, but sometimes we have to stop, or somebody makes us stop, like those prisoners," I said in agreement.

"With our high profile in this truck we can see better, but they can see us better too. No matter where we go or which way we go, we're bound to find trouble, it's unavoidable," I maintained. "If it's not eaters, it's somebody else."

"Yes, it's always something," Gin agreed, shaking her head.

"We need to think about some new tactics, we've been lucky so far. If those water stealers would have had guns and ambushed us, we would have lost that fight for sure," I suggested, as I again plowed over an inadvertent lumbering zombie, indiscriminately dissecting the slow moving cadaver with the underside of our truck.

Listening to our conversation, Billy interjected.

"Sooner or later, we're going to be clearing a room or building and find it infested with eaters. Maybe we should adopt some kind of military or police type of entry, you know, the same way the *Swat*, or *Seal* teams do it."

Mary, listening intently agreed.

"That's what we need to do; we need to be more efficient when we go into these places."

"Swat team style it is then, we'll enter in single file in the same order as we entered the surplus store. We'll keep our rifles to our shoulders so we won't have to waste time raising them up to shoot," I said.

"I don't know what the laws were in Texas regarding silencers before the plague, but if we happen across any at a gun shop, we could sure use them," I said.

"I thought silencers were illegal?" Mary said.

"Only in the movies," I answered with a smile. "If I'd known this apocalypse was going to happen, I would have done the federal paperwork and purchased a couple. The laws go state by state. With the proper paperwork, they were legal in Missouri and many other states. Of course now they're legal everywhere, everything is legal everywhere now."

"That's good to know, if they *were* legal in Texas we might be able to find some. I'll keep my eye out for them if we ever run across a gun shop that we feel is safe to stop at," Mary stated.

"Yeah, silent and long range both, that would be cool!" Jacob added with a smile, itching to get his hands on a sound suppressor.

"In the mean time, hand me that tomahawk you found," I said to Jacob. "I want to check out my new eater exterminating device."

We traveled south for a while, dodging abandon vehicles and observing packs of zombies stumbling through the countryside. Nobody said much as we drove along.

Then Mary asked me.

"You were curious about my friendship with Megan, so I told you how it is. Now I'm curious about something," she said.

266

"What?" I answered, as I concentrated on avoiding a group of relinquished cars.

"Back there at the surplus store you killed that man and that woman without giving them a chance. I wondered how you feel about that?" Mary asked coldly.

How I really felt, was annoyed at her question, but I tried not to show it.

"The man was stealing our water, and the woman was running at me with a knife, what would you have done?" I answered, nonchalantly. "Let him have our water, and let the woman kill you?"

"No," she answered sheepishly.

"Look Mary, we're trying to survive, and I plan to do anything and everything I have to do to keep us alive," I said sternly. "We've all had to do things we didn't want to do, things that we would have never even thought of doing a couple of months ago, and we've all made mistakes. If not hesitating to kill that man and woman was a mistake, that's just too bad for them. We learned early on, shoot first and clean up the mess later is the best way to make it through this hellish world we're in. Even if we regret doing something later, at least we're still around to regret it. Besides, not one of them made any attempt to communicate with us. They sneaked up behind that car while we were in the surplus store, because they weren't there when we pulled up to the front of the building. Then they tried to steal our water, so they got what they deserved," I said, casually aiming our truck at what looked to me like a *family* of three zombies in the middle of the road. The family consisted of the husband, a burly man while he was still alive, his wife, a well-built and probably good-looking

267

female in her more *lively* days, and their small male child of grade school age.

The thud of the already dead pedestrian's bodies hitting the large chrome bumper of our truck, and the slight jostle of the steering wheel as the front tires crushed my targeted victims, acknowledged my aim was true and I hadn't lost my touch.

"See everyone, that's how it's done, three less eaters we have to worry about, that's the way we have to look at it," I said. "If I could hit every single one of them I would."

"I would too!" Mary agreed, nodding her head.

The death of the undead family I had just run over, and my statement relating to the previous events that had just taken place that day, seemed to satisfy Mary's annoying curiosity about how I felt concerning my survival tactics, and ended our discussion of the matter.

We hadn't seen any predatory dogs since we had escaped the roving pack that had attacked us before crossing the bridge at Vicksburg.

As we journeyed southbound still heading toward the city of Galveston that scenario began to change.

The further south we got, the more we began to see feral dog packs, one of which was very large.

"Look over there!" Jacob shouted, alerting us to the distant danger. "Dogs, and a lot of them, look, passed those trees, you see um?"

Beyond a small wooded area about nine hundred to a thousand yards away from the freeway, Jacob had spotted a large pack of feral dogs.

"There must be fifty or sixty of them, and there're some more over there." Gin said, pointing to another smaller group that was trailing the main pack of wild mongrels.

"I think we'd need more than a mini-gun if we ran into a pack that size," I said, pushing the accelerator pedal down slightly.

"They're pretty far away, I don't think we have anything to worry about," Jacob said confidently.

"Those dogs would close the gap between us and them in a matter of minutes," Gin added, looking intently at the dogs.

"Well, we're not going to stop to find out," I said. "They're not paying any attention to us, they probably haven't noticed us, we'll just keep going and put some serious distance between them and us."

"That works for me," Gin insisted.

"Me too!" Mary added.

Houston was the biggest city we would have to go through on our way to Galveston, and it wouldn't be too awful long before we would be at its city limits.

"Clyde said not to go through Dallas, I wonder if Houston is going to be any better?" Gin asked.

I could tell by the look on her face that she thought she already knew the answer to that question. I didn't want to tell her that I was thinking the same thing, but I was.

"I hope it's better than Dallas, at least better than the way Clyde made it sound," I answered, trying to make Clyde's warning sound overblown. "He probably exaggerated a bit, you know how people are."

"I know how people used to be," Gin answered softly, and then she added. "I sure hope he was exaggerating."

"Besides," I said. "The Houston area is not nearly as big as the Dallas-Fort Worth area is, we'll have that going for us anyway."

Gin looked down at the map she had unfolded on her lap and said. "It's still a big city, and according to this, we're going to find out pretty soon one way or another."

Gin was absolutely correct, within two hours we were finding out, and what we found out, we didn't like.

We were inside Houston's city limits, about seven miles past highway 99, when there seemed to be an inexplicable shortage of discarded vehicles on the road. Gin was the first to observe the mysterious lack of obstacles in our path, and commented.

"This is nice for a change; we don't have to weave around a bunch of cars. I was getting sea sick with all of that swaying back and forth."

The whole time we had been on the road after we dumped the Morphodite, the only stretch of road that was not littered with wrecked or abandoned vehicles, was in the middle of nowhere as we drove toward Dallas. Now we were entering a large metropolitan area, and there were no cars on the road?

"Something not right, I've got a bad feeling about this, there're no cars, there're no trucks, and notice too, there are no eaters. I don't see any dogs either, something's up," I argued. "Everyone get your guns ready, something's going on."

The sound of metal slamming against metal filled the air inside our cab, as the slides of our firearms were racked and safeties were disengaged in preparation and anticipation of an imminent battle.

270

My sixth sense of impending doom was verified, when we rounded a turn after passing under the highway 8 overpass.

"There's the answer," I shouted, as we saw a huge blockade of cars, stacked one upon another, four cars high, and who knows how many cars deep.

The silhouettes of men with rifles lined the top of the stacks of cars, and clicking sounds could be heard as chips of paint and small pieces of metal ricocheted off our windshield, as bullets slammed into the hood of our truck.

Even though I had already slowed down while I tried to figure why there was such a lack of cars on the road. We were still going fast enough to cause the tires to send up a large plume of smoke and cause the truck to slide sideways when I slammed on the brakes.

We came to a stop, setting sideways in the middle of the road, surrounded in a cloud of white smoke from the friction-burnt tires. Sprays of steam shot from the front of the trucks grill caused by the bullet holes in the radiator, adding to the surrounding smoke screen.

"They're shooting at us," Gin screamed, already ducking down behind the dashboard.

With the damage the truck had already incurred, I knew that it wouldn't be in running condition for long. The attack had not stopped when I threw the truck into the third of eighteen gears available, and tromped down onto the gas pedal. I turned the steering wheel hard to the left, and amidst the hail of bullets still raining down on us from the towering lofts of our ambusher's scrap metal fortress wall, we took off back in the direction that we had came.

Streams of sunlight were now darting into the cab from the holes made by the bullets that penetrated the rear wall of our truck. We rounded the curve in the road that had previously hidden the ambuscade from us, and the ping of projectiles promptly ceased.

"Is anyone hurt," Gin quickly asked, setting up in her seat again.

"Mary's hurt, she caught one in her arm," Billy answered, poking his head out of the sleeper.

"How bad is it," I asked, now fighting to steer our crippled truck.

Mary stuck her head out of the sleeper.

"Not bad, I'll live," she said. "They just grazed me, it's just a flesh wound, I'll be all right."

"Is everyone else okay?" Gin inquired, concerned for the safety of her two sons.

"We're fine, but I heard a couple of bullets go by my head: that was a close one," Jacob answered, sticking his head out too.

"The truck's shot up pretty bad; it's not going to make it very far. It's got at least three flat tires, one of them is on the front, I can barely steer this thing. Our radiator is all shot up too, and we're losing water fast," I told them. "We're going to drive this thing as far away from those guys as it will take us. Then we'll be on foot again."

As far away as it will take us, was about three miles from those dry-gulcher's. By then, the tires that were flat were now shredded and we were riding on their rims, as we had done in the Hummer after the prisoners had attacked us. Two other tires were going flat and almost there. The radiator was completely out of coolant, and

272

the needle on the heat gage was pegged at its maximum. Our overheated engine was beginning to sputter as its pistons labored to fight against the friction and we came to a stop.

"That's it people, time to bail, the trucks done," I announced, turning the engine off. "Grab your stuff, just what you're willing to carry, leave everything else, and watch for eaters."

We got out of the truck, and after grabbing our essentials, we quickly surveyed the damage to the truck.

"Lots of bullet holes," Billy said.

"Yeah, lots of bullet holes in our water supply too," Mary added, adjusting the makeshift bandage Jacob had made from one of his mother's left over uniforms.

"We'll take what's left, we couldn't carry it all anyway," Gin said, stuffing several bottles into her pack. "Everyone grab some, as usual we don't know when we'll find more."

I was worried that the people that had ambushed us might decide to follow us, considering that we hadn't fired as much as one single shot back at them, they might feel emboldened because of it. Moreover, with the amount of bullet holes in our truck, I knew that they were serious assholes.

"We need to get away from here now, get your things," I ordered. "We need to get off the road."

Totting what supplies we could carry, we scurried off the highway, backtracking slightly.

"Stop here and get behind the safety guard rail, and put everything down except your guns," I said. "And do it quick."

I could hear the rumbling of a vehicle coming from the direction of the ambush.

"I think they're coming," Billy said, also hearing the rumbling sound.

"Get ready, let's see how they like being ambushed, and remember, if you're on the left side shoot the one on the left side and work your way to the middle, the opposite goes if you're on the right side," I told them.

As we waited, hidden behind the tall grass and weeds that grew underneath the safety barrier, the rumbling grew louder and then we could see them approaching. An open bed truck with several men in the back, all armed with assault rifles of different varieties.

"As soon as they stop, open fire," I whispered.

The truck heavily laden with bushwhackers began to slow down as it approached our bullet riddled and smoking semi-tractor.

"Find them!" A tall man wearing an army uniform bellowed.

The flat bed stopped, and as we had prearranged, before the first man could jump from the truck bed, we open fire on them.

Rapidly firing our semi-automatic rifles into the crowd that stood on the wooden platform of the truck, the ambushers had been taken completely by surprise and the men began to drop. Most were killed instantly, and many were wounded, however, some were able to jump down and find cover on the far side of their truck.

Our position offered us concealment, but not much cover, so I decided to move farther to my right in an effort to flank the remaining enemy before they could move to a more advantageous position.

"Keep your heads down," I yelled, motioning for them to move down to a lower area as I crawled into a flanking position.

I hadn't quite reached the optimum point where I could end this firefight, when I saw the first zombie stand up in the back of the truck, and then another, and another.

The ambusher's we had initially killed, had turned, and were now attacking the wounded and the men that had taken refuge from our bullets behind their truck.

There were two men inside the truck, the driver, and a passenger. Neither of them had exited the truck or fired a weapon at us. However, I could see that both men were starting to panic.

One of their previous living comrades had grabbed the driver while still on the deck of the truck, and was attempting to climb through the driver's window from there.

We had stopped shooting by now, and the remainder of the bushwhacker's that were still able to fire a weapon were busy fending off the ever growing population of zombies that were trying to *harvest* them.

With the driver incapacitated while fighting to defend himself, the truck did not move. The man that was riding shotgun could see the situation deteriorating rapidly; his companions were dying all around him, and then coming back to *undead life* and killing more of his friends. In his panicked state, while trying to release the driver of the truck from his former buddy's grasp, he fired his rifle at the groping zombie. At that moment, the zombie jerked on the driver's arm and pulled his head directly into the path of the bullet. The man's head literally exploded, covering the inside of the truck, along with the passenger and the undead intruder, with blood, clumps of hair, pieces of skull, and chunks of brain, (you know, the usual mess). This event sent the surviving man in the truck into an even greater panicked state, and sent his zombie friend into even more of a frantic feeding frenzy as it tasted some of the driver's blood that had landed in its mouth. This spelled doom for the man in the shotgun seat, for he was unable to fight off the unwavering advances of his famished former friend.

"There are more eaters coming up behind us!" Mary yelled, as she pointed in the direction of a group of curious zombies attracted by the gunfire and stumbling their way toward what they hoped would be their next meal.

Again, the sound of gunplay had alerted a horde of roving dead and hungry cannibals to our activity, and they were quickly making their way to our position.

"We're going to have to take care of all of them, we don't want any of them following us," I yelled.

The gunfire from the truck had ceased, all that had arrived alive, were now dead and undead, the only sound coming from the direction of the truck was the sound of the zombies snarling, slurping, and growling, as they chewed on and devoured their fallen brethren.

I motioned to the others to converge on the truck by pointing to my AK, and then to the truck. There were about seven eaters devouring the bloody remains of our attackers, with one or two more waiting in the wings to be reanimated and join the group of the hungry undead.

"Jacob, Mary, come with me, Billy you stay with your mother," I ordered, as I climbed over the guardrail.

"Head shots for all, let's get this done quick, the other bushwhacker's must have heard all the shooting. Hell, everyone else did."

With our guns at the ready, the three of us walked up to the zombie feast and delivered to each and every head, moving or not, a single bullet to the brain.

"Mary, go to our truck and grab the bolt cutters, and while you're at it, get one of the uniforms that didn't fit Gin. With that shirt you're wearing, you stuck out like a sore thumb in that green grass, we're lucky they didn't see us," I said, calmly, but firmly.

Jacob and I kept watch while Mary went back to our truck and retrieved the items that I had requested, she soon returned, and we all rejoined Billy and Gin.

"It's about time," Billy said snidely, half joking. "Those eaters down there are almost here, and there're some more on the other side of the road coming this way."

"Let's get our stuff, it's time to go back into silent mode," I said, picking up an ammo box, and pulling out my newly acquired, and as of yet, unused tomahawk.

We engaged the approaching small horde of zombies in a single file formation. I led the way carving a path through the middle of them, and dividing them into two even smaller groups as I christened my new tomahawk with the blood of the undead. The rest of our troop cut them down one by one as they stumbled their way around the fallen zombies that I had dispatched.

"This tomahawk is a good tool for eradicating eaters, it penetrates their skull far enough to kill their brain, but doesn't go in far enough to get stuck, works great," I admitted, while planting the small ax in the head of the last zombie in front of me.

"I'll stick to my sickle," Billy said, jerking the long concave blade vertically through the face of a once attractive twenty-something woman that had just snapped at his arm.

In moments, we had hacked down the rest of the zombies in the horde, and with the latest threat neutralized; we hurried to pick up our belongings and leave the area.

"I think it would be wise if we used a little bit of misdirection at this point," I suggested. "If those men we killed back there don't return to their base in a few minutes, their friends are going to come looking for them, and we don't want to leave a trail of dead eaters for them to follow."

"How are we going to misdirect them?" Jacob asked.

I slung my AK over my shoulder, picked up one of the bags containing our food, and began to walk west.

"We want to go south, so we'll walk west for a hundred yards or so," I shouted as I walked.

"What are you yelling for?" Gin asked, befuddled by my behavior.

"Yeah, Dad, I thought we were in silent mode!" Jacob contended.

"He's wants to draw in some more eaters," Mary asserted, in her usual monotone way.

"It's working, look, there are four more of them coming this way," Billy said, pointing to the northwest.

"Perfect," I said, turning toward the four approaching zombies and increasing my pace.

"Someone catch up and help me!" I shouted, once more dropping my supplies.

I stopped in an area under an on ramp that could be seen from the location of the two trucks we had just left. Partially covered with gravel, and where the grass and weeds were mostly shaded from the afternoon sun, it was the ideal place to butcher the oncoming zombies and try to mislead any ambushers that might try to follow us.

Mary was the first to join me, followed by Billy. The three of us waited in the small clearing for the four hungry zombies to arrive.

"Back to silent mode," I said, shaking my tomahawk in the air *Indian style* in a continuing effort to attract the approaching decomposing savages.

One by one, the zombies broke through the dense brush into the clearing, and one by one, they were destroyed with sharp forced trauma to their brains.

"Step in their blood, and follow me," I ordered Mary and Jacob, as I drenched the soles of my boots in zombie blood.

Without questioning my directive, they followed my lead and walked through the puddles of quickly coagulating blood.

We set out in the same northwesterly direction that the zombies had appeared from, leaving a trail of bloody footprints in the grass.

The zombie's blood soon was wiped from our boot soles by the tall grass, but we walked several more yards, crushing and bending down the brush until we came to the beginning of the on ramp under which we had eliminated the four zombies, and which ultimately led to the pavement covered streets of Houston.

Backtracking our way back to Jacob and Gin at the clearing, we resumed our journey south, being careful to leave no sign of our true direction of travel.

Twenty minutes later, the sound of a vehicle broke through the noise of our panting, as we trudged along lugging our supplies by hand.

"Hear that, it sounds like another truck," Gin said, stopping to listen.

We were traveling parallel to the interstate highway that we had been ambushed on earlier. Only a few hundred yards to the east, we could see another flatbed truck also filled with men, speeding down the road in route to the spot of our earlier firefight.

"Get down everyone," I ordered, dropping to one knee.

Everyone knelt down quickly, and we watched the truck pass by.

"I don't think they saw us," Mary concluded.

As the truck drove out of sight, Jacob stood up and said. "Yeah, they didn't see us, they would have stopped."

"Maybe," I said, standing up myself. "We don't know much about them, we know that they shot at us, and then sent more men after us when they failed to stop us at their road block. I think they cleared the highway of vehicles, and used those vehicles to build their wall of cars. I also think they cleared the area of eaters and feral dogs. If they have the resources to do that, we certainly don't want to under estimate them," I pointed out.

"We don't know for sure that they did all of that," Billy quibbled.

"That's right we don't, do you want to make camp here and see if they show up. I'm sure they'll be very pleased to see us, maybe we'll all sit around a campfire and sing Kumbaya together," I said sarcastically.

"I get it Dad, we can't take any chances," Billy retorted.

"While we're stopped here, Gin, you and Mary get into those camo uniforms, we didn't get them so you could carry them all over hell creation, we got them so you could wear them," I prompted, thinking we all might need a short rest anyway.

We turned our backs and the girls complied without an argument, which actually surprised me. They put on the uniforms and when they were finished, they started acting a little giddy.

They began to compare the air force camouflage pattern they were wearing, with my multi-cam pattern, Jacob's army digital camo, and Billy's old school Viet Nam camouflage. They said they thought theirs was a much better color, it went well with Mary's blue eyes, and they said how well it blended with the surrounding vegetation. I thought it might have been because in the new world we were in, anything that reminded us of how it used to be before the outbreak, like getting new clothes, was a welcome diversion from the gruesome reality we were living. It didn't really matter why they seemed happy, it was enough that the new uniforms gave them a bit of pleasure, and for a moment took their minds off whatever they might be imaging could be ahead of us, or behind us.

We now looked like a rag tag bunch of third world rebel soldiers, fighting against some oppressive banana republic government. But the reality of the situation was. We were one of many small oppressive governments across the nation, and probably across the world, fighting for our lives on a daily basis against a cannibalistic rebel enemy of unknown origin, unknown numbers, and unknown locations, which at times, unwittingly collaborated with other small oppressive governments just like us, in their effort to defeat us.

"You two look very paramilitary," I told Mary and Gin. "I'm proud to have you in my unit."

The girls giggled at my remark, and did their best to do a proper salute.

"Okay, enough messing around, we can't take any chances remember," Billy reminded, picking up his share of the supplies and ammo.

I bent down, reached for the items that I had been allocated to carry, and reiterated his comment.

"He's right; we need to get moving right now."

Walking in single file for what seemed like miles, I kept looking back over my shoulder checking for the bushwhackers that might be following us. After several hours of walking, we found ourselves far from the freeway, and far from any vegetation that vaguely matched any of our uniforms. We were in the heart of what you might call the uptown area. Small business storefronts, parking lots, drive thru banks and numerous other buildings ripe for the picking. However, with no means of transportation, we were already carrying as much as possible, and the load was wearing us down.

"Nothing but good news people, looks like we've found plenty of places to sleep tonight. Vehicles are starting to become abundant again," I said, pointing at the buildings ahead.

Just then, a very tall zombie appeared from an alleyway.

"I spoke too soon; there is some bad news right here in front of us."

I pulled my tomahawk from the matching multi-cam tactical vest that we had absconded with as part of the equipment we acquired from the military surplus store.

"Be ready, you know there's always more than just one," I warned, while approaching the giant stumbling menace.

I timed my swipe at the zombie so that my tomahawk impacted its skull between its off balance lurches. As the small ax dug a thin four-inch slit in the cranium of the zombie, two more of the undead appeared from the same alleyway.

These two new zombies were children; girls, one about eight, and the smaller one looked like it was barely old enough to be able to walk, maybe one and a half, or two years old at the most.

Mary had run up beside me ready to slay any zombies that might pose a threat, but seeing the baby zombie, she stopped dead in her tracks, paralyzed in some kind of self-induced trance.

Jacob stepped forward; leaped over the once towering zombie I had just put down, and stuck his sickle into the side of the eight year olds head.

The horizontal swing was powerful, but not well placed. Jacob's weapon had embedded itself directly behind the little girls jaw, and the point of the blade had exited out the other side of her face directly behind her jaw and right below her ear on the opposite side, completely missing her brain and leaving her a fully functioning pissed-off little zombie bitch.

Jacob was able to hold her at a distance by maintaining a firm grip on his sickle's handle, and keeping his arm straight.

Mary was still self-immobilized, frozen in some kind of panic, or fear, or disbelief, or something, whatever was holding her back from defending herself against the attack was irrelevant at that moment, although the baby was sickeningly freaky looking and small, it was still dangerous, and it was about to reach Mary.

My son Jacob, was struggling with his zombie, and losing ground. Billy and Gin were nowhere in sight now, and Mary was about to die at the hand of a vicious two year old miniature mutant.

I had to make a decision, I had to choose between saving my son I'd known and loved for sixteen years, or saving Mary, a girl I had met only a few days before.

This is the kind of situation that induces a phenomenon, called *Tacky Psyche*. I had experienced this phenomenon fully on two other occasions in my life. Once, when I accidentally pulled out in front of a car that was going about forty miles an hour, and another time during a sparring match at a karate class I was attending.

Tacky Psyche gives you the sensation or illusion of time slowing down. Everything around you begins to move in slow motion, some people say that time really does slow down; others say that it's an illusion, and that your brain just makes you think everything is slowing down.

I personally think that sometimes during times of extreme stress, or impending bodily harm, your brain speeds up its thought process so much in an effort to avoid the danger, that everything around you seems to slow down, and you seem to be watching the action, and reacting to the action, but you're detached from the actual time involved in performing the action.

In any case, when it does happen, Tacky Psyche allows you to do phenomenal things, things that you would not normally be able to do. It allows you to be in the "Zone" so to speak.

In an instant, I drifted into the realm of Tacky Psyche for the third time in my life; my choice was clear as I bolted toward Jacob. I seemed to be watching from a different dimension as my tomahawk smashed into the top of the eight year olds skull with astonishing speed and gargantuan force, stopping only when it collided with Jacob's embedded sickle.

Then I turned to the baby and watched her in slow motion fall and grab onto Mary's leg, and bury her teeth into Mary's shin. The pain of the bite quickly awakened Mary from her stupor, and with her left hand, she slapped the little girl as hard as she could in the side of her face, knocking her from her leg and onto the sidewalk face down.

Mary raised her left foot and stomped down hard on the back of the baby's head, slamming her small teeth into the concrete and flattening her nose. As Mary raised her foot again to give the baby zombie a second blow, I buried my tomahawk into the top of Mary's head, killing her instantly.

Then, just as sudden as it had begun, the Tacky Psyche phenomenon was gone. Mary's body dropped down across the two year old in real time, and pinned her to the ground. I lifted my foot and delivered the second blow to the head of the little zombie toddler, that I had denied Mary, crushing both the front and the back of the baby's skull, and putting an end to the macabre scene.

Don't misunderstand, Tacky Psyche doesn't turn you into a stone cold killing machine, killing Mary was my choice, and my choice alone.

Tacky Psyche is more of a state of mind. Your body reacts faster than usual because your brain is reacting faster than usual. The information that your brain is taking in is processed many times faster than normal, which kind of gives you a sense of having an out of the body experience, or like watching the action as if you were watching a television show close-up and in 3D. However, you still have complete control over your movements.

I then turned my attention toward finding Billy and Gin.

"Billy, Gin?" I called out in a loud whisper that received no reply.

I called again.

"Billy, Gin?"

"We're right here honey," Gin answered, stepping out of a doorway two storefronts behind me.

Relieved to see my wife, but concerned about my older son, I asked. "Where's Billy?"

"Right here Dad," Billy answered, as he too stepped out of the same doorway. "We had to deal with a couple of eaters that were about to come out of this store."

"What's wrong with Jacob? Is he all right, why is he kneeling down, is he hurt?" Gin asked looking back and forth at Jacob and me.

Jacob had watched while I put down the eight-year-old zombie with extreme bias, then planted my tomahawk into Mary's brain, and finally ended the battle by finishing off the maniacal baby with the heel of my boot.

He was now kneeling at Mary's side.

As we approached, Jacob asked. "Why did you kill Mary Dad?"

"She got bit son, you saw her get bit," I answered.

Jacob pulled Mary's pant leg up, exposing her leg.

"But, the bite didn't break the skin, see," Jacob answered sharply, pointing to Mary's unmarked bare leg.

"I saw the eater bite her; I thought she was infected, sorry. If she hadn't froze, she'd still be alive, she almost cost you your life. Better her than one of us, and if she was still with us, the next time it might have been one of us," I said in my own defense, feeling no remorse for what I'd just done.

Jacob looked up at me, obviously not pleased with my decision.

"You could have waited, and checked her wound before you killed her," he said.

"You know how fast they can change, and Mary was quite a good fighter, it was her or us, I chose us, it's that simple," I responded, starting to get annoyed. "She's dead now, there's nothing we can do about it."

"You two stop arguing, we need to find a place to sleep tonight, it'll be dark soon, we need to find someplace safe," Gin said, asserting her authority.

I helped Jacob to his feet as he grabbed Mary's machete, and we began to search for a place to sleep.

We decided that one of the stores in this neighborhood would have to do; as sunset was approaching quickly, and spending the night out in the open in a zombie infested urban environment was not an option, so we started looking for a shop that had a door that was still intact, and wasn't locked.

"Here, what about this one," Billy said in a low voice. "It's open and the door looks good."

Billy had found a shop that was just what we were looking for, it had a good unbroken door, and it wasn't locked. Plus, the shop had one more thing, transportation, it was a bicycle shop.

"This is perfect," Jacob said, already getting over Mary's premature death. "I miss my bicycle, are we going to ride bikes the rest of the way to Galveston?"

Looking at the large selection of two-wheeled transportation in front of us, I answered in the affirmative.

"I think we should give it a try, at least until we can find another car or truck. But first we need to make sure there aren't any eaters in here."

After searching through the shop and finding no zombies inside, we secured the front and back doors, and using what little sunlight that was left, we examined the assortment of bicycles that was now available to us. We each found a suitable bike that we thought would serve our purpose, and pulled it off the rack. Darkness fell as we separated our choice of new bicycles from the others and prepared an area to sleep.

The night passed, and we all got a good night's sleep for a change, no zombies came knocking, no one in the group died, well, not counting Mary, and no humans tried to kill or capture us.

The next morning, we woke up refreshed and ready to travel.

"My bike has a flat tire, no wait, two flat tires," Gin whined.

"They probably all do, there'll be a bicycle pump around here someplace," Jacob said confidently.

He looked around the room.

"Over there on the wall, there're a bunch of them."

We all walked over to the display wall and helped ourselves to one pump each; we retrieved the bike of our choice and began to inflate the tires.

"To bad we're not in a motorcycle shop," Billy remarked. "That would be really cool if we all had choppers."

"Personally, I think, except for extreme emergencies, you would have to be out of your mind to try to traverse a zombie apocalypse on a motorcycle, especially riding single on one.

There are several advantages that you would have riding a motorcycle. It's true you can go places that you couldn't go in a car or truck, you can maneuver through tight spaces that you can't in a larger vehicle, and being a lighter and more powerful machine (for the most part anyway, power to weight ratio and all) you could leave the scene of an attack faster. However, there are some huge disadvantages you would have while riding one solo.

One of which being, you have absolutely no protection around you, no doors, no windows, no nothing to keep the eaters away from you. Another being, it is very difficult to handle a weapon of any kind while trying to maintain control of a motorcycle, unless you're only going in a straight line and maintaining the same speed," I knowingly informed them, having at one time owned a motorcycle before the plague devastated our world.

"So, you want us to ride a bicycle?" Gin interjected, rolling her eyes.

"A bicycle is a different story. A bike is not nearly as heavy as motorcycle, you're able to ride a bicycle easily with one hand on the handlebars, and you can stop a bicycle faster, and either hold it up with your legs, or just jump off and fight on your feet if you need to, without getting hurt. A bicycle can carry a small amount of your supplies, strapped either to the handlebars, or on the back fender, or both. The only disadvantages that a bicycle has compared to a motorcycle, is speed, and of course, you have to pedal it. So when there's a choice between riding a bicycle, or riding a motorcycle, in my opinion the bike is the better choice. However in this case, the choice is between riding a bicycle and walking, I say we ride," I explained at length. "I'm tired of carrying all this stuff."

"I'm with you," Gin agreed.

"Me too," said Jacob, excited to get to ride a bike.

With the bikes packed and ready to go, we ate a small breakfast and checked the map.

"I think going that way is our best bet, what do you think?" I asked Gin, after showing her on the map the route I had chosen.

"Looks good to me, considering I have no idea what the roads are like, or how many hills we'll have to ride up, or any of that stuff, so of course it looks good to me," Gin said in a comical sarcastic tone.

I hoped she would be in the same good mood after the first hill we'd have to pedal up.

A quick check of the street, and the all clear was sounded; we wheeled our new rides out of the bicycle shop and into the street.

"I haven't been on a bicycle in quite a while, I'm a little rickety," Gin admitted as she rode along in a serpentine motion.

It wasn't long before we got to test my theory on how much easier it is to fight off zombies on a bicycle, as opposed to a motorcycle.

Three blocks from the bike shop, we ran into a rabble of the undead killers, probably twenty or so, I'm not sure of the exact number, we didn't bother to count them.

We stopped at first to assess the situation, and then decided that the best course of action was to ride through the thinnest part of the horde as fast as possible and dodge as many as we could.

"Get your cutting weapons ready, dodge them if you can, but don't take any chances, this isn't a game, if they get to close, slice them," I warned. "Stay together and pedal hard, let's go."

The zombies were scattered, not clumped in a tight group, which allowed us to maneuver through them at a fairly high rate of speed. As usual, our first weapon of choice was our silent edged weapons, saving the loud zombie attracting firearms for absolute emergencies.

This time I didn't lead the way, I wanted to bring up the rear so I could keep an eye on everyone else, and be there to help if needed.

Jacob went into the crowd first, and then Gin and Billy, followed by me.

Jacob weaved his way through the zombies quickly and without a problem. Gin's prowess on a bicycle left much more to be desired. She made it passed the first few lumbering zombies without putting herself in any danger; however, about a third of the way through, her lack of riding skill became apparent. She was starting to make some bad decisions on the best route to take to avoid the onslaught of assaulting dead ruffians of which most had seen us by this point.

As I watched her ride closer and closer to the menacing killers, I wasted no time in an effort to close the gap between us and keep from becoming a victim myself. I pulled up behind her, not daring to pull alongside her because of her wobbly movements. To collide with her in the middle of a zombie horde would mean certain death for us both.

However, riding behind her, all I could do was watch, so I decided to quickly go around her and fend off any zombies that were close.

As I rode by her, I yelled. "Follow me!"

Hoping that she could maintain her balance and I could lead her through the furious mob to safety, I aimed for a gap in the group of savage beasts. But to get to that gap, first I had to eliminate one of the zombies that blocked my way.

"Go around me!" I yelled to Gin, as I rode my bike directly into the zombie, planting my front wheel into the dead man's crotch.

Timing was critical; the impact caused the zombie to bend at the waist, forcing its slobbering mouth and snapping teeth over the handlebars directly at my face.

At the exact moment of the collision, I jumped off the back of my bike, pushing it farther into the famished dead brute's body. With the accuracy of a skilled surgeon, I swung my tomahawk diagonally across his head at the same time, chipping off the top of his skull and exposing the maniac's now partially dissected brain.

The zombie fell on top of my bicycle, pinning it to the street, leaving me without transportation.

Now on foot, I saw that my family had all made it to safety beyond the horde, and had stopped to wait for me. I on the other hand, had managed with my bicycle circus antics, to attract the attention of most of the hungry jaywalking barbarians who saw me as a very tasty morning meal.

"Hurry honey," I heard Gin scream, as the ferocious cannibals encircle me.

"There're too many of them Dad, use your gun," Jacob shouted, just before I heard his carbine's violent report.

Taking his advice, I reached for my pistol as the two zombies closest to me fell to the ground; Jacob's aim had been true.

I fired my pistol, dropping another zombie in its tracks.

Gin and Billy had now joined in the fight, and the sound of gunfire echoed through the streets bouncing off the hard surfaces of the buildings, and announcing our location to the world as numerous zombies fell around me.

With the now dead, undead scattered about, I pulled my bicycle from underneath the slain zombie that had trapped it there, and quickly rode to join my family.

Reaching my family, I said. "We need to find another way to travel, this isn't working for me."

"It sure isn't working for me," Gin said, frowning and shaking her head.

Billy mounted his bike and added. "All that noise is going to attract more eaters, let's go."

Billy was right; the noise did attract more zombies, and possibly something even worse. The sound of our gunfire had alerted the men that had ambushed us earlier, to the fact that we were in the area.

Although we didn't know it at the time, the ambushers hadn't given up, they were still tracking us. Our bloody misdirection ruse had only served to delay the inevitable, and they were able to find our true direction of travel despite our best efforts.

Because the ambushers hadn't caught up to us yet, we had naively thought that our deception had worked and they had no idea where we had gone. That wrong assumption could have been our ultimate undoing.

Maybe our bicycle ride that took a turn in a southerly direction due to another zombie attack was a blessing in disguise. It forced us almost immediately to realize that I had been wrong about traveling by bicycle, and compelled us to look urgently for a motorized form of transportation.

Setting out again, we pedaled hard to depart the area and distance ourselves from the epicenter of noise we had created during our most recent encounter with the living dead. Not to mention the few rotting corpses that we hadn't killed that were hot on our trail and still having visions of inviting us to brunch. Never realizing that we were also running for our lives from a group of men that were determined to catch us and get even for what, in their minds was the mass murder of their fellow comrades, even though it was their effort to dry-gulch us at their roadblock that had started the whole fiasco in the first place.

It's funny how that always seems to be the case, when it comes to revenge.

Our sprint to leave the area afforded us enough of a gap between both groups of killers, the group of homicidal maniacal zombies that were meandering around and following the sounds that their food source was making, and the group of homicidal maniacal humans that were trailing us, bent on inflicting their misplaced vengeance. It was due to that gap that we were able to stop frequently and check for a suitable vehicle to replace our bicycles.

"We need to find a company that used a fleet of vehicles, like a taxi company, or a delivery service," I said, hoping we would find something before we ran into another large group of zombies.

We rode along for a while longer, checking cars and trucks to no avail. Then Gin announced she had solved our problem.

"I've found the answer to our vehicle quest," she said, pointing to a post office a half a block away.

"That should do the trick honey, plenty of trucks, plenty of gas, and most important, plenty of keys," I contended.

Arriving at the post office, we rode to the back of the building where the mail trucks were parked.

"Jackpot," Jacob yelled, pointing to a tractor-trailer rig.

"Keep your voice down," Gin scolded. "Eaters will hear you."

"Sorry, jackpot!" Jacob said, this time whispering.

Jackpot it was, not only did the truck have a half-full tank of fuel; it also had the keys in the ignition and a charged battery.

"We're not going to get any luckier than this," Billy said, climbing behind the driver's seat. "No sleeper unit in it, but it's got an area back here that one or maybe two of us can sleep in."

"Gin, grab our stuff off of the bikes and put it in the truck, Jacob, come with me and I'll show you how to release the trailer from the fifth wheel," I directed, as I walked to the trailer.

I pointed out the crank on the trailer that raises and lowers the small steel wheels that allows the trailer to stand when you pull the tractor away.

"Crank this and lower these little wheels," I told Jacob. "They need to be lowered far enough to slightly raise the front of the trailer; that takes the pressure off of the fifth wheel."

"Are you the new drivers?" A voice blurted out from the loading dock. "I've been waiting for you to get here; we've got a lot of mail that has to go out."

A short rotund woman stepped close to the edge of the dock. She was dressed in an oversized letter carriers uniform that was *obviously* not issued to her. Her dirty brown hair hung down across half of her greasy pimple covered face. She swept it aside with her ink stained hand, only to have it fall back again impairing her vision on her right side.

"You need to get out of those civilian clothes and into your uniforms, you can't deliver the mail looking like that," she insisted, pushing her hair back again.

Billy and Gin stayed in the truck and said nothing, while Jacob and I walked slowly toward the woman.

"Yeah, we're going to get right on that," I answered.

"Well you need to hurry, the mails already late going out," she responded.

"She's crazy, just like that freak on the boat," Jacob whispered, trying not to move his lips.

"Indeed," I called to her, answering her and Jacob at the same time.

"Did they leave you to cover this shift by yourself?" I asked her, trying to see if she was alone.

"Yes they did, they let all of the slackers leave and told me to take care of everything, so now that you drivers are finally here, we'll get the mail moving. But you can't take those guns with you on your route, that's against the rules, you'll have to leave them here," she said, pulling her hair away from her eyes once more.

My tolerance for these roving nut cases had reached its limit. I smiled, and walked over to the edge of the four-foot high loading dock, and as I climb up, I asked the obviously fake postal worker.

"Where do you keep the uniforms?"

"This way," she said, turning toward the door.

Seizing the opportunity, I pulled my pistol from its holster, and stuck the barrel of the gun against the back of her head and pulled the trigger, firing one shot into the obese woman's brain execution style. Her dense oily hair blew away from her scalp as the blaze from the muzzle blast of my gun pushed it aside, and ignited the outer layers of her unwashed hair. The corpulent postal imposter fell forward, her arms at her side, and her hair now on fire.

"I didn't know that you could do that, must have been because of all the oil in her hair," I said, rejoining Jacob.

Gin and Billy had witnessed my impromptu execution of the woman and chose too mostly ignore the heinous act. The only comment made, was by Gin, who said. "Did you have to use your gun? Now we need to hurry and get away from here too."

Jacob had also watched the demise of the fat lady, and as usual added his two cents.

"Wow Dad, that reminded me of Mary," he said, shaking his head to show his disapproval.

Not disapproving of me killing the fat girl at the post office, and setting her hair on fire, but as a reminder of what I had done to Mary.

"Killing Mary was an accident, Jake, I told you, I was sure she had been bitten," I responded. "What I just did here was a mercy killing, partly for her, and partly for us.

I'm tired of dealing with these people that have gone insane, and having to wonder when they're going to completely snap, or if they already have snapped and are hiding some grisly secret that they've decided to share with us just before they make us their next victims."

"I get it Dad, mister nice guy has left the building," Jacob mumbled, as he stopped turning the trailer's crank and stated. "That should be high enough."

I finished the lesson on unhooking a trailer from a tractor by showing him the latch handle on the fifth wheel.

"Now all you have to do is pull this, and drive away," I instructed.

With the truck packed and the trailer released, we pulled away from the post office.

The woman I had killed was now totally engulfed in flames, her burning hair had caught her uniform on fire, and as it burned, it was acting as a candlewick. As the heat from the fire melted the copious amounts of blubber on her obese body, the cotton strands in her outfit absorbed the melted lard, which continued to feed the flames. A column of black sooty smoke rose into the air from her burning carcass, and unknown to us signaled our whereabouts to the trailing ambushers.

AMBUSHERS

Their flatbed truck was parked in the middle of twenty or so dead zombies that were being consumed by six other undead zombies that had been drawn to them by the sound of the gunfire that had put their meals down.

"Take care of these zombs!" A man ordered.

Several men immediately jumped from the truck and engaged the feasting zombies, prematurely ending their ghastly dining experience.

"These punks aren't too hard to track; they leave dead bodies everywhere they go. I bet if we follow that pillar of smoke in the distance, we'll find more of their handy work," said Russell, the leader of the group of trailing ambushers.

"Make sure all of these things are brain dead before we leave. Never forget Al." Russell reminded his men.

Al was a lifelong friend of Russell's; they had met in the fourth grade and became close friends, and they maintained their friendship all through school and beyond.

After the outbreak, Al and Russell were killing zombies and trying to survive just like everyone else. They were forced out of their hometown by a large drove of zombies, and had found themselves in a small one-horse town looking for a place to spend the night.

A local church was a prime candidate for their needs, but it was infested with victims of the virus. They decided to rid the church of its unholy visitors and use it for their own safe refuge.

However, in the process of clearing out the congregation of the dead, Al put down one without a clean head shot, only stunning the beast. The two of them dragged all of the bodies out of the church and stacked them at the side of the building.

The next morning, while Al was enjoying his breakfast while sitting on the church steps, he was attacked and bitten by the same stunned zombie he thought he had killed the day before.

When Al turned, Russell was forced to stick a butcher knife through his best friends eye socket to destroy his brain, and since then, Russell had become anal retentive about making sure every dead body was truly dead. So he always reminded his men of Al.

"All done boss, one of them, a girl, never was infected, someone just killed her," one of Russell's trusted minions reported.

"These people are a real class act," Russell replied.

"I saw another shadow, well, I didn't really see it, you know, when I turned my head it wasn't there anymore," the man reporting added.

"Just like the night lights, they're there when your eyes are closed, but seem to disappear as soon as you open your eyes, we've all seen them, well almost seen them," Russell acknowledged. "Everybody on the truck!" he yelled.

Once his men were on the truck, Russell tapped on the roof, leaned over to the driver's window and said. "Let's go find out what that smoke is all about."

"We've been tracking them for quite some time, Russell. What are you going to do to them when we catch up to them?" asked Lonnie, Russell's right hand man.

"I'm not sure yet, but if you have a weak stomach you might not want to watch," Russell warned, staring hard into Lonnie's eyes.

"Those people, whoever they are, killed my cousin Bobby. That was Bobby's first time out on a retrieval run, and they killed him," Russell stated, as tears began to flood his eyes. "I loved my cousin Bobby, and they forced me to splatter his brains all over the highway back there, and they're going to pay dearly for what they did."

The ambushers, guided by the rising smoke from the burning residue of the fraudulent postal worker, found their way to the post office quickly, and seeing the source of the smoke, Russell's blank expression turned to a scowl.

"Here we go again, was this one a zomb? Or did they just kill another citizen?" Russell asked, his body language showing his displeasure.

Lonnie jumped from the truck to check on the burning body.

"It's too burnt to tell boss, could have been a zomb, or maybe not," Lonnie answered, as he dodged the smoke changing directions in the wind.

"Doesn't matter, the same people did this, and we're getting close," Russell said, determined to catch the people that killed his cousin.

"Look at those bicycles over there, one has blood all over it, I'd say they rode them here after killing the girl we found in the street back there," Lonnie surmised.

"If you're right, then we need to be looking for a post office vehicle, probably one that's big enough to transport at least four or five people," Russell speculated.

"Which way now boss?" Lonnie asked. "They could have gone in any direction; we can't follow tire tracks on the pavement."

"We keep going south, that's the main direction they've been traveling since they massacred my men and murdered my cousin," Russell answered, with a stern look on his face.

"There's nothing we need here, get back up here and let's get after those bastards," Russell said, ordering Lonnie back onto the truck.

They left the post office with the crazy woman still on fire, and drove south checking their surroundings hopeful that one of them would get a glimpse of their elusive quarry.

"Everyone keep your eyes peeled, I want to catch these killers before nightfall," Russell barked, persistent in his determination to capture the people that had ended his cousin's life prematurely.

Catching their quarry before nightfall was easier said than done. The ambushers could travel only as fast as the road conditions allowed, for like their elusive prey, they too had to deal with the occasional zombie or two, or three, and the wrecked vehicles that cluttered the roadway, both of which limited their speed and agility.

Russell had always been somewhat of a lucky guy, once before the end of days arrived, he had won a small but substantial jackpot in one of the state lotteries. He was a pretty good poker player, though he didn't play on a regular basis, and standing over six feet tall, the ladies didn't find him hard to look at, so he did all right in that department too.

So, as luck would have it, one of the men in his bunch, just by chance, as he turned to the side and sat down to tie his shoelace, spotted a large postal truck.

"Over there, look over there, just beyond that gas station, that's got to be them," he said.

"That's them all right, it's got to be them, stop the truck," Russell ordered loudly, pounding on the roof.

"Give me those binoculars," he said gruffly, pulling the dangling field glasses away from the chest of one of his companions who had them hanging around his neck, and violently jerking the man's head against his body, pulled by the leather strap that held the twin spyglasses, as he looked intently through them.

The sun was beginning to set, and it would be dark soon.

"It looks like they've stopped," Russell said, staring into the binoculars. "I see two of them standing by their truck, these guys look like they're military."

"How many of them are there?" Lonnie asked.

"I can only see two of them and they're wearing two different uniforms," Russell replied, as he attentively looked through the field glasses.

"Maybe they're what's left of two units that fought the zombs in the beginning," Lonnie suggested apprehensively, feeling a little uneasy about attacking trained soldiers.

"It doesn't matter to me who they are or where they came from, we're going to kill them," Russell said, sounding more determined than ever.

******

Still searching for a place to spend the night...

"This looks like a good spot to bed down for the night, if there're no eaters in there," Billy said. "Dad, let's check the inside, if we can't stay here we'll need to find another place before it gets too dark to see."

"Okay, let's go in, honey the same formation as always," I said to Gin.

After our experience with Clyde, we had adopted the swat style of entry; guns at our shoulders and looking down the sights. That way no time was wasted raising our weapons and finding a sight picture.

We entered the building, which in its former life was a city jail, which sounded like a great place to spend the night, until we got inside.

The suburban jail stood alone in the middle of a small courtyard, and backed up to a large garage where the police cars had been stored and maintained, giving us the advantage of being able to see in a 270 degree span around the building, depending on our location within it. It also had a stairway that led to a hatch used to gain access to the roof, probably so the trustee prisoners in the courtyard could be watched.

As soon as we cleared the threshold of the jail, we began to hear moans and groans coming from the hallway where the prisoners were housed. The entry way and the main office was zombie free, but the familiar smell of rotting flesh became stronger as we continued down the corridor of the jail. When the dead became aware of our presents, the groaning gave way to the usual growling, snarling, and snapping that the undead always resorted to whenever they perceived an impending meal was nearby.

Opening the heavy steel door that led into the actual cellblock, the squeaking hinges on the door alerted all of the still incarcerated prisoners to our presents. Some of the prisoners had caught the virus and turned into zombies, just as millions worldwide had done at the start of the outbreak.

The outbreak of the virus was so sudden and overwhelming that most people including military and police abandon their posts in search of their loved ones. Very few jailers had the opportunity or the inclination to risk their lives taking the time to release their prisoners, so they were left in their cells, and with nobody to feed them, the prisoners that weren't affected by the virus slowly starved to death, died of thirst, or killed themselves. Their situation was similar to those that chose to incarcerate themselves in their vehicles in the beginning while they waited for help that never came.

In the end, all of the prisoners fell prey to the disease and were now extremely hungry for human flesh. In fact, most of them were so hungry that they had begun to gnaw on parts of their own bodies to satisfy their cravings, except for the ones that had used bed sheets, or some other means to hang themselves in their cells. They would have fed on their own body parts too had it not been for their method of self-execution. The weight of their bodies pulling down on the vertebra in their necks and spines for such an extended length (no pun intended) of time, had stretched their necks and backbone to the point that their head was separated so far from their torso that they could no longer reach their mouth with any part of their body except their finger tips.

Their giraffe-like metamorphoses may have been caused by the deterioration of their tendons and bone strength due to the zombie virus, in any case, their hanging bodies cast a bizarre, and unearthly form as their dangling feet nearly touched the floor.

With their rotting muscles having been deprived of any nutrients (human or animal flesh) during their incarceration, they were too weak to even raise their pathetically scrawny arms.

However, the muscles in their jaws seemed to be working just fine, as they continued to snap and snarl at us the whole time we were in the cellblock, causing them to sway back and forth on their makeshift tethers, which made the scene even more eerie.

"Well, sleeping in the cells is out of the question," Gin said.

"The smell is too much to deal with, even if we did remove them from their cells," Jacob added, holding his nose.

"Not to mention these incessant flies," Gin added, waving her hand in front of her face to shoo away the annoying insects.

"We'll have to look elsewhere," I said. "Billy, go get those weak excuses for binoculars we have, we'll go up on the roof and see if we can see a better place to go from there. Jake, you go with your brother. And both of you be careful."

Soon Billy and Jacob returned with the binoculars and we all headed up the steps to the roof.

The sun was nearly down as we scanned the area around the jail.

"All I see that's even worth checking is that gas station over there, it's small enough that we can clear it out in no time, that's if there are any eaters even in it," I said.

"What's that over there?" Gin asked. "Past the gas station a few hundred yards, you see it?"

I focused the spyglasses on the small bump on the horizon, and saw that it was a flatbed truck.

"What is it Dad," Jacob asked.

"We got trouble, big trouble, it's those ambushers again," I said, scanning the horizon for more signs of danger.

As everyone strained their eyes to see the distant bump in the fading sunlight, I again focused my attention on the tiny bulge too.

"It's a flatbed truck, and there are several men on it, but it looks like it's just setting there," I informed them before ordering. "Everybody down!"

"What are we going to do honey," Gin asked, visibly upset.

"They probably know we're here, probably saw our truck. They're most likely going to either wait till nightfall and come in under the cover of darkness, or bed down and hold off until morning, whichever way they decide, they'll be watching our truck. They might even try to disable it," I asserted. "We need to come up with a plan, and fast."

"We could leave the truck here and take off on foot," Jacob interjected.

"That will be our last option, if we run now we won't get five miles and they'll catch us before sunrise. That is if we're not a midnight snack for the eaters," I maintained.

Gin looked around, her eyes were wide open and she looked like she was almost to the point of panicking.

"We can't stay here, if we get trapped inside we'll be doomed for sure," she said.

"You're right, we can't stay here, but we might be able to make them think that we stayed here. I have an idea. Follow me!" I ordered, ducking down and making my way back to the roof hatch.

Back inside the jail again, I laid out my plan.

"We need some glass bottles and some kind of cloth," I instructed.

We found the bottles in a soda machine in the officer's break area, and tore strips of cloth, from some of the inmate's jump suits that Jacob found in a closet.

"Billy and Jacob, we need some gasoline, can you two go out on the street and poke a hole in the gas tank of one of those cars out there and drain some out?" I asked, not really wanting to send them out alone again, but seeing no other practical option. After all, they were both younger, faster, and more agile than me, and better suited for the job at hand. My skills would be put to better use as a sentry or guardian if you will, watching over them from a distance, ready to warn them of approaching danger, or simply putting an abrupt end to any threat that might seek to harm them.

I had already sent them outside to retrieve the binoculars, and they had done so without incident, but sending them to fetch gasoline from one of the derelict

309

vehicles was much more of a time consuming and dangerous job. Although the nighttime shielded their movements from the prying eyes of the ambushers, at the same time the darkness elevated the danger of a successful zombie attack considerably.

"Sure," Billy answered. "But we'll need something to drain it into."

"There was a janitor's bucket in the closet with the prisoner's outfits, I'll get it," Jacob said, as he hurriedly walked back to the closet.

"What do you want me to do," Gin asked, still wide eyed.

Breaking the front of the soda machine with the butt of my AK, and bending the mechanism that secured its contents with the barrel of my gun, I pulled a bottle out and handed it to Gin.

"Take these bottles out of the machine, and empty the soda out of them," I said.

I looked around and handed her a trashcan that was setting beside the desk.

"Empty them into this, I have another idea," I boasted. "I'm going to go with the boys and cover them from the doorway, get that done as fast as you can, we don't know how much time we have."

"Okay honey, I'm on it," Gin responded, as she popped the cap off the first soda bottle.

******

From their vantage point overlooking the jail, Russell gave his last orders of the day...

"Lonnie!" Russell summoned.

"Yeah Russell," Lonnie answered quickly.

"Make sure the men get fed, and that their guns are fully loaded. Post some sentries as usual, and I want somebody watching that truck every second, I don't want them slipping away during the night. We're going to wait until just before dawn to attack," Russell said, staring toward the jail as the last fading rays of the setting sun disappeared below the horizon.

******

With the janitor's bucket half filled, the boys returned to the jailhouse with the gasoline I had sent them to get...

"This should be enough; it's for Molotov cocktails isn't it?" Billy asked, voicing his uneasy confidence that he already knew the answer to his question.

Confirming his supposition, I answered. "That's right son, that should be enough, and it is for Molotov cocktails, let's get it to your mother."

When we joined Gin in the office, she was emptying the last bottle of soda into the trashcan on the floor beside her.

"You want to tell me this brilliant idea of yours? What are you going to do with all of this soda?" She asked, setting the last empty bottle on the desk.

"Well, first we're going to get busy and fill all of these soda bottles with gasoline, and stuff the strips of cloth into the tops," I explained.

"Yeah, Molotov cocktails, I get it, but what are we going to do with all of this soda?" She asked once more, expecting an answer this time.

"All right, here's the whole plan. We're going to lock the back door and somehow secure the roof hatch. Right before we exit the building we'll open the cell doors and let out the eaters, then as we head for the front door, we're going to pour the soda all over the floor making it slippery. We then leave the building with our bottles of gas, close the front door to keep the eaters from leaving, and we'll sleep in the truck. You and Jacob will anyway, Billy and I will keep watch from under the truck. That way we'll be there to protect the vehicle and watch the front door at the same time," I told them.

"What about eaters, you're going to stay out in the open all night with eaters prowling around?" Gin asked, not sounding too happy with my plan.

"One of us will be awake the whole time, we'll be able to take care of any small groups of eaters, and if a large horde shows up, then I guess we may have to jump into the truck and make a run for it," I explained, offering up the best answer that I could.

"What about the cocktails, when are we going to use them?" Jacob inquired.

I looked straight at him, and said. "If everything goes as planned, those men out there will think that we're inside the jail and not look too closely at our truck. When they charge through the door with guns blazing and are greeted by the ravenous eaters inside, the soda will make the floor slippery, thus making it harder for them to stop and turn around, and get back out of the building. That's when we toss the gas bombs through the front door and trap them inside. And we shoot any stragglers or rear guard that didn't enter the jail. That's the plan anyway, and only a thousand things can go horribly wrong," I maintained. "So we're all going to have to be alert, and when the time is right, we're going to have to get just plain downright mad dog mean, meaner than those men, meaner than the eaters, even meaner than a pack of feral dogs, just plain mean," I lectured, hoping to raise the bar on their fighting spirit.

We broke the lock on the back door to the jail, sealing the door closed; the roof hatch had been nailed shut by Billy and Jacob with tools that we found in a maintenance closet. As soon as our preparations were complete, we unlocked the cell doors and quickly spilled the soda onto the floor before running out of the building as fast as we could. I was the last one out and closed the door behind me, the trap was now set.

Once outside, Gin and Jacob quickly and quietly crawled into our postal truck, and Billy and I took our place under truck armed with our edged weapons, pistols, AK's, and Molotov cocktails.

The night passed slowly, neither Billy nor I could sleep as we waited for the impending attack.

Then a little after midnight Billy whispered.

"Dad, eaters, they're coming this way."

"We need to draw them away from the truck," I said, quietly crawling from under our vehicle.

Billy followed, and we ran across the street, the zombies hadn't seen us yet, so we were able to maneuver into a position that put us at a ninety degree angle from them.

This pack consisted of five zombies, three females, and two males.

"I'll take the women, you take the men," I ordered, pulling out my tomahawk.

We crouched low, and silently walked toward the wandering zombies under the cover of darkness, waiting to stand erect until we were within striking distance of them.

My first kill was a middle-aged woman of medium build, medium height, medium weight, and in fact, everything about her was medium. She was wearing a light blue sequin dress that sparkled somewhat in the dim pastel moonlight, making her easy to see in the dark.

I placed the blade of my weapon squarely between her eyes with such force, that the sound of her skull splitting echoed back to us off some of the surrounding buildings.

Out of the corner of my eye, I could see the method that Billy used to assault his first kill of the night. He leaped a few feet forward into the air before making contact with the zombie, using his weight and gravitational pull to enhance the downward force of his swing; he brought the point of his sickle down on the crown of the zombie's head, performing a classic zombie kill.

Both of our zombies dropped to the ground at the same time, and we pulled our weapons from their split craniums in sync. With the bodily fluids dripping from our weapons, we turned our attention to the remaining three hungry night stalkers.

I dispatched the other two female zombies in a similar fashion, as Billy finished off his lone male maniacal night prowler with a horizontal swipe of his sickle across the ferocious savage's eyebrows, detaching the top of its head and cutting its brain in half. We wiped the blood from our weapons on the zombie's clothes before hurriedly returning to our hiding place under our truck.

Once beneath our vehicle again, we both felt a sense of security, however, we both knew that feeling was false.

The rest of the night was uneventful, as we waited under the truck, anticipating the ambusher's attack.

******

An hour before dawn, just as Russell promised, the word went out around the ambusher's camp...

"Saddle up boys, we're going in, everybody up," Russell yelled, ordering his men to their feet.

Their plan was simple; they would ride slowly toward the jail making as little noise as possible. When they were about a half a block from the jail, the driver would speed up and they would use their truck as a battering ram against the front door. The assault force, which was everyone but the driver, would jump off the truck just before it smashed into the jailhouse door. The driver would then back up their truck giving the assault team enough room to enter the building. At that time, they would use their superior number of men and weapons, what Russell called a force multiplier, and run into the building killing everything in sight.

Their plan was simple, direct, and to the point, and Russell sensed his thirst for revenge would soon be quenched as the ambushers boarded their flatbed truck and began their slow trek to exact his misguided vengeance upon my family and me.

******

"You feel that Dad?" Billy asked. "I can feel a vibration, like a deep rumbling."

"They're coming," I said, tapping lightly on the undercarriage of the truck to alert Gin and Jacob to the impending danger.

We heard a dull thump as Jacob kicked the floorboard of the truck, signaling that they got my message.

We curled up behind the large truck tires, making ourselves as small as possible, and shook the gasoline cocktails to moisten their wicks with the flammable fluid inside the bottles.

"Here's the lighter, after the first one is lit, use it to light the others," I whispered, holding the lighter next to one of the gasoline bombs.

"We wait until they go inside, right?" Billy asked, trying to confirm the plan.

I answered his question with a quick affirmative nod of my head.

We watched as the ambushers rounded the corner and came into view, their truck began to gain speed and the rumbling got louder.

"They're coming right at us," Billy said. "I think they're going to ram *us*."

Thinking he might bolt from under the truck and give away our position, I grabbed his arm tightly and gave him a stern look, indicating to him that I was *not* going to run.

The speeding truck came within twenty yards of us, and then it abruptly made a hard right turn toward the front of the jail.

The turn had been so sudden and sharp that it threw two of the attackers from the bed of the truck. When they finally stopped rolling, they were so close to our vehicle, that it was a miracle that they didn't see us hiding under it.

Not wanting to be left out of the fight, the two men got to their feet quickly and ran to catch up to the truck that had ejected them.

The sharp turn their truck had made decreased its speed considerably, giving those men that had managed to stay on the flatbed, a chance to bail from the truck at a much slower speed before it impacted the jail door.

However, the momentum the truck carried as it slammed into the front door of the jail was more than enough to do the intended job.

As the driver backed the truck up, Russell led his rabble of minions that were fixated on our destruction, as they all scurried into the jail.

"Now," I said, lighting one of our gas cocktails.

Billy reached over with a bomb in each hand, and a gentle puffing sound was heard as both wicks ignited at the same time.

As I climbed from under our truck, I could see the passenger door open as Jacob emerged from the vehicle toting his carbine.

"Give me one of those bombs," he said, holding his hand out.

I didn't have time to argue with him, those bushwhackers were already inside the building and it wouldn't take them long to see that they had fallen into a trap.

"Here," I said, handing him a bottle of one of my flaming cocktails.

Billy had already begun to run toward the front door and was several yards in front of us, and Jacob easily left me behind as we ran, leaving me to bring up the rear.

The crackle of gunfire was now the dominant sound coming from inside the jail, heard over the shouts of "zombs" being called out by the panicking men as our would be attackers fought off the malnourished yet vicious monsters we had released.

Billy ran past their truck and hurled one of the Molotov cocktails into the doorway of the jail. We heard the glass bottle break and a low swooshing sound as the jailhouse doorway became engulfed in flames. He tossed his second bomb into those flames, and as we heard the glass bottle break inside the building, the sounds of roaring flames and of men screaming pierced the night.

Billy turned around, only to see the driver of the bushwhacker's truck had opened his door and was taking aim at him with his pistol. The man was aiming his gun at Billy through the gap between the door and the cab, but before the driver could get a shot off, a glass bottle slammed into the metal frame of the cab above him, and16 ounces of ignited gasoline rained down on his head and shoulders.

Shooting Billy now became much less of a priority to the man. As his gasoline soaked flaming head burned, his skin bubbled and the boiling blisters popped, his hair was quickly singed off and his eyeballs began to boil within the orbs of their sockets. In addition, every breath the panicked man inhaled served to ingest the petroleum-fueled flames into his lungs as he fell back into his truck screaming and slapping the living shit out of his own face in a futile attempt to extinguish the flames.

Jacob, still moving toward the man at a steady run after tossing his bomb onto the truck, jumped up and drop kicked the truck's door closed, trapping the burning man inside.

The sound of gunfire began to cease, as it was replaced by the sound of more men's screams as they were burned alive in the confines of the jail.

Sprinting the hundred feet or so, I quickly caught up to my sons. I then walked up as close as I dared to the front doorway of the jail and launched my single bomb as far as I could into the bowels of the flaming building.

Another swooshing sound drowned out the fading screams of the roasting men inside. Fire sprang from every window in the building now, and it shot up into the sky from the roof, soon the building became completely encompassed in flames and the intense heat from the fire forced us to move back to our truck.

"That guy that's on fire in the truck, when he finally burns out, he's going to be one ugly eater," Billy said laughing.

"The upper part of his body, especially his head is going to be burnt to a crisp. I don't think ugly is going to be the right word for what he's going to look like," Jacob added, giggling.

I knew they were laughing partly out of stress, and partly out of relief that they weren't killed, so I interjected.

"That was a stupid plan they had, slamming their truck into the building, not knowing what was waiting for them inside, let's face it, we got lucky again, and they died because they were stupid."

The sound of gunfire, along with the crackling and bright glow from the jailhouse inferno had attracted some of the zombies that were patrolling the area in search of food, as every zombie seems to be. We kept a close eye on them while we watched the fire and tried to calm ourselves, and as we did so, we made a few less than politically correct jokes about the man burning in the truck, which we began to refer to as "Match-Head".

Soon we began to see zombies converging on the jail in greater numbers, and with that new and yet ever present threat upon us again; we decided to climb into our postal truck and continued our drive south.

"One last thing," I said. "Everyone in the truck, I'll be right back."

As my family boarded our truck and prepared to depart. I braved the heat of the nearby burning building, and ran back to the flatbed truck and opened the driver's door. What was left of the man inside had stopped burning, the fire had probably sucked up all of the oxygen in the cab, but he was still smoldering and releasing steamy vapors from his chard and blistered skin. He had not reanimated into a zombie as of yet, but I knew that it wouldn't be long before he did. So I ran back and joined my waiting family in the truck and we continued on our journey, this time however, we traveled with the confidence of knowing that nothing capable of following us was on our trail.

"I saw you open Match-Head's door, why did you do that Dad?" Jacob asked, shaking his head in dismay.

"I thought it would be a pity to let such a lovely creation stay locked up inside that truck for the rest of eternity," I answered laughing. "I thought I'd let it out so that others might have the opportunity to enjoy that freak show at a later date."

"That was kind of a dangerous thing to do just for a joke honey," Gin scolded. "Don't do anything like that again, okay?"

"All right, but you've got to admit, at some point that thing is probably going to scare the proverbial holy living excrement out of somebody," I said laughing loudly.

"No doubt about that," Billy agreed, laughing too.

"I just hope it's not us, that get's the crap scared out of us," Jacob added.

"Well I'm sure we're going to get the crap scared out of us at some point down the road, we always do, it just won't be from Match-Head," Gin remarked.

"Okay, enough banter, I've got to concentrate on the road," I stressed, while swerving to add one more felony hit and run to my total by planting the right front fender of our truck deep into the left hip of an unsuspecting young male zombie that had staggered onto the road ahead of us. The impact of our semi-tractor's contoured fender, along with its heavy chrome-plated steel bumper smashing into the inattentive male *road zombie*, had dislocated one of its legs and disassembled its lower spine; giving new meaning to the term "Going Postal". My spontaneous and willfully heinous act had left the dead man sprawled out and thrashing around violently on the hard concrete surface of the road, awaiting the next felonious driver to come along and finish the gruesome *undertaking* (need I say it) that I had been so remiss in accomplishing.

THE GAS STATION

We hadn't been in the Houston area very long and we had already had several harrowing experiences, and on top of that, we had to get lucky a couple of times in order to stay alive. We were beginning to understand why Clyde had told us to avoid Dallas. I think better advice might have been to avoid big cities in general.

In the beginning, taking the river south kept us off the highways for most of our trip, which by default kept us from encountering very many non-infected humans. However, now that we were traveling mainly on the interstate highways and skirting the bigger cities, we were bound to run into more and more living people.

That in itself was a double-edged sword, or a flip of a coin, take your pick. Because we never knew which we might encounter: people like Frank and the Assassins willing to help you, or on the other side of the coin, there were people like the Ambushers, willing to kill you without blinking an eye just because you entered their turf.

We had already lucked out several times since the start of our journey, and as we drove along, all of the sudden, it looked as if we may have used up our allotment of good luck.

Pinging sounds against the side of our truck alerted us to the newest peril that was to befall our small troop.

"What's that?" Gin shouted.

I knew all too well what it was, it was the same sound that we had heard just days before when we were ambushed on another section of the freeway, it was a sound that I dreaded hearing.

"Someone's shooting at us again, just like before," I informed her. "But no road block this time, it's random gunfire from somewhere."

"Get down boys," Gin ordered.

"All of you get down," I yelled, slumping down across the steering wheel the best that I could while still maintaining control of our truck.

"All we can do is keep driving and hope they don't disable the truck," Gin speculated, crouching down behind the dash.

"There are only a couple of places that the gunfire could be coming from, either that row of trees over there, or somewhere in that group of storage buildings," I said, pointing to the two possible places that the shooter might be hiding.

"Billy, stick your AK out your mother's window and spray both those areas," I told him, still dodging abandon vehicles on the road, which most likely helped dodge some of the gunman's bullets.

Billy leaned over the seat and directed his mother to roll down her window. As Gin complied, Billy stuck his rifle out the window and fired it in the direction of the small cluster of buildings.

"You probably won't hit anybody, but you might deter whoever it is from shooting at us for a minute. Shoot into those trees too," I said, pointing again to a small wooded area in the distance.

Billy alternated his fire, several shots at the buildings, and then several shots into the woods, then back to the buildings again.

From the snipers nest our actions probably looked like a drive by shooting with no specific target in mind. More of the spray and pray method, or the accuracy through volume doctrine if you will, instead of any well-aimed precise shots.

What seemed like a lifetime passed in just a few seconds, and the sound of bullets hitting our truck ceased.

Remembering the prisoners and their roadblock, I slowed our truck to a crawl anticipating another blockade that I had yet to see.

However, the road was clear as far as we could see, except of course for the usual scattered derelict vehicles and a few stray putrid smelling regenerated flesh eaters that occasionally ambled onto the roadway, unknowingly putting themselves in the crosshairs of my always-willing homicidal truck's bumper.

Therefore, after a couple of hundred yards we began our normal cruising speed again. Only bothering to slow down enough to add three more *road zombies* to my current hit and run total.

"Unfortunately, I think we're going to run into much more of that kind of thing," I said. "If we do, sooner or later one of us is going to catch a bullet."

Gin looked at me, and I could see the confusion on her face.

"How are we going to avoid it?" She asked, with the look of confusion on her face beginning to turn to a look of fear in her eyes.

The stress of death around every corner every minute of every day and night was starting to take its toll on her, and I didn't have an answer. Our situation was starting to take a toll on all of us.

With pirates, ambushers, crazies, zombies, feral dogs, and now random people sniping at us, we needed to change our tactics and try a different approach.

What kind of different approach? I had no idea.

However, sometimes the more things change, the more they stay the same. And just like before the apocalypse, and to quote the greatest singer and song-writer that ever lived.

"Life is what happens to you while you're busy making other plans."

That's exactly what happened to us, we were busy trying to make other plans, and life happened to us, *apocalyptic life*.

I noticed that the fuel gage had dropped well below where it had been just minutes before.

"Something's wrong with our fuel tanks, I think we've got a leak."

Down the road a few hundred yards farther, on a stretch of road that had a gap between wrecked vehicles and meandering dead bodies, I stopped the truck to check our fuel tanks.

"We've got a leak all right, we've got nothing but leaks in this tank," I said, pointing to several bullet holes at the bottom of the tank.

"That's half of our gas, gone," Billy said, climbing out of the truck.

"What's next? How far can we get on just one tank?" Gin asked.

Looking down at the perforated fuel tank and the last reminisce of its contents dripping onto the road, I answered.

"I don't know, but our good tank, you know, the tank that doesn't have a bunch of bullet holes in it was the one that was emptying first, so it's got less fuel, and with all the holes in this tank, I'm not sure it's safe to drive this truck anymore."

Jacob climbed out of the truck, looked at the leaking fuel tank and declared.

"We need to find another vehicle; I don't want to end up like Match-Head!"

"Start unloading our stuff, it looks like we're on foot again," I said with a sigh. "And make sure we bring those bolt cutters, I think we'll probably need them."

"I got'em right here Dad," Jacob announced, holding the bolt cutters in the air.

On foot again, and burdened like pack mules, we lugged our supplies down the road in search of another means of transportation.

The ammunition and what little was left of our water was by far the heaviest burden we had to deal with. Our guns were heavy too, but in comparison to the weight and bulk of the water and ammo, they were much easier to tote, and their slings afforded us several configurations by which we could easily carry them in different ways.

Gin was wearing out the quickest, but we were all feeling the pain our cargo was inflicting upon us. The old military adage, *"Ounces equal pounds and pounds equal pain"* kept coming to mind.

"I don't know how much further I can go like this," Gin said, stopping to readjust her backpack. "At this point, I'll take any car, truck, wagon, bike, I don't care."

"Like always, we'll grab the first vehicle that we can get started, and worry about finding a better one later," I said, agreeing with her, and shifting my rife to my left side.

"We better find one before someone else shoots at us," Billy added.

We walked for the next few hours, stopping and resting each time while we checked abandon means of transportation that were not housing their former owners who were trapped and slowly decomposing inside.

Then, when we were at the point of total exhaustion and felt we couldn't take another step, we happened upon a minivan identical to the one that we used to own and had abandoned on the boat launch at the beginning of our journey.

Jacob, who had managed to walk slightly faster than the rest of us, was several yards ahead of the group and arrived at the minivan first.

"The keys are in this one!" he shouted.

"See if it will start," I replied, without much enthusiasm or hope.

To everyone's surprise, and relief, with one turn of the key the engine started.

"Unlock the rear hatch," Gin said, dropping her backpack on the ground behind the vehicle.

We opened all of the van's doors and hurriedly tossed our supplies in.

"How much gas does it have?" Gin asked, concerned that this ride might be a short one.

I glanced down at the gas gage.

"Not much, but enough to find a gas station, that is if we don't wreck it or get it shot out from under us first!"

Loaded up, and on four wheels again, the vigil to find a filling station began in earnest.

One thing about the American landscape, there never seems to be a shortage of gas stations, and the Houston area was no exception. Almost immediately, Billy spotted a familiar sign in the distance advertising the price of gas on the day our normal world ended.

"Over there, look, a gas station," he pointed out.

"With the electric out the pumps aren't going to work, how are we going to get the gas?" Gin asked.

"We brought that little squeeze pump with us, remember, it's in my backpack. It might take awhile, but we can pump the gas out of the underground tanks directly into the van," I answered, smiling and nodding my head.

Our newly acquired vehicle's tank was almost empty, and the plan was to pump as much gas into the tank as we could, and if the gas station sold gas cans, we'd fill up one or two and take them with us.

"The gas station is right up here, when we get there we'll have to be on the lookout for eaters, feral dogs, and feral people, and anything else that might try to kill us," I warned.

"So be on the lookout for the usual things, right," Jacob wisecracked.

Ignoring his remark, I continued.

"I'll fill up the tank and the rest of you cover me. If everything goes smooth, after the gas tank is full, we'll check for gas cans and fill them too."

"What about using the blades? Don't we need to be quiet? Gin asked.

"Only if there are one or two eaters, four at the most, any more than that we need to just shoot'em and find another gas station," I told her. "So, if I say shoot, you shoot, get me?" I said sternly.

They all replied. "Yes!"

"And you all should know by now that you don't have to wait for me to tell you to shoot, you go ahead and shoot if you think that you have to, right?"

Again, they all replied "Yes!"

"And if I say shoot all of them, you shoot every damn one of them that you can, whether *you* think they're a threat or not, get me!"

My family looked at me knowingly, and again, each of them replied. "Yes!"

"Remember, head shots on the eaters, and for everyone, or everything else, any hit is a good hit. Get me?"

The family nodded as Billy forcefully tapped his rifle's drum magazine twice to insure it was locked in place.

None of the nation's power grid was still intact by now, and we held out little hope that the gas station would have electricity to run the pumps, why would it, no place else did. Except for Frank's group, who knows, maybe we would get lucky...again?

However, the outbreak and subsequent societal break down had happened so fast, that it was almost a sure thing that the underground tank would be able to supply us with as much fuel as we could take with us.

We pulled into the gas station and I parked beside the small round metal covers where the tanker trucks filled the subsurface tanks. We leaped out of the van and everyone took their places guarding the van and my attempted retrieval of the fuel.

Prying off the metal cover on the covert fuel well with the pointed end of my tomahawk, I quickly gained access to the much-needed gasoline below. Wasting no time, I inserted the pump hose into the tank and began to squeeze the oval rubber bulb between the two miniature pump hoses, pulling gasoline up from the buried tank. I removed the van's gas cap and replaced it with the hose that was now spewing out gas from the subterranean fuel reservoir.

Turning toward her, Jacob announced to his mother.

"It's working Mom, Dad's filling the tank."

Gin glanced at me and then at Jacob, nodded her head and returned to her sentry duties.

"This is going faster than I thought it would," I said, steadily pumping the bulb. "A few more minutes and we'll be done."

"Eater!" Gin said, pointing to one of the dead coming around the corner of the building.

"I'm closer, I'll get it," Billy said, walking toward the lone zombie.

"Whack that zomb," Jacob jeered, before looking back at me and smiling.

"Hey, that's what those men back at the jail called them."

"Let's stick with "Eaters", less confusion that way," I sternly suggested.

"Okay!" Jacob replied.

"Whack that eater Billy!" Jacob called out softly, this time using his own families slang.

"Be careful Billy!" Gin beseeched him, as he approached the solitary zombie.

"Thanks Mom, I never would have thought of that," Billy replied sarcastically.

Billy did as Jacob had recommended, and split the zombie's head open with one swift blow, dropping it to the ground in front of him.

"Check the side of the building, but don't leave our sight, and be careful, remember they travel in packs," Gin ordered, reminding her son, and then scanning the area on the other side of the building for danger.

Just then a sputtering sound came from inside the station, and the gas pumps lit up.

Someone inside had started a generator.

Then a shadow moved passed the front door, the door opened and a crouching woman stuck her head out and yelled.

"That's our gas! You gotta pay for that gas?"

Upon hearing the sound of the generator starting, Jacob and Gin moved to the other side of the van and were watching the woman from behind it. Billy was checking the side of the building for more zombies, and had the woman flanked. While I stood alone in the middle of the gas station's parking lot, the perfect easy target for someone with minimal shooting skills.

"How much do you want for it?" I questioned.

"Don't want no money, money ain't no good no more, we're on the barter system now," the woman answered with a thick southern drawl. "What else you got that we might want?"

"We don't have much, a few bottles of water and a couple cans of tuna, that's about it," I answered, hoping she would let it go at that and let us leave without pushing the issue.

"First you steal our gasoline, and then you lie to us about what you got," the woman said angrily.

"I'm not lying, we've got next to nothing," I answered, trying to sound pathetic.

"Next to nothing, all you standing around with those fancy looking guns, you call that nothing, and yes, I can see those two behind that van," she hollered angrily.

In the middle of our conversation, my mind drifted away from the immediate peril I was in, and I thought.

"Now am I to believe that I'm the only person in America that had the foresight to possess some half-way descent firearms, the only one in these United States to

332

be vaguely prepared for an emergency of some kind?
What is with this obsession everyone seems to have with
my guns?"

Snapping back to the grim reality that confronted me, I replied to the woman.

"We can't give you our guns, traveling around out here without any firearms would be suicide," I pleaded, putting on the best whining routine I could muster, as I tried to think of a way to turn the tables on this woman.

"That sounds like a personal problem to me," she said, forcing a smile which revealed what was left of her yellow and rotting teeth.

"You keep saying things like, *our* gas; you lied to *us*, and what *we* might want. How many of you are in there?" I asked, trying to gain some operational information.

Before the woman could answer my question, I watched her face explode through the glass door she was kneeling behind, and then her body slumped through the hole in the door that her face had made on its way outside just moments before.

Before I could make a move, I saw Billy pushing the front door of the building open, dragging the woman's faceless body with it.

"It's okay everybody, she's alone in here."

During my conversation with the woman, Billy had sneaked around to the back door of the building (in blatant disregard for our rule number 4, I might add), which the woman had left unlocked, entered the building and shot the woman in the back of the head while I unknowingly distracted her.

"Are you sure nobody else is in there?" I asked, thinking that maybe the woman had tried to mislead us into thinking that she wasn't alone.

"There're only two rooms and a small hallway, I'm sure," Billy replied, as he walked toward me. "Nothing in there worth wasting our time over either," he added, as he pulled the siphon hose from van, and screwed on the gas cap.

"Then let's get back on the road before something else happens," I said, as I drained the remaining fuel from our small pump onto the ground and stuffed it back into my backpack.

"Too late honey, something else has happened!" Gin alerted, as her and Jacob came around from behind the van.

"Look!" She said.

I looked over at her, and she was pointing to a large group of zombies moving in our direction.

"There must be fifty of them!" Jacob yelled, as he raised his carbine and took an aggressive stance.

The *now* faceless woman in the gas station had unknowingly distracted us from the approaching danger of the large marching horde of rotting resurrected dead that was now upon us.

"Way too many of them to fight out here in the open, and no time to climb in the van," I screamed, as three zombies were already between our vehicle and us with a multitude of their friends close behind. "Get inside the station, hurry!"

It was a short run to the entrance of the building, Gin and Billy got there first, then Jacob, I brought up the

334

rear, and made it to the door at the same time as the zombie that was leading the pack did.

As we both converged at the doorway, I swung my elbow back and caught the revived dead man square in the temple; knocking him backwards just long enough for me to get inside the station.

The smell of the blood oozing from the anonymous carcass of the woman Billy had just killed, was guiding the less astute zombies (the zombies that hadn't witnessed us take refuge in the building) to our improvised sanctum sanctorum in search of their next meal. This made the crowd that was quickly gathering at the front of the gas station even larger. And to make matters even worse, the faceless corpse of the dead woman was unintentionally propping the door open, leaving a one-foot gap which was more than enough room for any zombie (except for maybe that corn-fed 400 pounder I dropped last week) to push its way through. Unfortunately for us, within seconds, that is exactly what they were trying doing.

Thankfully, because of laws that were first enacted in Chicago after a tragic theater fire in 1903, and nationally some five years later after the Collinwood school fire, where 175 people lost their lives, 172 of which were children. All exit doors on public buildings must open outward, allowing people to exit the buildings during emergencies without having to pull the door open against a rush of panicked victims.

Fortunately for us, even with the weight of the dead woman's carcass dragging on the floor, the mass of dead former humanity leaning inward on the door, effectively closed the door for us and stopped the onslaught of famished zombies dead in their tracks (no pun intended).

In addition, the woman's body served, at least for the moment, to plug the hole in the glass door that her face had made as it quickly exited the building just ahead of Billy's bullet.

"This broken glass isn't going to hold for long," I warned. "Billy, Jake, the two of you go to the back door and lock it, we don't need any surprises. Then get back up here quick."

Billy and Jacob ran to the rear door and made sure that it was locked, and then quickly rejoined Gin and I at the front of the building.

"How many do you think are out there?" Gin asked, turning a little pale.

"More than there were when we ran in here. I can't see past the ghouls squished up against the door," I answered. "But when that glass door breaks, we're going to have to do some very quick shooting."

"Want me to shoot some now?" Jacob asked, sticking the muzzle of his rifle up next to a zombie's face that was pressed flat against the glass.

"Don't shoot yet, we need to get ready first," I said.

"Ready, ready for what, to die?" Gin added softly, her face still very pale.

"Yeah, ready to die Mom, that's what we're getting ready to do," Billy snapped, annoyed at his mother's cynicism, and just as scared as she was.

"We're not going to die," I told them. "Not if we do this right."

Let's form a semicircle about ten feet from the door and two feet apart, the two of us on the ends will shoot across at the eaters on the opposite sides of the door. The two of us in the middle, will lay waste to the eaters in the middle. With all of the eaters trying to get to us, they'll climb over the one's we've already shot, then we shoot some more of them until the pile of dead eaters completely blocks the entrance. Hopefully, the sound of all our gunfire will draw any stray eaters that are not already here to the front of the building; we'll exit out the back door and run past the crowd of remaining eaters that are trying to get through the front door, we'll jump into the van and get the living hell out of this piss hole."

"The door can't stand the force of the eaters any longer, the rest of the glass is beginning to crack," Jacob yelled, as he moved his finger onto the trigger of his gun.

No sooner, did the last word leave Jacob's mouth, than the glass door shattered and the zombies that were pressed up against the cracking pane tumbled in.

We began firing our weapons as rapidly as we could. One zombie after another dropped to the floor, most of which were now missing a sizeable portion of the back of their heads. However, a select group that seemingly had softer skulls received our 9mm bullets that penetrated the front of their heads, and left a perfectly round 9mm hole, then traveled through destroying their brains, and exited leaving another perfectly round 9mm hole in the back of their skulls.

Although the mushy skulls of some of the undead allowed the 9mm projectiles to penetrate cleanly, our AK-47's were a slight bit messier, exploding the gelatinous cartilage like craniums, and splattering their festering insides over the surging mob of hungry killers that were pushing from behind.

As one zombie fell another took its place, each one having to climb higher as the pile of bodies grew. The plan was working; one or two minutes after the first zombie had fallen onto the floor in front of us, the pile of corpses had grown to such a magnitude that the doorway could no longer accommodate as much as one more body.

"Now might be a good time to test part two of your plan honey," Gin stated, no longer pale, the adrenalin having helped pump blood back into her face.

"Good idea, let's move," I ordered, firing two more shots into the mound of rotting corpses and disturbing the hundreds of buzzing flies that were landing on them, causing the flying insects to circle the pile once or twice and then land again.

Bursting into the alleyway from the back door of the gas station, we found that phase two of the plan was also working, so far anyway.

Rounding the corner and with the van in sight, we sprinted to it as fast as we could. A couple of lone stragglers were ghosting the van, but Billy eliminated both of them quickly with a swift stroke of his sickle, dealing each of them a dash of sharp force trauma to their diseased brains ending their hungry torment.

Once in the van more zombies came into view, it was as if a sporting event had just let out and flooded the streets with its patrons. But each and every one of these patrons were dead set (again, no pun intended) on having us as a four course meal for their cannibalistic style dining pleasure.

Seeing the massive gathering of the organic undead on all sides of us, swaying and stumbling in our direction, Gin screamed.

"Hurry! Go!"

Her spontaneous request was unwarranted, as I too had seen the substantial amount of raw flesh eaters that were converging on our position and surrounding our vehicle.

I slammed the van into drive and headed for the same driveway that we had used to gain entry to the station. This time however, as we negotiated the combination of entrance and exit we did so at a greatly increased speed, and plowed through a group of ten or fifteen zombies as we did so.

Severed arms and legs flew into the air, as sharp edges on the van's now damaged fenders sliced them off and hurled them in different directions.

Blood, intestines, feces, and an assortment of bodily fluids were also abundantly distributed across the front of our vehicle's fenders, hood, and windshield as our desperate escape attempt proceeded.

"Turn your wipers on honey; you can't see where you're going with all of the blood and guts all over the windshield," Gin said, showing little emotion as we drove through the bloodthirsty pack of predatory undead.

Which I found to be a little strange, considering minutes prior to this, when we were facing what seem to be certain death from an infinite number of these skin-devouring monsters, she was white as a ghost. Maybe she felt that now we weren't in any real danger. Personally, if that was the case, I thought she was wrong.

I reached down and set the wipers on high, and replied.

"Roger that!"

The wipers smeared the gory concoction back and forth across the window, occasionally catching a disemboweled intestine on the blade and dragging it across the windshield as well.

We were able to maintain our speed and not allow the zombies to compress in front of us and slow us to a stop. However, the down side to preserving our rapid speed was that arms and legs weren't the only things that were flung into the air. Sometimes, whole cadavers were sent airborne, bouncing off the hood and even the roof of our vehicle.

Then it happened, I hit a female zombie, one that was slightly overweight, she (it) wasn't what you would call grossly fat, but her nickname might have been *Pudgy* or *Chubby* before the outbreak.

The configuration of the front of the van caught her just right and launched her up into the air about fifteen feet, flipping her end over end, and when she landed, her head penetrated the windshield face first.

The impact crushed the front of her skull killing her inner zombie instantly, but left her head dangling through the window just below the rearview mirror, exposing part of her brain and dripping blood, and some purplish colored liquid that none of us could, would, or wanted to identify, onto the dashboard of our vehicle.

Our van plowed through what seemed to be a never-ending mob of the creophagous undead for several more blocks, crushing and crunching bones under our tires, and dismembering many of the monsters, even as I tried to dodge the bulk of this riot of the dead.

Then finally, as quick as it had begun, it was over, the zombie horde was behind us, and the road ahead was clear again.

Staring at the bloated carcass of the plump woman whose head now tilted up and down with every bump in the road, like a grotesque bobble-head doll, Jacob made a profound statement.

"I think we're going to have to find another vehicle."

"And soon," Billy added, swatting one of the tormenting flies that "Pudgy" had brought along with her.

"That'll work for me," Gin agreed, trying to poke the crushed head back through the hole in the windshield using the barrel of my rifle.

Having no luck pushing the corpse onto the hood, Gin asked. "Can I get some help here boys?"

Billy and Jacob quickly responded by adding the barrels of their guns to the effort, and with a powerful shove on the count of three, the pudgy one slid back through the windshield and down the hood. Pudgy was the last zombie to be squished under *this* vehicle, as she disappeared under the front of the van and became a speed bump on the road to hell.

"It stinks more now than it did with that head in here," Billy noticed, shooing a number of flies away from his face.

"That's because the air from outside is filled with the stench of rotting flesh, and the stink of the feces that is smeared all over the outside of the van is coming through the hole in the windshield too," I contended. "We'll just have to suffer for awhile longer, after all, we spent days on the river inhaling that putrid smell, I think we can tolerate this for a few hours until we can find another car or truck."

"Well let's at least roll down the windows and try to get rid of all of these flies," Jacob suggested, waving his arms in front of his face in an effort to disperse the nasty menacing insects.

The stink of the zombies, the harassing flies, and the hole in the windshield wasn't the only problem we had with the van. The constant pounding of the zombie horde being smashed against the front of the vehicle, had pushed the fenders in far enough that both the left and the right were touching the front tires every time the steering wheel was turned. The effect of this was that it was wearing down the sidewalls of the tires extremely fast.

"Every turn takes away more rubber from the tires," I said.

"We're not going to get very far, are we?" Gin asked, already knowing the answer.

"I don't think we're going to, not in this vehicle anyway," I answered, feeling compelled to say something.

Jacob and Billy were looking out the window, scanning the area for more danger when Jacob mentioned something that I had noticed earlier.

"It seems the further south we go, the more eaters we're running into. Has anyone else noticed that?"

Billy quickly answered his question.

"I've noticed the groups of eaters seem to be getting bigger, but none as big as the one we just drove through, not since we saw that giant bunch on the riverbank."

"Come to think of it, we *have* been seeing more eaters," Gin said in agreement, and nodding her head. "They were on us pretty quick when we set out on foot from those ambushers, then again when we rode through them on the bicycles, and then again at the jail, and finally at the gas station."

"It's probably because we're close to a large metropolitan area," I speculated.

"Maybe we should alter our course then?" Gin replied, reaching for the map.

"It's time for that change of tactics we spoke of, maybe go a little further west, and then cut south to Galveston?" I recommended.

"I think that might be a good idea," Gin agreed, scanning her map.

"Right after we find another ride," I answered.

THE TOWER

"I have an idea; see that water tower over there? It's not too far away, if we can make it there we'll use it as an observation post. We'll be able to see for miles in every direction," I insisted.

"Boys get the bolt cutters, we might need them."

As expected, the front tires didn't last very long. Moments after I made my request for the bolt cutters, the right front tire popped, pulling the van to the right and making it almost impossible to steer.

"That's it, now we walk again," I said. "We can't be burdened like we were before, this time we're going to travel light. Just take a couple of bottles of water and our ammo. Leave the food behind, we'll get more later, and we're bringing the bolt cutters too. Let's go!" I ordered.

We quickly grabbed our ammo and water and exited the vehicle fearing that the sound of the tire popping would alert any roaming zombies that were close. We left the van in the middle of the road thereby adding one more abandoned vehicle to the many that were already littering America's highway system, and began to walk toward the water tower.

"How far do you think the water tower is from here?" Gin asked, sounding depressed.

"It's not that far Mom," Jacob answered confidently. "We'll be there in no time, that is if we don't have to fight our way through a mass quantity of eaters."

"Thanks son, your mother needed that little bit of encouragement," I commented sarcastically, thinking my wife had already started to sound depressed, and we hadn't been out of the van five minutes.

The water tower was a little farther than it looked, and having to cut our way through several fences along the way did nothing to hasten our journey to it. However, within three hours of abandoning the van, we found ourselves standing outside the chain link fence that surrounded the once distant water tower.

"I'll chop the lock off," Billy said anxiously.

Billy broke the lock off the gate, and we gained access to the ladder that was attached to the side of one of the tower's support columns.

"You want me to climb all the way up there?" Gin asked, shaking her head no.

"No Mom, you can stay down here and fend off all of the eaters that happen our way," Jacob said in his usual wise guy manner.

"I guarantee you'll be safer up there than you'll be down here honey, I'll follow you up the ladder, and catch you if you fall," I said, knowing that if she fell, she'd take me with her and probably kill us both.

By now, Billy was already one quarter of the way up the ladder, and softly yelled down to us.

"What are you waiting for; there are eaters just past those apple trees over there," he said, pointing to the east.

"Go Jacob, get up the ladder, we'll be right behind you," I insisted, urging Jacob to climb up the ladder.

"Come on honey, you're next," I said, as I now urged my wife to ascend the water tower's ladder, unaware that soon I would come to regret the guarantee of safety that I had made to her.

Gin moved slowly toward the ladder, she knew that she had no choice but to climb to the narrow platform that encompassed the tank that comprised the tower.

"Just grab the rungs tight and don't look down, and keep moving, you'll be at the top before you know it," I suggested, hoping that would help ease her fear.

Gin began to climb, and as she did, I could hear her counting the rungs as she went. As scared as she was Gin

345

managed to move steadily up the ladder and before long the four of us were standing on the three-foot wide platform one hundred feet in the air.

"I can see forever," Jacob said.

"Forever is a long time," Billy responded, trying to match Jacob's gift for sarcasm.

"I can't believe I made it," Gin said panting. "That's just as hard as it looked."

"Well, we're all up here now, so we need to start assessing the surrounding area, looking for cars, trucks, eaters, you know, the usual things we have to look for," I stated. "Let's spread out and see what's out there. Jacob, you take the south view, Billy, you take the west, I'll take the north, and Gin, you take the east. Once you get to your spot, you had better lie down. Remember, if we could see this water tower from a long way off, so can everyone else," I reminded them, as I quickly walked to the northern side of the tower, and began to question my idea of climbing up onto the tower.

Little did we know that even as I spoke the warning we were being watched. Not only by the zombies in the area; but also by humans as well.

The group of undead that Billy had spotted beyond some trees as he climbed up the ladder had seen us, and had joined with another bunch of the diseased cannibals that had been lingering out of sight under the canopy of those same fruit trees several hundred feet away.

The moans and groans of the ever-growing horde of zombies was attracting more of their kind, possibly through some kind of zombie communication, or maybe it was just the sound that was bringing them together.

Whether or not it was the noise of the group, or some remedial speech pattern that was consolidating the horde, the fact was, they knew where we were, and they were moving slowly toward the water tower.

Meanwhile, humans had also watched us ascend to the top of the ladder, and were assembling a formidable group of assaulters to investigate our presents on what they considered their property. Soon it would become all too clear; I had made a big mistake.

"See anything worth anything?" Jacob asked. "Because I sure don't!"

"Not much to report from here, except I can see a lot of houses scattered about, we might be able to commandeer a car at one of them," Billy answered.

"Honey, you better come and see this, this doesn't look too good!" Gin said, sounding quite alarmed.

I crawled over to her vantage point, where I saw a large group of zombies making their way up the grassy slope from the apple grove to the base of the water tower.

"That's not good," I said. "It's not as big of crowd as we saw on the riverbank, or after we left that gas station, but it's still pretty big," I commented, thinking this was not a good situation for us to be in.

"We're trapped up here aren't we?" Gin complained, looking rather somber.

"Yes, it looks that way, this was a big mistake, climbing up here was a big damn mistake, I should have known better," I confessed, thinking to myself. *"How could I have been so stupid?"*

Billy and Jacob had heard us talking and crawled over by us.

"Can eaters climb a ladder Dad?" Jacob asked, glancing over the edge of the catwalk and looking down on the assembled zombie horde that was looking up at him.

"I don't know, but we're going to find out real soon," I answered, trying to think of some way out of the mess I had gotten us into.

The hungry horde gathered at the foot of the tower, and several of the zombies groped at the ladder but had no luck figuring out how to climb up it.

However, wouldn't you just know it, there's one in every crowd. A young zombie, well, one that would have been young if he had lived long enough, who was dressed in a high school band uniform, clamped onto a rung as high as he could reach and pulled himself up, accidently putting one of his feet on the bottom rung.

Showing what seemed to be a glimmer of intellect, most likely just desperation to have us for lunch; the young flesh-ingesting maniac grasped the next rung up, and began his climb to the top.

Other zombies followed his lead, and before you could say "*Zombie Apocalypse*", the ladder was teeming with slobbering zombies ascending skyward.

As the young band member arrived at the pinnacle of the ladder with several flies orbiting his head, I pulled my tomahawk from my tactical vest once more, and with one vertical blow to the top of his head, I opened a three-inch gaping hole in his skull.

The zombie immediately toppled from the top of the ladder with most of its circling flies following close behind, flipping head over heels and slamming into five or six other zombies below him on his way down, taking them with him as he fell.

At the base of the tower the impatient horde that crowded together like sardines in a can grabbing at the rungs of the ladder, were bombarded by the bodies of the falling undead, leaving a pile of bloody twisted and mangled living corpses at the base of the water tower.

That horrific scene had no effect at all on the zombies that had not been hit by the plunging cadavers; they were driven by nothing more than hunger for our delectable tasting skin.

If anything, the pile of inhuman corpses served as a staircase at the base of the ladder, giving the determined zombies a ramp of mangled body parts that allowed them to gain access to the rungs of the ladder that were several feet higher off the ground.

One by one, more zombies climbed onto the ladder, and one by one, when they made it to our platform, our edged weapons indented their skulls, and one by one, they fell.

Occasionally some of the zombies were so intent on grabbing us, that when they reached the top, they would let go of the ladder as they reached for us, and fall to the ground on their own.

And every once in a while, a swift boot heel to the face would aid their ten story vertical plunge to the ground without the help of my tomahawk.

"We're going to have to do this all night!" Gin announced. "This could get dicey in the dark!"

"I got us into this, and I'm going to get us out of it," I responded. "Remember the eaters that freaked out in the river when they fell into the water, and how they all crammed themselves together under the trees to avoid the rain? Let's see what happens to this bunch when they get wet."

I pulled a bottle of water from one of the backpacks and removed the cap, and as I sprinkled the water down the ladder, we watched the zombies go into their hydro-panic mode.

As they did on the river, their fear of the water caused them to forget about us, and their hunger for a moment, and flail their arms about in an attempt to avoid the liquid.

As droplets of water sprinkled down on them, they dropped from the ladder like the flies that surrounded them (just another way of saying they dropped like flies), and quickly joined their twisted and squirming compadres at the base of the tower, thereby adding to the ever-growing pile of broken and disfigured corpses wallowing there.

"That works great Dad," Jacob said, with a hint of hope in his voice.

"Yes honey that works great, but we only have a few bottles of water with us. Not enough to hold them off all night," Gin asserted.

"That's for sure, not nearly enough bottled water to keep them off the ladder all night long, but we do have plenty of un-bottled water," I reminded her, as I reached for my tomahawk again.

I took my tomahawk and swung it as hard as I could, piercing the skin of the water tank with the pointed end of the weapon. Upon withdrawing my tomahawk from the steel tank, a small stream of water squirted out over the ledge above the ladder and fell like rain drops over the climbing zombies.

Panic ensued once more, and one by one, the remaining zombies released their grip on the ladder as they tried to escape the counterfeit waterfall.

The water cleared off the ladder and forced the crowd of zombies at the bottom that weren't part of the pile, to spread out in a circle around my somewhat man made waterfall.

"They're off of the ladder now, but we'll have to fight our way out if we climb down," Billy said, shaking his sickle in a threatening manner at two of the flies that still lingered near the top of the ladder.

"The water got'em off the ladder, but the situation is still grave," I said. "It seems we have two choices, we can stay up here over night, and hope there's enough water in the tank to last until morning, which there probably is, and then fight our way through the eaters down there. Or, we can climb down now, fight our way out, and hope we can find some place reasonably safe to spend the night."

"We only have two or three hours at most before sundown, I don't want to be out in the open over night, that's way too dangerous," Gin said. "If we can't find some place to stay we might not make it."

"The flies might not be as active in the cool morning hours, and that will be one less thing that we have to contend with, plus we will be rested and have all day to find a vehicle if we stay up here overnight," I said, stating reasons to choose one of our options.

As we weighed the pros and cons of spending the night on the tower, or making a break for it before sundown, our decision was made for us.

"Look!" Jacob yelled, as he pointed down at the zombies below.

While the zombies were preoccupied with avoiding the artificial rainfall that we had manufactured, and watching what they hoped would be their next meal (us on the water tower), the humans that had watched us climb to the top earlier were attacking the loitering horde.

"There's almost as many of them as there are eaters," Billy asserted gleefully.

"Don't get too lathered up, we could be out of the frying pan and into the fire, we don't know who these people are," I said cautiously.

"The eaters are almost all killed off," Jacob announced, as he watched the people on the ground slice their way through the remaining members of the zombie mob.

Just before the last zombies were dispatched, we heard.

"You on the tower, come down now!" Said a man's gruff voice through a bullhorn.

"They don't seem to be too worried about attracting eaters," Gin said. "What are we going to do?"

I looked directly into her eyes and said. "We don't have much of a choice, we have to do exactly as they say, and you know they could have just shot us off this water tower."

Again, the man behind the bullhorn blasted his orders.

"You on the tower, come down now, and keep your hands away from your weapons."

"Billy, you go down first, Jacob next, I'll go third, and honey you come down last, that way if you fall I'll be under you to catch you," I said, again hoping that she wouldn't fall.

We proceeded down the ladder in the order that I had prescribed, and again Gin counted each rungs as she descended. At the bottom, a welcoming party of men and women armed to the hilt met us.

As we stumbled over the pile of dead and maimed zombies stacked at the base of the water tower, a stocky red haired man that was preoccupied with giving the others in his group orders approached us.

"Climb over that mess, and be careful not to get bit, they're not all dead yet," he said, stomping the heel of his boot into the side of a snapping zombie's head. "Hand over your weapons and be quick about it, we don't have all day."

At that point, four others in the group stepped forward and relieved us of all of our weapons.

"The ammunition too," ordered the red headed man. "What's your name, why are you here, and what in the hell are you doing destroying my water tower?"

His total focus was now upon us, and I could tell that this man was in no mood to play games, yet there was something vaguely familiar about him, but I just could not place it.

"My name is Jack, this is my wife Gin, and these are my two sons Billy and Jacob," I told him.

The man stared at me with a steely glare and said. "Next question, what are you doing here?"

353

"We're just traveling through, our van broke down a ways back, and we climbed the tower to escape these eaters that you and your people just put down," I answered, with my own steely glare fixed on him.

"Why did you poke a hole in one of *my* water towers?" he asked, still glaring at me.

Again, I glared back at the man.

"My family and I are from the St. Louis area, we floated down the Mississippi River to Vicksburg, and along the way we found that the only thing these creatures seem to be afraid of is water."

"You should have seen the way some of them freaked out when they fell in the river," Jacob interrupted.

A seething glance from me got the message across to Jacob to just stand there and keep his mouth shut.

"So, when we found ourselves trapped up there, and the eaters somehow managed to climb the ladder, I poked a hole in the tank and that kept them from climbing up," I continued. "We didn't realize that it was *your* water supply."

The man didn't answer, he didn't say anything, he just stared at me, and after a while he said. "There's something about you, what was your name again?"

"Jack," I answered sharply.

The man squinted his eyes and continued to stare for a moment, and then a slight smile came to his face.

"You didn't happen to be in the Corps, did you?"

The memories came flooding back to me at that moment.

"I didn't get your name," I said, as a slight smile crossed my lips.

"Ron," he said. "But you can call me *Sarge,* everybody else does."

At that instant, we both knew what was familiar about each other. Years ago, we served in the military together.

"You old *"Devil Dog"*, how have you been?" Ron asked, now grinning from ear to ear.

"I been doing all right Sarge, well until all of this started," I said, pointing to the pile of fly infested zombies at our feet.

"Give them back their weapons," Sarge ordered his men. "This guy can out shoot all of you; at least he could back when we were in the Marines."

"I'm getting a lot more practice nowadays," I said re-holstering my pistol.

"I guess we all are," Sarge added, motioning for me to follow him. Let's get the hell away from these damn flies.

"Indeed, the eaters are bad enough," I agreed, following closely behind the Sarge.

"We've got a nice little setup not far from here; it's pretty secure, and has enough room for all of our people, enough room for you and your family if you'd like to join us. I can't believe we ran into each other, it's been a long time Jack, a really long time," Sarge said.

"I never would have guessed it was you at the bottom of that water tower, we didn't know what to expect when we came down," I responded, waving for Gin and my sons to keep up with us.

The former sergeant abruptly stopped, turned to me, and said. "You're damn lucky it was me at the bottom of that water tower. We've ran into people that would have killed you for your hat, hell there might be one or two of my men or women that would do that. After they saw you poke that hole in the tank, some of my people wanted to just shoot you off that tower and ask questions later.

I told them they might miss and put more holes in the tank, even though I knew that they *wouldn't miss*."

"I'm glad you were so convincing, you always were a smooth talker Sarge," I admitted, nodding my head.

The sergeant briefly turned to one of his men and pointed to the hole in the water tower.

"Donny, you and Paul climb up there and plug that leak!"

He turned back to me.

"Jack, what in the hell were you thinking, climbing up that ladder in broad daylight, in full view of everything in hell's damn creation?" Sarge asked, with a very concerned look on his face.

"Must be from fatigue, we've been traveling almost from the minute the world went to shit, I guess I'm just tired, I'm not thinking straight, I've lost my edge," I answered sheepishly, still embarrassed about my mistake.

"Well, I've got to admit, you certainly do look like shit, but don't worry, I'll make sure you and your family gets some rest, and I'll keep the meaner ones under my command away from you for awhile, until they can see that you're not a complete idiot."

"I'd appreciate that, and thank you for not summarily killing us all, and oh yes, thank you for another emotional scar with that idiot comment," I said, trying to add a little levity to the conversation.

The sergeant turned away smiling and said. "Same old Jack, kills ya with laughter, or kills ya with his gun, but one way or another he'll kill ya."

We walked for a while talking of old times in the Marine Corps, and watching his people kill small random groups of zombies along the way.

"Well this is it Jack, what do you think of it?" Sarge asked, as we hiked across a large, formally well-manicured lawn that was now overgrown with weeds and tall grass.

The building that stood in front of me was constructed of red bricks with stone windowsills that sat ten feet above the foundation. The complex had a seven or eight foot high chain link fence surrounding most of the facility, and a parking lot that was capable of holding a couple of hundred vehicles, but only had eighty or ninety in it at that time.

"It's a YMCA building," I said. "And a fairly large one at that!"

"Large indeed," Sarge said. "We've got a swimming pool, gym, two basketball courts, and we converted one of the three hand-ball courts into a movie theater."

"Where do you get your electricity," I asked.

"Same place we get our hot water for our showers, that's the best part, we have a huge gasoline generator that runs everything that's electric, lights too," Sarge said proudly.

"Sure sounds like a sweet setup," Gin said, overhearing our conversation as she followed.

The sergeant turned around to Gin and said. "Sweet indeed little lady, sweet indeed. It would be even sweeter if we didn't have to go out into the world and collect supplies and gas and, well you know, things like that. But we're getting pretty good at gathering up stuff."

He turned back to me and said. "While we're out there, we figure we might as well do our part to bring back the world from the brink, and kill as many of those things as we possibly can, so that's what we do.

Part of our mission when we came for you was to clear out that bunch that had you trapped. We'd been watching them assemble for a couple of days before you showed up. When you climbed onto that water tower, we figured that was a good excuse to mosey over and take care of them and deal with you at the same time, you know kill two birds with one stone so to speak."

We reached the front of the sergeants stronghold where they had parked a tour bus in front of the doors, leaving about three inches of space between the bus and the building, and having to back it up a few feet to the right to gain access to the building, and then move it forward to block the doors again.

"Jack, you and your family go get cleaned up, we'll get you some clean clothes and get those filthy rags you're wearing washed and rustle you up some grub. I bet it's been awhile since you people have had a chance to take a hot shower," Sarge said smiling.

"It's been forever," I answered, smiling back at him.

"Johnny will show you around, I've got some things to take care of, I'll join back up with you at dinner, okay?" Sarge said, as if asking my permission.

"Roger that, Sarge," I answered, as we followed Johnny down the hall.

We spent the next hour taking a tour of the facility; it was almost like Johnny was trying to sell us a membership to the Y.

After we had taken a long hot shower, we were each given a plush bathrobe with a monogrammed YMCA logo embroidered on the pocket, and what seemed to be pants from a one size fits all martial art gi left over from a karate school that had used the place for their classes.

Once we were clean, dressed, and alone, Gin asked me a question.

"How well do you know this man, are we safe here, I mean, from these people?"

"From these people, I don't know. From Sarge, let me put it this way. If it weren't for the Sarge, I wouldn't be here. He has saved my life as many times as I have saved his. I would trust my life to him anytime, as I have many times in the past, we fought together during the war. And it looks like we may fight together again during this new war," I explained, conveying my confidence in my tone.

"What about his people, he said that they're pissed about the water tower, I heard him," Billy asked, duly concerned.

"I heard that too," Jacob noted, as he admired his new bathrobe.

"He seems to be in control of the others, and there's probably nobody here that has had to do anything worse than we've had to do out there, so let's try and be nice and get along with everyone, but keep your eyes and ears open, and as usual stay on your toes. We'll decide later, whether or not we're going to stay here. Let's go find the

Sarge and get something to eat, I'm starved," I answered calmly.

It wasn't long before we found Johnny, who led us to the cafeteria where Sarge and about thirty others were gathered for their evening meal.

"There you are, I'm glad to see you're still carrying at least some of your guns," the Sarge said, pointing to Jacob's carbine.

"It's a little hard to carry everything wearing these bathrobes, so we thought we would just bring our rifles," I answered, holding my AK-47 up for display.

The stocky ex-marine laughed and jested.

"Good choice Jack, we never want to bring a pistol to a rifle fight."

"Not unless we have to Sarge," I maintained. "My family has some rules, and one of them is, always have a gun within reach, so we always do, I mean unless your men take them away from us," I quipped smiling.

"Don't worry Jack, that will never happen again, ever," Sarge answered, as the smile ran away from his face. "We feel the same way, look around you, everyone has a gun whether you can see it or not. This place is as secure as it gets outside of Cheyenne Mountain anyway, we can't take the chance of one of them getting in, and us not being ready for them. All it would take is for someone to die of a heart attack during the night, and we could lose dozens before sunrise. So everyone carries a gun all of the time, just like you."

"Eaters are everywhere!" Jacob announced rather loudly trying to join the conversation.

"Where were you headed before we met up?" Sarge asked.

"Galveston," I answered.

"Galveston is overrun with the dead, we've got several people who came from there, they say it's a lot worse there than it is here, and it's pretty bad here, so it's really bad there, you don't want to go there Jack," Sarge pleaded.

We continued to talk and discuss our options, when four women carrying trays approached our table.

"Here you go, we hope this will be to your satisfaction," one of the women said.

All four trays were each brimming with food, and in the middle of each tray was a large, one-inch thick porterhouse steak.

"Steaks! Holy crud, where in the world did you get steaks Sarge?" I asked, thinking of Frank and his membership store full of food.

"I thought you might like that, one of my men was a butcher back in the real world, and cows aren't infected, none of the animals are as far as we know, except for maybe dogs, and anything that eats meat, and we're not eating dogs or any other carnivores.

We have quite a group of diversified people here, but just like the Corps, everyone is a warrior first and a tradesman second," he insisted. "Dig in Jack, you too boys, it's much better hot. Anything else we can get *you* little lady?" Sarge asked Gin, waving to one of the women who had brought the steaks to us.

"Well there is one thing," Gin answered hesitantly.

"Dessert, I bet it's dessert, bring some dessert, and bring enough for me too please," Sarge shouted to the woman.

"I could use some more ammo, that is if you happen to have any you can spare, and some dessert wouldn't be bad either," Gin said nonchalantly answering Sarge's question.

"We *are* running short on ammo," Billy added.

"We have about every kind of ammunition there is; we raid gun stores every chance we get, I think we can spare a little. I see you probably need AK bullets, what other caliber do you need?" Sarge asked.

Jacob raised his carbine and said. "I could use some 9 millimeter if you've got any?"

"If I've got any, why we have more of that than anything else, you can have as much of that as you can carry," Sarge insisted.

"We don't know if we're staying or going yet, so there's no big hurry," I said.

A tall blonde woman carrying a tray approached our table.

"Here's your dessert Ron," the woman said as she sat the tray on the table. "If you want anything else, just let me know."

"Okay Helen," said Sarge, watching her walk away.

"Apple pie, my favorite," Jacob proclaimed, as he grabbed a plate of dessert.

"You and your people seem to get around pretty good; have you lost many on your supply runs?" I asked.

"In the beginning we lost more than I care to admit, because we run into those diseased sons-a-bitches around every corner, we still have a few close calls here and there," Sarge answered. "But over time we developed somewhat of a system. We can charge car batteries with our generator so there's never a shortage of vehicles. We acquired some maps of the underground so we travel unseen much of the time," he explained.

"Underground, what do you mean by the underground?" Gin inquired.

"The sewers, we walk through the sewer to get to where we want to go. There are hardly any, what did you call them Jacob?"

"Eaters!" Jacob quickly answered.

Sarge continued his explanation.

"Yes eaters, there are very few eaters in the sewer system. Most of the time we can spot the ones that are down there long before they can surprise us, because they're so noisy with their constant snarling and growling. And we're totally out of sight of the hordes that are becoming more prevalent on the surface, and any rogue snipers or gangs that take pot shots at us from time to time. Hell, we can literally travel for miles undetected that way."

"What if you meet up with one of those rogue gangs in the sewer, what do you do then?" Billy asked.

"Well son, so far that hasn't happened, but when we travel anywhere we do it in a fairly large and well armed group. So if we do run into a formidable force down there, we'll be able to either talk our way out using the mutually assured destruction argument, or inflict some serious damage on them," Sarge guaranteed us.

The sergeant paused for a moment, and then announced.

"There is one thing Jack, if you stay with us, you'll need to be an asset to the group in some way, that goes for everyone, nobody gets a free ride here, nobody, is that understood?"

Jacob looked puzzled.

"What kind of an asset?" He asked.

"Anything that benefits the group, some are cooks, some wait tables like Helen, some are perimeter guards, mechanics, and some of us like me, collect supplies and specialize in killing those monsters out there, or as Jacob calls them, *Eaters*. It's up to you what you want to do, but you have to do something," Sarge insisted.

"That's not a problem, if we decide to stay, we'll pull our weight," I said.

"Right!" Gin added, as Billy and Jacob nodded their heads in agreement.

The Sarge and I spent the rest of the evening talking and reminiscing about old times. We shared our adventures dealing with the events of our new world; while my family enjoyed being *really* clean for the first time since we left our home on the outskirts of St. Louis. Gin and I even drank a couple of cold beers with the Sarge to celebrate our timely meeting.

Just before we retired for the evening, two young men approached us carrying a pile of folded clothes.

"Sir, we washed your family's uniforms, they're clean now, but we couldn't get out all of the blood stains."

"I'm sure they'll be just fine, thank you," I said, taking a pile from the taller man.

"After all, they are camouflage, the stains will blend right in," Gin added, reaching for the garments the other man was holding.

The next day, we sequestered ourselves in what used to be one of the offices, and after several long talks with my family members, we all decided that at least for the time being, it would be in our best interest to stay with this group of people.

After all, they have a reasonably secure facility, with electricity, hot water, and food. Not to mention a swimming pool, gym, and several other amenities that would make life in the apocalypse somewhat bearable.

We also decided that during our stay, however long that would be; our contribution to the group would be the same as the Sarge's, we would go out and collect supplies and kill zombies. After all, that's what we had been doing, and we were getting pretty good at it.

Two months passed, and by day we spent our time going on supply runs, killing zombies, and learning the sewer system around the former YMCA, and at night, we made good use of the swimming pool, basketball courts, and movie theater.

We were getting to know the people at the Y, and between the basketball games, and saving some of their lives, not to mention them saving ours on occasion, we began to develop close bonds with many of the people. Even some of the meaner ones!

THE ARMORY

"Hey Jack," the Sarge yelled from down the hall. "Come here for a minute."

"What's up Sarge?" I asked, thinking he was going to challenge me to some kind of contest, handball, or a game of horse, or something like that.

"Tomorrow we're going a little farther away than usual. There's a National Guard armory west of here a few miles, we're going to go over there and see if we can obtain some serious weapons, maybe a even a tank or something," he said, looking at me with that steely stare he used when he was dead serious (no pun intended).

"How far is a little farther?" I asked.

"About one hundred miles," he answered, still giving me his steely glare.

"I take it we're not going to be walking on this supply run," I concluded, returning his steely glance with one of my own.

"That's right Jack, we'll be driving to the armory, and we'll be taking a school bus on this expedition.

Fred and Jeff, along with a few others have been working on some pertinent changes to the bus for a couple of weeks now, and they just about have them completed," Sarge informed me, nodding his head and plastering a shit-eating grin on his face.

"How big is this school bus you're planning to drive a hundred miles," I asked, remembering our life on the road.

The sergeant canted his head to the left, and squinted his eyes slightly.

"It's a forty footer Jack, you kind of sound like you might have an issue with this plan, do you?" He asked softly.

"It's just that me and my family have been on the roads, they're littered with crashed and ditched vehicles, eaters come out of nowhere, and then of course there're the snipers. Not to mention we ran into road pirates who had built a barricade across the freeway and were stopping everyone that came by, you remember, I told you all about it," I said, expressing my concern.

"Sure I remember, I even remember you telling me about Match-Head and that gang of rogue dip-shits he was with," the Sarge informed me.

"So with all of that in mind, what modifications are Fred and Jeff making to this 40-foot school bus of yours?" I asked, curiously awaiting his answer.

I'll tell you what, let's go over to the garage area and take a gander at it," Sarge answered, as he turned and began to walk toward the back of the building.

"We're not going into this totally blind; do you remember Jill and Tommy? They joined the group about three weeks ago. Remember, they showed up here on that beat to hell motorcycle, saying that they would never ride a motorcycle again, as long as they lived?" Sarge said, recalling the two new comers.

"I remember them, I shared our experience on the bicycles with them, vowing never to use a bike every again, what about them?" I asked.

"They came in from the west, right passed the armory. Tommy said there were a lot of abandoned cars on the road, but nobody took any potshots at them, and they didn't run into any trouble. Well, except for the zombies and that damn shadow thing, but you can't really call that trouble, nobody has seen it well enough to even tell what the hell it is," Sarge said, shaking his head.

"We've seen it too, I mean kind of seen it. Everyone we've ran across that wasn't trying to kill us that is, has told us that they have experienced it too, along with the lights at night," I informed the Sarge.

"Lights at night?" Sarge asked, again tilting his head and squinting his eyes.

"Yeah, they're just like the day shadows, you never really get to see them, they don't make any sense either," I answered.

"Well this is it Jack," the Sarge said, opening the door to the garage.

"Hey Fred, hey Jeff, you guys about done?"

"Just finished putting on the last of the window tint, we're ready to go, just say the word," Jeff answered proudly, as Fred nodded his head in agreement.

"Good, give Jack here an update of what you changed on this bad boy, he'll be coming with us," Sarge said, looking over the completed bus.

I liked the way the Sarge had volunteered me (and my family) for the mission before I'd given him my answer one way or another. I decided to keep my mouth shut and inspect this school bus of theirs before I made up my mind whether or not I would be joining them on this very dangerous, and possibly suicidal mission they were about to undertake.

"Well, first we made sure it's in tip top running condition, we changed the oil and filters, checked and bled the brakes, and topped off all of the fluids. But the real changes are the ones that are going to get us there and back. We salvaged this huge blade from a snowplow that was being transported on a northbound train when the plague hit, turned it upside down, and welded it on to the front bumper mounts. The idea being, any of those monsters out there that we scoop up will be discarded to the left of the bus, and not tossed over by the door," Jeff explained, very pleased with his work.

"Sounds good," Sarge agreed, stroking his chin. "What do you think Jack, sound good to you?"

"How strong is the blade, will it hold up to crashing into and pushing vehicles out of the way?" I asked, impressed with Fred and Jeff's workmanship.

Fred piped up at this point.

"That was my concern too, so I welded supports onto the frame, they're made out of chrome steel, they'll hold up to just about anything," he said, almost arrogantly.

Jeff then added.

"We just got done tinting the windows, that's so any snipers that are out there won't be able to get a clean shot off, and we even tinted the windshield and encapsulated the front and sides of the driver's seat with 3/8 inch steel plates. Just in case any shooters try to guesstimate where the driver is seated. We painted the bus black as you can see; I figured a big yellow school bus would stick out like a sore dick in a snow storm."

"Anything else?" Sarge asked.

"We cut holes low along the sides near the floor at two foot intervals, just big enough to shoot a gun through, and as you can see we welded steel panels across and in front of the wheel-wells to protect the tires and keep any zombies you might run over from getting stuck in the wheel wells. We even added an escape hatch in the floor, just in case for some reason you end up flipping the bus over."

"Don't forget the extra fuel tank," Fred reminded. "We put an extra fuel tank about fifteen feet away from the original one, in case you start leaking fuel from it."

"Are you two going to be going with us?" I asked.

"No they're mechanics and welders," Sarge interjected quickly.

"Good," I said. "Then you two won't mind working through the night and adding something for me."

"Anything for the cause," Jeff said, surprisingly happily. "What is it that you would like added sir?"

"Don't call me sir; I'm not your dad!" I answered smiling, just before I shared with everyone our experience running from the pack of dogs just after we had left the river. And how we periodically would see packs of dogs in the distance as we made our way across the country. I also informed them of how we managed on several occasions to get ourselves surrounded by large groups of zombies that seemed to come out of nowhere.

I told them that we would need two ports cut into the middle of the roof of the bus. One close to the front and one close to the back, ports that we could close and lock if need be, and that were big enough to crawl through if we had to. Also we would need platforms to stand on that were high enough that we could get our upper torso through the ports so we could shoot at any attackers, whether they were dead or alive, or animals, or all of the above.

"We'll have it done before dawn," Jeff insisted, nodding his head and looking at Fred.

"Considering that we've already taken out most of the seats, this shouldn't be too much of a chore," Fred agreed, smiling.

"Great, then we leave at dawn," the sergeant announced loudly.

As the sun rose, and we entered the garage the following morning, the Sarge and I found Jeff and Fred sleeping on the floor under the bus. However, true to their word, they had completed the assignment that I had given them, and had even added steps to the platforms, and a rope to pull the hatch covers closed from inside the bus.

"Wake up you two," the Sarge bellowed. "I didn't mean you had to sleep here!"

Crawling out from under the bus, and wiping the sleep from his eyes, Jeff said. "We know, but we wanted to make sure that we did the job to your satisfaction, so we decided to wait for you here."

I wasted no time boarding the modified school bus and climbing onto one of the shooting platforms. I pushed the port cover open and stuck my head out, standing up I was able to move freely in all directions, and after pretending to fire my rifle from the perch, I signaled to the sergeant my approval by giving him the thumbs up, and acknowledging my approval to Jeff and Fred by saying.

"I see you even padded the edges of the hatch, you two did a great job."

"Thank you sir," Jeff replied, not remembering my mandate from the night before which was not to call me *sir*.

"If it's all the same to you, we're going to go get some real sleep now, this concrete floor is not the most comfortable place to sleep," Fred added, as Jeff nodded his head in agreement.

"It's time we get going Jack, go wake up your family, eat some breakfast, get your gear, and meet me back here in exactly one hour, I'll get the rest of the crew," Sarge ordered, as he left the garage.

I made my way back to our sleeping quarters, not really pleased with the thought of traveling a hundred miles one way, through "*Eaterland*". But the Sarge and the rest of the group had been good to us, and the school bus modifications looked sound, and the prospect of gathering some military weapons and perhaps a tank, was enough to convince me that the reward might be worth the risk.

"Wake up everyone, it's time to get ready, wait until you see the vehicle we'll be traveling in today," I said, trying to sound cheerful.

"Are we going to the armory today like you and the sergeant talked about last night, honey?" Gin asked, sitting up and stretching her arms.

"Like I told you last night, the Sarge kind of volunteered us, so indeed we are, it's only one hundred miles away, and if all goes well, we'll be bringing back a lot of serious firepower," I answered, trying to sound like the whole trip was no big deal.

"Dad, can you tell me when everything has gone well since this whole thing started?" Jacob asked, again sarcastically.

"We're still alive, that's gone pretty well hasn't it?" I retorted back sarcastically.

372

"Point well taken," Jacob replied.

"Enough messing around, we leave in less than an hour, let's get our gear together and then go get some breakfast," I suggested, calmly. "We can bring more ammo than usual; considering that we'll be riding this time, instead of walking."

With our gear organized. We went to the cafeteria and consumed a fine breakfast that consisted of steak and eggs, and when we had had our fill, we retreated to our quarters to collect our gear.

"Everyone better make a facilities check before we leave, we're going to be on the road for a while, and as you know, there aren't many restrooms out there, and even if there were, I doubt if the Sarge is going to want to stop every five minutes to let you take a squirt," I warned.

"I'll be right back," Billy said, as he turned and ran back toward the cafeteria.

"Hurry up, we've only got a few minutes before we leave," I yelled down the hallway to him.

When I came out of the restroom, I saw Billy coming down the hallway pushing a food cart.

"Since we'll be riding today, we can use this to haul more ammunition to our vehicle, that is, if there's enough room in the vehicle to carry all the ammo this cart can haul!" Billy said, expecting me to say there was a limited amount of space, as he was unaware of the size of the vehicle we'd be traveling in.

"Good idea son," I said smiling. "There's plenty of room for as much ammo as we can bring along."

Another quick stop at the ammunition room to load the food cart to its capacity, and we set off to meet up with the Sarge and the rest of the bus crew.

"Okay, is everyone ready for this?" I said, just before opening the door to the garage.

"We're ready," Jacob said, while the others nodded their heads in agreement.

Trying to set a tone of excitement to take away from the real danger of the upcoming mission, I swung the door open and shouted. "Ta-da!"

"Are you kidding me?" Jacob exclaimed. "That's cool Dad."

"Yeah, that's really cool Dad," Billy added, grinning from ear to ear.

"All right you're here, right on time, let's get this monster machine loaded and hit the road shall we?" the Sarge said, acting as if we were about to embark on an excursion to the local park for a picnic.

"Can we stop somewhere and pickup a couple of twelve packs of beer for the journey Sarge," I quipped, trying to add a little humor to the moment.

"I don't think a couple of twelve packs will be enough, we better get a couple of cases," Sarge answered laughing.

Everyone's mood was upbeat as we pulled out of the garage and made our way along the driveway, through the parking lot and onto the main road.

"No shooting at anything unless we need to, we don't want to bring unnecessary attention to ourselves," Sarge ordered, as our driver Dave plowed into the first of many zombies we would run into on our journey, literally.

"This snowplow blade works great, did you see that monster get shoved to the side, I mean the part of it that didn't get sheared off at the ankles," Dave said giggling, with a maniacal look on his face.

"Jack and his family call them *Eaters*," Sarge said giggling too, only without the maniacal look on his face.

"That works for me, "Eaters" it is," Dave replied, still giggling as he plowed into another zombie (get it, *plowed* into).

By the sergeant's order, Jeff and Fred had left nine seats intact in the bus including the driver's seat. Everyone going on this mission was chosen for it because of a unique talent they possessed, and the extra room left by extracting the unnecessary seating was going to be needed to haul back the weapons we hoped to acquire at the armory.

Four of the seats were filled by my family and me, we were chosen because of my past with the Sarge, and because of our prowess with firearms, accept for Gin, I had asked for her so that there would be no chance that my family would become separated, and besides, she wasn't exactly a bad shot.

The other five seats accommodated the driver Dave, who drove a school bus for a living before the apocalypse, and told everyone. "If you ever have to drive a school bus for a living, just kill yourself first, it'll save everybody a lot of trouble!" The Sarge, well someone needed to lead the mission. A stocky guy named Bruce, who in his former life was a locksmith. A man named Rich who didn't say much, but always carried a 12 gage tactical shotgun, and who had been an armored vehicle mechanic in the army and claimed he knew how to drive a tank. And last, but certainly not least, a cute small framed little blonde girl in her late twenties named Beth, who was sporting a .22 caliber version of an AR-15, who everyone seemed to think was some kind of psychopath. I guess you never know when one of your psycho friends will come in handy.

After we had ridden for a while, I thought it might be a good idea to get to know the people on the bus that I was going to have to trust with my life, and vice versa, besides my family of course. I had seen all of them at the Y on occasion, but never really got to know them. So I smiled, trying not to offend her, and asked Beth.

"Does that .22 do the job on eaters?" She smiled at me and answered.

"Usually I take one shot, and I get one kill, but sometimes I add an extra couple of shots just for fun. The .22 is quieter than most guns, so I feel I can take more shots without making too much noise."

"With that kind of attitude, you'll get along well with my son Jacob," I divulged, still smiling at her.

"Jacob and I get along just fine, we met a few weeks ago at the swimming pool, it'll be nice to do some eater killing with him, I'm a supplier too. We've just never had the pleasure of going on a run together until now," she said confidently."

"Jack everyone here is an experienced supplier, they've all killed more eaters than I can count, so don't worry, you're in good hands," Sarge added, as he scanned the horizon with a pair of 20x50 binoculars.

"I'm just trying to get to know everyone, that's all Sarge," I maintained.

As I was beginning to start up a conversation with Bruce, Dave yelled.

"Here we go people!"

Immediately we heard dull thuds coming from the front of the bus. Zombies were careening off the snowplow blade and causing it to make a low vibrating twang. First, one or two, then three or four more, then so many that it was impossible to discern any gaps between the thuds and the twangs.

"We're plowing through a pretty big horde of um," Dave yelled, his knuckles turning white as his grip tightened on the steering wheel.

Blood now splattered over the windshield as severed body parts, crushed skulls, and broken bones, bounced off and over the plow blade, leaving a trail of the crimson liquid in their wake. So much in fact, that the red ooze drifted along the sides of our bus, making our already tinted windows opaque, and soon totally obscuring our view of what was happening outside the bus.

"Lucky for us, Jeff and Fred topped off the windshield washer fluid, at least I can see what we're about to hit with this big black beast," Dave stated, not sounding very confident.

The wipers slapped back and forth for what seemed like an eternity, smearing the bodily fluids and other assorted hunks of mutilated zombies across the windshield as more and more of the undead slammed against the plow blade. As body parts were tossed all around us, the only pieces that were conspicuously missing were the feet of the undead, which were being sheared off at the ankles and bouncing against the floorboards of our bus, adding an uneven drum roll to the melody of carnage already being played.

"Even with the washer fluid, I can barely see out, it's too bad those guys didn't think to put new wiper blades on this machine," Dave hollered out, turning the wheel to avoid an abandon truck. "I missed that one, but we're going to hit these other two at full bore."

A sickening crunch echoed through the interior of the bus, as the two vehicles Dave had referred to were pummeled by the large plow blade, followed by the powerful inertia of the forty-foot school bus.

"We're still rolling, and the plow blade is still attached, I guess that chrome steel reinforcement held," Sarge boasted, with a smirk on his face.

"I guess so," I said, agreeing with him.

The others had remained relatively quiet until now, no screaming or yelling, nothing to distract Dave while he drove through the onslaught of obstacles.

That wasn't a big surprise, we were all seasoned veterans of the zombie apocalypse, we'd all seen our share of mayhem and gore, and we'd all been in many tight situations where we thought we were probably going to die at any moment.

So ramming our way through a large group of nomadic reanimated dead homicidal maniacs in a five-ton vehicle with a converted snowplow blade attached to the front of it, was just another day at the office for us.

All of the sudden, Beth leaned over and pointed her .22 rifle at one of the side holes.

"Look, fingers, they're grabbing a hold of the bus," she said, firing three rounds into the fingers sticking out of the hole.

The zombies hand retreated quickly, but left two of its digits twitching on the floor of the bus with several flies hovering around them.

"Check the other holes," Jacob shouted, itching for some action.

He found fingers reaching through two of the other small gun ports, and hacked at them with his machete, leaving even more fingers twitching on the floor.

"Look!" Billy yelled. "As soon as we whack the fingers off, they're replaced by another eater trying to stick their hand inside."

"So don't worry about them, they can't get to us through those holes, we'll take care of them after we're clear of this mob scene we're dealing with now," I said. "And besides, their fingers squeezed in those holes are keeping some of the flies out of the bus."

By now, we had mangled countless zombies and spewed gallons of blood from their bodies, which now covered the road, making our bus begin to lose traction.

"There're too many of them out in front of us, the tires aren't gripping the road, I can feel the bus fishtailing and we're slowing down," Dave yelled, with a flair for the dramatic. "If we stop we're through! Done for! Finished!"

As fast as I could, I climbed onto the forward platform with my AK, and opened the front top port hatch.

"Somebody take the back port, and shoot the eaters in front of us on the right side," I shouted, pointing toward the front of the bus.

In a flash, Jacob jumped onto the rear platform, opened the hatch, and began firing his carbine into the crowd of zombies on the right side of our bus that we were about to hit. I could hear the whizzing sound of Jacob's bullets fly past my head as I too began to drop the attacking zombies along the right side of the road in front of the bus.

I emptied my drum magazine and ejected it from my rifle, and narrowly avoided being hit by a zombie's severed left arm that flew by me as I ducked back into the bus. Beth had already handed Jacob a loaded magazine, and now stood at the base of my platform with two of my fully loaded drum mags in her hands. I sat my empty magazine on the platform and snatched a loaded one from her right hand. Back through the top hatch I went, and began to engage the rabble of zombies again.

Between the snowplow blade shoving the hungry monsters to the left side of the road (except for some of their detached limbs, intestines, and cut off feet), and the attrition rate that Jacob and I were inflicting on the horde on the right side of the road, the bus was gradually gaining speed again as Dave's felony hit and run tally began to diminish.

Through the gunshots and sound of bones being bashed against the plow blade, and the low bass tone made by the feet being battered against the bottom of the bus, I somehow heard Dave screaming at the crew.

"It's working; I think we're going to make it!"

We continued to shoot and plow our way through the horde of the dead for the next two hundred yards or so, and as the quantity of zombies began to subside, Jacob and I retreated back into the school bus and secured the hatches, allowing only a few flies to follow.

Looking around the bus, I caught a serious gaze from Gin, as if she was saying to me.

"Who was it that thought this was a good idea?"

Dave was giggling again, most likely nervous laughter. Rich sat there seemingly unfazed by the event. Bruce smiled at me undaunted by the harrowing experience.

Surprisingly, Beth was the first to say something, usually it's the Sarge or myself that come up with the first quip after some hair raising incident.

"Well, that's one way to thin the herd," she said, as a smile broke through her serious demeanor, and she made her way from one gun port to the next, blowing off the fingers of the zombies that were still clinging to the side of our bus.

The Sarge wasn't in as much of a jovial mood as the rest of us.

"What the hell happened back there Dave, didn't you see that giant crowd of homicidal maniacs blocking the road, or did you just decide to the test our bus on the biggest group you could find to see if it was up to the task at hand?" he said angrily, glaring at Dave.

"They were gathered together on the other side of that hill, we crossed the crest of the hill, and there they were, there was nothing I could do, they weren't there and then they were there. They just appeared," Dave replied, no longer giggling.

"From now on, when you come to a hill, slow down so we don't end up in the middle of that kind of mess again. Get me?

By the way, I want to thank you for the smell we have to endure for the rest of this trip now that our vehicle is covered with rotting body fluids and entrails.

And look at Jack and Jacob, I'm sure that they thank you too, I mean do you think they enjoy being splattered with all sorts of stinking zombie remains? I'm not even going to mention these damn flies all over the inside of the bus, get your act together Dave," Sarge insisted, as he began to calm down and swat at some of the buzzing insects harassing him.

Feeling the tension in the bus, Billy thought he would try to lighten the mood.

"Are we there yet?" he asked, smiling.

His imitation of a road wary child seemed to do the trick; the salty old Marine Corps veteran could not hold back his laughter even as one of the tormenting flies landed on his face.

"Like father like son," he teased. "Jack, that's your son all right."

"I have taught him well," I said jokingly, and then added. "I think Dave might just have broken my record of felony hit and runs!"

That comment brought a smile to everyone's face, even Rich's.

We drove on for miles, taking that time to reload our magazines, and kill the remaining marauding flies that had invaded our bus. We encountered small groups of zombies along the way, and observed Dave timidly use them to increase his felonious total under the watchful eye of the Sarge, and tried to avoid, although not always successfully, a plethora of abandoned and derelict vehicles parked on the road.

At each occurrence, our blood stained modified school bus passed muster with flying-colors, dispatching zombies and vehicles alike from the road.

"We're almost there," Sarge announced, picking up his rifle and the biggest crowbar I had ever seen.

"Wow, that's a huge crowbar," Jacob said. "Where did you get it?"

"Picked this little baby up at the railroad yard, they used it to pry up railroad ties, it does wonders on doors and windows, but it's too heavy to carry around most of the time. I thought it might come in handy for breaking into a military facility like a National Guard armory," Sarge responded, holding up his humongous steel tool.

We all followed suit, picking up our weapons, and assorted specialized equipment, such as lock picks, and mechanic's tools and prepared to go into the armory.

Dave turned our bus onto a short asphalt street, and announced.

"There it is, just up ahead."

Dave brought our bus to a stop in front of the armory and we prepared to disembark.

"Everyone knows what to do, so do your job and we should be in and out in no time, let's go," the Sarge ordered, as he opened the school bus door.

We filed out of the bus, and Rich, Dave, and Bruce separated from us immediately and disappeared around the side of the building in search of the area where the vehicles might be parked.

Sarge and the rest of our group went directly to the front of the building where we found the front door securely locked. The Sarge jammed his gargantuan crowbar into the narrow crack between the door and the doorjamb close to the top hinge.

"Watch this; this should be a piece of cake," he said, tugging hard on the opposite end of the steel bar.

A loud crack broke the precious silence we coveted, as the top of the door separated from the frame.

"One more and we're in," Sarge bragged, while sticking the crowbar in beside the lower hinge.

Another loud cracking sound was heard, which was quickly eclipsed by the horrendous noise made by the heavy wooden door falling onto the concrete walkway.

"Eaters!" Gin said calmly, alerting us that the noise we had made was drawing zombies toward us.

"We'll take care of this," Billy said walking in the direction of the small cluster of zombies. "Come on Jake, let's get'um."

I had come to trust my boy's competence in the art of killing zombies, so I wasn't overly concerned when they set out to drop a small band of these deadly maniacs, apprehensive yes, overly concerned no. As long as I didn't see them becoming too cocky, which seems to always turn to carelessness, and being careless will get you killed in our new world.

Billy and Jacob quickly and silently did away with the approaching zombies using their edged weapons, which reinforced my confidence in them, and then they rejoined the rest of us waiting by the front door.

We all entered the building, and once inside we quickly located the arsenal that was one of the objectives of our mission.

"All of the guns are locked in these racks," Gin announced, seeming rather frustrated. "I thought all we would have to do is pick them up and leave."

"Soldiers steal too," I said, expecting to find them secured.

"Yeah, but soldiers don't carry five foot long crowbars," Sarge added, tearing the lock and hinge assembly off a rack with one swift tug.

"Jack, see if you and your boy's can find some ammo for these M-4's, and anything else for that matter," the Sarge ordered, while ripping the lock off another rack.

"Gin, come with us, we're going to need all the help we can get," I explained.

We found the ammunition locked in a cage in the next room.

"Jacob, run back and get the sergeant's crowbar, quickly," I said.

Jacob ran back and returned with the crowbar, and with Beth.

"I don't think leaving the Sarge by himself is a good idea," I mentioned, while breaking the lock off the ammo cage door.

Beth shrugged her shoulders and replied. "Neither do I, but he insisted I help you guys, and we don't have time to sit down and debate it."

"These ammo boxes are heavy," Gin complained, as she lifted one of the boxes.

"Yeah, we're going to need a cart or a dolly or something, otherwise this will take us forever," I admitted, looking around for something to use to transport the burdensome ammunition.

"What about this?" Billy asked, pointing to a steel-wheeled heavy wooden flatbed cart.

"I think that's the reason it's here, duh," Beth mocked sarcastically, showing that she could be just as big of a wiseass as the boys.

We loaded the flatbed with as much ammo as possible, keeping in mind that we still had to be able to move it once it was loaded.

"That's it, we've got 5.56, 7.62, 9mm, and some 50 cal. for that big sniper rifle I saw in the next room," I grunted, trying to push the cart by myself. "A little help would be nice boys."

With the help of Billy and Jacob, we pushed the ammo cart past the rifle depository room, to the front door, where we left it to return and help the Sarge.

The Sarge had found a flatbed of his own, and had it piled high with M-4 rifles and M-9 pistols.

"If I put anymore on it they just slide off," he said smiling.

"I can carry two *or* three," Jacob volunteered, sliding two pistols into his pockets, and picking up three more rifles. "Or I can carry both the rifles and the pistols?"

"Me too," said Gin, as she grabbed two more M-4's.

"Give me some," Billy added, not wanting to look like a slacker. "Never mind, I'll carry this heavy ass .50 cal. Barrett rifle."

"I'll make sure we don't get our asses killed," Beth muttered, heading for the door.

With both carts full, we maneuvered them out the front door and down the walkway to our parked bus.

"Let's get this stuff into the bus," Sarge ordered, pointing to a half dozen slobbering zombies stumbling toward our school bus.

As we loaded the weapons and ammo into the bus as fast as we could, Beth calmly stepped between the approaching flesh-eating maniacs and us; pulled a plastic water bottle out of her pocket and unscrewed the cap. She took a small sip, and then emptied the rest of the water onto the street in front of her.

"What are you doing Beth?" the Sarge screamed. "Shoot'em, shoot'em now!"

Beth nonchalantly looked at Sarge and gave him a sultry wink. She then proceeded to stick the muzzle of her .22 rifle into the empty water bottle; she gripped the neck of the bottle hard, took two steps toward the closest zombie, and shot a round through the bottom of the bottle and into the forehead of the slobbering maggot infused beast. The fly larva that was infesting the hungry monster sprinkled onto the ground around its body, as it slammed down hard onto the asphalt.

She had effectively created a homemade suppressor (silencer) in a matter of seconds, which had muffled the sound of her rifle by at least two-thirds. Beth continued on, systematically neutralizing the hungry dead cannibals, while we finished loading the newly acquired weapons and ammo onto the bus.

After dusting off the approaching undead killers, Beth returned to the bus as if nothing had happened, brushing off some hitchhiking maggots from her arm as she approached.

"That's a neat trick Beth, where did you learn that," Billy asked.

"From my first real boy friend, he was somewhat of a bad boy; you know the type, right Gin?" She answered, looking at Gin knowingly.

"I know the type all right, I should, I married one," Gin replied.

"Hey honey, you can't be talking about me, can you?" I asked, looking as pitiful as I could.

"The one and only," was her answer.

"We need to find the others, and get out of here," Sarge stated, looking in the direction we last saw the other men.

"What's that?" Gin said, listening intently to an unfamiliar sound.

"It sounds to me like the boy's found themselves an armored vehicle," I said. "And here it comes now."

The rattling, clanking, clicking, and clattering sounds of tank tracks, gave way to the visual interpretation of the noise, as an M1 Abrams third-generation main battle tank rounded the corner of the building and headed straight for us.

We could see Bruce sitting behind a "Ma Duce" 50 caliber machine gun, as Rich steered the tank in our direction, while Dave staffed the main gun.

"Lucky we picked up a few boxes of the 50 cal. ammo," Billy said.

"Yes, it does look that way," Beth added, as she found another maggot to brush from her sleeve.

The tank pulled up beside the bus and Bruce said. "Hey guys, you'll never guess what else we found."

"Probably not, so why don't you tell us before the noise of that tank brings more of the dead our way?" Sarge urged sternly.

Bruce held up the gun group and hose of a World War II, M2-2 Flamethrower.

"It's a flamethrower, and it's full of fuel too," Bruce said proudly. "I have no idea what in the hell the National Guard was doing with this, but it's ours now."

"Maybe they were going to use it in a demonstration or something, who knows, but like Bruce says, it's ours now," Sarge declared, climbing onto the bus.

"Billy, climb up there and grab that Flamethrower, and let's get it loaded onto the bus," Sarge ordered.

Turning to Bruce, he then asked. "How much fuel does that tank have in it?"

"We just filled it up; they've got a fuel pump back there. The pump had a weak tit excuse for a padlock on it, but Bruce and his lock pick made short work of that. There's a bunch of stuff back there, there's a garage, and a bunch of other vehicles too," Bruce proclaimed, boasting of his discovery.

"Sarge, I think we should check out the back, if there's a lot more stuff back there, I'd hate to leave it, after all we're already here," I told him, thinking I wouldn't mind getting a hold of another Hummer.

"You've got fifteen minutes, not a second longer, and don't make me have to come and find you, you hear me Jack?" Sarge said in an uncompromising tone.

"Yes sir, we hear you, fifteen minutes," I answered.

"I'm not kidding Jack, fifteen minutes," the Sarge reiterated.

"Let's go, you heard the Sarge," I said to my family.

Just as Billy climbed down from the tank, and was about to hand the flamethrower over to the sergeant so he could join us in our endeavor, Bruce's head exploded.

Resulting in pieces of blood soaked skull, grayish-tan and pink colored pieces of brain, and clumps of his brown hair being scattering all over the tank's turret, and leaving a crimson mist of blood floating in the space that his head had once occupied.

As Bruce's headless body slid down into the tank, the Sarge screamed. "Sniper!" as he dropped to the floor of the bus.

"Get behind the tank!" I yelled, as we scrambled to take cover behind the large steel behemoth.

"Jack, can you see the sniper's position?" the Sarge called out.

"He's got to be shooting from one of those three tall buildings to the east of us," I yelled back, as the pinging sound of another one of the sniper's bullets ricocheted off the armored skin of the tank.

"Rich, Dave, can you hear me?" I shouted.

"We can hear you, what do you want us to do?" Rich yelled back through the open turret as he pushed Bruce's lifeless body off his lap.

"You see the three tall buildings to the east of our location; the sniper's position has to be in one of those buildings. Do you think that you can bring down those buildings with the tank's cannon?" I asked, hoping for an affirmative answer.

"Should be a piece of cake," Rich answered, as the tank's turret slowly turned toward the building on the far left.

Moments later the barrel of the tank's big gun rose slightly and we heard Dave yell.

"If I were you, I would cover my ears; this is going to be loud."

Not being able to hear Rich and Dave from their position on the bus, the Sarge and Beth covered their ears when they saw me signal them to do so, just moments before the 120 mm smoothbore cannon released its powerful report.

The shock wave from the gun's blast shook the modified school bus as the mighty tank cannon stirred up a dust cloud that engulfed the bus. And as the slight southerly breeze slowly pushed the dust cloud to the side, we could see that Dave's aim had been true.

The 120 mm high explosive projectile had impacted one of the main vertical support beams and exploded, tearing a large chunk out of the southwest corner of the building about one third of the way up. Which was just above the rooftops of the smaller buildings setting in front of it that were blocking our view of the lower third of the building. The destruction of the that main support beam caused the structure to first slowly tilt to our right, and the further it leaned, the faster it began to fall, until the edifice broke off at the point of the shell's contact and crashed to the ground, flattening several smaller structures that had been built around it. A gigantic cloud of dust rose into the air, as the demolition of the first building was complete.

Now the ricocheting bullets came at an increased pace, confirming that the building that had been destroyed, wasn't the one that the sniper had picked to do his deadly deed.

"Hit the next one, we're still taking fire," I yelled, as I dragged an exposed part of the flamethrower behind the tank.

"Roger that," Rich shouted, as we watched the cannon take a bead on the next building.

When the barrel stopped, we again covered our ears. I couldn't help but think of the hearing protection that we had used for target practice on the river, and that we had lost because of abandoning most of our supplies on our way to the water tower. And how it sure would have come in handy about now.

Again the powerful armament sounded off, and again a large hole was blasted close to the base of the targeted structure, however, this time the building didn't tilt, it didn't lean, and it didn't fall, this time the explosion had ignited a fire, which was quickly engulfing the upper floors.

"Put another one into it," Billy screamed, still hearing bullets bouncing off the tank.

The turret moved once more, and again the mighty Abram's main gun blasted another huge hole into the burning building.

The second shot did the trick, now with a whole section of the front of the building missing; it toppled almost straight down compacting floor by floor, until it disappeared into a massive cloud of dust and debris.

With two high-rise buildings destroyed, and the sniper's bullets still landing all around us, it was clear that the remaining building was where the sniper had made his nest.

"Two down, and one to go," I yelled to Rich and Dave.

"You guys just keep your heads down for a couple more minutes, and then we can pack our trash, and blow this popsicle stand," Rich bellowed from the bowels of the tank.

Again, the turret on the colossal mobile artillery piece began to move. As the muzzle of the big gun on 68-ton beast leveled on the remaining building, and the sniper's bullets continued to drop on the tank, Rich and Dave prepared to eliminate the last bastion of the deadly sniper that had killed Bruce and seemed to be determined to kill us all.

The horrendous ground shaking roar of the Abrams cannon had sounded three times, and the sound of two buildings crashing to the ground a few blocks away, added to the racket that we were producing, which for all intent and purposes was like ringing a giant dinner bell for all of the starving zombies roaming the area for miles around.

"Dad! There're eaters everywhere," Jacob screamed, crouching down even lower behind the tank.

I had been occupied with the sniper, and my attention focused on trying to help direct Rich and Dave as much as I could. When I turned around and saw what had Jacob so alarmed, I too became alarmed.

Hundreds of zombies were staggering toward us from all directions and at varying speeds, some of which had maggots dripping from their slobbering mouths and some did not, but all were besieged by a forbidding black cloud of houseflies. We were pinned down behind the tank, and we couldn't risk climbing into it for fear of ending up headless like Bruce, and between us and the bus lied several yards of no man's land; a snipers paradise.

We were trapped, our choices were clear, we had but two options; option number one, we could run and most likely catch a sniper's bullet in the head, and then be eaten by zombies, thereby dying a horrible death one way or another.

Option number two, we could stay where we were, and be eaten alive by the same zombies mentioned in option number one, thereby cutting out the middle man (the sniper), and still dying a horrible death.

Either way we were bound to end up in a pile of zombie defecation, provided that zombies do indeed defecate, as of yet I hadn't seen that happen, but in this brave new world, and with the smell of some of those undead bastards, it seemed that anything and everything was possible.

Until Rich and Dave pulled the trigger on the big gun once more, and collapsed the sniper's refuge once and for all, our only hope was to fend off the horde and try to make our way to the bus (option number one). There was always a chance, no matter how slight it might be, that the sniper would miss his mark, and we would all make it to the safety of the bus.

On the other hand, the odds were astronomically high, that the hundreds, if not thousands of zombies that were approaching us, would miss their mark when they would inevitably overrun our position.

Therefore, I hoped that the boys inside the tank would hurry and eliminate the sniper's hiding place, so we could make our way to the safety of the school bus without worrying about losing *our* heads in the process.

The turret of the tank began to turn once more as Dave lined up the barrel of the cannon with the third and last building that needed to be destroyed in order to kill the sniper and hopefully save our sorry asses in the process.

"Ka-Boom!" A deafening explosion ripped through the breach of the Abram's cannon. Once I recovered from the shock and surprise of the cannon erupting, I yelled to Rich.

"Rich, are you and Dave all right?"

No answer came from inside the tank. Billy then tried to contact the men inside the tank. He beat the metal butt stock of his AK-47 against the tank's steel hull and yelled.

"Dave, Rich, can you hear me?"

Again, there was no answer from the men in the tank, only smoke spewed from the top of the turret.

"What in the hell happened?" Gin asked.

"I think the sniper put a round down the barrel of the cannon just before Dave had a chance to pull the trigger," I answered. "See the bulge in the side of the barrel?"

As I finished my explanation to Gin, I heard the Sarge's voice.

"Sorry Jack," I heard him yell, as the bus pulled away. "We can't wait any longer, we gotta go!"

That was the last thing that I heard the Sarge say, before he and Beth drove out of sight, plowing through scores of zombies, and leaving us to fend for ourselves.

My parting gift to the Sarge was several well placed shots into the rear tires of his bus, hoping to give him the same chance of surviving the massive horde as he had given to us.

I did feel a little bit sorry that I had put Beth in that same predicament; however, sometimes sacrifices must be made.

Now short on ammo, surrounded by zombies, thousands of zombies, and still pinned down by a sniper, my family looked at each other knowing this was the end, nothing short of divine intervention could save us now.

"We're not going to give up just yet," I shouted. "If we're going out, we'll take as many of these rotten sons-a-bitch'in eaters with us as we can."

As quick as I could, I strapped on the fuel tanks of the World War II era flamethrower, and picked up the gun group of the frightening weapon. Somehow, I managed to light the pilot flame, and when I pulled the trigger, twenty feet of flaming petroleum shot from the nozzle.

I pointed the weapon at the top of the tank turret and set it on fire, the billowing black smoke and orange flames gave me temporary concealment from the sniper's view.

I then walked several feet from the back of the tank and met the first of the attacking living corpses.

Swinging the nozzle in a semi-circular motion, I covered a row of forty or fifty zombies, three, or four deep. With that first swing, I ignited somewhere between one hundred, and one hundred and fifty zombies, along with tens of thousands of flies, and sent them all preapproved, straight back to hell where they belonged.

As many zombies as I had set on fire on my first offensive advance, I knew that there were far more attacking maniacs than the fuel tanks in my M2 flamethrower could possibly repulse.

However, I was determined not to go down without a fight, and too die with my boots on.

So, with the stench of burnt and decaying zombie flesh, and with the smell of the fuel from the flamethrower searing my nostrils, I continued to hose down the overwhelming zombie horde with the flaming liquid, resolute in my commitment to take as many of them to hell with me as I possibly could.

END OF DAYS AND NIGHTS

"Krmwya aipel ersaao, riuedo baere aipels ytyhdf!" Babbled a junior grade ensign third class.

"English, speak English!" Captain Xarr shouted, after overhearing his inferior talking in his native tongue. "We were not shipped out to Anunnak University for six cycles of Oraiya to become proficient in every language on this hellish planet so we could speak the mother tongue of the Anunnaki fatherland on this mission.

Therefore, Lieutenant Commander Jol, until this mission has reached its full conclusion, every officer, every enlisted person, male and female, including those four gynandromorphs that spearheaded our expeditionary force to observe and gather intelligence on the test subject groups that were ultimately picked as the primary coterie for this particular mission."

"They are quartered up on deck 69." Lieutenant Commander Jol interrupted as he recalled, thinking he was informing his captain of the location of the Anunnaki gynandromorphs.

"Yes Lieutenant Commander Jol, you are correct, I had them housed there to separate them from our *normal* Anunnaki crew members. Especially that one that was stationed near the earther's city called St. Louis to report on the progenitor of test subject group 32452013 before our experiment commenced, it is the worst one of the four.

"It is the worst one by far Captain Xarr." Lieutenant Commander Jol agreed. "As you are well aware of Captain, that particular gynandromorph is guilty of the unauthorized use of its *mesmerizimic gland* to further its own sickening agenda, by enrapturing and having clandestine illicit galactic interspecies sexual relations with test subject group 32452013 progenitor's former employer."

"Yes Lieutenant Commander Jol, I almost feel sorry for the test subject group 32452013 progenitor's former employer. *Almost* being the key word here Lieutenant Commander. Nonetheless, I intend to report the gynandromorph's deplorable and potentially dangerous behavior to the "Supreme Being" of the Anunnaki Confederation upon our return to the home planet."

"Yes, Captain Xarr!"

"Until then Lieutenant Commander Jol, using one of this planet's dialects, and once more employing the regions currently popular vernacular, all I can say is.

Yikes! *Better that employer than me, have you seen that gynandromorph?"*

"Yes I have, and I totally agree with you Captain Xarr!" said the Lieutenant Commander, because he had been thinking the same thing himself. "However, in this particular case I feel that the term you used in the regional vernacular may be grossly understating the obvious, sir."

"I agree Lieutenant Commander Jol, and the next time I will choose my words more carefully," Captain Xarr answered, cringing at the mere thought of sexual relations with any gynandromorphs. "In the mean time, keep all of them sequestered on deck 69 for the duration of this mission and the return voyage home, unless otherwise notified, we don't want any of their hermaphroditic social indiscretions to infect the rest of the crew. Now do we Lieutenant Commander Jol?"

"Absolutely not Captain Xarr!" Lieutenant Commander Jol answered with fervor.

"Oh, and Lieutenant Commander Jol."

"Yes Captain Xarr?"

"If you ever again interrupt me, or make an attempt to correct me, or question my opinion, my orders, or my authority in any way, you will without a doubt find yourself encapsulated, and treading the liquid in a deep chromium plated vat of cold *kimchi,* that is if you're lucky, and I'm in a good mood that day. Do I make myself perfectly clear on this issue Lieutenant Commander Jol? Or should I say, soon to be Private Jol?"

"You have made yourself perfectly clear Captain Xarr, it will never happen again."

"See that it doesn't Lieutenant Commander!"

"Yes, Captain Xarr!" Lieutenant Commander Jol quickly answered, feeling the sweat in his armpits begin to drip profusely down both sides of his torso.

The captain then resumed spouting his orders to Lieutenant Commander Jol and the ship's bridge crew.

"Everyone on this ship *will* speak the language of the indigent people of the land mass that we are hovering over at the time. Is that clear Lieutenant Commander Jol?" The intergalactic spaceship's captain directed loudly.

"Yes Captain Xarr, completely clear," the Lieutenant Commander acknowledged fervently as the rest of the crew nodded in agreement. "I will make sure that order is carried out immediately sir."

"Good! See to it that you do. But first, your report Lieutenant Commander Jol!"

"Captain Xarr, the glitch in our visual dispersion anomaly generator has been rectified, so our ship will no longer leave a tell tale luminance during the night, or solar blocking glimpses during the daylight hours that the test subject groups had been seeing."

The Captain, pleased with Lieutenant Commander Jol's report replied.

"Excellent Lieutenant Commander Jol! However, next time do not take so long in your rectification program."

"There will not be a next time Captain Xarr, immediately after the engineer in charge of that section had the device in proper working order, and thoroughly tested, I had him executed for his initial incompetence." Lieutenant Commander Jol quickly responded.

"Excellent Lieutenant Commander Jol!" Captain Xarr said, nodding his head in approval. "As you know, there is no latitude for incompetence on this mission."

"There's more Captain Xarr," Lieutenant Commander Jol mentioned hesitantly.

"Let's hear it Lieutenant Commander Jol, the rest of your report," said the captain spurting out his diaphoretic order.

Although knowing that the captain would not be pleased with the remainder of his report, Lieutenant Commander Jol had no choice but to proceed.

"Well Captain Xarr, it is about test subject group 32452013."

Annoyed with the hesitant behavior of his subordinate, the Captain snorted. "What about test subject group 32452013?"

"Test subject group 32452013 is totally surrounded by the control subjects," the Lieutenant Commander answered, feeling his sweat drenched uniform clinging to his body.

"Is that all Lieutenant Commander Jol? From your tone and tentative nature, I thought you were going to report something serious," the captain chuckled, not realizing the gravity of the test subject's situation.

"Test subject group 32452013 has done well since the commencement of the extinction *experiment*. They work well as a team, they are resilient, innovative, and battle tested, and they are devolving into what these earthers call, stone cold killers, so just keep monitoring their progress Lieutenant Commander Jol. Is that understood?" the captain counseled, noticing, but choosing to ignore his Lieutenant Commander's overly moist uniform.

"No Captain Xarr, you do not understand. They are surrounded by *thousands* of control subjects, plus one of their own species is nearby in an elevated position trying to eliminate them using one of the planet's primitive projectile launching devices similar to the ones that test subject group 32452013 uses!" Lieutenant Commander Jol explained, well aware that he had again pointed out a correction that needed to be made in his captain's opinion. "They are very low on their own projectiles, and at the moment they are busy holding off the attack of the control subjects with some kind of barbaric petroleum based radiation expelling device that was used in one of their many past planetary wars. I estimate that their current life expectancy is now between three and four earth minutes in duration."

After hearing the pertinent details and now understanding their perilous predicament, Captain Xarr was now concerned for the safety of test subject group 32452013, not because of any compassion for the earthers, but because of the possibility of the massive global experiment, i.e., top-secret mission, failing under his watch.

"Lieutenant Commander Jol, have I ever told you why, out of the hundreds of experienced, competent, combat tested, battle fleet commanders, I was chosen to lead this mission?"

"No Captain Xarr, I assumed that it was because you were the best qualified for this operation."

"Lieutenant Commander Jol, that is one reason of course, but I also had a major advantage over the other candidates. Lieutenant Commander Jol, are you aware of the history of the Xarr family name?"

"Captain Xarr sir, I know that the Xarr family name has a long lineage of distinguished military and scientific service to the Anunnaki cause," Lieutenant Commander Jol answered.

"That is correct Lieutenant Commander Jol, however your generic description of my ancestral exploits leaves many facts untold, and also leaves me to wonder just how it is that you were chosen for the position that you now hold aboard this vessel?"

The Lieutenant Commander said nothing for fear he would say the wrong thing to his captain, and end up joining the aforementioned former engineer in forced early retirement down in the ship's morgue.

"Lieutenant Commander Jol, listen, and listen well, I shall now enlighten you with the knowledge of my families pedigree. It will serve you well to remember everything I am about to tell you. Is that clear?"

"Yes, Captain Xarr." Lieutenant Commander Jol answered, stammering nervously.

"Many generations ago, my ancestor, a very high ranking fleet commander much like myself, built what the inhabitants of this planet call the Great Pyramids; they had been built to last many hundreds of millennium. When first completed, on days when this world's sun radiated to the surface of the planet unencumbered by cloud cover, its rays would reflect off of the polished white limestone veneer of the monumental edifices, and could be seen sparkling like precious stones for well over a hundred earth miles in every direction, including up. That is right Lieutenant Commander Jol, at one time the pyramids served as beacons that could even be seen from outside this planet's thick oxygen-nitrogen atmosphere. Of course, they look nothing like that now, thanks to those ignorant, self-centered, lazy, small-minded earthers. Those primitive untamed idiots striped the glossy limestone off the pyramids to build themselves small pathetic dwellings that no longer even exist, leaving my ancestor's great accomplishments standing there in the middle of that sandbox they call a desert, looking like the piles of dilapidated rubble that they are today, just pitiful shells of what they once were."

Captain Xarr gritted his teeth in anger as he continued to tell the history of his ancestor's triumphs to his Lieutenant Commander.

"Lieutenant Commander Jol, my ancestor was a proud Anunnakian and a great military leader, scientist, and explorer. He was so confident in his abilities, that as a tribute to the fine work that he and his crew were going to accomplish on this, how do these earthers say it, *god-forsaken* planet. That on his forth mission to this solar satellite, he commissioned a statue of himself to be erected using the available primitive slave labor force he called the "*followers gang*", his statue was meant to figuratively stand guard majestically over the future magnificent edifices prior to them being constructed nearby; which was scheduled to happen on the sixth tour of his many missions to this world.

The earthers now call that monument to my legendary military ancestor, the *Sphinx*. That is right Lieutenant Commander Jol, the face on the monument called the Sphinx by this planet's lowly inhabitants, at least what is left of it, is the face of one of the greatest Xarr's in Anunnaki history."

"Yes, Captain Xarr!" Lieutenant Commander Jol shouted as he snapped to attention.

"So that brings us to me."

"Yes Captain Xarr!" The Lieutenant Commander again shouted.

"Here I am, many centuries later, using the same almanac to guide our timetable so that our superior Anunnakian race can maintain the precise schedule set at the beginning of our 1st Baktun by my storied relative from the distant past, Admiral Pacal Xarr, also known as the Zaktor Lion."

"That is why the base of his monument is in the shape of a lion's body," Lieutenant Commander Jol hesitantly interrupted once more.

"Very astute of you my young Lieutenant Commander," Captain Xarr acknowledged, choosing to ignore another one of Lieutenant Commander Jol's untimely interruptions.

"While living deep in the jungle between the two continents on this rocky and miserably wet orb that are now known to the earthers as North and South America, my great, great, great, great, great, well you get the idea Lieutenant Commander."

"Yes, Captain Xarr!" Lieutenant Commander Jol repeated loudly for the third time in a row, and repeated at a decibel level that was starting to annoy his ship's captain.

"Yes…indeed, Lieutenant Commander Jol." Captain Xarr continued, glaring at his subordinate.

"As did the missions of Pacal Xarr so many eons ago, my mission also has dictated that I travel several hundreds of thousands of parsecs away from my homeworld to the same, as I said before, *god-forsaken* planet, and deal with the same sub-intelligent barbaric earther savages that my fabled ancestor dealt with during the ancient past.

Only this time things are different. This is not some wayward scientific scavenger hunt out in the far reaches of the universe. It's not another pathetic nation building expedition to a distant star system intended to stroke the Supreme Beings ego. Or for that matter any of the many devil may care military exercises that are the norm in these times of political discourse on our planet.

This sole mission could possibly end up becoming responsible for ending all hostilities between the Anunnaki people and our dreaded hedonistic galactic enemies once and for all.

As a current member of the most elite branch of the *military tentacle* of the Anunnaki Confederation, you as well as all military personnel like yourself who hold the highest level of all restricted confidential classifications of which our Ministry of Warfare issues, that of *Mega Clandestine Enigmatic*, should know that the further continued propagation as well as the future of the entire Anunnaki race could very well be affected positively or negatively depending on the success or failure of our mission."

"Yes Captain Xarr, I am well aware of these facts that you have just summarized," Lieutenant Commander Jol, interjected.

"Failure might always be an option in your world Lieutenant Commander Jol, however, neither my existence nor my career allows for a lack of success in any degree, especially, on this most crucial of all assignments.

I will not fail in my mission on this ugly sphere, just as Admiral Pacal Xarr did not fail, or for that matter, any of my ancestors that came before me. None of them failed to accomplish their missions on this planet or any other, and I do not intend to be the first commander in the Xarr family lineage to disgrace our fine name. Do you understand me Lieutenant Commander Jol?"

"Yes, Captain Xarr!" Lieutenant Commander Jol barked; still standing at attention as small beads of perspiration began to glaze his alien forehead.

"However, most importantly, I refuse to fail the Anunnaki population who are depending on us to do our duty and our job; do I make myself perfectly clear Lieutenant Commander Jol?" Captain Xarr scolded.

"Indeed Captain Xarr, *perfectly clear*," the junior office echoed.

"In other words Lieutenant Commander, my family's gene pool was a major factor in my becoming the *predominant commander* of this particular mission."

"I completely understand the thought process of the Supreme Being in this most important matter Captain Xarr," Lieutenant Commander Jol proclaimed, nodding his head and thinking. *"It's not what you know, it's who you know!"*

"Somehow I find that statement very hard to believe Lieutenant Commander," Captain Xarr, professed vaguely smiling. "However, as you know, if for any reason we *do* fail to accomplish our mission to the complete and utter satisfaction of the Anunnaki Supreme Being, I can assure you; that deep chromium plated vat of cold *kimchi* that I mentioned earlier will seem like a pleasurable dip in a mineral spring during a trip to one of the day spa's somewhere in the Gorlan asteroid belt sector." Captain Xarr stressed.

"Admittedly so, Captain Xarr, my awareness of these things that you speak of is most acute." Lieutenant Commander Jol concurred.

"Well then, I suggest that we go and deal with those useless earthers in test subject group 32452013 before they are exterminated and I am forced to hold you entirely responsible for their demise," Captain Xarr, urged. "Or before I start to remember your monumental ineptitude concerning your knowledge of my family tree, shall we?"

"Yes, Captain Xarr." Lieutenant Commander Jol loudly barked once more to his superior's vexation.

Shouting to the pilot, Captain Xarr ordered.

"Put us over the test subject group 32452013's position immediately!"

Within seconds, the alien spacecraft hovered invisibly, high above the embattled National Guard armory.

"Give me a visual," the Captain ordered, almost too late, as a crew member had already began the process of putting the event taking place below them onto their plasmatic viewer.

The scene on the ground confirmed Lieutenant Commander Jol's report that test subject group 32452013 was in a hopeless situation, the sound of the battle tank's gun firing had drawn what the Anunnaki crewmembers called control subjects (zombies) to the armory in vast numbers.

The aerial view showed so many control subjects, that for blocks in every direction it was difficult to see even one square foot of flat, ground level terra firma that wasn't occupied with a hungry and slobbering control subject, most of which were displaying at least some maggots somewhere on their person. In addition, hundreds more of the control subjects were converging on the site every minute, bringing their personal swarm of flies along with them.

"Lieutenant Commander Jol, I didn't come half way across this galaxy, all the way to the Saxfox Major constellation, leave my female companion and our off springs, spend the last three Kronal sections setting up this *experiment* on this ugly green and blue rock, just to see test subject group 32452013 eliminated prematurely," the Captain reeled angrily.

"What are your orders Captain Xarr?" Lieutenant Commander Jol asked apprehensively, knowing that the penalty for any failure on his part would be prolonged torture and then death, if he were lucky.

"Signal four of the phase-three transport ships to rendezvous at this location immediately," Captain Xarr answered. "Make that three phase-three transports, and one phase-four transport Lieutenant Commander Jol."

The Lieutenant Commander complied with his captain's orders, and within moments, four transport ships were hovering beside the Mother ship, fifty thousand feet in the air over the embattled Texas National Guard armory.

"Lieutenant Commander Jol, insert a genetic differentiation chip into each of the pre-extinction bipedal carnivorous creatures prior to their release onto the planet's surface. We want to make sure that we don't accidently eliminate test subject group 32452013, or for that matter, any of the other test subject groups either," Captain Xarr ordered. "And release them immediately, test subject group 32452013 can't maintain their current status much longer."

"Yes, Captain Xarr," Lieutenant Commander Jol responded, signaling to lower ranking crewmembers to comply with the Captains orders immediately, or else.

Not wanting to meet the same ghastly end as he had arranged for one of the ship's engineers, the Lieutenant Commander quickly followed up on the orders he had conveyed from the Captain, making sure that those orders were being followed to the letter.

"Captain Xarr, your orders have been complied with. The genetic differentiation chips have been inserted, and the release of the pre-extinction bipedal carnivorous creatures is complete," Lieutenant Commander Jol proudly informed his captain. "I have ordered our subatomic molecular evaporation cannon to be prepared for firing, and we will soon eliminate the human threat that is plaguing test subject group 32452013 from the elevated location that the earthers allowed to remain intact."

"Excellent, Lieutenant Commander Jol," the captain spouted. "Your independent initiative and the initial action taken to cope with the rogue earther that is harassing test subject group 32452013 is most impressive... *for a change*. Under my tutelage you just might make it to the rank of Sub-Prime-Lieutenant Commander one of these days after all."

"Thank you Captain Xarr, I shall continue to endeavor to persevere toward that goal," Lieutenant Commander Jol replied panting, as he stood on the bridge of the spaceship, relieved that he wasn't being taken into custody, or even summarily and publically executed for his individualistic thinking.

******

Meanwhile, back down on the planet's surface...

"This thing is about out of fuel, and they're still coming, they're climbing over the burnt carcasses to get to us," I yelled, feeling the weight of the flamethrower's fuel tanks diminishing.

"Ammo count?" I hollered.

"I've only got four round left!" Gin yelled back.

"I got five!" Jacob shouted.

"Two!" Billy stated, as he launched his last two bullets into the faces of two approaching zombies at point blank range, flinging several of their clinging facial maggots into the air.

"I'm out!" he yelled.

The M2-2 flamethrower was now beginning to sputter and spit. No longer was it hurling twenty-foot lengths of flaming death in the direction of the attacking cannibalistic brutes; now only three to five foot squirts of fire left the nozzle of the once devastating device.

"We're about done here," I yelled, trying to prepare myself for the horrible death that was imminent.

411

"Holy crud," Jacob shouted as loud as he could. "That can't be real?"

Before I had time to turn and see what had prompted Jacob's announcement, I uttered the same words myself only with a slight variance.

"Holy shit in an argyle sock, that can't be real?" I said in amazement, as I watched a prehistoric velociraptor tear off the heads of two zombies that had managed to avoid the flames, and that were about to pounce on me. Then with its six-inch long talon, unzip another determined zombie from its sternum to its crotch, dumping its internal organs on the ground in front of me.

The phrases "Holy crud", and "Holy shit," seemed to echo repeatedly, depending on which one of us used the verbiage, as each one of us saw more and more velociraptors mauling the horde of zombies that surrounded us.

Out of the corner of my eye, I caught site of a beam of light split a large cumulus cloud and quickly descend down upon the third building that was still standing; reminding me that even if we somehow managed to escape the carnage that was happening all around us, we still would have to deal with the hidden sniper.

At the moment that the beam hit the building, the building glowed for a split second, then it turned a powdery white color and crumbled to the ground silently. With that, the sound of bullets ricocheting off the tank immediately ceased and the sniper was no longer a threat.

As I turned from watching the sniper's nest disintegrate, to check on my family members, I saw

412

another site that boggled my imagination. What I saw was another prehistoric animal that couldn't possibly be terrorizing the planet at this moment in time, for it too had been deemed extinct for millions of years.

What I saw, was a Tyrannosaurus-Rex wreaking havoc through the multitudes of zombies along with the raptors. Some of the raptors were very close to us, it was almost as if they were forming a protective semi-circle around us to fend off the attacking zombies, the Tyrannosaurus-Rex was ripping apart zombies in the outer circle, and was soon joined by three more vicious Tyrannosaurs.

Body parts were being tossed indiscriminately into the air. Thick pools of blood were forming around us and oozing under our feet. Intestines of the undead were being flailed back and forth in the prehistoric animal's mouths, and were being flung onto us and everything else in the surrounding area, as the dinosaurs mutilated thousands of zombies in their path, and left an unbelievable amount of carnage in their wake during the grisly spectacle that was taking place just feet from us and the disabled tank.

"When they get done with the eaters, we'll be next," Gin screamed, totally in panic mode.

"Right, we're next, they're not eating the eaters, they're just tearing them to pieces, and I bet we're next!" Billy yelled.

Jacob climbed up on the tank, which now had stopped burning, and said. "I'm not waiting to find out!"

"There're three dead bodies in that tank Jacob, and one of them hasn't got a head," Gin screamed, in a panicked hysteria.

413

"Yeah; and there're thousands of dead bodies out here, most of them without their guts, arms, legs, or heads either," Jacob replied, swiping a four-foot long bluish green large intestine off his shoulder.

"He's right, just because up to now the dinosaurs haven't torn us apart, that doesn't mean that they're not going too," I said expressing my concern, while I too wiped off a collection of small intestines that were hanging from my right arm, which had been flung onto me by a nearby frenzied raptor.

None of us really wanted to close ourselves inside a burnt out battle tank with three dead bodies in it, but under the circumstances we all felt that we had no other choice.

Jacob went first, firing his last round into Rich's head. Rich had been killed by the concussion of the shell exploding inside the barrel of the cannon, but had not sustained a head injury; therefore, he had reanimated into a member of the undead shortly after his death. However, after becoming a zombie and being too stupid to climb out of the tank, he waited anxiously for his first live feeding in the darkness of his own armor-plated death trap.

Dave on the other hand, had had the right half of his skull torn off in the blast along with the right side of his face, which now dangled limp from one of the tank's guidance controls. He would have been pronounced "dead at the scene" by the county coroner (I mean, if there had been a coroner present at the time) so he was not a threat. And of course, Bruce's head had been shattered into a thousand pieces by the sniper's bullet, so there was nothing to worry about there.

After Jacob had entered the tank, Gin followed crying her eyes out, and then Billy climbed onto the tank and crawled inside. Then taking one last look around, and after seeing the hundreds of meat eating dinosaurs that were mutilating the thousands of fearless maniacal zombies, I too entered what I thought of as our steel coffin, and I reluctantly closed the tank's turret hatch behind us.

THE END?

Be sure to check out the sequel to this book.
Zombie's Doom? Chronicles of Jack Doom
@
http://www.amazon.com/dp/B012BTJAOE/

Don't forget to visit my author page!
@
http://www.amazon.com/Will-Lemen/e/B00O17RZ3S/ref=dp_byline_cont_pop_ebook s_1

www.ingramcontent.com/pod-product-compliance
Lightning Source LLC
Chambersburg PA
CBHW020928020726
47495CB00002B/403